TOUCHED BY A TRAITOR

The Daring Damsels
Book 1

Mihwa Lee

ARE YOU SIGNED UP FOR DRAGONBLADE'S BLOG?

You'll get the latest news and information on exclusive giveaways, exclusive excerpts, coming releases, sales, free books, cover reveals and more.

Check out our complete list of authors, too!

No spam, no junk. That's a promise!

Sign Up Here

www.dragonbladepublishing.com

Dearest Reader;

Thank you for your support of a small press. At Dragonblade Publishing, we strive to bring you the highest quality Historical Romance from some of the best authors in the business. Without your support, there is no 'us', so we sincerely hope you adore these stories and find some new favorite authors along the way.

Happy Reading!

CEO, Dragonblade Publishing

To my ARC readers

You inspire me to do better

PROLOGUE

31 December 1830—London

HAD ANDREW CRESWELL foreseen his impending encounter with Charlotte Grace this evening, he would have remained firmly ensconced in his bedchamber. Instead, cruel fate had orchestrated their meeting, and now they stood in stony silence within Madam Tansley's lavishly appointed parlor.

The establishment occupied a grand Georgian townhouse in one of London's more respectable districts, its exterior betraying nothing of the commerce conducted within. Inside, Turkish carpets covered polished floors, while crystal chandeliers cast warm light over silk-draped walls adorned with paintings of dubious virtue. The air hung thick with the mingled scents of French perfume, expensive tobacco, and the lingering aroma of roasted fowl from the evening's repast.

Andrew's calloused hands, more accustomed to hauling cargo than holding crystal, tightened around his brandy glass. The woman beside him possessed the bearing of an aristocrat fallen on hard times, judging by the way her fingers worried the worn wool of her skirt with barely contained agitation.

Miss Grace was undeniably striking—a study in quiet dignity amidst the brothel's calculated opulence. Her dark hair was swept into a simple chignon, a few rebellious tendrils framing features that spoke of good breeding despite her circumstances. Large eyes, dark as winter nights, held a keen intelligence that set her apart from the painted courtesans who moved through the room like exotic birds.

Though of average height, reaching just below his chin, her presence commanded attention. Her figure was slim and graceful beneath the modest woolen dress that stood in stark contrast to the revealing silks surrounding them. The high neckline and long sleeves only served to fuel Andrew's imagination, while her posture suggested steel beneath the delicate exterior.

The issue wasn't her beauty—far from it. The problem lay in her gaze, sharp as a winter wind, that swept over him with the practiced disdain of those born to privilege. Her eyes catalogued his rough-hewn clothing with silent judgment, each glance an indictment of the calluses beneath his cuffs and the working man's cut of his coat.

Andrew savored another swallow of brandy, silently conceding that Madam Tansley's excellent spirits might be the only thing saving this woman from his temper. The conniving procuress had orchestrated this meeting, then vanished, leaving him trapped with Miss Grace's glacial company.

Around them, the evening's revelries continued. Gentlemen in fine evening dress conversed in hushed tones with women whose painted smiles never quite reached their eyes. A pianoforte tinkled in the corner where a blonde courtesan entertained a portly MP with a ribald song, while servants in pristine livery moved silently between the guests, ensuring glasses remained full and plates laden.

"Tell me," Miss Grace said suddenly, breaking their brittle silence, "are you a man of substantial means?"

Andrew released a derisive breath. "Good Lord, how refreshingly direct. Do you always fortune hunt at a brothel or is this a special occasion?"

Color flooded her cheeks, but her chin lifted defiantly. "You mistake my meaning entirely. I'm not seeking a husband."

"A patron then? A keeper? Or are we conducting a census?"

She hesitated, her composure wavering for the first time since their introduction. When she spoke again, her voice carried careful calculation rather than desperation. "I find myself requiring… a business arrangement. Something mutually beneficial for parties of discerning taste."

"And what sort of business might that be? Your ability to assess a man's worth by his coat, or making dockworkers question their life choices?"

Instead of looking chastened, one corner of her lips curved upward in genuine amusement. "I see you have a gift for sharp observation, sir. I could certainly offer equally pointed rebuttals if that's how you'd prefer to spend your evening."

Andrew studied her carefully. "And what would you consider a proper use of such an evening, Miss?"

"Well," her long eyelashes fluttered as she adopted an air of mock consideration, "cataloguing men's shortcomings, delivering uncomfortable truths, reading legal texts when the company grows tedious…" Her voice grew more serious but retained its edge. "Or perhaps offering something that might genuinely interest a man of means."

His brows drew together. "I hope you're not peddling stolen goods, Miss. I have expensive tastes but simple ethics."

"Nothing stolen," she said with a wry smile that didn't quite reach her eyes. "My virtue, sir. For the right price."

Andrew recoiled as if struck, brandy sloshing dangerously close to the crystal's rim. "What in God's name—"

"Two hundred pounds," she pressed on, desperation fracturing her careful facade. Her fingers worried the fabric of her skirt with violence. "Perhaps you know someone who might meet such a sum?"

For a moment, he could only stare, mind struggling to reconcile her refined bearing with such a brazen proposition. This woman, with her aristocratic features and eyes that burned with wounded pride, was offering herself like common chattel? Yet the raw desperation threading through her voice rang with unmistakable truth.

The way she held herself—spine rigid as if facing an executioner rather than negotiating—suggested this degradation cost her more than she was willing to reveal.

The air between them grew thick with tension. Andrew found his attention drawn to the elegant line of her throat, the subtle quickening of her breath beneath the modest neckline of her gown. He remained so transfixed that Madam Tansley's approaching footsteps registered too late.

"Ah, I see Andrew has assumed his banker's countenance," Madam Tansley purred, her smile predatory as she materialized beside them like a silk-clad specter. "Already discussing terms, are we, dear girl? What sum did you name?"

"Two hundred pounds," the woman answered, staring at her feet.

Andrew gritted his teeth. Madam had targeted him for this negotiation.

A laugh like poisoned honey spilled from Madam's painted lips. "Oh, my sweet child. You should request more. Much, much more."

Andrew rounded on his surrogate mother, muscles tightening with barely contained frustration. "I want no part in this sordid business."

"No?" Madam's words dripped with maternal mockery. "You've been an ill-tempered brute these months past. I imagine one evening with a sweet girl like Miss Grace should remedy that disposition entirely."

"Mother." The word scraped from his throat like gravel, heavy with warning.

Miss Grace's composure cracked at last, her eyes going wide with dawning comprehension. "Mother? You're her—"

"Not by blood," Andrew cut in sharply. "It's… complicated."

Madam's sharp features softened to genuine affection beneath the calculated exterior. "I found him stealing bread as a scrawny lad. Took him in, raised him proper. Now look at my boy—master of the Sovereign Seas Trading Corporation."

The change in the woman was instant and electric. Gone was the haunted desperation, replaced by keen intelligence as her mind seized upon this revelation. "The Sovereign Seas? The shipping enterprise?"

Her voice carried a note of recognition and something more calculating.

"Why, yes," Madam said distractedly as her attention wavered. "Ah, the duke beckons. Do try not to devour each other, children." With those words, Madam drifted away.

In the vacuum of Madam's absence, Andrew found himself trapped in Miss Grace's calculating gaze. The cool disdain had vanished, replaced by something far more dangerous—hope tempered with shrewd assessment.

"Have you reconsidered my proposition, Mr. Creswell?" Her voice took on a velvety tone, though he noticed how her hands trembled slightly as she smoothed her skirts.

"No."

He turned to escape, but her fingers closed around his wrist like a shackle. The touch blazed between them unexpectedly, and Andrew stared at the point of contact, transfixed by how small and delicate her hand appeared compared to his. Her skin was soft but cold, as if she'd been standing in winter air.

"Please," she breathed, and the word cracked open something in her carefully constructed facade. "I need your help. I have a plan—something that could change everything. But I can't manage it alone."

For just a moment, her mask slipped entirely. He saw not the calculating aristocrat or the woman offering her virtue, but someone achingly young and afraid, clinging to hope by her fingernails. The vulnerability in her eyes reminded him of his own reflection in shop windows during those hungry years on the streets.

"What sort of plan?" The words escaped before wisdom could catch them.

Her eyes darted across the crowded parlor, taking in the various gentlemen who might overhear. "Not here. Is there somewhere we might speak privately?"

Before Andrew could respond, a booming voice cut through his contemplation like a blade through silk.

"Creswell!" Lord Wilson approached with the particular swagger of inherited wealth, his smile as genuine as a counterfeit sovereign. The man's evening dress was immaculate—black tailcoat perfectly fitted, white cravat tied with mathematical precision, gold watch chain gleaming across his considerable waistcoat. "I've been meaning to discuss a rather lucrative opportunity with you."

Miss Grace withdrew her hand, though the ghost of her touch lingered like a brand upon his skin. "Lord Wilson."

"I couldn't help but notice the remarkable growth of your enterprise." Wilson's tone suggested he was bestowing a great honor by merely acknowledging Andrew's existence. "My associates and I would be willing to invest substantially. Say, ten thousand pounds for a quarter share?"

"You're most kind," Andrew replied with careful politeness, "but Sovereign Seas isn't seeking investors at present."

Wilson's smile tightened at the corners like poorly stretched leather. "Come now, Creswell. Surely you understand the advantages of having friends in the right circles? One never knows when the tide might turn against a man."

"The tide has served me well enough these past years," Andrew said evenly, though his shoulders tensed at the veiled threat.

Wilson's gaze slid to Miss Grace with predatory interest, his eyes cataloguing her form with the same calculation he might apply to a prize horse at Tattersall's. She instinctively shifted closer to Andrew, seeking shelter in his shadow.

"Speaking of treasures… what a lovely creature. If you're not making use of her particular charms, perhaps I might arrange a more suitable introduction?"

Andrew's jaw clenched, the muscle ticking beneath his skin. The casual way Wilson spoke of her, as if she were cargo to be traded, made his blood sing with protective fury. Whatever this woman's circumstances, she deserved better than to be discussed like livestock.

"You mistake the lady's station, Wilson. Miss Grace is a gentlewoman under my protection."

The lie rolled off his tongue with surprising ease. Something about her desperate courage demanded his defense, even if he didn't fully understand why.

Wilson's eyebrows shot up, a knowing smirk playing at his lips. "Is she indeed? How convenient. Though I must say, Creswell, for a man of your humble origins, you play the gallant protector rather convincingly." He adjusted his cravat with manicured fingers. "Still, should you tire of the role, my offer for both ventures stands. Good evening."

As Wilson sauntered away, Andrew became acutely aware of Miss Grace's warmth against him, of how she'd pressed herself into his shadow like a frightened dove seeking shelter. The subtle scent of jasmine and vanilla clouded his senses, but beneath it he caught something else—genuine fear.

"Your private audience, Miss Grace. Now."

He guided her through the crowd, his hand hovering protectively at the small of her back without quite touching. They wound through the brothel's maze of oriental screens and velvet drapes toward a private parlor, away from watchful eyes and listening ears, where perhaps she might finally reveal what desperate plan had driven her to such extremes.

CHARLOTTE WATCHED THE door close with a soft click, her heart drumming an unsteady rhythm against her ribs. The private parlor was smaller than the main room, more intimate, with burgundy silk wallpaper and a single crystal lamp casting warm light over polished mahogany furniture. A fire crackled in the marble hearth, its glow dancing across Persian carpets and gilt-framed paintings of pastoral scenes—a far cry from the bawdy artwork adorning the public spaces.

Mr. Creswell's presence seemed to fill every corner of the room—all six foot two of him, his shoulders broad beneath a coat of rough brown wool that spoke of dock work rather than drawing rooms. The garment was well-made but practical, its sleeves bearing the subtle wear of honest labor. His white shirt, though clean, was simple linen rather than fine cotton, open at the throat where she glimpsed the strong column of his neck. The firelight caught the strong line of his jaw, transforming his weathered features into something almost noble.

She'd expected to feel nothing but cold calculation during this encounter. Instead, warmth pooled in her stomach as she watched him move, each gesture speaking of hard-won strength. When he'd defended her against Lord Wilson's crude suggestions, she'd felt something crack open in her chest—a dangerous flutter of gratitude she couldn't afford.

"Please," he gestured to a velvet armchair near the fire, his voice a deep timbre that seemed to resonate in her bones. Charlotte perched carefully on the edge of the seat, her worn woolen skirts settling around her ankles.

She studied his face in the firelight, her mind racing. Andrew Creswell—owner of Sovereign Seas Trading Corporation. The irony wasn't lost on her that the man she'd approached in desperation might be the very person who could benefit from her hard-won knowledge.

"Mr. Creswell," she said, her voice taking on a new quality of purpose, "now that I know who you are, I believe I might have information that could be of considerable value to your business. Perhaps we might… renegotiate our arrangement?"

His eyes narrowed and Charlotte's nerves threatened to crumble under his scrutiny.

"Your proposition…" he said, finally.

She straightened, steeling herself against the intensity of his gaze. This was business, she reminded herself, even as her heart hammered against her ribs. "Five hundred pounds."

"And what exactly," he leaned forward, elbows braced on his knees, "does this newfound worth purchase?"

She swallowed and forced herself to meet his gaze. "My virginity, yes," she said with a slight tremor in her voice, "but also, information that could fill your coffers or keep you from the gallows."

She watched his eyes widen at her boldness, saw him lean forward despite himself. The firelight caught the sharp angles of his face, and for a moment she glimpsed skepticism, perhaps even concern in his expression.

"Do we have an agreement, Mr. Creswell? Five hundred pounds?" she breathed, fighting to maintain her composure as his proximity threatened to undo her carefully constructed facade.

When he extended his hand, Charlotte noticed the roughness of his palm, the strength in those fingers that had built an empire from nothing. Instead of taking it, she turned her own palm upward, suddenly vulnerable. "Three hundred now, for the knowledge I'm about to impart. The remainder when you've… claimed your prize."

The words tasted like ash in her mouth, but she forced them out. For a moment, her carefully constructed walls cracked, and she wondered if he could see the truth in her eyes—not just the fear of what she was offering, but the desperate hope that somehow, this degradation might purchase her freedom.

His eyes raked over her form, and Charlotte felt it like a physical caress. Even as her pulse jumped wildly, she maintained her pose.

"I don't carry such sums," he said, his voice rough in a way that made her shiver. "Wait here while I speak with Madam."

As he turned to leave, Charlotte released a shaky breath, pressing a trembling hand to her chest. What was wrong with her? This was supposed to be simple—a transaction to secure her future. She wasn't supposed to feel this flutter of attraction, this dangerous wish that things could be different.

When Mr. Creswell returned, notes crackling in his grip,

Charlotte's fingers shook as she accepted them. His eyes lingered on her tremors, something unreadable flickering in their depths. For a moment, she thought he might ask if she was truly certain, might offer her some alternative. The thought both terrified and thrilled her.

But pride was a luxury she'd pawned along with her late mother's jewelry.

Steeling herself, she leaned forward, dropping her voice to urgent whispers. "Mr. Creswell, are you familiar with Priestley versus Fowler?"

His brow creased. "The labor dispute? I've heard rumblings, but—"

"It's far more significant," Charlotte cut in, grateful to focus on something she understood. "This ruling could bring your shipping empire to its knees."

Interest overcame wariness as he shifted closer. "Explain."

As she outlined the legal vulnerabilities, Charlotte felt herself coming alive. This was what she was meant for—not bartering her body but wielding her mind like a sword. For the first time since entering this place, she felt truly herself.

"The court's decision on employer liability contains a fatal flaw—one that leaves you vulnerable to smuggling operations. Your company, Mr. Creswell, is exposed."

He blanched, rising to pour brandy with less than steady hands. "These are damning claims. How did you come by such knowledge?"

"I've been studying law in secret and... your company," she confessed, accepting the crystal glass. "The money... it's for passage abroad. To continue my studies."

Andrew regarded her with wonder warring with doubt in his expression. "If accurate, you've earned every pound. My solicitor will verify this... before his dismissal."

He settled beside her, his thigh a line of heat against hers. Charlotte's breath hitched as he turned, bringing their faces a few feet apart. This close, she could see the kindness there, carefully hidden beneath layers of hard-won caution.

"You speak like one born to privilege," he murmured. "Who are you really, Miss Grace?"

For a moment, Charlotte considered lying, spinning some tale that would preserve the last shreds of her dignity. But she was too exhausted for such effort. What did it matter what he thought of her? She'd never see him again.

She drew herself up, aristocratic pride burning through her circumstances. "I am the daughter of a viscount, granddaughter of an earl. My mother's mind shattered when I was sixteen. Father sold everything to spare her the asylum's horrors. After she passed, he followed her to the grave from a debtor's cell."

The words came easier than expected, perhaps because his presence reminded her of his own humble beginnings. Something in Mr. Creswell's expression thawed, and she saw not pity but understanding—the recognition of one survivor to another.

"Why not seek employment as a governess?" His voice was rough velvet in the dim light.

Bitterness flooded Charlotte's chest, but also vulnerability she rarely allowed herself to feel. "Society shuns the daughter of a madwoman. And the noble houses…" Her mouth twisted. "Their masters believe a fallen aristocrat makes for easy prey."

She'd learned that lesson the hard way, in a dozen drawing rooms where men's eyes had lingered too long, where offers of "protection" came with prices she couldn't bear to pay.

Andrew turned toward her, and Charlotte felt something shift between them. "And here?"

"I keep house," she added quickly, then felt compelled to add, "Madam is kinder than most. She offers work without asking for more than I'm willing to give."

"How did you survive before?" The words were gentle, inviting confidence.

Her fingers whitened around her glass as memories threatened to surface. "A kind vicar offered shelter and education until he married. I searched for work but…" She shook her head, surprised by how much she wanted to share with this man. "They all feared I carried my mother's affliction."

"Wouldn't marriage offer security?"

The question struck her to the core, and she found herself answering more honestly than she'd intended. Her voice dropped to a whisper. "What man would wed a woman with madness in her bloodline?"

The admission hung between them, more naked than any physical revelation. Charlotte felt exposed, vulnerable in a way she hadn't since her parents' deaths. Yet Mr. Creswell's presence didn't make it unbearable.

She looked up, catching him studying her with an intensity that made her cheeks warm. "How is it you command the language of privilege but wear it like borrowed clothes?"

His laugh rolled through the room like warm brandy, genuine and unguarded. "I'm common as dirt. No schooling to speak of, but Madam wouldn't have her boy sounding like a dock rat."

The ease with which he shared his origins, the lack of shame in his voice, made something in Charlotte's chest loosen. Here was a man who'd risen without forgetting where he came from. She edged closer, drawn by his openness. "How old were you? When she caught you stealing?"

"Twelve. My parents were in the ground from consumption, and I had my two-year-old sister on my back. Word was Madam had a soft heart beneath her sharp edges."

Something in Charlotte's chest cracked open at the image—a boy barely older than a child himself, carrying even greater burdens. Gone was the calculation of moments ago, replaced by an understanding. "To lose them so young, with a sister to protect…"

"How did you manage?" she whispered. "With your sister and being so young yourself?"

"I'd trade street findings for whatever I could get—always searching for food for Daisy. Her smile…" He paused, lost in memory, and Charlotte found herself leaning toward him, genuinely invested in his story. "It kept me human when the streets tried to make me savage. Having her to protect made me cleverer, stronger."

Without conscious thought, Charlotte's fingers found his wrist, a gossamer touch that anchored them both. The contact sent warmth spreading up her arm, but more than that—it felt right, natural, as if they'd known each other far longer than a few hours.

He stared at the point of contact before slowly, deliberately, threading his fingers through hers. The simple gesture made her heart race.

His voice continued steady, though his thumb had begun tracing idle patterns on her skin that sent sparks dancing along her nerves. "I learned to fight, claimed the best corners for selling papers. Madam watched Daisy while I defended my territory. Three years of saving bought us a room with a schoolmistress which was better suited for Daisy."

Charlotte found herself drifting in twin currents—the hypnotic caress of his thumb and the revelation of his past. Something shifted between them, a bridge built of shared wounds and iron resolve. She recognized in him what she saw in her mirror—someone who'd clawed their way up from the depths, wearing their scars like armor.

"Mr. Creswell," she breathed his name like a prayer, the distance between them dissolving gradually. "It's incredible what you've built from nothing but courage and will. And from what I've heard, you founded your empire on honor rather than exploitation."

The admiration in her voice was entirely genuine. Whatever had brought her to this moment, she couldn't deny her respect for what he'd accomplished.

He turned to her, something raw and wondering in his gaze. "A man alone can fight his way up. A gentlewoman alone?" His voice roughened with emotion. "That's a different kind of battlefield. You must have ached for your family."

The understanding in his voice nearly undid her. Charlotte felt tears threaten, surprised by how desperately she wanted to share her burden with someone who might comprehend it.

"I miss the dream of family," she said carefully, her voice barely above a whisper. "But the reality? I lived among strangers who resented my refusal to trade on my charm for their gain. Father saw only Mother's shadows in me. His love was admirable, but his failure to secure my future was not."

Andrew's arm settled across her shoulders, solid and warm. Charlotte froze, caught between instinct and yearning. The gesture was so natural, so protective, that for a moment she allowed herself to imagine what it would be like to have someone truly on her side.

"What kind of parents leave their daughter defenseless when they had the means to protect her?" Anger threaded through his words, and Charlotte's heart twisted at his protective fury on her behalf.

"Is that why you turned to law?" he asked softly, his breath warm against her temple. "Your parents?"

She stilled, struck by his insight. No one had ever understood her motivations so clearly. "Yes. I want to fight a world that treats misfortune as a crime."

As the tension slowly drained from her spine, Charlotte found herself melting into his embrace. This was dangerous territory—she couldn't afford to trust, to hope, to feel anything real for this man. Yet wrapped in his arms, listening to the steady beat of his heart, she felt safer than she had in years.

Catching her wandering thoughts, she blurted, "Why are you unmarried?"

Andrew captured her free hand, studying her work-roughened fingers with gentle consideration. His touch was so different from what she'd expected—not grasping or demanding, but almost reverent.

"I've waited for someone rare," he said, his voice pitched low and intimate. "A woman who sees past my origins, accepts all I am, and can walk between worlds as I do… but with more grace."

As he spoke, Charlotte looked up at him, and his eyes met hers with newfound intensity. She felt pinned by his gaze, her body humming with nervous energy and something deeper—a recognition that terrified her.

"Someone like you," he murmured, the realization dawning in his voice.

His arm slipped to her waist, drawing her against him until no space remained between them. Charlotte's breath stuttered as she realized what was happening—this wasn't part of her plan, this growing warmth between them that had nothing to do with transactions or desperation.

"As I spoke of what I seek in a wife, I found myself describing you," he whispered into her ear.

The words hung between them, weighted with possibility and danger. Charlotte pressed her palm to his chest, finding his heartbeat steady beneath linen while her own pulse raced wild as a hunted deer.

"You might be exactly what I need," he said, his words carrying the gravity of revelation. "Sharp-minded, able to move between worlds, intimate with life's cruel lessons. Add your beauty and courage, and you're everything a man could want in a wife."

Color flooded Charlotte's cheeks as his words scattered her thoughts like autumn leaves in a storm. Surely, she had misinterpreted, or perhaps the brandy had addled her wits entirely. This wasn't how transactions were supposed to unfold—with genuine feeling creeping in to complicate everything.

"We could…" he ventured, uncertainty threading through his voice like silver.

Charlotte straightened, her heart hammering against her ribs. "What?" The word emerged strangled; her usual wit abandoned her entirely.

"Join our lives," he said softly, his hand moving to cup her cheek with devastating tenderness. "I think we'd make a formidable match."

The room spun like a child's top. Charlotte blinked hard, certain she must be lost in some fever dream. This man—this powerful, dangerous, captivating man she'd known only for an evening—was offering marriage?

"I… I don't understand," she whispered, even as part of her soul sang at the possibility. "We're strangers, Mr. Creswell."

His grip tightened fractionally at her waist. "Are we? You've shown me more of your true self in hours than most reveal in years. You challenge everything I thought I knew about women, Charlotte."

Her name on his lips sounded like a prayer. She'd come with clear intentions, none of which involved marriage—especially not to a man who might actually see her as more than a burden or a prize.

And yet…

She couldn't deny the current running between them, the way her skin sang at his touch, how their minds sparked against each other. For one dizzying moment, Charlotte let herself envision it: a life shared with Andrew Creswell, their combined strengths wielded for change. The possibility was intoxicating and terrifying in equal measure.

This could be her salvation—from poverty, from solitude, from vulnerability. But also from her dreams, from the future she was willing to sacrifice herself to achieve.

"I want to believe that's possible," she whispered, and realized she meant it more than she'd ever meant anything.

Something darkened in his gaze as he turned to her fully. The air crackled between them like lightning about to strike. Charlotte balanced on the knife's edge between terror and wild hope while Andrew watched her, desire warring with concern in his eyes.

With startling ease, he gathered her onto his lap. She gasped, instinctively gripping his shoulder as he tightened his arm around her waist, the other hand resting casually on her thigh. His words came rough with emotion: "Charlotte, I mean every word. The streets taught me to protect the vulnerable. I'm steadfast, and I'd guard you with my life. We're cut from the same rare cloth, you and I. We could find happiness… perhaps even love."

The sincerity in his voice nearly shattered her resolve. This was something real, something that could change everything. Yet even as hope bloomed in her chest, reality intruded.

"Andrew… your offer overwhelms me. A marriage proposal is beyond my wildest dreams." She drew a steadying breath, steeling herself against the warmth in his eyes. "But I must pursue law, even as your wife. You can't imagine what I might achieve, though I'd still be everything you desire in a bride. We need only endure four years apart while I earn my degree."

His eyes widened in shock. "Four years?"

"Yes, but I am only one and twenty. I'll be ready to bear children after graduation. Consider it an extended betrothal."

"Impossible," Andrew said, his voice gentle but unyielding as iron. "A wife in trade would destroy every social connection I've fought to build."

Charlotte felt the hope in her chest wither like frost-touched flowers. The careful warmth they'd built between them cracked under the weight of reality. "I want more than hearth and nursery," she said softly, unable to keep the disappointment from her voice.

He shifted, drawing her closer even as his words pushed her away. "Where would you even find such education?"

"A progressive academy in Boston, United States." Charlotte's voice cooled to winter as she realized the impossible gulf between them. "I suppose that settles matters. I shall proceed as planned. Shall we return to our original arrangement?"

The fragile web of understanding between them dissolved, leaving only the stark reality of their clashing dreams. Andrew's face was a battlefield of opposing impulses—desire and propriety locked in combat. Charlotte waited, wrapped in dignity like a shield, while her heart broke quietly in her chest.

She'd been a fool to hope, even for a moment, that someone might want her dreams as much as they wanted her body. The lesson stung, but she'd learned worse.

Yet as Andrew's hands moved to his neckcloth, something shifted in the air between them. Charlotte watched him with growing wonder as he loosened the white linen with ease, his coat following to a nearby chair.

Her eyes widened, lips parting softly as he began unfastening his shirt buttons. She held her breath with genuine amazement. She'd known this could happen with her proposition, but she had never thought she'd be on a man's lap while he undressed and looked at her with such reverence, as if she were precious rather than merely convenient.

"Andrew," she whispered, her voice trembling with uncertainty, "I don't know if I can... I've never..." The admission cost her, color flooding her cheeks as vulnerability cracked through her carefully maintained composure.

Tenderly, he cradled her chin, his thumb tracing the velvet curve of her bottom lip. His touch was so gentle, so different from what she'd steeled herself to expect, that tears pricked at her eyes. "We don't have to do anything you don't want," he murmured, his voice rough with restraint. "Tell me to stop, and I will."

The kindness in his words nearly undid her. When had anyone given her such a choice? When had anyone cared more for her comfort than their own desires?

"Perhaps," he continued, his gaze searching her face with concern, "I could persuade you otherwise. But only if you truly want this, Charlotte. Not because you feel you must."

Before she could second-guess herself, Charlotte reached up to cup his face, marveling at the rough texture of his evening stubble beneath her palm. "I want to understand what this could be," she whispered, surprised by her own confession. "Not the transaction I planned, but this. Whatever this is between us."

Her admission seemed to unlock something in Andrew. He dipped his head, his breath warm against her skin for a heartbeat before his lips met hers. The first touch was gentle—a question asked in the softest whisper—but as she yielded, the kiss transformed into something that consumed her entirely.

His mouth moved against hers with reverent hunger, his lips firm yet tender as they coaxed a response she didn't know she possessed. When his tongue traced the seam of her lips, requesting entry, Charlotte gasped, and he took advantage, deepening the kiss.

Heat bloomed low in her belly, spreading through her limbs like honey warmed by fire. Her fingers found the lapels of his coat, clutching the fabric as if it were the only thing keeping her tethered to earth. The taste of him—brandy and something indefinably masculine—made her head spin with a dizzying rush that had nothing to do with the wine she'd consumed.

His hand cradled the back of her neck, his thumb stroking the sensitive skin there in a rhythm that sent shivers cascading down her spine. She could feel the thundering of his heart where her palms pressed against his chest, matching the frantic pulse that hammered in her throat.

When he finally gentled the kiss, drawing back just enough to rest his forehead against hers, Charlotte's lips felt swollen and tingling, her breath coming in short, desperate gasps. In his arms, she felt like a woman awakening to desires she'd never dared imagine.

"I shall fund your education," Andrew's voice resonated with quiet certainty, his words making her heart stutter to a stop. "No conditions attached. If your heart isn't fully present, Charlotte, you're free to go. I couldn't bear knowing our connection stemmed from obligation rather than mutual desire."

Charlotte stared at him, emotions warring in her chest. "You would do that? Even knowing I might leave?" Her voice cracked with disbelief. "Even knowing I've offered myself to you like… like common chattel?"

"You're not chattel," he said fiercely, his hands framing her face. "You're brilliant and brave and deserving of every dream you've ever harbored. If helping you achieve them is all I can offer, then that's enough."

The generosity of his offer, the respect in his voice when he spoke of her dreams, shattered something inside her. For so long, she'd been told her ambitions were unnatural, unwomanly. To hear them spoken of as worthy, as valuable...

"Why?" she whispered, tears spilling freely now. "Why would you help me when you gain nothing in return?"

"Because you matter," he said simply. "Your mind, your dreams, your happiness—they matter. Not because of what you can give me, but because of who you are."

Time suspended between heartbeats. Then, with trembling hands, Charlotte reached for him, bridging the space between them with a kiss that held all the sweet hesitancy of innocence, yet beneath it ran a current of grateful affection that felt dangerously close to something deeper.

This wasn't part of her plan. She wasn't supposed to feel this overwhelming gratitude, this unexpected tenderness for a man who saw her as more than the sum of her desperation. Yet as his hands moved with reverent care, as he whispered her name like a prayer, Charlotte found herself surrendering not to obligation, but to genuine desire.

"I've never known kindness like this," she confessed against his lips, her voice barely audible. "I thought... I thought all men would see me as damaged goods, tainted by my family's disgrace."

"Then they would be fools," Andrew murmured, his lips trailing down her throat with devastating tenderness. "You're not damaged, Charlotte. You're a survivor. There's a difference."

When he began to unlace her corset, his movements were slow, careful—asking permission with every touch. Charlotte found herself nodding, not because she felt she must, but because she wanted to. Wanted to feel beautiful under his gaze, wanted to experience this connection that felt so different from the cold transaction she'd planned.

As her corset fell away and he gazed upon her shift-covered form, Charlotte instinctively moved to cover herself. But Andrew caught her hands gently. His eyes hovered over her mounds, the faint shadow of her nipples showing through the thin fabric.

"You're exquisite," he said, his eyes darkening with need tempered by respect. "But only if you want this. Only if it's your choice."

"I want this," she whispered. "I want to feel wanted. For myself."

When he removed his shirt, Charlotte found herself studying the play of muscle and sinew with genuine appreciation. This man had worked for everything he had, had built his empire with his hands. The calluses on his palms spoke of honest labor, of a man who understood struggle as intimately as she did.

"You're beautiful," she said softly, surprising herself with the admission. "I didn't expect… I mean, I thought this would be…" She trailed off, blushing.

"Cold?" he supplied gently. "Mechanical?"

She nodded, unable to meet his eyes. "I thought all men were like the others who pursued me. Men who saw only what they could take."

"And now?" His voice held carefully controlled hope.

Charlotte looked at him then, really looked—at the genuine concern in his eyes, the way he held himself in check despite his obvious desire, the reverence with which he touched her. "Now I see a man who gives rather than takes. Who offers rather than demands."

The wonder in her voice seemed to affect him deeply. When he kissed her again, it was with renewed tenderness, as if her trust was a gift more precious than her body.

ANDREW FELT SOMETHING shift within him at her words. Despite the desperate circumstances that had brought her here, despite the transaction that lay between them, there was genuine feeling in her voice—surprise, perhaps even relief. She hadn't expected kindness, and the realization that she'd been treated poorly by other men sparked a protective fury in his chest. Her courage in the face of such circumstances, her refusal to let desperation break her spirit, commanded his respect in ways he hadn't anticipated. The desire that had been simmering beneath his careful control now blazed hotter, fueled not just by her beauty but by admiration for her strength.

He pulled on her shift to expose her breasts and groaned when they became bared to him. He covered one of the rosy peaks with his mouth and grasped the other breast with his hand. He squeezed and kneaded the generous flesh, enjoying her nipple puckering and swelling under his care as his arousal surged. He held her body writhing and bucking against him as he used his tongue, teeth, lips and fingers to stimulate the peaks.

Releasing her breasts, he raised his eyes to hers, noting the beautiful orange glow of the lantern light on her flushed face. Charlotte's eyes fluttered open, widening with breathless wonder as he repositioned her on his lap to unfasten his falls. The heat of her gaze, the unabashed hunger that sparked in those luminous depths, sent a lightning bolt of lust sizzling through Andrew's veins. His balls tightened, drawing up hard against his body as a coil of tension wound ever more tightly in his groin.

"Do you pleasure yourself, Charlotte?"

Her large eyes stared back at him with shocked innocence; she shook her head. He leaned forward a little, his lips brushing against the tender skin behind her ear, traversing lower to tickle her neck. "I won't take your virtue, Charlotte. Not now. As much as I want to claim your innocence and force you to stay, I want a wife who chooses me above all else."

With his hands lifting the hem of her shift, Andrew coaxed her to adjust her position while he slowly revealed her stockings.

His eyes riveted on the pale skin of her thighs as they emerged. She tried to cross her legs in an attempt at modesty, but he gently laid a hand on her knee. "I want to watch you touch yourself, Charlotte, and I hope you'll allow me to pleasure myself."

He waited patiently while she processed his request.

Slowly, she parted her legs, the apex of her thighs shrouded in darkness beneath her shift. The anticipation had his breath hitching in his throat, his eyes transfixed on the shadow beneath the hem.

"Do you know what to do?" he asked, one hand gently stroking her bottom while the other rested on her thigh.

She shook her head, her arm around his neck tightening.

"Pull up the hem of your shift so I can see you."

She did his bidding shyly. Andrew inhaled deeply, then swallowed his breath when her sex came into view. The center of her heat, pretty and pink, glistened with moisture.

"Blast it, you're beautiful," he murmured.

Raising his eyes to hers, he carefully reached for her hand and moved it toward her bud.

"Here is your pleasure center," he said. "Massage it to stimulate it. If you haven't felt it before, the pleasure can be surprising, overwhelming…"

Once she had her finger on her clitoris, he released her hand. He watched her for a moment, before replacing her hand with his own and stroking to demonstrate. Soft moans left her lips while he stroked her bud. He chuckled quietly when she protested upon him removing his finger. She then resumed the ministration, moaning faintly. With his arousal surging, he reached into his breeches and gripped the thick shaft swelling along his thigh.

Charlotte paused her movements to watch his member come into view. Her eyes opened wide and fixed on his length as he stroked it slowly. Pulling her to him, he took her mouth in his once more and pulled in her tongue. They consumed each other's breaths and moans as Andrew laid her on the divan. Spreading her knees apart, he knelt between her legs and stroked himself while his eyes fixed on her cunny.

"Christ, you're exquisite," he said, meeting her shy eyes. Her cheeks were flushed, and she began to lift her hips, the muscles in her inner thighs flexing and releasing. "Good. That's it. Come for me. I want to see your cunny weep."

He spread her legs wider apart, his knees touching her ass as she opened wider for him. He bunched up her shift higher to just below her breasts so he could spend on her stomach.

"Andrew…" she moaned. "Is this…?"

A smile curved his lips briefly before he was overwhelmed by his climax cresting. "Not if you can speak, sweetheart."

Then with a sharp intake of her breath, she lifted her hips off the divan, the muscles in her thighs stiffening. A moan scraped out of her throat, her eyes closed shut and her mouth opened wide as she rode her first orgasm. The passion behind her moans thrust him into his own climax as he lurched forward, the hot and creamy liquid spilling onto her stomach, then dripping down her quim.

With one hand braced against the arm of the divan, Andrew remained still for a long time, a mix of elation and despair mingling in his chest.

Finally, he opened his eyes to gaze upon the woman who had rewritten his world in a single evening. Her eyes remained closed, her breathing soft and steady.

As THEY CAUGHT their breaths in each other's arms, Charlotte found herself laughing softly at her own responses, amazed by the pleasure he coaxed from her inexperienced form. "I never knew," she breathed. "I never imagined it could feel like this."

"Like what?" he asked, his own breathing shallow.

"Like joy," she whispered, the sentiment startling her.

As they lay entwined afterward, Charlotte traced patterns on

Andrew's chest, her mind reeling from what had transpired. She understood now why this felt different—why he wasn't like the other men who had pursued her with calculating eyes and grasping hands. Here was a man who had raised his sister from childhood, who had built an empire from nothing but determination and calloused hands. A man who offered rather than demanded.

"I don't understand how you can be so generous," she said quietly. "Offering to fund my education with no guarantee I'll return to you."

"Because it is what you need," Andrew replied, his arms tightening around her. "Because you matter to me in ways I'm only beginning to understand. Please Charlotte. Stay and let us discover what we can be to each other."

Charlotte felt her heart fracture. The temptation was overwhelming—to sink into his strength, to let him shelter her and provide for her. But the reality of marriage loomed stark in her mind. As his wife, she would become his property entirely. Her money, her body, her very existence would belong to him. If he tired of her, if he took a mistress, if he simply decided she was no longer worth providing for, she would have no recourse, no escape.

"I wish I could," she whispered, her voice thick with unshed tears. "I wish I were brave enough to trust that your kindness would last a lifetime. But I've seen what becomes of women who depend entirely on a man's goodwill." She met his eyes. "If I don't pursue my studies now, I may never have another chance. And if I don't become the woman I'm meant to be—one who can stand on her own—I'll have nothing to offer you but my dependence. I cannot put myself in that vulnerable position."

The words tasted bitter, but they were true. How could she trust a man she'd known for mere hours with her entire future, no matter how gentle his touch or sincere his promises?

Andrew's jaw tightened, but he didn't argue. Instead, he pulled her closer, tightening his arms around her. "Then go," he said roughly. "Become the brilliant barrister you're meant to be. But know that what we shared tonight was real, Charlotte. Whatever happens, that was real."

As dawn broke, Charlotte dressed with shaking hands, her heart breaking with every moment that brought her closer to leaving. She paused at the door, looking back at Andrew still lying languidly upon the settee, and nearly lost her resolve.

"Thank you," she whispered. "For seeing me. For helping me. For giving me a choice."

"Charlotte," he called as she reached for the door handle. When she turned, he said simply, "You're worth fighting for. Don't let anyone convince you otherwise."

She nodded, unable to speak past the lump in her throat, and slipped away into the morning light—carrying with her not just the means to pursue her dreams, but the knowledge that she was worthy of love, even if she couldn't claim it yet.

LADY DAISY

30 September 1836—London

ALMOST SIX YEARS after that fateful night when Andrew had bargained for Charlotte Grace's future, he found himself again at the negotiating table—though this time as the Earl of Carlisle, and with his beloved sister's fate hanging in the balance. His fingers bit into the polished mahogany of his desk, knuckles blanching white as he wrestled with an impulse toward violence that would have scandalized his newfound peers in the peerage. This negotiation, unlike the intoxicating parley with Charlotte, left nothing but ash and bile in his mouth.

"You dare speak such filth in my presence?" His voice emerged as a predator's growl; wolfish eyes boring into Viscount Byron's carefully composed face. The nobleman held still, but his quivering throat betrayed his fear.

"I wish I spoke falsely, but the doctor has confirmed your sister's… compromised state."

"Two physicians verified her virtue not a month past!" Andrew's roar filled the study. Byron's gaze fixed on Andrew's whitened knuckles with mounting unease behind his gilt spectacles.

Andrew leaned forward, using every inch of his imposing frame to advantage. Dark eyes glinted beneath windswept hair as he fought for control. A measured breath. Then, in a low rumble: "Explain why you ordered another examination without my consent. What prompted this… violation?"

"Whispers reached me of your sister taking a lover. I wrote to you, but you were days from return. I couldn't wait. Lady Daisy consented. Everything was done according to her wishes."

Andrew rose to his full height, his voice deadly calm. "The betrothal stands. Your unauthorized examination means nothing. And her virtue was never a condition."

"It wasn't specified because it was assumed!" Byron shot back, his face flushing red with indignation. "What man would accept her after she's taken a lover during our engagement?"

"Read your contract," Andrew said. "If it mattered, you should have included it. We've broken no terms."

Byron's hands trembled with rage as he gripped the arms of his chair. "How can I take her as wife? If she's with child, how can I know it's mine?"

"Then wait to bed her until you're certain she isn't," Andrew replied with cold practicality, watching Byron's face turn purple with fury.

"Your logic is depraved!" Byron exploded, springing up so violently that his chair crashed backward against the wall.

The sound of splintering wood seemed to snap something in Andrew. He stalked around the desk with predatory grace, his dark eyes fixed on Byron until he stood close enough that his breath stirred the smaller man's hair. Byron instinctively stepped back, his earlier bravado crumbling under Andrew's towering presence.

"Choose your next words very carefully," Andrew said quietly, his voice carrying the promise of violence. "You insult my sister, threaten to destroy her reputation by breaking the betrothal, and now impugn my honor. I pray you're prepared for a lifelong enemy, my friend. I'll never forgive this violation of Daisy's dignity, and I will have justice. Leave now, before I redecorate your pristine shirt with your own blood."

The viscount drew himself up like a ruffled peacock. Andrew half expected a display of chest-thumping, but the man merely turned on his heel and stormed out.

Andrew waited until the front door's echo died before bellowing for his sister. She materialized in his doorway instantly, the picture of innocence. "You summoned me?"

His prepared words died on his tongue. Daisy remained an enigma, her mind as sharp as a blade and twice as dangerous. He never knew when she was playing him like a fiddle.

"Byron threatens to break your betrothal."

"I suspected he might." Butter wouldn't melt in her mouth.

"Why does he believe you've taken a lover?"

"I tried explaining that a woman's… condition… might change for reasons unrelated to… relations with a man."

"Are you saying the rumor is false?"

"Naturally!"

His brow furrowed deeply. "You passed the first examination. Care to explain what changed?"

"Perhaps jumping fences with Blaze wasn't wise." She had the grace to look slightly abashed. "I know you think me reckless, Andrew, but I couldn't bear being cooped up like a prized hen while Byron paraded me before his friends."

The flash of vulnerability beneath her careful composure reminded him of the frightened girl he'd once comforted through nightmares. "What possessed you to submit to such an offensive examination? You could have refused or waited for my return."

"I'm of age now—no longer your ward. I wanted to prove my innocence. Besides," she added, her voice dropping with distress, "his harassment grew tiresome. The way he looked at me, spoke to me… as if I were already his property to command."

Andrew collapsed into his chair, suppressing the urge to hunt Byron down. His sister's admission revealed more than she perhaps intended—the fiend had been pressuring her, making her feel trapped.

"Am I still to marry Lord Byron?"

"You seem remarkably untroubled for someone whose reputation hangs in the balance," he said, eyes narrowing.

"You know my feelings about marriage. I'd rather practice medicine." Her mask slipped further, revealing the passionate, determined woman beneath. "Andrew, I've worked so hard to earn my credentials. The thought of abandoning it all for a man who sees women as breeding stock…"

"Yes, yes. While I hoped for this match, I won't let a snake like Byron have you. I mistook him for a man of honor." Andrew's shoulders sagged with the admission, his jaw working as he fought back his anger at his own poor judgment. His voice gentled as he saw the relief flood his sister's features, her rigid posture finally relaxing. "Still, Byron claims your conduct is questionable."

"What course will you take?" Daisy asked, leaning forward slightly, her hands clasped tightly in her lap.

"Hold him accountable for his false accusations and contract breach," Andrew said, his fist clenching against his thigh as he spoke.

"You mean pursue legal action? Is such extreme action necessary?" For the first time, Daisy looked genuinely worried, her brow creasing as she reached out to touch his arm. "Andrew, I couldn't bear it if this damaged your standing in society."

Andrew's expression hardened, his eyes flashing with protective fury. "He'll whisper his doubts to every ear in London. Your reputation will be beyond salvation if we don't fight with every weapon at our disposal."

"I'm hardly concerned," she murmured, though her fingers twisted anxiously in her skirts, betraying her words.

"A woman's tainted reputation will poison your medical career. No one trusts a corrupted woman—especially other women," Andrew said, his voice heavy with the weight of societal reality.

Daisy's face crumpled, her composure finally breaking. "What medical career?" Bitterness laced her words, her voice cracking. "You've forbidden me from practice since the day I earned my license." Her hands fell limp in her lap, defeat written in every line of her body.

The accusation hit home, and Andrew felt the familiar weight of guilt. "My investors are traditional men. I can't have them questioning my principles. If you insist on practicing medicine, you'll need your husband's blessing."

Daisy's shoulders slumped, and for a moment she looked far younger than her years. "Can we weather such scandal? Taking him to court only draws more eyes to our shame."

"You'll be ruined regardless—Byron will see to that. A legal complaint paints us as victims of injustice. Once we engage a barrister, absolute truth becomes vital. You might as well start now and spare me the trouble. Is there anything you wish to confess about these accusations?"

"No. I'm innocent," she declared firmly, meeting his gaze with renewed steel.

She held his stare steadily, but doubt gnawed at him. The memory of her forged signature and stolen seal on those papers to study under Dr. James Barry in Jamaica still haunted him. His brilliant, willful sister was capable of almost anything when her goals were threatened.

That evening, despite his weariness, Andrew hurried through London's rain-slicked streets, his Hessians splashing through puddles. His mission—rescuing exploited courtesans on behalf of Madame Tansley's rescue mission—couldn't wait. Time was critical to identify any victims at the gentleman's club near Inner Temple before they disappeared into the night.

He cursed softly upon entering the club's ornate doorway. Late. Fisher, the butler, approached with reverence. "Lord Carlisle, might I be of assistance?"

"Quite all right." Andrew forced pleasantry. "Have you noticed any unusually small or slight women?"

Fisher's eyes widened marginally. "No, my lord. The ladies present are rather… substantial."

Pressing a crisp note into Fisher's palm, Andrew continued his search. These rescue missions for Madam Tansley had taught him strategy—listen for genuine merriment or troubling silence.

The east wing proved unremarkable, but an unnatural quiet

pervaded the west. Concern mounting, Andrew seized a candlestick and affected an intoxicated weave. The first door revealed only startled faces through opium haze.

Muttering drunken apologies, he staggered to the second door, allowing his feigned unsteadiness to seem natural.

"Devil take you! This room is occupied!" a voice snapped, the speaker barely turning.

Darkness cloaked the chamber until Andrew raised his candle, revealing a couple in the far corner. The woman faced the wall, unnaturally still, while her companion stood partially disrobed in the flickering light.

The woman's rigid posture and refusal to turn drew Andrew's attention. He approached, lifting the light to better see the gentleman's face.

"Chatham?" He recognized the duke's distinctive rings.

The man turned further, eyes widening. "Carlisle! What devil's madness brings you bursting in? Lost your companion?"

"My deepest apologies, Your Grace. I search for her, though I've forgotten her name."

Andrew strained to glimpse the woman concealed behind the duke. "She bears a striking resemblance to your companion. Miss, might I see your face?"

"I assure you, Carlisle, this isn't your lady. She's been in my company this hour past."

Her reluctance to reveal herself only fueled Andrew's unease. "Miss, I mean no harm. Your Grace, would you step aside?"

As Chatham moved with reluctance, the woman turned. The candlelight caught porcelain skin and dark eyes that seemed to pierce Andrew's very soul. Time stopped, the world narrowing to her face alone. His knees nearly buckled with the shock of recognition.

In those first years after her departure, she had haunted his dreams relentlessly. He'd searched for her in every passing face, his heart leaping at each dark-haired figure that crossed his path, chasing phantoms born of desperate hope.

Time had eventually dulled her image to a watercolor memory, details lost to the years. But now, standing before him in flesh and blood, there was no doubt. This was no trick of grief-addled imagination.

Reality struck him, leaving him dizzy and breathless. His gaze darted between Charlotte and Chatham, taking in the duke's hastily restored attire, his shirt missing and falls still agape.

Andrew pressed his palm to his brow, turning away, unable to bear the tableau before him. Whatever thoughts churned behind their silence, they granted him a moment to gather his scattered wits.

"Charlotte…" The name scraped from his throat like desert sand. He spoke barely above a whisper, as if speaking too loudly might shatter this cruel apparition. "Are you… well?"

"Yes," she answered, her voice husky with emotion he couldn't interpret. The sound of it—so familiar yet changed—sent a knife of longing through his chest.

Steeling himself, he turned back, raising the light to study her features. He searched for signs of mistreatment but found none.

Though thinner than memory painted her, she carried a new maturity in her bearing. Her skin still bore the bloom of her youth, but something haunted lurked behind her eyes—the look of one who had weathered too many storms.

"How do you know one another?" Chatham asked, bewildered.

Andrew ignored the duke, his entire world narrowed to Charlotte. "Are you here by choice?"

"Yes," she whispered, her gaze never leaving his face. "The duke and I… we have an arrangement. A partnership of mutual protection and… understanding." Her voice caught slightly. "Albert's own circumstances require discretion, as do mine. We shield each other from society's expectations."

"Well, then…" he managed.

Andrew fled, his heart thrashing against his ribs like a caged animal. He stumbled through the doorway, vision swimming as his carefully constructed composure crumbled. The corridor air grew thick and suffocating, pressing in from all sides until he could scarcely breathe.

Breaking into the night air, he gulped great desperate breaths, trying to clear his head and ease the vise crushing his chest. He sagged against the building's rough brick, eyes clenched shut as rage and anguish threatened to overwhelm him.

The knowledge that she had found sanctuary with another—that whatever arrangement they shared kept her safe but lost to him—was a poison he couldn't purge from his system.

With a trembling exhale, he pushed away from the wall and began walking, each step heavy as lead as he vanished into London's shadowed streets.

"ANDREW!" THE NAME tore from her throat before she could stop it. She lurched toward the door, her hands scrabbling at the handle. "I have to explain—he has to understand—"

"Charlotte, wait." The Duke of Chatham's gentle hands caught her shoulders, steadying her trembling form. "Think. What would you tell him? How could you possibly explain without revealing everything?"

She crumpled to the floor, heedless of dignity, her breath coming in ragged gasps as emotion overwhelmed her. The duke's words didn't ease the desperate ache in her chest. Six years. Six long years since that night she had offered herself to Andrew. The memory of his touch, his whispered devotions, had been her anchor through the lonely years that followed—a secret flame she'd nursed while masquerading as a man to study law. Even now, her body burned with the phantom sensation of his hands, his lips, the way he had looked at her that night as if she were precious beyond measure.

"Albert... he looked at me with such... such disgust," she

whispered, sinking back against the door. "As if I were something vile."

Charlotte's mind flashed unbidden to darker memories. She had abandoned her plan to study law in the United States when she received her acceptance letter from Cambridge, albeit under the guise of being a man. This had seemed the safer option rather than traversing foreign lands alone. She had been barely three and twenty when she desperately tried to maintain her disguise as a man while pursuing her legal studies. A monthly payment had ensured one student's silence, but then the dean had summoned her to his office late one evening. Her heart had nearly stopped when he'd revealed he knew she was a woman.

"I have no interest in your meager funds, Miss Morton," he'd said, his eyes raking over her form with calculated intent. "I require… other forms of payment."

The memory of those monthly meetings made bile rise in her throat—the musty office, the sound of the door locking, her quiet sobs muffled by her own hand. She had endured it silently, knowing that to refuse meant losing everything she'd sacrificed for. Until that final night, when another professor had walked in unexpectedly. The horror in his eyes had quickly transformed to fury as he'd pieced together what was happening.

The next day, Albert had offered her sanctuary. His quiet devotion had become her shield—born not of romantic love, but of mutual understanding. Two souls who required society's protection from their own truths: hers, the dangerous ambition to practice law as a woman; his, the equally dangerous truth of where his romantic inclinations truly lay.

"My dear," Albert said gently, settling beside her on the floor, "you rather understated your feelings for Carlisle when we began this arrangement."

Charlotte's throat constricted with unshed tears. "I thought I had buried them. I thought if I could just avoid him, pretend that night never happened…" She pressed her hands to her face. "But seeing him again, the way he looked at me—as if I'd betrayed everything good between us."

"Perhaps," Albert said carefully, "it might be worth considering whether our arrangement has served its purpose. You're established now, Charlotte. You have your law degree, your barrister's credentials. Perhaps it's time to—"

"No." The word came out sharper than she intended. "Albert, you don't understand. He would never accept what I've become. That night, six years ago, he offered to fund my education—when I refused, when I chose my dreams over his proposal..." She laughed bitterly. "How could I explain that I've spent four years living as a man, that I've had to endure... compromising the virtue he'd tried to protect... just to earn the right to practice law?"

"He might surprise you," Albert said quietly. "Love can be more forgiving than we expect."

"Love?" Charlotte's voice cracked. "He doesn't love who I am now, Albert. He loved the grateful, desperate woman who would have been content to be rescued. But I'm not that woman anymore. I can't be."

Yet even as she spoke the words, her heart rebelled against them. The way Andrew had looked at her tonight, before shock and hurt had replaced recognition—there had been something there. Something that suggested the intervening years hadn't dimmed whatever had existed between them.

"I should have run after him," she whispered, surprising herself with the admission. "I should have tried to explain, regardless of the consequences."

Albert's expression softened with something approaching pity. "And what would you have said? That our relationship is one of convenience and protection?"

"I would have told him the truth," Charlotte said fiercely, then deflated. "If I were brave enough."

The duke sighed, raking fingers through his disheveled hair. "My dear, you are many things, but a coward is not one of them. Perhaps it's time to prove that—to yourself and to him."

She sank her head to her knees, shoulders bowing under grief's weight. Her feelings for Andrew ran deeper than she'd ever intended to acknowledge. What must he think of her now? The thought brought a sorrow so profound it threatened to drown her. Yet Albert had been her only ally, her sole hope these past years. How could she risk that safety for a love that might not survive the truth?

"He thinks I chose you over him," she said quietly. "That I refused his proposal only to become another man's mistress."

"Then perhaps it's time he learned otherwise," Albert replied. "The question is: Are you prepared to fight for what you desire?"

Charlotte's eyes flashed. "Albert, we made promises to each other. Sacred ones. I can't simply abandon you because—"

"Because you've found love?" His voice was gentle but firm. "Charlotte, I won't be the chain that binds you to a life of shadows."

"And I won't be the reason you're exposed and ruined." Her voice cracked with emotion. "If anyone learned the truth about your… nature… it wouldn't just mean social death. The law itself would destroy you."

"My status will grant me some protection. You know this." Albert's face grew somber. "I cannot care more for my reputation than your happiness."

"But you ought to," Charlotte said fiercely. "We both knew the risks when we began this arrangement. I won't let my feelings for Andrew become your downfall."

"And I won't let my secrets become your prison."

Charlotte closed her eyes, Andrew's face—shocked, hurt, disgusted—burned into her memory. "What if he can't forgive me? What if I tell him everything and he still looks at me like I'm something to be ashamed of?"

"Then at least you'll know," Albert said gently. "And you'll have fought for what matters most."

As silence settled between them, Charlotte found herself torn between the safety of her current life and the terrifying possibility of reclaiming what she'd lost. The memory of Andrew's kiss, his gentle hands, his promise to fund her education with no strings attached, warred with the reality of what she'd become—a woman who'd had to live as a man, who'd endured degradation for her dreams, who'd found protection in deception.

CRUEL FATE

3 October 1836—London

TWENTY BARRISTERS HAD dismissed him outright upon Andrew's request to represent his sister. Despite his painstaking letters to London's finest legal minds, each response brought only polite rejection. Even his friend, Nicholas Preston, had declined.

The message was clear—domestic cases were beneath their dignity, inviting only scorn from peers and bench alike.

Yet Andrew hadn't risen from dockworker to aristocrat by accepting defeat. His will had never bent, and it wouldn't start now.

Andrew maintained his mask of polite interest, befitting his position as Earl of Carlisle and honorary bencher, as new barristers were presented at the Grand Hall.

The Grand Hall's solemn pageantry faded to a meaningless swirl of black and white, each new barrister's bow a distant echo, until—there. His heart raced, recognizing her before his mind could catch up. That particular way she held herself, proud yet somehow vulnerable, the same bearing that had first bewitched him in Madam's parlor six years ago. The graceful arch of her neck, once pressed against his lips, now bent in reverence to the court.

Charlotte Grace.

So, she had completed her law degree. She'd achieved everything she'd dreamed of. The realization brought with it a wave of bittersweet memories he'd thought safely buried. Then, unbidden, came the memory of her compromised form beside the duke.

The thought burned like acid in his throat. Six years of waiting for her letter wondering if she thought of him, and now he knew—she'd found comfort in another man's protection. The generous funding, the blessing to pursue her dreams, all of it apparently meaningless beside this evidence of her... arrangement.

The Master of Bench, Lord Alford's voice cut through the chaos in his mind. "Gentlemen, I present Miss Charlie Morton, called to the Bar."

Andrew's breath caught as truth struck him. The woman who'd haunted his dreams had been a fiction. He hadn't even known her real name.

Morton. Not Grace.

She stepped forward, chin held high, defiance radiating from every line of her body. The traditional robes seemed to mock the very institution they represented.

Their eyes met across the sea of faces. Recognition flickered in her gaze, followed by something that looked almost like hope—quickly masked by studied indifference that couldn't quite hide her fear.

Despite the turmoil in his chest, he couldn't deny her raw courage. Dark tendrils escaped her severe wig, framing a face grown sharper with time, more beautiful somehow in its maturity.

Whispers turned to hisses in the crowd. "Preposterous," one voice spat. "A mockery," another cut deliberately loud.

Her expression hardened and her chin lifted as their eyes locked again. She was magnificent but utterly doomed.

Lord Alford called for silence. "Miss Morton has met all requirements with distinction. She is legally entitled to practice."

"By law, perhaps," someone shouted, "but what of tradition? Of natural order?"

The crowd pressed closer, faces twisted with righteous anger.

Fear flashed across Charlotte's face, and something ancient and protective stirred in Andrew's chest. He wouldn't watch a mob form regardless of his personal feelings.

Stepping forward, he raised his voice. "Gentlemen. We are men of law and order. We must respect the law and the Master Bencher's decision."

The crowd hesitated, many turning to him in surprise. Though his honorary bench position came from wealth rather than legal expertise, his word carried weight.

Charlotte's eyes found his, brimming with gratitude that made his chest tighten painfully.

"However," came a silk-smooth voice from behind Andrew, "one must question whether respect for law should extend to… perversions of it." Lord Naylor, one of Parliament's most influential voices, stepped forward. His gaze swept dismissively over Charlotte before fixing on Andrew with pointed interest. "Surely an earl understands the importance of maintaining proper standards? The Crown depends on men of traditional values."

The threat was delicately veiled but unmistakable. Andrew felt the weight of a dozen influential gazes upon him, measuring his response. His position in the peerage was still fresh, his political influence dependent on these men. A single misstep could destroy everything he'd fought to build—not just for himself, but for Daisy, for his workers, for everyone who depended on his success.

Choose, Naylor's eyes seemed to say. *Her or your future.*

Andrew's jaw clenched as he felt the familiar sensation of the ground shifting beneath his feet—the same helpless rage he'd felt as a boy when larger forces controlled his fate. But he was no longer that powerless child. He was an earl with responsibilities that extended far beyond his own desires.

Forgive me, Charlotte.

"Don't mistake intervention for approval, Miss Morton," Andrew heard himself say, his voice carrying across the silent hall with cold authority. "Your presence here mocks centuries of tradition, but we must abide by the law which permits you. Even if these halls do not welcome you."

The moment the words left his mouth, Andrew regretted them. The flash of pain in Charlotte's eyes cut deeper than any blade, but his pride—and political survival—wouldn't let him take them back. He watched her absorb the blow, saw her spine straighten with that familiar defiant grace that had first captivated him.

Fire flashed in her eyes before ice claimed them. "I don't seek your approval, Mr. Creswell. My apologies… Lord Carlisle. I forgot your earldom is so… recent," she said, the barb aimed precisely at his common roots—and finding its mark with devastating accuracy.

Even as it stung, he couldn't help but admire her tactical brilliance—she'd reminded the entire room of his common roots in a single, perfectly aimed blow.

"I merely wish to prove my worth," she continued, her voice steady despite the hurt he'd inflicted.

Her words were like a knife twisting in Andrew's gut. The political victory felt hollow as ash, purchased with Charlotte's pain.

"Let us return to our duties, gentlemen," Andrew said, his voice carefully modulated. "The law waits for no man… nor woman," he added, the pointed emphasis drawing satisfied murmurs from the traditionalists.

As the crowd dispersed, he watched her standing alone, spine straight as steel before a room of men who craved her failure. The sight of her solitary defiance made his chest ache with unwilling admiration and fear in equal measure.

Her courage was both magnificent and terrifying—she was walking into a lion's den with nothing but her wits and determination to protect her.

With practiced casualness, he threaded through the thinning crowd, ignoring Naylor's knowing smile. Fear flickered across Charlotte's face before neutrality claimed it. Andrew inclined his head—a gesture that could be interpreted as either courtesy or condescension, depending on one's perspective.

"Miss Morton?" he said for nearby ears, ensuring his tone carried the proper distance. "Might I escort you out? I have questions regarding… the Halsbury case."

Understanding flashed in her eyes—recognition that he was offering what protection he could without compromising his position. "Your lordship is most kind."

As they walked, Andrew positioned himself to shield her from the most venomous stares, his presence a buffer against the worst of the hostility. When they reached a secluded alcove, he finally allowed his mask to slip slightly.

"Charlie Morton. Surely not your given name," he said evenly, though his pulse quickened at their proximity.

"It is. On my birth document at Father's insistence. I suppose it soothed Father's pining for a son. Mother always called me Charlotte, however."

"If your parents wished for a son, they partially succeeded."

She cut him a sharp glance, and he caught a flash of hurt beneath her defiance. "I'm unchanged from six years ago. Did your lordship question my sex then?"

The memory of their intimacy struck like lightning—her soft gasps, the way she'd trembled in his arms, how she'd kissed him with such sweet desperation. His body betrayed him with instant recognition, desire warring with the fresh wound of seeing her with Chatham.

His body's response mocked his wounded pride. Six years, and she could still unravel his composure with nothing more than proximity.

"You're clever, Miss Morton, but heed this advice," he murmured, closing the distance between them until he could smell the faint scent of jasmine that clung to her skin. "Be wise. Don't tempt me."

A ghost of a smile touched her lips, and for a moment he saw the Charlotte he remembered—bold, challenging, utterly fearless.

"It seems my very existence tests your control, my lord."

His throat tightened at the truth of her words. She had always been his weakness, his one moment of complete abandon. Forcing gravity into his voice, he asked, "Who trained you?"

"The Duke of Chatham."

"Naturally." Bitter laughter escaped him before he could stop it. "That explains the scene I witnessed. What else could have persuaded His Grace to champion you against Parliament's fury?"

She lifted her chin, folding her hands. "I assure you, my legal acumen equals—perhaps exceeds—that of my male peers. Which reminds me, did you verify the accuracy of my warning from our first encounter?"

"Yes," he admitted, the word tasting of defeat and grudging respect.

Charlotte's lips curved into that sweet, dimpled smile he remembered too well, triumph and something deeper flickering in her eyes. "How fortunate I could assist before your solicitor had the opportunity."

She straightened her spine, and her jaw set in a hard line. "I thank you for your escort, Lord Carlisle. Good evening." As she turned to leave, Andrew felt something fracture inside his chest. The distance between them felt vast—an ocean he'd helped create.

She retreated into the garden, each step away from him costing him more strength than the last. Andrew remained frozen, his hands clenching and unclenching at his sides as he watched her solitary figure disappear into the shadows.

Every instinct screamed at him to follow—to ensure her safety, to apologize, to somehow undo the damage his words had inflicted. The garden was poorly lit, and London's streets grew dangerous after dark.

But following her now would only compound his betrayal, make him appear even more duplicitous than he already was. She'd made it clear she wanted nothing from him—not his escort, not his concern, certainly not his presence.

THE COOL NIGHT air did nothing to calm Charlotte's flushed skin or the storm of emotions churning in her chest. She wrapped her arms around herself, trying to still her racing heart. Despite all that had transpired between them, she couldn't deny the electric awareness that still crackled whenever he was near.

The contradiction left her reeling. He'd defended her from the crowd's anger only to deliver his own with surgical precision.

His appearance at the ceremony had shaken her more than she cared to admit. Though thinner and paler than she remembered—the weight of his new responsibilities evident in the sharp angles of his face—he remained devastatingly handsome. His broad shoulders and strong jaw stirred feelings she thought long buried.

But more than his physical presence, it was his behavior that left her reeling. The man who had once promised to fund her dreams with no strings attached had publicly humiliated her. The same hands that had touched her with such reverence now gestured dismissively at her presence.

The soft crunch of gravel made her turn sharply, her heart leaping at the unexpected sound. In the moonlight, she recognized Andrew's tall silhouette immediately—the broad shoulders, the familiar way he carried himself. Relief and wariness warred within her as he drew closer, the cool night air suddenly heating her skin.

"The gardens are lovely at night," he said softly, his rich baritone sending an involuntary shiver down her spine.

The gentle tone—so different from the cold dismissal he'd shown her in the hall—ignited her anger. Charlotte turned to face him, no longer able to hide behind politeness. "Are they? I find them rather cold," she said, her voice sharper than intended. "Much like the reception inside."

She saw him flinch slightly at her words, a crack in his carefully maintained composure. Good. If she was hurting, she wanted him to know it.

"Charlotte," he began.

"Miss Morton," she corrected icily. "We must maintain proper standards, after all. Isn't that what you said?"

Andrew's jaw tightened, and she caught a glimpse of something raw in his eyes—pain, perhaps, or regret. But it was gone too quickly to be certain.

"You don't understand the position I'm in," he said quietly. "The politics, the expectations—"

"I understand perfectly," Charlotte interrupted, years of frustrated hurt finally finding voice. "You told me to pursue my dreams, Andrew. You funded them. You blessed my path. And now that I've succeeded—now that I've become exactly what you said I should become—you treat me like a pariah."

"That's not—" He stopped, his shoulders sagging as the fight went out of him. "You're right. What I said in there was deplorable. I was supposed to protect you, and instead I..." He raked a hand through his hair, his composure finally cracking. "Christ, Charlotte, I was terrified. Terrified of losing my position, my influence, everything I've built. But that's no excuse for what I did to you."

The raw honesty in his voice caught her off guard.

"Then why?" she whispered. "Why throw it all away for politics when you once believed in me enough to fund my dreams?"

Andrew's jaw tightened, his gaze dropping to the ground. "Because everything has changed since then, Charlotte. When I funded your education, I was nobody—a merchant with ambition but no real standing. Now..." He gestured helplessly. "The earldom, the investments, the position in Parliament—it's all built on sand. One wrong move, one perceived betrayal of their values, and it all crumbles."

His voice grew strained. "I have hundreds of employees depending on me, Daisy's future to secure, obligations I never had before. The men who made me an earl can just as easily unmake me. And supporting you publicly—" He stopped, the words seeming to stick in his throat.

"Would mark you as a radical," Charlotte finished quietly, understanding dawning in her eyes.

"I was a coward," he said simply. "I chose security over principle. Over you." His voice turned bitter. "But perhaps it was easier to justify because I'd already lost you, hadn't I? You'd found yourself a protector who could offer you more than I could—respectability, connections, the freedom to practice law without consequence. What was I compared to that?"

The pain in his voice, the way he saw himself as somehow lesser than the duke, made her heart clench. "Andrew," she said more gently, taking a step toward him. "You don't understand about Chatham and me. Our arrangement isn't what you think—"

"Isn't it?" His laugh was harsh, self-mocking. "Then explain it to me, Charlotte. Help me understand why the woman who showed me what love could be—who made me want things I'd never dared dream of—chose another man's protection over mine. I tried to find you, but I couldn't locate a Charlotte Grace anywhere in London. Now I understand why. I didn't know your real name. No letter, no attempt to contact me. You walked away."

The question hung between them, weighted with years of hurt and misunderstanding. Charlotte felt the old familiar urge to tell him everything—about Cambridge, about the dean, about Albert's true nature and her own desperate need for safety. But the words stuck in her throat, trapped by years of necessary secrecy.

How could she explain that Albert's protection came at the cost of guarding his most dangerous secret? That admitting what the dean had done to her would mean confessing she'd traded her body for her education when Andrew had so reverently protected it? She'd felt so ashamed, so unworthy of the man who'd treated her with such tenderness, that she'd convinced herself he was better off without her.

"I can't," she whispered, hating herself. "I wish I could, but I can't."

Something died in Andrew's eyes at her words. When he spoke again, his voice had returned to its earlier formality, though she could hear the anger beneath it.

"Then I suppose we have nothing more to discuss, Miss Morton. I wish you success in your endeavors."

He turned to go, and Charlotte felt panic rise in her throat. Her hand reached out instinctively, fingers grasping at empty air.

"Andrew, wait," she called, the words escaping before pride could stop them. When he paused but didn't turn back, she continued desperately. "I know you must think the worst of me. I know what it looks like. But please… please don't think I took your generosity lightly. What you gave me—the chance to pursue my dreams—it meant everything. It still does."

For a moment, his shoulders sagged with some invisible weight. When he finally looked back at her, his expression was unreadable in the moonlight.

"It's late," he said quietly, his voice stripped of emotion. "Allow me to escort you back to the Inner Temple. You can find a cab from there."

The offer was proper, practical—and devastatingly distant. Charlotte nodded, not trusting her voice. As they walked in tense silence through the London streets, she felt the weight of all her unspoken truths pressing against her chest.

When they reached the familiar gates of the Inner Temple, Andrew turned to her one final time. He then simply tipped his hat with cold formality.

"Good evening, Miss Morton."

The formal address, after everything they'd shared, cut deeper than any cruel words that had been hurled at her by strangers. She watched his figure disappear into the London fog, and felt the bitter taste of his judgment and the terrible knowledge that she'd lost him twice now—once by choice, and once by circumstances beyond her control.

Charlotte sank onto a nearby bench, finally allowing herself to weep for everything they'd lost and everything they could never be.

THE LAST-DITCH EFFORT

9 October 1836—London

FOR THREE MONTHS, Andrew had circled the borders of the Inner Temple like a man skirting the edges of madness. His excuses to avoid the legal district had grown increasingly elaborate—anything to escape the maze of narrow streets where Charlotte now built her new life. He couldn't trust himself within those ancient stone walls, couldn't predict whether seeing her would ignite the smoldering remains of his desire or fan his temper into murderous rage.

But when Lord Alford's messenger arrived bearing a letter adorned with urgent red seals, Andrew's resolve crumbled beneath the weight of obligation. One did not refuse the man whose influence had secured him the naval contract—that precious agreement to supply warships which had paved his path to the peerage. The earldom now shielded Andrew from the whispers and accusations that had once dogged his steps, a protection he could not afford to squander. No, he would do His Lordship's bidding provided it did not require him to grovel.

The late afternoon sun spilled through the leaded windows of Lord Alford's chambers like molten gold, painting the oak-paneled walls with an otherworldly glow. As Andrew crossed the threshold, his curiosity momentarily overcame his dread.

"Ah, Carlisle," Lord Alford gestured to a chair. "We have a rather delicate matter to discuss."

Andrew sat, spine rigid with anticipation. "How might I serve you, My Lord?"

Lord Alford leaned forward, fingers forming a steeple. "The Inner Temple's charity debate for Bertram Orphanage approaches. It's vital—not just for the children, but for our institution's standing. We must present a united front, showcasing our finest. I'd like you to participate."

"Surely there are more seasoned debaters among the benchers?"

"Indeed." Discomfort flickered across Lord Alford's features. "However, we face a unique situation. I've decided to pair you with Miss Morton."

Andrew's voice turned to steel. "Miss Morton? Surely you jest. I cannot possibly—"

"I understand your reservations," Lord Alford sighed wearily. "But this arrangement serves multiple purposes. It shows the public—particularly the common folk and Whigs whom King William favors—that we embrace progress. Meanwhile, it gives Miss Morton the chance to prove herself publicly. Should she succeed, it will vindicate my decision to call her to the Bar and silence my critics."

Andrew surged to his feet, pacing like a caged lion. He uttered the words that he didn't believe in but his political position required him to speak. "My views on her presence here are well known. I cannot support this charade."

"Carlisle," Lord Alford's voice sharpened, "would you prefer her paired with someone who might humiliate her—and us—before the other Inns? Despite your objections, I know you can show more reason in dealing with her."

Andrew stilled, weighing the implications. Working with her would be maddening but watching another intentionally shame her was unbearable.

"Consider her a weapon for our advantage," Lord Alford pressed. "Succeed, and you've raised funds for worthy children while proving your ability to transcend personal feelings. You emerge noble either way."

Andrew's jaw tightened. "My lord, I must voice my concerns.

Working publicly with Miss Morton will compromise my standing with my investors and could damage my position in Parliament. My shareholders are already uneasy about any association with progressive causes."

He paused, inhaling deeply. "However, I owe you a considerable debt. Your influence secured me the naval contracts, and your recommendation earned me my seat in the House of Lords. If you believe this course is necessary…" He trailed off to massage his temple and organize his thoughts. After a moment, he nodded stiffly. "Very well. I shall do your bidding but note my protest. Understand that I do this out of loyalty to you, not conviction in the cause."

Relief softened Lord Alford's features. "Noted. I trust you'll handle this delicately. The debate is in a sennight. Best find Miss Morton and begin preparations."

As Andrew turned to leave, Lord Alford spoke again, hesitation threading his voice. "Not to add pressure, but rumors say certain members seek my removal for allowing a woman at the Bar. If Miss Morton fails to win public favor and some benchers' approval, I fear my position becomes untenable."

Andrew's head fell forward, a weary sigh escaping him. "You're right—I hardly needed that additional weight."

He strode from the office, his mind churning with resentment at the elegant trap he'd been maneuvered into. Yet beneath his frustration lurked an unwelcome spark at the prospect of seeing Charlotte again. Despite every effort to quash it, a current of anticipation hummed through his veins.

FINALLY SHAKING OFF the incessant thoughts of Andrew, Charlotte immersed herself in documents for the child labor debate, knowing her arguments would face twice the scrutiny of her male colleagues. A sharp knock interrupted her concentration.

"Enter," she called, not lifting her eyes.

Andrew's presence filled her small office like storm clouds before thunder. Her breath caught as she took in his imposing figure.

"Miss Morton, am I interrupting anything of vital importance, or merely your usual pursuit of tallying my many failings?"

Charlotte willed her features to stillness despite her racing pulse. "Lord Carlisle. How delightfully presumptuous of you. I was preparing for our debate—a novel concept, I realize, given your apparent preference for angering the beast before ambushing."

His laugh rumbled low. He settled across from her with infuriating nonchalance as if they were intimate friends. "Your thoughts on child labor in factories, then? I confess myself curious to hear your solution, though I suspect it involves more heart than pragmatism."

"As opposed to your callous arguments wrapped in a pretense of caring but rooted in self-serving objectives?" she countered. "Not to worry, my lord. I shall prepare you by dismantling your profound observations, if we're being charitable with definitions."

One corner of his lips curved up in an infuriatingly amused smile. "I welcome your analysis, Miss Morton."

She shot daggers at him with her eyes which could have felled him where he sat. "It must end," she said sharply. "Children belong in schools, not dangerous factories. Though I suppose a man who profits from such arrangements might find my position inconvenient."

"Some argue these children support their families," he said mildly. "But pray, don't let economic realities trouble your noble sensibilities."

His patronizing tone sent heat through her despite her determination to remain unmoved. She caught herself leaning forward and jerked back.

"Ah… I still affect you," he observed, eyebrows arching with insufferable satisfaction.

"Not in the manner you imagine, Lord Carlisle. Your ego is simply overwhelming. This office wasn't designed to accommodate persons of your considerable... pig-headedness."

His chuckle resonated through her bones. "Your blush suggests otherwise, Miss Morton. Unless you've suddenly developed a fever from the exertion of thinking?"

She bristled. "This is my domain, my lord. Perhaps you should return when you're capable of discussing serious matters without resorting to... whatever this performance is meant to accomplish.."

"Performance?" His voice dropped to velvet mockery. "My dear Miss Morton, if I were performing, you'd know it. This is merely friendly counsel." His eyes traveled deliberately down her throat. "I advise you to cease provoking powerful men and retreat to Chatham's protective embrace. Some battles cannot be won through sheer bloody-mindedness."

"Bloody-mindedness?" Charlotte's voice rose an octave. "Is that what you call principled conviction? How terribly unfashionable of me."

"Your principles are admirable," he said, rising with predatory grace. "Your survival instincts, however, leave much to be desired." He perched on her desk with deliberate casualness. "I wish you wouldn't keep stumbling into my path, Miss Morton. My capacity for rescue has its limits."

"Rescue?" She laughed, a sound like breaking crystal. "From my perspective, Lord Carlisle, you appear more akin to the dragon than the knight."

His smile turned positively wicked. "How perceptive. Though I confess, the role of dragon has its... compensations."

"Such as?"

"Dragons, my dear, always get to keep the treasure."

Charlotte shot to her feet, pushing the chair back, heart thundering against her ribs. "Lord Carlisle, this is inappropriate," she whispered, but she didn't step away. Couldn't step away.

For a moment, they stared at each other, six years of longing suspended between them like a taut wire. The air crackled with unspoken words, with all the passion they'd tried to bury.

Then he reached for her, one hand sliding around her waist while the other caught her wrist, pulling her against the solid heat of his body. The world dissolved into sensation—the bitter burn of brandy on his tongue as it swept into her mouth, the bruising grip of his fingers digging into her ribs, the helpless whimper that tore from her throat as denial and desire exploded in a kiss that was equal parts punishment and plea.

Her knees buckled, forcing her to clutch at his coat for support, her fingernails scraping against the wool as her body betrayed every rational thought. Heat pooled low in her belly, spreading like liquid fire through her veins until she could barely breathe. His stubble scraped against her chin, rough and masculine, while his other hand tangled in her hair, tilting her head back to deepen the assault on her senses. She could taste desperation on his lips, could feel the heat seeping through the fabric where her chest pressed against his. Her own pulse hammered so violently she was certain he could feel it too.

The kiss deepened, years of denied passion crashing through carefully constructed walls until Charlotte could barely remember her own name. His hands traced fire down her spine, and she arched into him with a soft gasp that seemed to ignite something primal in his touch. Time lost all meaning in the storm of sensation—the ridge of his hard length against her hip, his large hand exploring her body with abandon, the way her fingers had somehow found their way into his hair.

Reality crashed back like ice water when his hand found her bare thigh. Charlotte wrenched herself away, chest heaving. "Stop," she gasped, pressing trembling fingers to her lips. "I can't... Chatham—"

"Chatham?" Andrew rose to his feet and stepped toward her until her back met the bookshelf. He braced both arms against it, caging her with his body. "Don't hide behind that excuse when what burns between us could set London ablaze."

Color flooded her cheeks, but this time from anger rather than passion. "Hide behind?" The words cracked like a whip. "The duke has shown me nothing but respect and devotion, which is more than I can say for other men who claimed to care for me. I will not dishonor or hurt him."

"Respect? Devotion?" Andrew's eyes flashed dangerously as he leaned closer, his breath hot against her cheek. "Tell me, Charlotte, does your devoted duke make you tremble like this?" His fingers traced up her arm, leaving gooseflesh in their wake. "Does your breath catch when he enters a room? Does your heart race at the mere thought of him?"

"You have no right—"

"I have every right when you kiss me like that," he growled, the raw need in his voice making her shiver despite herself. "Like you've missed this as much as I have." His thumb brushed her lower lip, still swollen from his kiss. "Tell me you feel nothing when I touch you. Tell me you can kiss me like that and still claim to feel anything real for him."

Charlotte forced steel into her spine, even as her body still hummed from his touch. "My loyalty lies with him," she said, smoothing her skirts with hands that trembled. "This was a moment of weakness brought on by old memories and your..." she gestured vaguely at him, hating how her hands still shook, "your particular talent for provocation."

His jaw clenched, a muscle ticking beneath his skin. "Is that what you tell yourself? That I merely provoked you into feeling something that isn't there?"

"What I feel for the duke is real," she insisted, though the words felt like ash in her mouth after the fire they'd just shared. "He offers me security, protection, a future where I can practice law without fear—"

"Protection?" Andrew pushed away from the bookcase, releasing her. His laugh was harsh enough to make her flinch. "From threadbare clothes and shoes with more holes than an anthill? What kind of protection leaves you looking half-starved?"

The casual observation stung her pride more than she cared to admit. "He has offered financial support, but I had to decline. What's more important is that he understands me, supports my ambitions—"

"Because he sees you as a novelty, a curiosity to parade before society!" Andrew's words crackled with fury as he paced the room. "I see you, Charlotte. I see the fire that burns in you, the passion that consumes everything in its path. I feel it every time you're near me, and you can't tell me you don't feel it too."

"What I feel," she said, forcing ice into her tone despite the heat in her body, "is gratitude toward a man who has shown me nothing but kindness and acceptance."

"And do you love him?" Andrew's voice dropped dangerously low as he stepped closer, close enough that she could see the flecks of gold in his eyes. "Look me in the eye and tell me you love him. Tell me what you feel for him is anything like what just passed between us."

Charlotte lifted her chin, meeting his gaze even as something deep in her chest cracked. The lie came harder this time, each word a betrayal of her own heart. "I do love him," she said, each syllable measured and precise. "What happened between us was… a mistake. A momentary lapse in judgment that will not be repeated."

The silence that followed was deafening. She watched the fury drain from his face, replaced by something far worse—a cold, empty acceptance that made her want to take back every word.

"A mistake," he repeated, his voice devoid of emotion. "Well then, Miss Morton, I shall endeavor not to make any more… mistakes… with you." He stepped back, his withdrawal like a physical chill. "I wish you every happiness in your sensible, secure future."

He turned sharply on his heel, pausing at the door without looking back. "We begin tomorrow. Nine o'clock."

The door closed behind him with quiet finality, just as devastating as if he'd slammed it. Charlotte sank into her chair, pressing shaking hands to her face as the phantom taste of his kiss lingered on her lips and the terrible knowledge settled in her chest that she may have lost him for good this time.

THE DEBATE

14 October 1836

"I TRUST YOU'RE prepared, Mr. Creswell," Charlotte said, her voice carefully controlled. "I won't have your... personal feelings compromise our success."

Andrew's laugh was dark as his fingers languidly stroked the spot on his shirt where her hands had clutched at him just days before. "Fear not, Miss Morton. My 'feelings' are remarkably well-behaved in professional settings." His voice dropped to a teasing whisper. "Though I notice you're gripping that quill as if it might escape."

Charlotte glanced down at her white knuckles and deliberately loosened her hold. "I am merely... ensuring proper penmanship."

"Ah yes, because nothing wins an argument like strangled writing instruments." Andrew settled into his chair with maddening ease. "Tell me, do you also throttle your legal briefs into submission?"

"Only when they refuse to cooperate," she replied tartly. "Rather like certain earls of my acquaintance."

"Touché. Though I should point out that my cooperation has been exemplary. I haven't mentioned your tendency to pace when nervous even once."

"I do not pace when—" Charlotte caught herself mid-stride and froze. "And you stare out the window like a housecat admiring sparrows."

"Just studying my prey. But of course I never get nervous," he said, tugging at his coat sleeves.

"Shall we begin, or would you prefer to shoot down some sparrows first?" Charlotte asked, finally taking her seat and arranging her papers.

"How thoughtful of you. Keep your bonnet on, Miss Morton. They have an excellent aim for exposed weaknesses."

Her eyes met his with a flash of silver fury while his answering smile held satisfied glee. But as they took the stage, something shifted. The familiar rhythm of intellectual combat overrode their personal animosity. Whatever lay between them, they both wanted to win.

Charlotte's voice rang out clear and strong, and Andrew found himself caught in the familiar spell of her brilliance. The woman before him commanded the room with a presence that made his chest ache with pride and regret in equal measure.

Throughout the debate, her quick wit and razor-sharp rebuttals repeatedly caught him off guard. Despite their personal turmoil, they found an unexpected rhythm. Each cutting argument felt like an extension of their private battle, their shared passion transmuted into intellectual fire.

Watching her dismantle their opponents' defense of child labor, despite himself, Andrew found his resentment giving way to grudging respect. Her passionate gestures, the fierce light in her eyes, her absolute command of the room—this was the woman who had first captivated him, the brilliant mind he'd been fool enough to let slip away.

When his turn came, he matched her intensity instinctively, their mutual fury channeled into devastating logic. His economic arguments wove seamlessly with her moral appeals, and for brief moments, their eyes met across the podium. In those glances lay everything they couldn't say—respect, regret, and something far more dangerous.

Their opponents from Gray's Inn wilted before their unexpected alliance. But during a heated exchange on education reform, Higgins made the mistake of launching a personal attack.

"While Lord Carlisle's arguments merit consideration," Higgins sneered, wiping his brow, "I cannot take seriously any position advocated by a… lady. A woman's place is nurturing children, not in a court of law. It goes against the natural order…"

The words died in his throat as both Charlotte and Andrew turned to him with identical expressions of cold fury. In that moment, their private war forgotten, they were once again a united front.

Charlotte stepped forward. Her face was marble-smooth, but her eyes blazed with controlled fury that made Higgins step back.

"I may be a woman, sir," her voice carried with quiet authority, "but I stand here by virtue of my mind and conviction—the same qualities that built this institution you guard so zealously."

Her gaze swept the room, commanding attention.

"You speak of natural order, Mr. Higgins, but order evolves. Your predecessors once argued against educating the poor as unnatural. Yet here we debate expanding that very education."

Her voice grew in strength.

"I earned my place through the same rigorous study and examination as any man. My presence doesn't diminish these halls—it enriches them. In denying half of humanity the chance to contribute their intellect, we deny ourselves the full measure of human progress."

She turned to address the entire audience.

"Gentlemen, today's question isn't whether women belong in law. It's whether we, as a society, can afford to squander the contributions of any mind capable of advancing justice and the rule of law, regardless of their sex."

The room erupted into both a storm of applause and contentious murmurs. Andrew stood transfixed, seeing Charlotte as if for the first time. Where others might have crumbled under such a personal attack, she had transformed it into a masterful argument that not only defended her place but elevated their entire purpose.

As she turned to him, triumph playing at her lips, he offered a slight nod—a warrior's acknowledgment of a worthy opponent.

Their eyes held as the judges announced their victory and the substantial sum secured for the orphanage.

In the celebrations that followed, Andrew found himself drawn to her orbit, keenly aware of her proximity. "We make quite the team, it seems," he said, his voice softening.

She glanced up, eyes dancing with victory and mischief. "Indeed, though don't let it inflate your ego. I still find you thoroughly insufferable."

Andrew's laugh rumbled low. "The sentiment is entirely mutual, Miss Morton."

As they parted that evening, he felt the ground shifting beneath his feet. Whatever his public position demanded, he could no longer deny what he'd witnessed tonight. She belonged here—thrived in this world of intellectual combat and legal brilliance—while he remained trapped in a world that demanded he deny her excellence.

How could he reconcile the woman who commanded respect through sheer force of intellect with the political reality that required him to publicly dismiss her achievements? His shareholders, his fellow lords, his entire carefully constructed position depended on maintaining traditional values that would see her brilliance as a threat to the natural order.

He was left with impossible choices. Loving her meant choosing between her happiness and his survival in a world that would never accept them both. And that terrified him more than anything else.

OUT WITH THE NEW

20 October 1836—London

DESPITE LORD ALFORD'S best efforts and Charlotte's stellar performance, the emergency meeting crackled with barely contained fury. The Master of Bench presided at the oak table's head, his composure a thin facade over chaos. Andrew and Charlotte stood at opposite ends, unlikely allies watching hostility swirl around the man who'd dared challenge tradition.

Lord Symon heaved himself up, jowls trembling with rage. "Gentlemen, we face a crisis that threatens our very foundations. Lord Alford's decision to admit… a woman," he spat the word like poison, "borders on institutional sacrilege."

Approving murmurs rippled through the chamber. Andrew stepped forward, his voice slicing through the din. "While I share concerns about women in this institution, I cannot watch us sacrifice a man of Lord Alford's caliber over what some view as progress."

The Duke of Chatham joined Andrew's defense. "Lord Alford's decision wasn't made lightly. The law doesn't explicitly bar women, and Miss Morton's admission rested purely on merit."

Andrew's jaw clenched as he watched the duke speak with such passionate conviction about Charlotte's abilities. The man defended her with the very courage Andrew should have shown, and the bitter irony wasn't lost on him. Here he stood, making tepid arguments about institutional politics while another man—his rival for Charlotte's affections—championed her cause with the fervor she deserved.

"Merit?" Lord Symon scoffed. "What merit could a woman bring? Lord Alford's judgment is clearly compromised. He must step down for our institution's sake."

Chaos erupted, opinions flying like arrows. Andrew glanced at Charlotte, noting her calculated silence as she let Chatham champion her cause. Smart, he thought grudgingly, even as resentment churned in his gut. She was letting the duke fight her battles while Andrew stood by like a coward, torn between protecting his interests and protecting her.

"My Lords," Andrew's voice thundered over the din, "consider the cost of forcing Lord Alford out. We'd set a dangerous precedent, valuing blind tradition over justice and equality under law."

Chatham nodded. "Is this not our sworn duty? The law, in its purest form, knows no sex."

Their words seemed to land, several benchers' expressions turning thoughtful as Lord Alford straightened in his chair. Andrew found himself simultaneously grateful for the duke's support and disgusted by his own relief at having an ally— especially this particular ally.

Andrew's gut twisted as Lord Conrad rose, the ancient bencher's movement drawing every eye in the chamber. The silence that fell made his skin prickle with foreboding.

"I've witnessed many changes in my years," Conrad's voice quavered but held firm. "But this... this goes too far. Lord Alford, you've served admirably, but here you've erred grievously. For our beloved institution's sake, you must step aside."

The words settled over the chamber like a funeral pall. Andrew watched faces turn, one by one, toward Conrad's position. Even those who'd nodded along to his earlier arguments now wore masks of grim acceptance. The tide was turning.

His chest constricted as he glanced at Charlotte, seated ramrod straight beside Lord Chatham. She'd earned her place through merit, not privilege. Now they would strip it away through backroom politics rather than law.

Charlotte rose suddenly, her voice cutting through the murmurs. "My Lords, if I may speak."

The chamber fell silent, surprise rippling through the room.

"Lord Alford showed courage in admitting me based on qualifications alone. If that courage is now seen as error, what does that say about your commitment to justice?" Her voice remained steady despite the hostile stares. "I ask not for special consideration, but for the same standards applied to any barrister. Judge my work, not my sex."

She sat back down to uncomfortable silence, her brief intervention hanging in the air like a challenge none seemed willing to meet.

Lord Alford rose then, dignity settling over him like armor. "If this body demands my resignation, so be it. I stand by Miss Morton's admission. History will judge us all for what transpires here today."

Andrew's eyes met Charlotte's across the chamber. In that moment, their personal drama fell away. This was about something larger than both of them.

The vote, when it came, was crushing but not surprising. Andrew watched the numbers mount, each raised hand another nail in progress's coffin. Lord Alford would step down immediately, and with him would go Charlotte's strongest ally.

As Alford departed with quiet dignity, an uneasy silence settled over the chamber. Andrew felt it pressing down on his shoulders.

Lord Conrad broke the stillness, his victory making him bold. "Gentlemen, we must address the matter of appointing a new Master. Our reputation hangs by a thread."

Andrew's fingers tightened against his chair arm. The old snake wasn't even trying to mask his triumph.

Lord Grady's reedy voice cut through the chamber: "What of Dean Wilson from Cambridge Law? He's been most vocal about preserving our traditions."

Andrew's stomach lurched as approval rippled through the

room. Wilson. The same man who'd recently invested in his shipping company after circling like a vulture, whose eyes held calculated hunger when he'd first seen Charlotte six years ago. His appointment would be an executioner's axe hanging over her career.

"Gentlemen," Chatham spoke, "while Dean Wilson's traditionalism is noteworthy, consider the broader view. The legal world watches us. We need leadership that can balance tradition with inevitable change."

Lord Conrad's gaze stabbed toward the duke. "And who would you suggest, Your Grace? Someone more sympathetic to your dalliance with Miss Morton?"

Andrew felt an unexpected surge of fury. How dare they reduce Charlotte's achievements to a mere dalliance? But before he could speak, the Duke of Chatham's voice cut through the chamber like a blade.

"Your mental faculties appear to be deteriorating as rapidly as your manners, Lord Conrad," the duke's tone could have frozen hell itself. "I trust you meant to say 'alliance'—unless you're suggesting impropriety, in which case I'd be delighted to discuss your insinuations privately. My cousin the king has always been most interested in matters of honor among his subjects."

The threat hung in the air like a sword. Andrew watched Conrad's face drain of color as the duke continued with silky menace.

"As for my suggestion, perhaps we need someone with the intellect to recognize merit regardless of its packaging—a quality that seems increasingly rare in this chamber. But pray, don't let wisdom trouble your aged sensibilities."

Andrew found himself both impressed and irritated by Chatham's ruthless deployment of his royal connections. The man wielded his privilege like a weapon—birthright and royal connections deployed with surgical precision—while Andrew sat paralyzed by his own conflicted interests. Chatham fought with the very advantages Andrew had never possessed: noble blood, family influence, the casual arrogance of those born to power. Andrew had clawed his way up from the docks through wit and ruthlessness, but here, watching another man defend Charlotte with weapons Andrew could never wield, his self-made fortune felt like fool's gold.

But even the duke's formidable influence meant little to men fearing for their way of life. Wilson's momentum grew like a gathering storm. Andrew watched faces turn one by one, seeing not just Charlotte's future dimming, but something larger—the death of possibility itself. Chatham had fought magnificently for her, using every weapon at his disposal, while Andrew had offered nothing but hollow procedural arguments.

When Lord Conrad called the vote, the "ayes" thundered through the chamber. In his mind, Andrew's silence felt louder than any protest he could have voiced. He watched triumph etch itself into Conrad's ancient face while Chatham's jaw tightened with barely contained rage.

As the meeting dissolved into self-congratulatory murmurs, Andrew remained seated, his world tilting on its axis. This wasn't just about Charlotte anymore, or his confused feelings for her, or his resentment of the duke's bold advocacy. This was about justice itself—merit versus privilege, progress versus comfortable tradition.

Charlotte appeared at his side, her voice pitched low but sharp enough to cut glass. "How fascinating to witness such passionate advocacy, Lord Carlisle. Your evasion of mentioning my name was positively thunderous."

Andrew's head snapped up to meet her gaze—cool, assessing, disappointed.

"One might almost think," she continued with devastating politeness, "that you were weighing your principles against your portfolio. How fortunate that your investments emerged victorious. I do hope you look back on this day fondly."

Andrew rose slowly, his jaw working as he struggled between justification and shame.

"You don't understand—"

"Oh, but I do," Charlotte interrupted softly. "I understand perfectly. The question is: do you?"

PROTECTOR

27 October 1836—London

ANDREW WATCHED AS David clicked his tongue disapproving-ly at the coarse jacket Andrew had chosen for his dock work. The garment was an affront to everything the valet held sacred in men's fashion.

The rough wool hung shapeless on his master's frame, while the trousers did nothing to flatter his lordship's physique. Even the scuffed boots seemed to personally offend David's refined sensibilities.

"This attire, my lord, does you a grave disservice. It renders you rather… drab," David pronounced the last word as if it tasted bitter.

Andrew's brow creased. "Drab? I cannot imagine a greater insult from your lips, David."

The valet's expression pinched with exasperation. "Why persist in wearing such garments, my lord?"

"They serve well enough for manual labor. I'm usually in my shirt after a few minutes anyway."

David's hand flew to his mouth in horror. "In your—!" He cut himself off with a martyred sigh.

Andrew clapped his shoulder consolingly. "Take heart. Next month, you shall have free rein to dress me for a soiree as you see fit."

David's eyes lit up like a child at Christmas. "A soiree, my lord? And I need not seek approval?"

Andrew eyed him warily. "You're frightening me, David. Yes,

a gathering for the benchers and Temple members."

Leaning on his crutch, David circled his master, mind already spinning with possibilities. "I envision it perfectly—a mustard-yellow floral waistcoat, a royal-blue tailcoat. You'll command every eye in the room."

Andrew blanched. "Floral? I'm hardly suited to dandyism. I'll look ridiculous."

"Your masculine frame suits anything, my lord. You'll look magnificent. It will certainly brighten your complexion."

"I wasn't aware my complexion needed brightening."

"Well," David mused solemnly, "it's only as dull as your mind permits."

"Dull? Splendid," Andrew drawled.

"Perhaps a large sapphire pin and gold pocket watch to complete the ensemble," David continued, enthusiasm mounting.

"Excellent."

"Pumps with a white cravat in the ball-room style!" David's eyes sparkled with possibility.

"I can hardly contain my enthusiasm," Andrew said with a wince. But for now, he craved the distraction of physical labor, hoping sweat and strain might quiet his restless thoughts.

The parade of potential brides had intensified since his elevation to earldom. Yet each introduction only reminded him of what he'd lost in Charlotte—her fierce intellect, her unwavering principles, her refusal to accept the world as it was.

The hypocrisy cut deep, and he knew it. He admired her for the very qualities he'd failed to defend publicly.

"GOOD DAY, MY lord!" Felix's greeting carried across the dock. The man had worked Andrew's docks since the early days, one of the few who remembered when Andrew himself had hauled cargo for daily wages.

"Felix! I'll be joining you this morning," Andrew called back cheerfully.

The men rose, doffing caps until Andrew waved away the formality.

Felix's face darkened. "We're short-handed, my lord. Several down with dysentery after taking food from doxies. They were famished after twenty hours without proper meals."

"Why weren't they fed?"

"The old bread seller's taken ill herself."

Andrew surveyed the exhausted faces. "Any man who needs it, get your meal at the bakery today. Use my name. I'll arrange terms for future provisions."

With gestures and murmurs of gratitude from his workers, Andrew threw himself into unloading lumber, his secretary Cooper scurrying alongside with paperwork, looking like a fastidious sparrow among hawks as he clutched his ledgers and dodged flying wood chips with practiced efficiency.

As sunset painted the docks golden, Andrew straightened, muscles protesting the day's labor. The ship stood nearly empty, lumber awaiting stacking, his men wearing the satisfied exhaustion of honest work.

Wiping sweat from his brow, his gaze drifted to the gathering women lining the dock's edge. A figure stood out among them, incongruous in her bearing, and Andrew's breath caught.

Charlotte.

She moved among the women with purpose, speaking earnestly with several. Her threadbare cloak and worn boots spoke of her financial struggles, yet she carried herself with the same dignity he remembered.

Andrew approached slowly, unwilling to startle her or draw unwanted attention to her presence.

"Miss Morton."

She turned, surprise flickering across her features before composing herself. "Lord Carlisle."

The women around her cast curious glances between them,

sensing undercurrents they couldn't name.

"What brings you to the docks?" he asked, though he suspected he already knew.

"I was discussing employment opportunities with these ladies," she replied with quiet dignity. "Laundry work, household service, or in Sophy's case"—she nodded toward a pregnant woman—"wet nursing."

Her work here revealed the same compassion that had first drawn him to her, the same desire to fight for those society ignored. Yet concern overwhelmed admiration.

"And your own safety? These docks are no place for a lady alone."

Charlotte's chin lifted slightly. "These women face far greater dangers than I do. Besides, who else will offer them alternatives?"

The simple question struck him silent. Who indeed? While he and his peers debated tradition and progress in comfortable chambers, Charlotte worked among those society had forgotten.

"Do you regularly visit here?"

"I move between various locations where women gather. With few paying clients, I believe my time better serves this cause."

"Few paying clients? Surely Chatham provides—"

The words escaped before he could stop them.

Her expression cooled. "That's rather personal, Lord Carlisle."

The rebuke stung. He'd lost all right to such concerns.

Resignation flickered in her expression but her voice carried a sharp edge. "He's offered. I declined."

"Why refuse? You deserve adequate compensation for your work."

Something flashed in her eyes—hurt, perhaps, or anger. "Because accepting would mark me as his mistress rather than his colleague. Discovery would mean instant disbarment. Now they may suspect but cannot prove our relationship extends beyond mentor and student."

The explanation hit him like a physical blow. She was protecting not just her reputation but her very right to practice law. Every comfort she refused was a sacrifice for her dreams.

"I should return to my work," she said, moving to take her leave.

"Take my carriage," he said.

She paused. "Will you accompany me?"

"No. I have work yet to finish." He gestured toward his driver. "James will see you safely home."

As they walked toward the carriage, Andrew noticed again the threadbare state of her cloak.

"The money I gave you years ago—"

"I've had to use it for… various necessities since beginning this path." Something in her tone warned him away from pressing further.

The carriage door opened, and Charlotte turned to him. For a moment, her composed mask slipped, revealing exhaustion and something that looked like loneliness.

"Thank you," she said quietly. "For the carriage. And for… understanding."

She stepped inside, the door closing with a soft click. As the carriage pulled away, Andrew stood watching until it disappeared, his heart heavy with the knowledge that loving her meant more than wanting her for himself—it meant defending everything she stood for, even if she could never be his.

⊰➤➤➤❮❮❮⊱

CHARLOTTE PRESSED HER forehead against the cool carriage window, tears blurring the London streets. That single night six years ago still haunted her—Andrew's gentle hands, his whispered understanding when her world was crumbling. He'd been light in the darkness, never knowing how desperately she'd needed it.

Now his bitterness about Chatham cut deeper than he could

know. Each barbed comment about her "flimsy connection" to the duke reopened wounds she'd thought healed.

If only he knew the truth—that her relationship with Chatham had been born of desperate necessity, not love or ambition. Chatham had become her shield after that horrible night at Cambridge, when she'd learned that her body was currency in a world that saw her dreams as aberration.

Her fingers pressed against the glass until they ached. How she longed to tell Andrew everything—to see understanding replace the bitter disappointment in his eyes. But the cost was too high. Her position at the Inner Temple, the women who looked to her as proof that change was possible, the duke's secret that wasn't hers to tell—all balanced on her silence.

The carriage hit a rough patch, jolting her from her thoughts. Charlotte straightened, wiping away tears with practiced efficiency. She had survived Cambridge. She had built a life from those ashes. She would survive this too, even if it meant watching Andrew slip away like sand through her fingers.

Because despite everything—the secrets, the impossible choices—she loved him. That love would have to be enough, even if she could never act on it.

AFTER A DAY that should have numbed him with exhaustion, Andrew's mind raced with thoughts of Charlotte.

"What's troubling you, brother?" Daisy's unexpected appearance in his study startled him from his brooding. She stood radiant in her new walking dress, the colors as vibrant as her irrepressible spirit.

Andrew rubbed his temple. "Do I look troubled?"

Daisy tilted her head, eyes dancing with mischief. "You've aged a decade since this morning. Every line's working overtime."

"How flattering," he muttered.

"Perhaps you need a wife," she said, settling into the chair across from him. "You haven't courted anyone seriously in years."

Andrew's gaze sharpened. "How is it you speak of such matters so freely? It's hardly proper."

Daisy waved dismissively. "Don't be absurd. I'm six and twenty, not sixteen. Besides, marriage would solve your melancholy."

"Perhaps you're right. It's time I wed."

Maybe a wife would fill the growing void in his chest, silence the thoughts of Charlotte that had renewed their torment.

Daisy's face brightened. "How wonderful! I know several suitable candidates."

Andrew's eyes widened in horror. "I've met your friends, Daisy. They hold no appeal whatsoever."

"Then we must expand your circle. Perhaps my birthday celebration—I could invite eligible ladies from town."

"Perhaps," Andrew murmured, though the thought held little attraction.

Daisy studied his face, then suddenly straightened. "Speaking of solutions—have you found a barrister for my case yet?"

Andrew's mood darkened. "None will take it. They claim domestic matters are beneath their dignity."

"Surely one barrister in London would accept good money. We're not even asking for victory, just competent representation."

"They fear becoming their profession's laughingstock."

Daisy's eyes suddenly blazed with inspiration. "What about the female barrister? The one who fooled everyone by studying as a man? Such determination!"

Andrew choked, memories of Charlotte flooding back unbidden. "She's not an option."

"Why not? She's fully qualified."

"No."

"Because she's a woman," Daisy said, her voice cooling.

"It's not that simple." Andrew ran a hand through his hair. "If my investors learned I'd engaged England's first female barrister, it would signal support for her cause. Lord Pemberton and his allies are already watching my every move, waiting for me to step out of line."

"So this is about politics."

"It's about survival, Daisy. One misstep and I lose everything—my position in Parliament, my business contracts, my ability to protect our family. Wilson's appointment to the Inner Temple isn't coincidence. He's positioning himself to destroy anyone who challenges the old order."

"And yet I heard you defended her at the ceremony."

Andrew's jaw tightened. "That was different. I prevented a mob, nothing more. Hiring her would be a declaration of war against men who could ruin us both."

"So you'll sacrifice my future to preserve your standing with those same men?"

"I'm trying to protect us both!"

"By letting them win?" Daisy's eyes blazed. "You've already stripped away my medical career for the same reasons. Now you'll let my reputation be destroyed rather than risk their disapproval?"

Andrew slumped in his chair. "We'll never agree on this."

"You've already stripped away my joy, my passion, my purpose!" Daisy's voice rose. "I was born to be a physician, risked everything for those credentials! Now what fills my days? Shopping, menus, reading about medicine I can't practice!"

"A woman's place—"

"Don't!" She slammed her palm on the desk. "I don't diminish motherhood, but you diminish me! I could be mother, wife, and physician—but you won't allow even the attempt!"

Andrew watched his sister's anguish with growing discomfort. When had he become the enemy in her eyes?

"If I can't live my dreams," Daisy continued, her voice dropping to steel, "I'll fight for the woman brave enough to carve her place in this world. Hire her, Andrew."

"No."

Daisy's fists crashed onto the table, fury vibrating through the room. When she spoke again, her voice carried a quiet venom that chilled him.

"Hire her, Andrew. My reputation, my case, my future hang in the balance. Hire her, or I swear I'll disappear and destroy what's left of my reputation myself. At least then the scandal will be of my own making."

The threat hung between them like a blade. Andrew stared at his sister—this brilliant, passionate woman he'd tried so hard to protect—and realized he might have been protecting her from the wrong things entirely.

THE SCOUNDREL

2 November 1836—London

THE GREAT HALL of the Inner Temple hummed with tension as members gathered for the formal introduction of their new Master of the Bench. The air was thick with the scent of polished wood and leather-bound books, mingling with expensive colognes and snuff.

Lord Wilson strode into the hall, his presence immediately commanding attention. His silver hair was immaculately coiffed, and his robes of office hung perfectly from his tall, imposing frame. As he took his place at the head of the room, a hush fell over the assembled barristers and benchers.

"Gentlemen," Lord Wilson began, his voice resonating through the hall, "I stand before you today with a solemn duty to uphold the traditions and integrity of this esteemed institution."

His gaze swept the space, pausing briefly on Charlotte, who stood near the back, her spine straight despite the palpable tension. Wilson's eyes narrowed almost imperceptibly.

"We find ourselves at a crossroads. The world outside these hallowed halls may be clamoring for change, but it is our responsibility to stand firm in defense of the principles that have guided English law for centuries."

Several of the older members nodded in agreement, while others shifted uncomfortably.

"It has come to my attention that certain irregularities have been permitted in recent months." His gaze fixed directly on Charlotte. "Miss Morton, you are trespassing. You're not invited, as I do not recognize you as an official Temple member."

A shocked murmur rippled through the assembled crowd. Andrew studied Charlotte's expression—disgust and determination carefully masked behind a concealment of polite interest. Just as he took a step forward in her defense, Charlotte's voice carried clearly across the suddenly silent hall.

"I am a barrister approved by the Inns of Court, whether you personally approve or not, Lord Wilson. Unless you see yourself as above the Court." Her tone grew honeyed with poison. "Though I suppose that would explain your rather creative interpretation of legal precedent."

Andrew coughed to hide his chuckle.

Wilson's jaw ticked, his face reddening like a man on the verge of apoplexy. "Do not think you can trap me with amateur theatrics before this assembly. I have never accepted you as a barrister and never will. I suggest you vacate my property before you're thrown out."

"How fascinating," Charlotte replied with mock scholarly interest, her voice pitched to carry to every corner of the hall. "I had no idea personal acceptance was required for legal qualifications. Shall I inform the Court that you've appointed yourself the sole arbiter of professional standing? I'm certain they'll be enlightened by your innovation."

Andrew's chest swelled with pride at her brilliant riposte, even as his jaw clenched with the effort of remaining silent. The assembled crowd watched in rapt attention, some nodding at Charlotte's logic, others looking scandalized.

"The lady speaks the truth, Wilson. I suppose you'll be throwing me out too for training her," a familiar voice rang from the back of the hall.

Andrew's stomach tightened as the Duke of Chatham appeared, moving to stand beside Charlotte, his presence immediately shifting the dynamic in the room. Andrew felt something shift in his chest—an uncomfortable recognition. Here was a man who wielded his privilege like a shield on her behalf.

Perhaps she deserved someone who didn't have to weigh her worth against his own interests. Someone who could stand beside her with real authority—the protection of his birth.

Wilson's face contorted as he found himself facing not just Charlotte, but Chatham's formidable influence. "Your Grace, this is a matter of institutional integrity—"

"Indeed it is," the duke interrupted smoothly. "And Miss Morton's presence here speaks to the very integrity you claim to defend. Unless you're suggesting the Inns of Court lack the authority to determine membership?"

The confrontation hung in the air like smoke from a fired pistol, with Wilson's face cycling through shades of red as he struggled to respond without directly challenging Chatham's authority. Eventually, he dismissed the assembly with terse formality, though his glittering eyes promised this was far from over. Andrew watched Charlotte and the duke exit together, their quiet conversation and shared purpose a stark reminder of Chatham's advantage.

The evening's formal ceremonies, however, were far from over. Despite wanting to flee the Inner Temple entirely, Andrew settled into his seat at the round table for the benchers' meeting, Cooper taking his place behind him. This meeting was tedious but necessary—essential for garnering support and protecting his business interests.

"Carlisle." Lord Wilson's voice cut through the conversation as he claimed the seat beside Andrew.

"Wilson."

"I think you know what I want to discuss." Wilson fixed him with a pointed look.

Andrew's brow furrowed. "Your investment concerns?"

"Your association with Morton."

Andrew paused, surprised by the directness. "Ah, is that what's keeping you awake at nights? I'm flattered by your concern for my social calendar."

"She represents dangerous precedent. One female lawyer

today, ten tomorrow. Your association lends her credibility." Wilson leaned forward. "Do not engage her."

Andrew's jaw tightened at the man's audacity but drawled casually, "Good heavens, Wilson. Ten female lawyers? However shall we cope? Can we afford their meager salaries?"

Wilson continued as if Andrew hadn't spoken. "Your sister is betrothed. Do you want her associating with someone of questionable reputation?" Wilson's eyes gleamed with malice. "Morton received the highest marks in her class—ahead of judges' sons, dukes' heirs. One wonders how such achievements were… earned."

The implication hung in the air like poison. Andrew's hands clenched beneath the table, but he forced a laugh. "My dear Wilson, are you suggesting that Cambridge's finest minds were so easily… distracted? How embarrassing for them. Though I suppose it does explain why so many of our colleagues struggle with basic logic." He turned to look intently into Wilson's eyes. "You appear to be taking my association with Miss Morton more seriously than is warranted. Is there something I should know?"

Wilson's smile faltered slightly. "Based on your reputation, you're likely privy to intelligence before I am."

Andrew's gaze sharpened as realization dawned. "You've already spoken to my shareholders." His voice carried mock surprise. "How industrious of you. Tell me, did you use your charming personality to win them over, or did you simply bore them into submission?"

Wilson cleared his throat, eyes darting away.

Wilson wasn't just attacking Charlotte—he was positioning himself to take control of Andrew's company, using her as a weapon against him.

"Only months after investing in my company," Andrew mused, his voice deceptively mild. "I wonder what motivated such… urgent concern. Perhaps you've developed a sudden passion for corporate governance? How admirably civic-minded."

Andrew forced himself to laugh, schooling his features into

nonchalance. "On a more pleasant note," he began, "I saw Lady Lidia at Hyde Park yesterday. Charming girl—though I do hope she's inherited more of her mother's wit than her father's... strategic thinking."

The mention of his daughter made Wilson preen with paternal pride. Perhaps there was a way to turn Wilson's ambition against him—a strategic marriage alliance to neutralize the threat.

"She is lovely, both inside and out," Wilson said. "Properly raised, devoted to convention. Her sights are set on someone of elevated station." He leaned in conspiratorially. "Speaking of which, Carlisle, you ought to be considering marriage yourself."

Andrew inclined his head with a wry smile. "That seems to be the prevailing opinion."

"Look no further, Carlisle. My daughter would be perfect for you."

Andrew paused, as if considering. "Perhaps. While I have no immediate plans to wed, I can see the potential for an advantageous union."

The words tasted like ash, but they served their purpose. Wilson's eyes gleamed with satisfaction, temporarily distracted from his machinations.

As they sat in loaded silence, Andrew reminded himself that this was just another business negotiation. But the hollow feeling in his chest suggested that this particular dance might cost him more than he was prepared to pay.

THE SOIREE

DAVID'S EXPRESSION WAS one of pure, unadulterated glee as he maneuvered around his master on his crutch, his keen eyes examining every detail of his sartorial handiwork. With a deft touch, he plucked an invisible fiber from Andrew's shoulder, his fingers as delicate as a surgeon's. Stepping back, he clapped his hands in unabashed admiration, his face alight with pride and satisfaction.

Andrew, however, was less than thrilled by the attention. "Are you quite satisfied?" he asked impatiently.

"You look absolutely marvelous, my lord," David exclaimed.

"I shall have to take your word for it." Andrew glanced down at his attire and a crease appeared between his brows. "David, is this large sapphire truly necessary?"

David merely waved a dismissive hand. "It might serve to soften your rough exterior, make you less… dour."

Under the weight of Andrew's withering gaze, David merely puckered his lips. "I did save your life, if you recall."

Andrew rolled his eyes. "And I thought I had repaid that debt with a lifetime of friendship, wealth, your own personal tailor, and fabric shipped from the far corners of the world. I wasn't aware I was also expected to dress for your amusement."

But even as the words left his lips, Andrew felt a flicker of fondness for his impertinent valet. David had been by his side through thick and thin, a constant source of support and companionship in a world that often felt cold and unforgiving.

"You did promise…" his valet said softly.

Andrew's shoulders slumped. "Why are you in my employ again? Surely you have better things to do with your wealth?"

David's face lit up with a smile that was equal parts adoration and mischief. "Nothing gives me more pleasure than to dress you, my lord. Your physique is a masterpiece. Oh, I do have a floral cravat—"

"No!" Andrew cut him off before David could suggest more embellishments, marching toward the door.

An hour later, Andrew disembarked from the carriage and strode into Lord Wilson's recently acquired townhouse—a purchase made possible by profits from Andrew's own company. The irony wasn't lost on him. After handing his effects to the butler, he suppressed a frown at the parlor's decor. The fabrics matched his waistcoat so perfectly he might blend into the furniture.

"Carlisle, you're as pretty as a spring flower," Rogers called out over the pianoforte.

"You're not to my taste, Rogers," Andrew said flatly.

"Indeed, you would make a fine nest for mama birds," Wilson added, his laughter echoing.

Andrew growled, his patience thinning.

Collins interjected. "Shall we conduct business before supper? I'd prefer clear heads for our discussions."

Andrew followed Wilson to his study with the other investors, accepting a measure of brandy before turning to face them with a steely gaze. "State your grievances, gentlemen. The no-nonsense version, if you please."

Collins cleared his throat. "It's straightforward, Carlisle. The Whigs tread carefully around the Tories since this Reform business. The Duke of Chatham sneaking a woman into the bar has already enraged them. If you hire her for legal services, you declare revolt against the Tories. We need their support for our port development."

Andrew nodded. "Gentlemen, I agree on every point. However, I have family matters to consider. If I cannot locate a barrister to represent my sister, I may have no choice but to turn to Miss Morton." He looked pointedly at Wilson. "Should you wish to assign a barrister to my sister's case, I'd happily relinquish any professional association with the lady."

Wilson shifted uncomfortably. "I'm afraid I cannot force anyone's hand. Not with my tenure being only weeks old."

Andrew knew he walked a delicate line, balancing business, family, and politics. Taking a deep swig of brandy, he met their gazes. "Very well. I have no intention of jeopardizing our gains, but I will not abandon my sister. However, there may be opportunity here—one that could make the Tories grateful."

The men waited expectantly.

With a sigh, he muttered, "I shall become familiar with her first. Her work ethics, habits, methods."

"You brilliant devil!" Murphy exclaimed. "You mean to use her for your needs, then discredit her afterward?"

Andrew let them draw their own conclusions. "That remains… an option." He had no such intention, but buying time required letting them believe what served his purposes.

"You could thoroughly ruin her reputation!" Rogers added with glee.

The group erupted into laughter. Andrew swallowed his disgust at these men who found humor in a woman's potential destruction. "Let us maintain civility. Miss Morton is protected by the king's relative. We cannot afford Chatham's ire."

Before Wilson could respond, a sharp rap sounded on the door.

"I beg your pardon, Lord Wilson," the butler said. "Miss Morton requests admission to the Inner Temple soiree, but she's not on your guest list."

At her name, Andrew's stomach lurched—a reaction most unwelcome. He held his breath until she appeared, her presence filling the room like electricity.

His gaze drifted over her dark-blue dress, modest yet elegant, the shimmering fabric highlighting her curves. Her hair was pulled back in a severe chignon, and she carried herself with the quiet dignity of someone who refused to apologize for her presence.

Charlotte held Wilson's gaze steadily while he spoke.

"You are correct, Neville. She is not on the guest list. Please see to it that the interloper leaves the premise."

Andrew's blood began to boil at his insolence when the Duke of Chatham appeared beside her, his arm casually hovering near Charlotte's waist in subtle possession. The gesture sent a stab of pure possessiveness through his chest that left him breathless with its intensity.

Wilson stammered, suddenly devoid of bravado. "Your Grace, I thought you were engaged elsewhere."

The duke fixed Wilson with a glacial stare. "When I learned Miss Morton wished to attend her rightful Temple function, I changed my plans. She always brightens dull gatherings with her conversation." His voice carried dangerous quiet. "But it seems you disapprove of my decision regarding Barrister Morton. Please enlighten me. What errors have I committed?"

The room fell silent although Andrew could think of nothing but the way Chatham's hand lingered protectively at her back, the intimate familiarity between them—it ignited something savage and possessive in his chest. He could still picture her beneath him all those years ago, still remember her gasps of pleasure. Now another man claimed those privileges, and the thought made his hands clench into fists.

Wilson, sensing the duke's displeasure, quickly backpedaled. "I wouldn't dare disapprove, Your Grace. In fact, we were discussing how Carlisle ought to hire Miss Morton for Lady Daisy's case."

Both Charlotte and Chatham turned surprised gazes on Andrew, but he barely registered their expressions. The jealousy coursing through him was like acid, burning away rational thought.

"Is that true?" Charlotte asked.

"Aye," Andrew managed, his voice rough. "However, no barrister has been willing thus far. Perhaps you wouldn't either—apparently it would be professional suicide."

Charlotte's eyes sparked with interest, and Andrew felt another twist of pain as he watched the duke smile proudly at her courage.

"Well, I'm intrigued," she said. "Shall we discuss it privately?"

Andrew moved toward the door, desperate to take her away from Chatham. "We shall use your small library, Wilson. See that we're not disturbed."

As he passed Chatham, Andrew couldn't help but catalog the man's golden hair, handsome features, and fashionable attire. Everything Andrew was not—born to privilege, refined, able to champion Charlotte openly without consequence.

Andrew offered Charlotte his arm, noting how the duke's eyes followed the gesture with sharp attention. When she took it with her gloved hand, she quirked a brow at finding his hand bare.

"I detest gloves," he said, flexing his calloused fingers deliberately. "My hands are already too large for most refined tasks."

Let Chatham see what real strength looked like, what real work was. He was no pampered aristocrat who'd never earned his position through anything more demanding than an accident of birth.

As he led Charlotte toward the library, Andrew tried to focus on Daisy's case rather than the warmth of her touch or the knowledge that soon she would return to Chatham's side—and Chatham's bed. The jealousy burned steady and dangerous in his chest, a poison that would only grow stronger with time.

CHARLOTTE STEPPED INTO the library with trepidation, her

emotions warring between excitement and fear. Andrew stood by the window, his matching coat and breeches molded to his form with impeccable tailoring. At two and thirty, he was even more magnificent than the man who had haunted her dreams for six years. The years had etched fine lines at the corners of his eyes—evidence of battles fought and won, of a boy who had clawed his way up from the docks to claim an earldom through sheer force of will.

The library was a quaint space with only a handful of shelves and a cozy seating area. She walked around the room, pretending to admire the ornate bookshelves while trying to calm her nerves. Alone in this small space, she felt Andrew's presence intensely.

Taking a deep breath, she settled gracefully into a plush chair near the window. He sat directly across from her, and she fought to maintain her composure. Her eyes settled on the dainty flower patterns adorning his waistcoat, and she couldn't suppress a smile.

"What is amusing?" he asked gruffly.

"This look is certainly different from your usual. I didn't take you for a dandy."

To her delight, he shifted awkwardly. "It's my valet's doing. He demanded that I let him 'express his artistic vision.'"

"And you surrendered to a valet?"

"The man saved my life. Apparently, that grants him eternal power over my wardrobe." Andrew tugged at his sapphire pin with obvious discomfort. "He assured me it would 'soften my rough exterior.'"

"Well, you certainly won't blend into any shadows tonight."

"Please," he said with mock severity, "my dignity has suffered enough for one evening."

Charlotte laughed despite herself, the sound seeming to ease some tension in the room. "Forgive me. How may I assist you, Lord Carlisle?"

Andrew's expression grew serious as he launched into his sister's situation—the broken betrothal, Lord Byron's damaging accusations, and the threat to both Daisy's reputation and his business ventures. His fierce protectiveness spoke volumes about his love for his sibling, stirring a profound envy in Charlotte, who had grown up alone.

When he finished, he handed her a document. While she reviewed it, Charlotte could feel his gaze on her, making her acutely aware of her simple dress and modest appearance.

"The other barristers were correct that courts typically avoid domestic cases unless unlawful conduct is evident," she said, lifting her eyes. "Has Lord Byron taken further action since withdrawing his offer?"

"He's spreading accusations within our social circles. This threatens both Daisy's character and my investors' confidence in a family accused of lacking moral fiber."

Charlotte nodded, her fingertip trailing across her lower lip as she studied the papers. "How curious that instead of providing a dowry, Lord Byron was to fund your port expansion."

"He believed shares would prove more lucrative than traditional arrangements."

"If port construction delays result from this broken engagement, financial repercussions would far exceed the initial two thousand pounds," she mused.

After studying the documents intently, she looked up with growing excitement. "I can build a case and present it to the court."

"You can?"

"Before I outline my strategy, I require a retainer of one hundred pounds, another hundred for the first half, and the final hundred held in escrow until conclusion."

"Three hundred pounds!" he exclaimed. "That's outrageous! Even my most esteemed London barrister wouldn't dare charge such a fee!"

Charlotte rose gracefully, handing back the document. "I urge you, my lord, to engage your esteemed barrister then."

"Sit down, Miss Morton," Andrew said, recognizing he had

no choice. "Surely you're familiar with negotiation?"

"My fee is not negotiable," she said pleasantly, though she resumed her seat.

"You must concede three hundred pounds is astronomical for a single case."

"Did I say three? I meant five hundred, for old time's sake, Lord Carlisle." Her eyes sparkled with mischief. "A fitting amount, considering I'm the only one willing to defend your sister's honor."

Andrew regarded her with grudging respect. "You need this case as much as we need you. We're lending credibility to your practice."

"A case everyone else calls professional suicide and is too humiliated to represent." She tilted her head. "Self-destruction commands a premium, my lord."

They stared at each other, neither yielding.

"This case requires five months of dedicated effort," she continued. "Four hundred pounds plus the retainer—equal to one Season's wardrobe, or perhaps two of yours, given your recent economical choices in attire."

Andrew leaned back, obviously suppressing a smile. His unwavering gaze made her pulse flutter, but Charlotte met his stare, refusing to yield in this silent contest.

"The agreement must include my right to dismiss you if your performance proves unsatisfactory. You keep the retainer but return the remainder."

"Naturally. Though I should warn you, my definition of 'satisfactory' may differ from yours. I consider it satisfactory if we both survive the experience with our reputations marginally intact."

Charlotte drafted the contract with efficient strokes, her deliberately masculine script contrasting with her feminine bearing. Andrew extracted two hundred pounds from his leather pocketbook, sliding them across. "I shall consider this a down payment on what I suspect will be a very expensive education."

Though she tried to remain composed, her trembling fingers betrayed her relief as she secured the notes.

"We'll assert Lady Daisy's innocence, arguing Lord Byron fabricated accusations to escape port development obligations. Guilt becomes credible when paired with motive—financial desperation resonates universally. We'll pursue this under common law within the fortnight."

Andrew signed with decisive strokes just as a sharp knock interrupted. A footman announced supper, but Andrew dismissed him with a curt nod. As the servant's footsteps faded, Andrew rose and quietly turned the key in the lock, the soft click echoing in the sudden silence.

Charlotte's eyes followed his movement, her pulse quickening at the gesture. The professional distance they'd maintained began to feel fragile, gossamer-thin.

"The contract is concluded," she said, gathering the papers with hands that trembled slightly. "I should rejoin the gathering before—"

"Charlotte..." Her name fell from his lips, stripped of all formality, heavy with longing and regret.

The sound of it—spoken with such raw need—made her pulse quicken. Gone was Lord Carlisle, the shrewd businessman. This was Andrew, the man who had once held her with such reverence, who had whispered her name against her skin in the darkness of that parlor so long ago.

She stood abruptly, her chair scraping against the floor. "We should return to the others."

Without looking at him, she moved toward the door, her heart hammering against her ribs. This was dangerous territory—the professional facade she'd worked so hard to maintain was cracking, revealing the vulnerable woman beneath who had never stopped loving him.

"You were to be mine, Charlotte." His voice was rough with pain, and she heard him approach from behind.

She halted but didn't turn, her hand reaching for the door

handle. "You had your chance. You demanded I sacrifice my dreams to protect your interests."

"I thought what we shared was worth more than the security another man might provide." His footsteps advanced slowly, deliberately. "I believed our hearts had room for no one but each other. How could you give yourself to someone else?"

"Because it was too agonizing not to," she whispered, her voice breaking.

She felt him behind her now, his presence like a flame at her back. When his hand appeared beside hers on the door, not quite touching but close enough that she could feel the heat of his skin, her resolve wavered.

"I waited for your letter," he said, his breath stirring the hair at her nape. "For months, I hoped you wouldn't end our association."

"I stayed away," she admitted, her voice barely audible. "Because I knew if you asked me to come back to you, I would have said yes. And I would have hated us both for it."

The confession hung between them like a bridge neither dared cross. Charlotte's fingers pressed against the door, torn between fleeing and turning into his arms.

"You speak of him with such devotion," Andrew said, and she could hear the pain he tried to hide.

"Andrew, please—"

"Because I dream of having yours." His voice dropped to a whisper that seemed to caress her very soul. "Every night since the day we met, I've dreamed of your hands, your voice, the way you looked at me that night as if I were the only man in the world."

Charlotte closed her eyes, fighting the tears that threatened to spill. "You don't understand. What I have with Albert—it's not what you think. It's protection, companionship, but it's not..."

"Not what?" he pressed gently.

"Not love," she breathed. "Not the way I loved you."

The admission escaped before she could stop it, hanging in

the air between them like a confession that changed everything. She felt Andrew go still behind her, heard his sharp intake of breath.

"Loved?" he asked, his voice barely above a whisper. "Past tense?"

Charlotte's composure finally shattered. She dropped her head as tears streamed down her cheeks. "How can you ask me that when being in the same room with you makes it impossible to breathe?"

Slowly, she felt his body cage her in, his hard chest brushing against her back with each inhalation, and a growing firmness pressing against her spine. His heat surrounded her as his hot breath ghosted over the sensitive skin of her neck before he rasped, "I believe you're still mine, Charlotte."

She gasped as she felt the length of him flush against her, his arousal evident as it dug into her back.

"I've tried so hard to forget," she continued, the words tumbling out like water through a broken dam. "I've told myself a thousand times that we were impossible, that our dreams could never align. But seeing you again, working beside you, pretending I don't feel what I've always felt—it's killing me."

For a moment that stretched like eternity, they simply stood, breathing hard as years of denial and longing crackled between them like lightning about to strike.

Suddenly, he was everywhere—his warmth enveloping her like a summer storm, the comfort of his embrace making her head spin with long-denied desire. Andrew's arms tightened around her body, his large hands spanning her waist with a possessive grip that made her knees weaken. The hard planes of his chest pressed against her back, every inch of him solid muscle and barely restrained power. When he buried his face in the crook of her neck, his lips brushing her skin with devastating tenderness, Charlotte's breath caught in her throat.

"Stop pretending," he whispered, his thumb brushing away her tears. "Stop running from what we both know is still there."

Charlotte leaned back against him despite every rational thought screaming at her to step away. "Andrew, we can't. Too much has changed. Too much stands between us."

"Has it?" His other hand found her cheek, turning her face toward him until barely a breath separated them. "Because right now, in this moment, it feels like nothing has changed at all."

His lips were so close she could feel his breath against hers, could see the gold flecks in his dark eyes that had haunted her dreams. "If I kiss you," she whispered, "I won't be able to pretend anymore. I won't be able to go back to the way things were."

"Then don't," he said, his voice rough with need. "Don't go back. Don't pretend. Just… be here. With me. The way you were meant to be."

His hot breath came shallow and labored against her neck, sending shivers cascading down her spine. The rasp of his evening stubble scraped deliciously against her sensitive skin as he traced a path from her shoulder to her ear, each kiss warmer and more urgent than the last.

"God help me," she breathed against his lips, "but I've missed you so much."

Their mouths met in a kiss that was six years of longing distilled into a single, searing moment.

The subtle bite of his teeth, followed by the soothing warmth of his tongue, drew a helpless whimper from her lips. His fingers pressed into her stays, the rough calluses of his hands catching on her gown. She could feel the thundering of his heart against her back, matching her own frantic pulse. She clutched desperately at his forearms, her body arching into him of its own accord.

Charlotte reached behind her and gripped his thigh, thick and hard like marble. He brought one foot forward to position her deeper between his legs, pressing his throbbing length against her backside. With a moan, she began to grind against him, the ridge of his arousal digging into her with a delicious ache.

"I've missed you," he breathed, his voice low and rough with desire.

A whimper escaped her throat as her body purred with relief. Finally, after countless lonely nights dreaming of his warm embrace and the safety of his protection, she was in his arms once more.

Her hand tugged at her skirts, lifting the layers, then finding her heat swollen and wet. She began to pleasure herself, gently stroking her aching bud as he had taught her all those years ago.

"Christ, Charlotte…" he groaned, caressing the cleft of her quim with his long finger while she continued her self-ministration.

"Andrew… I ache…" she breathed.

His breathing grew shallower as the tip of his finger entered her cunny, her muscles clasping it greedily. A husky grunt left his throat.

Sliding back and forth inside her, he stroked and eased the throbbing. Charlotte turned her head and kissed him until her moans reverberated in his mouth. She stroked her swollen bud faster, harder—Andrew's finger keeping pace with her.

"Andrew… deeper… please," she breathed. "I'm close…"

"Come for me, darling. Come around my finger," he grunted, his breath coming in shallow pants.

As the arousal accumulated, Charlotte rode his finger, moving her hips to deepen the penetration. Sensing her need, he gave her more, burrowing into her silken flesh, his breaths quickening in her ear. With one sharp inhale, she stilled as her orgasm broke, her inner muscles pulsing fiercely around his digit. She muffled her scream of pleasure by biting onto his arm while her body trembled with the force of her release.

"Charlotte," he hissed through clenched teeth, then stiffened abruptly, his breath catching in his chest. With a sharp exhale, he lurched against her, pressing his pulsing manhood hard against her ass. As his draughts of air slowed and his muscles began to relax, he removed his finger slowly from her quim. Barely able to stand on her shaking legs, Charlotte leaned her forehead against the cool wood of the door. Her hand reached for his, wanting his arms to tighten around her, but Andrew withdrew, releasing her completely.

The chill surrounded her once more, raising gooseflesh on her sensitive skin. Her mind thrashed against the cold. She wanted him, wanted the warmth and comfort of his embrace.

She turned around and froze at the darkened spot in front of his breeches. A snort of laughter escaped before she could stop it. But as the humor faded, reality crashed back—what had they done? What did this mean?

"Are you all right?" he asked, schooling his features to collect his scattered dignity.

"Perfectly," she managed, though her gaze remained pointedly fixed on his breeches. "Well. That's certainly… obvious."

Andrew winced. "Ah. Yes. Well." He cleared his throat. "Do I owe you an apology? I must admit, I don't regret what happened, although my valet may feel differently."

Charlotte pressed her lips together, fighting another laugh. "Your poor valet. Does he often have to attend to such incidents?"

"Good God, no." Andrew's face flamed. "That is to say… this is rather unprecedented."

"Unprecedented?" She arched a brow, her composure returning as his crumbled. "My lord, are you suggesting I've introduced you to something new?"

"Charlotte," he warned, though his lips twitched.

"I'm merely concerned for your household staff. Perhaps you should include hazard pay in their wages?"

Andrew's jaw muscles flexed. "You're enjoying this far too much."

"Am I?" She tilted her head innocently. "I'm simply being practical. Someone will need to explain this to the poor soul who handles your washing."

"Charlotte…" His voice rumbled low.

"I will send a footman to attend to you," she said sweetly, "while you attend to… that."

She gestured vaguely at his breeches, grinning wider at his groan of mortification.

By the time Charlotte entered the dining room, the meal was well under way with glowing yellow and orange in the dozens of candles. The duke was seated next to Wilson while Andrew's chair remained vacant. An empty chair waited for Charlotte at the far end of the table. The men beside her scowled as she took her seat, clearly unhappy about her presence.

Charlotte was left out of the conversation, the men talking over her when she tried to speak. She didn't mind being ignored—it gave her time to savor the feast, having subsisted on the bare minimum in recent years. After she was satiated, she looked up to find Andrew entering, wearing borrowed breeches that were scandalously tight. Without looking in her direction, he seated himself.

Chatham's voice cut through the din. "I do believe that query is best answered by our sole lady barrister."

Charlotte's heart pounded as she realized she'd missed the question entirely. "Please forgive me, gentlemen. I'm afraid the question eluded my attention."

Chatham's eyes glimmered with mischief. "Lord Wilson believes a lady barrister would find herself partial to her own sex, compromising her objectivity due to an inherent capacity for empathy."

Charlotte fixed her gaze on Wilson, who had clearly been drinking heavily. "Does not the same hold true for gentlemen barristers when representing their fellow men?"

Wilson's countenance darkened. "Nay, Miss Morton, for men are not prone to sentimentality. We possess the fortitude to maintain objectivity."

She managed a faint smile. "Is it not men who, consumed by wounded pride, engage in brawls and wars? I daresay it is the masculine temperament more easily swayed by emotion. If women were truly the irrational sex, there would scarcely be a husband left alive."

Laughter rippled through the room but was quickly silenced by Wilson's flushed face. "Do you find the murder of husbands a suitable subject for jest?"

"No, my lord, I do not," Charlotte replied steadily.

"To make light of such grave matters only highlights your own ignorance!" Wilson barked.

"I thank you, Lord Wilson," she said with graceful composure.

Wilson stiffened in bewilderment. "Have you partaken too heavily of the spirits?"

"Nay, my lord. I merely expressed gratitude for your unwitting confirmation of my assertion. While your temper slips from your grasp, I remain in full possession of my faculties."

Wilson's face flushed crimson. The duke intervened smoothly. "Tell us, Lord Wilson, what entertainment have you arranged for this evening?"

Wilson's smirk returned as he replied loudly, "We shall be diverted by ladies of the night, Your Grace. Their charms will provide ample distraction." His gaze roved over Charlotte with deliberate insolence. "Perhaps you would care to join the festivities, Miss Morton? Your talents may well extend beyond the courtroom."

Laughter echoed around her while Charlotte's cheeks burned with indignation. But before she could respond, Andrew's voice cut through the din.

"Miss Morton is a lady of quality, and I shall not abide any man treating her with less than the utmost respect."

Charlotte's heart swelled with gratitude, even as she felt heat at the memory of their recent encounter.

"Her presence here is entirely unsuitable," Wilson said while glancing at Chatham nervously.

Andrew's eyes narrowed. "Indeed, you are correct, Wilson. Miss Morton's civility and grace far surpass the company present."

He strode purposefully toward Charlotte, his hand outstretched. "Miss Morton, would you do me the honor of accompanying me for fresh air? The atmosphere has grown rather rancid."

Charlotte's gaze swept the room, taking in the amused and shocked expressions. With a nod, she placed her hand in Andrew's, feeling comforted by his strong grip as she rose.

As they stepped into the corridor, voices grew louder behind them. Andrew turned to her. "I shall escort you home."

Before Charlotte could respond, the Duke of Chatham appeared, his attire resplendent with jeweled buttons.

"Miss Morton," he called, approaching with his usual grace. "I must ensure you're comfortable with Lord Carlisle as your escort. Should you prefer, I would be honored to see you home."

Charlotte felt the weight of both men's gazes upon her. The safe choice would be the duke—returning to their established arrangement, their careful distance. But Andrew's defense of her, the memory of his touch in the library, the way he'd looked at her with such longing…

She drew a steadying breath. "I am most grateful for your concern, Your Grace, but I believe Lord Carlisle and I have matters to discuss."

Something flickered in the duke's eyes—surprise, perhaps, or approval. "Very well, my dear. I bid you both good evening."

Andrew's expression showed careful restraint, but Charlotte caught the flash of satisfaction in his eyes as he offered his arm.

The carriage rolled through London's darkened streets, the clip-clop of hooves and creak of wheels the only sounds breaking the charged silence between them. Charlotte sat rigidly upright, acutely aware of Andrew's presence beside her in the intimate confines of the coach.

"Thank you," she said finally, her voice barely above a whisper. "For defending me in there."

"Wilson's a damned fool," Andrew replied gruffly. "His behavior was inexcusable."

Silence stretched between them until Charlotte spoke with

deliberate lightness. "Well, I suppose you'll miss Wilson's evening entertainment. Though I imagine you're quite familiar with such... diversions."

Andrew's jaw tightened, and she immediately regretted the jest. When he spoke, his voice carried unexpected vulnerability.

"Actually, I've never... that is, I don't frequent such establishments. Never have." He stared out the window at the passing gaslight. "Madam Tansley saved my life when I was twelve. She and Daisy were the only family I knew. When she summoned me the night we met, I thought perhaps one of her girls was in trouble."

Charlotte's breath caught, realizing her assumption had been entirely wrong. "You mean you weren't there for... companionship?"

"My days were consumed by work, leaving neither time nor funds for such pursuits. From my youth, I learned to deny myself such gratification." His gaze found hers in the dim light. "Your presence was... an unexpected gift."

The admission hung between them, raw and honest. Charlotte felt her assumptions about him crumbling, replaced by something far more dangerous—understanding.

"I thought..." she began, then stopped, color flooding her cheeks.

"What did you think?"

"At first, when we were standing in that parlor..." she said softly, "I thought you saw me as just another woman offering herself for coin. Another sordid transaction in a place built for such things."

Andrew turned to face her fully, his eyes intense in the flickering light from the streetlamps. "I was terrified," he admitted. "Terrified of what you were offering, terrified of how much I wanted it—and you. What happened between us that night wasn't what either of us planned."

"No," she whispered. "It became something else entirely."

"And tonight in the library?"

"Tonight felt like…" she paused, searching for words.

"Recognition," he said simply. "Of something I've been searching for."

The carriage hit a bump, jolting them closer together on the bench seat. Neither moved away.

"What are we doing, Andrew?" Charlotte asked, her voice thick with emotion. "This is madness. We can't… there's too much standing between us."

"Is there?" His hand found hers in the darkness, his thumb tracing gentle circles over her gloved knuckles. "Because sitting here with you, it feels like the first time I've been able to breathe properly in six years."

Charlotte's resolve wavered as his words echoed her own feelings. "The duke… my position… your reputation. I am hardly the sort of woman an earl should be seen championing."

"What about what you want, Charlotte? Not what's practical or safe or proper—what do you want?"

The question hung in the air between them, weighted with possibility and peril. Charlotte stared into his eyes, seeing her own longing reflected there, and felt the last of her defenses crumble.

"I want," she whispered, "to stop pretending that what's between us doesn't exist. Even if it's only for tonight."

Andrew's breath caught, and for a moment that stretched like eternity, they simply looked at each other. Then his free hand rose to cup her cheek, his thumb brushing across her skin with devastating tenderness.

"Then don't pretend," he murmured, leaning closer until his breath mingled with hers. "Not tonight."

The carriage rolled on through the London streets, carrying them toward an uncertain future, but for now, in this moment, nothing existed but the space between their hearts and the promise of what might be possible if they were brave enough to reach for it.

OBSESSION

1 December 1836—London

T HE TASTE OF forbidden fruit lingered on Andrew's tongue, a phantom sensation that haunted him still. The memory of Charlotte's lips refused to fade, tormenting him with exquisite clarity. In the sanctuary of his mind, he found himself once again in that fateful library, her lithe form pressed against him, her clean scent intoxicating his senses.

With each passing day, the certainty grew within him—a possessive, almost primal urge that whispered he could never let her go. The thought of another man holding her sent a surge of determination through his veins, hardening his resolve.

As the clock struck nine, a looming figure darkened Andrew's office doorway. Adams, an exiled foreign nobility and his friend, now served a more complex purpose in Andrew's intricate web of surveillance including watching over Daisy. Despite his imposing stature, Adams possessed an uncanny ability to blend into the shadows—a talent that had kept Daisy blissfully unaware of his presence.

Andrew's lips curved into a wry smile as he contemplated his sister's obliviousness. If Daisy had even an inkling of Adams's watchful eye, her inability to keep secrets would have surely betrayed her. But today, Andrew's thoughts were consumed by a far more pressing matter—Charlotte.

Adams appeared in the doorway of Andrew's study with his usual quiet efficiency, straightening his waistcoat with the practiced air of a man who'd spent years perfecting the art of appearing unremarkable.

"Adams, my man, where's my sister wreaking havoc today?" Andrew drawled, rising from his desk to shake his friend's hand with genuine warmth.

"The modiste's with Miss Grantham, attempting to bankrupt you one silk ribbon at a time," Adams replied, his deadpan delivery complementing the slight twitch at the corner of his mouth.

Andrew chuckled, settling back against his desk with arms crossed. "Any scandals to report?"

"Shockingly conventional behavior, I'm afraid." Adams clasped his hands behind his back, adopting his most serious expression. "She hasn't caused a single diplomatic incident this week."

"Well, there's always tomorrow," Andrew said, then paused, suddenly finding great interest in the paperweight on his desk. "Tell me, what do you know of Miss Charlie Morton?"

Adams's eyebrows rose fractionally—the equivalent of wild surprise from the usually impassive man. "Ah, the infamous lady barrister. Causing quite the stir among the old guard, I hear. Fascinating woman, by all accounts."

"Indeed." Andrew's fingers drummed against the desk's edge. "I need someone to keep an eye on her."

"To protect or to spy?" Adams tilted his head with the air of a man solving a particularly interesting puzzle. "With your track record, I suspect both."

Andrew had the grace to look sheepish. "Your perception wounds me, Adams. But yes, both. Report any peculiarities straightaway."

"I'll put Moncton on it," Adams said.

"Moncton?" Andrew's brow furrowed. "Is he the best we have?"

Adams drew himself up with mock indignation, straightening his shoulders. "Second only to myself, naturally."

"Just ensure he doesn't fall in love with her," Andrew muttered, turning to stare out the window.

Adams's lips twitched with barely suppressed amusement. "Speaking from experience, Carlisle?"

Andrew's hand flew to rub the back of his neck. "Perhaps."

"Is that so?" Adams leaned forward slightly, eyes gleaming with mischief. "Perhaps I should take the assignment myself. It'd be a shame not to make the acquaintance of such a special lady."

"Don't you dare!" Andrew spun around, pointing an accusatory finger at his friend.

Adams chuckled. "It'll cost you extra if I need to murder your competition."

"Don't be ridiculous." Andrew waved a dismissive hand, though his scowl remained. "I could commit the deed myself if that were the case. No, I need you to investigate her Cambridge degree. Find out whom she had to charm or… bribe."

The last word came out with distaste, Andrew's jaw tightening as he said it.

"Consider it done," Adams said, his tone returning to business efficiency.

"And arrange half a dozen guards for Daisy's birthday festivities."

"Still concerned about Byron's vindictive streak?" Adams asked, his tone sobering slightly.

"The man's been spreading rumors for months. I wouldn't put it past him to cause a scene at her celebration, especially with half of London society in attendance."

"Understood. Discreet positioning around the ballroom?"

"Exactly. She shouldn't even notice them, but I want every entrance covered."

Adams nodded approvingly. "Consider it handled." He turned to leave but hesitated at the door.

Andrew looked up from his papers. "Out with it, old friend. Your face suggests either indigestion or particularly juicy gossip."

Adams's shoulders relaxed as he turned back with a conspiratorial grin. "Lord Bridgewater's betrothal has ended rather spectacularly. The lady apparently found her protection officer more appealing than his lordship."

Andrew's eyebrows shot up, and he set down his pen entirely. "Reliable source?"

"When have I ever led you astray?" Adams asked, straightening his cuffs with exaggerated precision. With a knowing smile and a bow that was more friendly than formal, he took his leave, pausing only to add over his shoulder, "I do so enjoy watching you in the throes of... professional interest."

Andrew grabbed his quill and threw it at the closing door, Adams's laughter echoing down the hallway.

As Andrew dismissed Adams, across town in the Inner Temple, Charlotte's quiet morning was about to be disrupted. Her small office, usually a sanctuary of legal texts and case files, was today filled with the low murmur of laborers, brought in by the reluctant Mr. Philips, the solicitor.

Mr. Philips, an unhappy man forced into working with Charlotte by the Duke of Chatham, stood amid the bustling scene.

As barristers customarily did not solicit clients directly and rarely interacted with them, maintaining connections with solicitors was of utmost importance. When Mr. Philips had initially refused to work with her as all others had, the duke had unleashed a torrent of threats, breaking the poor man's resolve. Despite his numerous irritating habits, Mr. Philips was undeniably skilled in his work.

Charlotte was deep in thought, contemplating the best approach to present Lady Daisy's case, when Mr. Philips opened the door to her private office. A handsome brunette breezed into the room, her arms outstretched in greeting. She was dressed in an exquisite deep burgundy wool gown, adorned with lace trim.

"Miss Charlie Morton, I am absolutely thrilled to make your

acquaintance," the lady exclaimed, clasping Charlotte's hand with both of her own. "I am Daisy Creswell, and this"—she turned to a woman who had gone unnoticed until that moment—"is my dear friend, Miss Susie Grantham."

Miss Grantham offered a shy smile and a polite bow. She was the opposite of Lady Daisy, with golden-blonde hair and warm hazel eyes. Charlotte found herself immediately taken with the open and down-to-earth demeanor of both ladies.

"Lady Daisy, Miss Grantham, it is an honor to make your acquaintance," Charlotte said. She gestured for them to take a seat and rang for tea, though she held little hope that Mr. Philips would have the time to prepare it.

"I must apologize for this intrusion, Miss Morton," Lady Daisy began, her voice filled with enthusiasm. "Susie and I were in the vicinity, and we simply had to meet you. Not only are you representing my case, but we've been following your career with great interest since you were discovered to be a woman. Not for the sensationalism but for giving all women hope we may travel the paths destined for us."

"How kind of you to take an interest in my career," Charlotte replied, genuinely touched.

"Andrew has told me all about your brilliance and your breathtaking beauty," the lady continued, her smile radiant. "I see now he was entirely correct. You are absolutely stunning."

"Oh my, that is quite the compliment," Charlotte said, doubting Andrew would have paid her a compliment so openly to his sister.

"Those were his words, not mine," Lady Daisy clarified with a sly grin.

As the three women settled into a comfortable conversation, the earlier bustle of the parlor faded into the background.

"Miss Morton, I cannot express how thrilled I am that you are taking on my case."

"The pleasure is all mine, my lady."

Lady Daisy reached into her reticule and produced an envelope, presenting it with a flourish. The shy Miss Grantham applauded lightly with excitement.

"I would be most delighted if you could join us for a three-day gathering at Andrew's estate in Whistable in a fortnight. The festivities will include dancing, musical performances, a delightful picnic, and a scavenger hunt. Your presence would bring us the utmost joy." Turning to her companion, she sought confirmation. "It shall be a rather intimate gathering, will it not, Susie?"

Miss Grantham, her demeanor shy, nodded in agreement before saying melodically, "Indeed, we anticipate no more than two dozen esteemed guests."

The thought of seeing Andrew thrilled her, but Charlotte couldn't afford the cost of transportation. "I am truly honored by your invitation, Lady Daisy. However, I'm afraid my work keeps me quite occupied here in the city, even on weekends."

"Nonsense!" the lady declared, waving away Charlotte's concerns with a graceful sweep of her hand. "You can bring your work with you to the cottage. A change of scenery will do you a world of good. I assure you, there will be no shortage of entertainment, wealthy guests, or delectable feasts. I insist on sending a carriage to collect you on Friday afternoon. You can work and dine during the day and join us for entertainment in the evenings. And you'll be among familiar faces—my brother, Miss Grantham, the Duke of Chatham."

"I did not realize you were acquainted with the duke."

"Yes, indeed. He will be chaperoning his niece, Lady Gloria. In fact, I shall ask Gloria to personally escort you in her carriage. One more thing…" Lady Daisy examined Charlotte's attire before she said, "I shall give you a few frocks I no longer wear. We're around the same height. You are slimmer, but I shall assign a girl who is excellent at alterations as your lady's maid."

Before Charlotte had time to respond, Lady Daisy rose to her feet, ending the discussion. The whirlwind of ladies took turns embracing Charlotte warmly before departing as swiftly as they had arrived.

Charlotte stood motionless, staring after them, her mind faltering with the unexpected turn of events. She glanced down at her attire—the serviceable wool dress that marked her as firmly beneath the notice of the silk-clad ladies who would attend. The garment, though clean and well-mended, might as well have been a banner announcing she did not belong in Andrew's glittering world. In fact, with each passing day, her circumstances drove her further from the gilded path he walked.

And yet… three days—three days of warmth and comfort, of feasting at a table laden with delicacies she'd nearly forgotten the taste of. Three days of sleeping in a proper bed, with soft linens and downy pillows. Three days of… him.

Charlotte pressed her fingers to her temples, trying to silence the treacherous whispers of her heart. She would not permit herself to dwell on how her skin tingled at the mere thought of sharing the same roof with Andrew, of catching glimpses of him across candlelit rooms, of possibly hearing his deep laugh echo down marble halls. She would not acknowledge how her pulse quickened at the prospect of their paths crossing in quiet corridors, or how her dreams might betray her beneath those promised soft sheets.

No. This was about survival, about seizing a brief respite from the grinding wheel of poverty. The soft bed, the abundant food—these were the true temptations. Not the way Andrew's voice still caressed her ears like warm honey, or how his presence filled a room like summer heat.

Not the memory of that night in the library, when he had enveloped her in his embrace, his hot breath against her neck, his powerful body pressed against her back. The ghost of his lips still haunted her skin—how he'd traced burning kisses from her shoulder to her ear, the rasp of his evening stubble a delicious torture. Even now, days later, she could recall with perfect clarity how his hands had spanned her waist, how the thundering of his heart had matched her own frantic pulse.

The food and shelter. That was all. It had to be all.

HOUSE PARTY

9 December 1836—Whistable

"**T**HIS IS QUITE an interesting development." The Duke of Chatham smirked as the carriage jostled along the uneven road. "You say Lady Daisy extended the invitation?"

Charlotte narrowed her eyes and sent a silent warning. "What are you implying, Your Grace?"

"Nothing at all, Miss Morton." Chatham grinned innocently.

Lady Gloria, seated beside Charlotte, spoke. "Uncle, do you suspect Lady Daisy of playing matchmaker? It would make sense, given that she is an independent woman who likely admires a fellow female with professional aspirations."

"Is Lady Daisy an aspiring professional?" Charlotte asked.

"Oh, yes," Lady Gloria said. "She ran away to Jamaica to study medicine under a physician. Lord Carlisle went after her, but to everyone's astonishment, he allowed her to remain and finish her training. She returned to England only a year ago."

"That is admirable," Charlotte said. The revelation stirred something warm in her chest—further evidence of Andrew's capacity for understanding, despite how he presented himself.

Lady Gloria fixed her attention on Charlotte, a mischievous glint in her eye as she glanced at her uncle. "And what is your opinion of Lord Carlisle?" she whispered.

The Duke of Chatham interjected. "He is not a suitable match for you, Gloria."

Lady Gloria sat up straight and schooled her features to nonchalance. "What makes you think I want to be matched with

Lord Carlisle?"

Chatham quirked a brow. "Your feelings are quite evident in your expression. You would make a poor card player indeed."

She bristled, her lips forming a petulant pout. "Very well, then. Hypothetically speaking, why is he unsuitable for me? If it's his age, he's only fifteen years older than me. Besides, he looks healthier than any man I've ever met."

"It is not the age. Your parents require you to marry into an old, established title with a long lineage. Carlisle only obtained his title a year ago. Regardless of his wealth, it will not satisfy your parents' expectations."

Gloria slumped in her seat, her displeasure evident.

Chatham turned his attention back to Charlotte, his gaze holding a teasing glint. "Well, Miss Morton?" he prompted. "What is your opinion of the esteemed Earl of Carlisle?"

Charlotte's fingers tightened in her lap, memories of Andrew's hands, his whispered words, flooding back unbidden. She forced her voice to remain steady. "The earl appears to be fiercely protective of his sister, and his mannerisms can be somewhat... direct. It is abundantly clear that he does not mince words."

Gloria's countenance brightened like a flower revived by a refreshing shower. "Oh, he is ever so lovely to Daisy. Beneath his tough exterior lies such a tender heart." Her eyes sparkled with admiration. "And he is so handsome and strong."

Charlotte felt her breath stall despite herself. She knew exactly how strong he was, how gentle those calloused hands could be.

Chatham's brows shot up in alarm. "How do you know about his tenderness and strength? Is there something you should tell me?"

"Not at all!" Gloria hastily replied. "I've only drawn these conclusions from what Daisy tells me. She mentioned he works at the docks every week, regardless of his busy schedule, lifting nearly a hundred pounds for hours on end. And he always brings her the most thoughtful gifts when he returns from his travels. A man like that would make a wonderful husband."

"Is that so?" Chatham threaded his fingers together, looking unimpressed. The gems adorning them glimmered in the light, matching the silver stitching of his attire. "And you, at the tender age of seventeen, fancy yourself an expert on such matters? Has Lord Carlisle shown any impropriety toward you?"

The direct question shocked both Charlotte and Gloria, who shook her head vehemently. "Not in the slightest! His lordship scarcely acknowledges my existence, treating me as if I were nothing more than a child."

"From his perspective, my dear, you are precisely that," Chatham said, visibly relaxing. He then turned his attention back to Charlotte, his expression growing thoughtful. "Though I must say, Miss Morton, a man in Carlisle's position faces complicated loyalties. His business has grown considerably, and with growth comes obligations to rather influential investors." He paused, studying her reaction. "I merely hope you're aware that such men often find themselves caught between personal desires and financial necessities."

Charlotte's chest tightened. The duke's words warred with her memory of Andrew's vulnerability when he had spoken of waiting for her letter. Surely the man who had held her so reverently could not be capable of such calculation? Yet doubt crept in—what did she truly know of his business dealings?

"How do you think he might go about fulfilling his obligations to his investors?" she asked, her voice carefully neutral.

"It is hard to say. Take his sister's case, for example. If you were to fail, it could be enough to destroy your hard-earned career which is precisely what his shareholders are hoping for."

"I shall not fail," Charlotte said, perhaps more fiercely than necessary. "It is shocking that no one else had considered this line of defense. It is well-founded."

Chatham nodded approvingly. "I have the utmost faith in your skills where law is concerned. It is your history with him that might blind you to traps."

History. If only Chatham knew how recent—and how intimate—that history had become. Charlotte's fingers unconsciously traced her lower lip, the ghost of his kiss making it seem tender. "I have considered it. When it comes to the case, my failing becomes his as well."

The duke nodded. "This assembly should be interesting," Chatham said, his eyes sparkling with hidden meaning.

Charlotte turned her gaze to the passing scenery, but her mind drifted to that dimly lit library, to Andrew's voice rough with desire when he had said *do not pretend*. The memory sent traitorous warmth spreading through her body. She pressed her kerchief to her lips, fighting the conflicting emotions that threatened to overwhelm her.

Could Chatham be right? Was she walking into a trap of Andrew's making? Or was the trap simply her own heart, already ensnared by a man who might never be able to choose her over his empire?

In any case, she suspected she was already caught.

CHARLOTTE STEPPED OUT of the carriage, her mouth agape at the sight of the grand mansion rather than the quaint cottage she had envisioned. Tall oak trees lined the driveway, with moorland and gardens surrounding the imposing structure.

Daisy descended the front steps with a squeal of delight, enveloping Charlotte and Lady Gloria in a warm embrace. "Miss Morton, how wonderful that you have come! I simply cannot wait for you to meet my friends!"

"I'd be delighted to make their acquaintance," Charlotte said with a smile.

Upon entering the house, Susie greeted them in the entrance hallway, beaming quietly in a lovely peach-colored dress. Daisy buzzed about like a bumblebee in bright-yellow silk, her barely contained merriment a sharp contrast to her brother's surprised and gloomy countenance as he watched from a distance.

"What on earth is in your trunks? They must be heavy if our strongest footman is struggling!" Daisy's eyes followed the two footmen carrying Charlotte's belongings upstairs.

Charlotte chuckled. "I'm moving my office here for the weekend. They're mostly filled with papers and ink."

"That's a relief. I thought you were hiding a body in there." The ladies laughed while Charlotte's gaze drifted to Andrew, who was shaking the duke's hand with careful politeness.

"I'll show you to your rooms," Daisy announced. "Most of the guests have arrived and are enjoying champagne in the parlor."

Once Charlotte was deposited in her luxurious chamber, a giggle escaped her lips. Before her stood a large, beautiful bed with the prettiest counterpane of pink silk. On it lay several dresses of bold colors—Daisy's generous offerings. Charlotte threw herself onto the feather mattress with unladylike enthusiasm, rolling about until she was wrapped in the comforter like a sausage roll.

A gentle knock sounded, and a maid entered. Upon seeing Charlotte's undignified position, she let out a soft giggle.

"My name is Hannah, Miss Morton. Lady Daisy asked me to assist you during your stay."

"Did she? How kind of her."

"That is a mighty fine bed, ain't it, Miss?" Hannah remarked, her eyes twinkling.

"Yes, it is. I could spend the rest of my life in it."

"I've never seen a lady act like you, Miss."

"That's because I'm a lady who can appreciate the small things, Hannah."

As Hannah unpacked Charlotte's meager belongings—frowning at the slight defects in the garments—Charlotte luxuriated in a warm bath. The steaming water soothed her weary soul, and she felt she might melt into blissful contentment.

When she emerged, glowing and refreshed, Hannah began

the transformation. With deft fingers, the maid coaxed Charlotte's dark hair into a loose chignon, soft curls framing her face. A touch of powder and rouge enhanced her natural beauty, making her eyes sparkle.

Charlotte had chosen the most daring gown—deep-red silk that complemented her dark hair and skin. The neckline dipped low from off-the-shoulder cuffs, offering a tantalizing glimpse of her décolletage. It was bold, but in a room full of strangers and critics, she refused to disappear into the walls.

"You're a true beauty, my lady," Hannah said, adjusting the final threads of her alterations.

Charlotte's fingers drifted to her bare throat, thinking of her mother's necklaces she'd been forced to sell. "Do you think this might be too revealing?"

"Not at all, my lady. Why, Lady Sotheby caused quite the scandal last Season when her cuffs slipped to expose her corset!" Hannah giggled.

A sharp knock interrupted them.

Hannah moved to answer, but Andrew was already stepping inside, his presence filling the room. Charlotte's breath caught— he looked magnificent in his evening attire, but his expression was tense.

"Hannah, allow Miss Morton and me a private word?" he said.

The maid curtsied and withdrew, closing the door behind her. Andrew's eyes immediately found Charlotte, drinking in the sight of her in the crimson gown. His jaw tightened.

"You look..." He stopped, his gaze darkening and roaming over her form. "Exquisite. Dangerously so."

Charlotte felt heat rise in her cheeks. "Andrew, what are you doing here? If someone should see—"

"That's precisely why I'm here." He moved closer, his voice dropping. "Charlotte, tonight will be... difficult. Wilson is among the guests, and he's been watching me closely. My investors grow suspicious of my interest in you."

Understanding dawned in her eyes. "I see."

"I may need to seem dismissive, even cold, and I may need to feign an interest in Wilson's daughter." The words clearly pained him. "I cannot bear the thought of you believing it genuine."

Charlotte nodded slowly. "I understand. And I must maintain my facade with the duke. Any sign of familiarity between us could ruin both our reputations."

"Precisely." Andrew stepped closer still, close enough that she could smell his cologne, feel the heat radiating from his body. "But before the pretense begins..." His hand rose to cup her cheek, thumb tracing her lower lip.

"Andrew," she whispered, her resolve crumbling at his touch.

"I know I shouldn't," he murmured, his other hand settling at her waist. "But seeing you in this gown, knowing I must ignore you all evening..."

He leaned down, capturing her lips in a kiss that was desperate and tender in equal measure. Charlotte melted into him, her arms wrapping around his neck as he pulled her closer. The kiss deepened, the threat of separation making it more urgent.

When they finally broke apart, both were breathing heavily.

"Can you do this?" he asked quietly, his forehead resting against hers. "Can you bear to ignore me?"

Charlotte summoned a rueful smile. "I've endured worse, my lord. The question is whether you can manage to look bored in my presence."

He chuckled softly. "A considerable challenge, I admit."

"Then we are both about to discover our talents for deception." She stepped back reluctantly. "You should go. Hannah will return soon."

Andrew nodded, though his hands lingered at her waist a moment longer. "When this charade is over, Charlotte..."

"When it's over," she said softly, "we'll speak honestly."

He pressed one final, brief kiss to her lips before stepping away. "Remember—nothing you witness tonight is genuine."

"I shall remember. I pray you do as well." Despite her words, a flicker of pain stabbed at her heart before she composed herself.

As the door closed behind him, Charlotte pressed her fingers to her lips, still tingling from his kiss. Hannah returned moments later, chattering cheerfully about the evening ahead, but Charlotte barely heard her.

Her heart was already dreading the performance to come.

Approximately two hours after Charlotte's presence had surprised him, Andrew stood beside his sister in the greeting line, smiling while he tried to confront his sister delicately. "You failed to mention you were inviting Miss Morton to this gathering."

"It must have slipped my mind. My apologies, brother."

"That is what I thought. You wouldn't dream of playing matchmaker between the notorious bluestocking and myself, expecting her to advance your cause in medicine, would you?"

"Andrew!" Daisy's eyes and mouth gaped open. "How could you imagine me capable of such a scheme?"

Andrew narrowed his eyes at her, and her lips quirked into a mischievous grin. "I can invite her but cannot force her heart. That, you'll have to do yourself."

"What on earth are you about?"

Instead of answering his question, Daisy's face broke out into a wide grin, her teeth showing and eyes twinkling. "Doesn't she look absolutely marvelous? A woman possessed of such beauty and intelligence must be rare indeed!" Daisy emphasized her sentiment by clasping her hands together.

Andrew's attention shifted sharply to their subject of discussion, who was glowing radiantly yet clung appropriately to the Duke of Chatham's arm. The duke's niece occupied his other side, but Andrew's chest tightened at the sight of Charlotte's hand resting so naturally on Chatham's sleeve.

Remember—nothing you witness tonight is genuine, he reminded himself, even as jealousy clawed at his insides. She was playing her part perfectly, just as they'd agreed.

As the threesome approached to pay their respects to the host, Andrew steeled himself for the performance of his life. His gaze traced the neckline of her dress, dipping low and revealing the supple mounds he'd kissed before. The deep-red hue of Charlotte's gown seemed to mock him—a beacon of everything he must pretend not to desire.

Gathering his wits, Andrew drew in a steadying breath and summoned every ounce of aristocratic indifference he could muster. When Charlotte extended her gloved hand, he took it with calculated coolness, bowed perfunctorily, and released it with deliberate haste—as if touching her meant nothing at all.

The hurt that flashed across her features nearly undid him, even though he knew she understood the necessity. Her eyes darted about the room, and he recognized the performance for what it was—she was playing the part of a woman dismissed by her social superior.

Christ, we're both too good at this, he thought grimly.

Turning to the duke, Andrew offered a more genuine handshake—it was safer to be cordial with Chatham than risk appearing jealous. When Lady Gloria curtsied, he bowed over her hand with precisely the same indifferent courtesy he'd shown Charlotte, though the child's fluttering eyelashes made him inwardly cringe.

As the duke led the ladies away, Andrew fought every instinct screaming at him to follow. Charlotte looked magnificent in that crimson gown, the silk accentuating every curve he'd memorized. But he forced himself to remain motionless, to appear utterly unaffected by the vision she presented.

This is necessary, he told himself as Wilson's calculating gaze swept over him from across the room. *Protect her reputation. Follow the plan.*

But watching Charlotte lean into Chatham's protection, seeing how naturally she fit at the duke's side, Andrew wondered if he was protecting her—or simply handing her over to a better man.

The performance had begun, and already it was torture.

A FEW HOURS after she felt Andrew's calculated indifference, Charlotte held out her plate to the servers, swallowing at the sight of the heaps of food piled upon it. Gingerly carrying the plate, she ordered wine from a footman and looked around the dining room buzzing with impeccably dressed people. Not recognizing any faces, she headed toward the parlor and saw an empty seat where Daisy and Chatham were engaged in conversation with several young people.

As she approached, Daisy interrupted the discourse to enthusiastically wave her over. Charlotte gratefully sat between her hostess and a blonde woman who had one slice of meat and three slices of carrot on her plate.

Charlotte ate with quiet desperation, not having had her belly filled since Wilson's soiree. She half listened to the nearest conversation but snapped to attention when she heard her name.

"By supporting Miss Morton, Your Grace, are you not proclaiming your support for women's rights to work?"

Daisy's provocative question commanded attention. Charlotte found solace in the fact that she wasn't the most controversial person in the room for a change.

"I believe in the inherent equality of all individuals," the duke replied.

"Daisy, allow His Grace a moment to savor his meal. I daresay he feels quite like the main course himself with your relentless interrogations." A familiar drawl elicited chuckles from the guests. Charlotte looked up to acknowledge the jest, then noticed Andrew standing across from her, behind the seated guests.

Her heart betrayed her with its racing, though she knew he wouldn't acknowledge her. From her vantage point, she observed Andrew as his glance deliberately strayed toward the pretty blonde seated beside her—a calculated display for Wilson's benefit, no doubt.

The young woman in pale-green silk beamed radiantly in Andrew's direction, clearly encouraged by his attention. Charlotte recognized the performance for what it was, even as jealousy clawed at her chest.

Daisy leaned toward her conspiratorially. "Are you acquainted with Lady Lidia?"

"No, I have not had the pleasure," Charlotte replied, smoothing imaginary wrinkles from her gown.

"She is Lord Wilson's daughter."

Of course she is. Charlotte managed a neutral smile. "I see. She is very beautiful."

"She is, if one likes a greenhouse rose. I believe Lord Wilson is quite keen to become part of our family." Daisy's displeasure was evident in her cool tone.

Charlotte's chest tightened, though she reminded herself this was merely Andrew's strategy to placate Wilson. "Is your brother searching for a wife, then?"

"I believe so. He is—"

"I have no ambition other than being a loyal wife and mother," Lady Lidia announced loudly, clearly performing for Andrew's benefit. The conversation ceased as all attention turned to her.

Charlotte fought to appear unaffected as Andrew regarded Lady Lidia with what seemed like keen interest.

Daisy chuckled pointedly. "That's very admirable, Lady Lidia, but men often prefer women with ambitions outside the home— opera singers, for instance."

Lady Lidia gasped. "Surely if men sought such women, they would pursue them for matrimony!"

Andrew's expression grew stern toward his sister before

transforming into a gracious smile for Lady Lidia. "Please forgive my sister. I can assure you that men of influence desire women who free their minds for household matters. Women who venture outside the home inadvertently cause disruptions in our careers."

The words stung, even knowing they were part of his performance. Charlotte watched Lady Lidia beam gratefully, elongating her graceful neck for Andrew's apparent admiration.

Her stomach wrenched at the convincing display.

When another gentleman approached Lady Lidia, she skillfully transferred her attention, leaving Andrew free to move away. Charlotte found herself following his departure with her eyes, hating how much she missed his presence even knowing it was all pretense.

"Are you well, Miss Morton?" Andrew's voice rumbled unexpectedly close.

She turned to find him leaning over the settee with a concerned host's expression. "Yes, my lord. Very well, thank you."

He inclined his head formally—maintaining proper distance, just as they'd agreed. Then he addressed his sister quietly. "Her father is an important investor and ally. Mind your manners."

As Andrew walked away, Charlotte felt the profound loneliness of their necessary charade. As such, when the duke's bejeweled hand appeared before her, offering silent comfort, she took his arm gratefully.

"Let us walk about the house, shall we?"

In the secluded corridor, Chatham's voice was gentle. "The performance grows difficult, does it not?"

Charlotte's fingers tightened on his arm. "It is… more challenging than I anticipated."

"You could end this pretense, you know. Confess your feelings."

"No. This protection serves us both." She drew a steadying breath. "Besides, Andrew plays his part convincingly. Perhaps Lady Lidia truly would suit him better."

"He watches you when he thinks no one notices."

Her heart raced treacherously. "That could mean many things."

"Charlotte." His serious tone made her stop and face him. "Have you seen the columns about us in the scandal sheets?"

"No, what do they say?"

"They speculate that you are my mistress. They claim you compromised yourself to graduate. My darling, our arrangement has protected me brilliantly, but I fear your reputation cannot survive much longer."

Charlotte's hand flew to her stomach. "What are our options?"

"We could marry."

Her eyes widened. "His Majesty would never accept such a controversial figure into his family."

"Perhaps he would view it as the lesser evil." The duke's smile was melancholic. "It would be easy for us, seeing we already love each other."

Charlotte stared at him, weighing the safety of his offer against the dangerous hope Andrew's glances had kindled. In the distance, she could hear the murmur of the dinner party continuing—Andrew maintaining his performance, just as she was maintaining hers.

But for how much longer could either of them sustain this charade?

ANDREW HAD WATCHED when Chatham escorted Charlotte out of the parlor for their private conversation. Almost an hour later, he was keenly aware of their re-entry, both wearing expressions of renewed intimacy that made his chest tighten with dread.

They're playing their parts well, he told himself, even as jealousy clawed at his insides. Too well, perhaps. The sight of Charlotte's radiant smile directed at the duke—genuine affection rather than mere performance—pierced through his carefully constructed defenses.

A quartet filled the air with pleasant melodies, and liquor flowed freely, but Andrew suddenly felt as though the walls were closing in. Despite his best efforts to appear captivated by Lady Lidia's simpering, his attention remained fixed on Charlotte. Every graceful movement, every melodic laugh shared with Chatham, reminded him of what he was pretending to reject.

"Whose murder are you plotting with that glare, Carlisle?" a smooth voice inquired.

Andrew turned to find the Marquess of Hereford and the Duke of Lancaster flanking him, their gazes fixed appreciatively on Charlotte.

"It appears he's quite taken with the lady in red," Lancaster observed with a knowing smirk.

"Isn't she a true beauty, Hereford? Just look at those dark curls cascading over her silky skin. Why, she must bathe in—"

"Utter another word about Miss Morton's bathing habits, and I'll break every bone in your body," Andrew growled, his voice low and menacing.

"A bit possessive for a man showing such marked interest in Wilson's vapid daughter, are we?" Hereford interjected, raising an eyebrow.

Andrew's jaw clenched. "What took you lot so long? You were to arrive this afternoon."

"As higher-ranking peers, we arrive when we please," Hereford replied with mock hauteur. "That, and we were delayed procuring Daisy's birthday gift."

"Which is?"

"Other than our magnificent presence? What was it Daisy said, Lancaster? 'You are the brother I always hoped for but never had'?"

"Touching sentiment," Andrew muttered, then stiffened as he caught sight of Chatham's arm sliding around Charlotte's waist.

The duke pulled her closer, raising his glass in what seemed like a subtle toast in Andrew's direction.

Bastard knows exactly what he's doing.

"Daisy begged us to knock some sense into you about Miss Morton," yet another voice announced. "Called you a 'stupid, stupid man,' if memory serves."

"Preston!" the two men exclaimed, greeting their friend with enthusiasm while Andrew remained transfixed by the intimate tableau across the room.

"We hardly dared hope you'd grace us with your presence," Lancaster grinned.

"Lucky for you, I managed to clear my exceedingly busy schedule," Preston replied grandly. "Though I must say, Carlisle seems rather distracted by the entertainment."

"Indeed. Shall we retire somewhere he can brood in private?" Hereford suggested, steering the group toward Andrew's study.

"But he simply must maintain surveillance of his lady love," Lancaster teased.

"Easily remedied," Preston declared. "I've found that declaring one's intentions publicly works wonders for securing a woman's affections."

"Have you three quite finished?" Andrew growled as they entered his study.

The men settled around the hearth as a footman poured drinks. "Not remotely," Hereford replied cheerfully. "Tell us, Carlisle, have you made an offer for Miss Morton's hand?"

"Don't be absurd. Why would I do such a thing?"

"Because, according to our highly reliable source—your sister—you harbor certain tender feelings for the lady," Preston said.

"We shared… an acquaintance years ago. Nothing more." Andrew drained his glass in one swallow.

"I must say, I'm relieved to hear you hold no tender feelings," Lancaster drawled meaningfully. "It would pain us to see you pining when it's too late."

Andrew's blood turned to ice. "Too late for what?"

The three friends exchanged loaded glances.

"Out with it, damn you!"

"Well," Hereford began gravely, "word has it that our friend Chatham has accessed the family vault."

"And retrieved his grandmother's ruby ring," Lancaster added helpfully.

Andrew's stomach plummeted. "The man collects jewelry like a magpie. What of it?"

"That particular ring," Preston said solemnly, "has only one traditional purpose."

Andrew felt the blood drain from his face, his chest constricting as if someone had wrapped iron bands around his ribs. Marriage. The duke was going to propose to Charlotte.

"Surely he must marry within his station," Andrew said weakly.

"No matter," Preston said, affecting relief. "Since you're entirely uninterested."

"Indeed. Thank goodness we needn't mention the other development," Lancaster sighed dramatically.

"What other development?" Andrew demanded.

"Not worth discussing if your heart isn't engaged," Hereford said, producing a cigar with theatrical nonchalance.

"I know what you scoundrels are doing! Tell me!"

"Very well," Preston grinned. "I wagered these fools that you'd admit your feelings within ten minutes."

"You bet on my emotional state?" Andrew roared as money changed hands.

"Indeed. And judging by your thunderous expression, I've won handily," Preston said, pocketing his winnings. "The question remains: What do you intend to do about it?"

Andrew shot to his feet, his friends' laughter following him as he strode toward the parlor. His mind raced with possibilities, each more desperate than the last. The pretense that had seemed so necessary now felt like a noose tightening around his throat.

As he reentered the gathering, his gaze immediately sought Charlotte. She stood beside Chatham, radiant in her crimson gown, looking every inch the duchess she might soon become. The sight of them together—so natural, so right—made his chest ache with longing and regret.

But watching her animated conversation with the duke, seeing the genuine affection in her eyes, Andrew wondered if in trying to protect his interest and respect Charlotte's loyalty to the duke, he might have handed her directly to a better man.

And yet, as he observed Chatham's protective stance, his obvious devotion to Charlotte's well-being, Andrew couldn't help but wonder if perhaps that was exactly what she deserved.

GARDEN LIGHTS

10 December 1836

THE COTTAGE HAD been full of activities all day, with staff rushing to prepare for the concert that night, rooms filling with candles and arrangements of herbs. Charlotte had stayed away from it all, needing to work on her cases. As evening approached, she finally descended the stairs, her eyes weary from hours spent poring over legal documents.

The servants bustled about with renewed urgency, carrying trays of crystal glasses and silver platters toward the dining room. The air hummed with anticipation for the evening's entertainment—first dinner, then a musical performance in the drawing room. Charlotte paused at the bottom of the staircase, observing the organized chaos with a mixture of admiration and exhaustion.

Through the frost-etched windows, something caught her eye—a glimmer of light in the garden that seemed too deliberate, too beautiful to be mere moonlight. Curious, she made her way to the French doors leading to the patio.

The sight that greeted her took her breath away. The garden, typically barren in the depths of December, had been transformed into a winter wonderland of light. Hundreds of lanterns, their delicate glass domes gleaming like frozen teardrops, stretched as far as the eye could see. Each one housed a tiny, defiant flame that danced and flickered, casting an otherworldly glow across the frozen landscape.

Without thinking of the cold, Charlotte stepped onto the patio and began walking along the illuminated path. The lanterns hung from bare branches, lined frost-covered walkways, and nestled among holly bushes heavy with crimson berries. Their warm light caught the edges of icicles, setting them ablaze with golden fire.

She had walked only a short distance when she spotted a tall figure standing near the greenhouse, his face tilted toward the star-filled sky. The orange glow of a cigar tip punctuated the darkness as Andrew drew deeply, exhaling a stream of smoke that disappeared into the night air.

He turned at the sound of her footsteps on the gravel, and his expression immediately shifted from contemplative to concerned.

"Charlotte, what are you doing out here without a coat?" he chided, already moving toward her. "You'll catch your death in this cold."

Before she could protest, he was shrugging out of his own coat and draping it around her shoulders. The wool was warm from his body heat and carried his familiar scent that made her pulse quicken.

"Come," he said, his hand hovering at the small of her back without quite touching. "Let's get you somewhere warm."

He guided her toward one of the glass structures she had admired from afar. Up close, she realized it was a miniature greenhouse, glowing with warmth from strategically placed lanterns.

"This is extraordinary," she breathed, stepping inside the heated space. "Andrew, this garden is truly remarkable."

A faint smile touched his lips as he watched her turn in a slow circle, taking in the artful arrangement of light and glass. "I'm glad you approve. I've spent considerable time perfecting it."

"You created this? It's like something from a fairy tale," she said softly, then looked up at him. "But you must be freezing without your coat."

"I'm fine," he assured her, though she noticed he moved closer to one of the warming lanterns.

For a moment, they stood in comfortable silence, the magical garden surrounding them like a glittering cocoon. Then Andrew's expression grew more serious, his gaze studying her face in the lamplight.

"Tell me about your relationship with Chatham," he said, his voice carefully controlled but with an undercurrent of tension.

Charlotte's eyes flashed with surprise. "What do you mean?"

"I mean exactly what I said. What is the nature of your relationship with the duke?"

She straightened, her chin lifting slightly. "We are friends. Close friends, and professional colleagues."

"Friends," Andrew repeated, his tone skeptical. "The man is in love with you, Charlotte."

"That may be true," she admitted quietly. "I don't doubt that Albert loves me as a friend."

He paused, seeming to steel himself for the next question.

"If he were to propose marriage? Would you accept him?"

Charlotte hesitated, her fingers twisting in her skirts. "He... he has mentioned it. Last evening, in fact."

The relief that had begun to settle over Andrew's features vanished instantly, replaced by something fierce and possessive. "And?"

"I'm not certain," she whispered.

"You're not certain?" Andrew's voice rose, his careful control finally snapping. "How can you not be certain when you know how I feel about you?"

"What do you expect from me?" she shot back, her own anger flaring. "You're too busy manipulating the *Ton*, appearing to protest against my career, hiding any association with me. What am I supposed to do to guard my security when you won't even acknowledge me publicly?"

"I must work slowly to convince these powerful men," he said through gritted teeth. "I need a contingency plan in place before I can reveal my true feelings. These are dangerous waters, Charlotte. One wrong move and—"

"And what? You'll lose your precious shareholders?" She

stepped away from him, pacing to the window. "Meanwhile, the scandal about Albert and me grows daily. It may ruin my reputation entirely. I need to make a decision before that happens."

"How can you even consider him?" Andrew demanded. "How can you ponder marrying another man when you're in love with me?"

Charlotte whirled around, her eyes blazing. "Because you make it impossible to believe that love is enough! You say you love me, but you won't fight for me. You won't stand by me publicly. Albert offers me partnership, respect, and protection without conditions."

"And what of passion? What of the fire that burns between us?"

"Fire can consume as easily as it can warm," she said, her voice breaking slightly. "Perhaps I'd rather have the steady flame of respect than risk being burned by your ambition."

Andrew crossed the room in two strides, grasping her shoulders. "You don't mean that."

"Don't I?" she whispered, even as her body betrayed her by leaning into his touch. "You've shown me where your priorities lie, Andrew. And they're not with me." She shrugged off his coat and thrust it against his chest. Andrew grasped her hand, the contact sending a jolt through her.

"Charlotte, don't leave like this."

"I believe I've heard enough for one evening. I should return to the house before I'm missed at dinner."

She walked away, swallowing her tears while Andrew looked on and watched her slip away.

UNCOVERING

ANDREW ENTERED THE ballroom after dinner, Charlotte's words in the garden still ringing in his ears. He immediately reached for a glass of champagne to quell the emotions raging within him. The effervescent liquid did little to soothe his frayed nerves as his eyes were inevitably drawn to Charlotte and the duke, their heads bent together in intimate conversation.

With each passing moment, the sight became increasingly unbearable. Andrew turned away from them as his grip on his champagne flute tightened, his knuckles turning white as he fought for control. He drained the glass in a single gulp and reached for another.

"Carlisle." The Duke of Chatham's voice came from beside him as His Grace picked up his own flute of champagne, a large diamond glittering on his finger.

"Your Grace. How delightful that you could join us."

"Come now, Carlisle. There's no need for pretense. I'm well aware of your feelings toward me," the duke remarked good-naturedly.

Andrew bristled. "I may not agree with you paving the way for a female barrister, but I do believe you to be a decent fellow."

"How generous, considering you funded her education and hired her yourself."

"Hiring her was an act of pure desperation."

"Is that all?" The duke's eyes pierced through him. "I find it hard to believe you could hire Miss Morton against your investors' wishes without some ulterior motive."

"You give those men far too much credit."

"Perhaps, but you are quite creative with your schemes. It would be a shame to lose control over your own company."

Andrew's jaw tightened. "I suppose I'm not entirely opposed to the idea of female professionals, but the practical application is complex in a society not yet ready for such change."

"Only if you choose to complicate the matter." The duke's smile radiated warmth. "What is the point of life without a little idealism?"

"Speaking of life's meaning," Andrew said, his tone turning cool, "do you love her?"

The duke met his gaze unflinchingly. "I do. Do you?"

"As much as I'm capable."

"There's an honest response. You acknowledge you're not capable of loving her as she ought to be loved."

"I have hundreds of employees to consider. Losing my company would harm more than just myself."

"I imagine that's exactly how Charlotte feels." The duke stepped closer, lowering his voice. "I suspect your attraction to Charlotte is part of some scheme to appease your shareholders. I will not look kindly upon anyone who attempts to harm her career."

Andrew smiled coldly. "You ought to learn the facts before making accusations regarding your charity."

"I know the facts. And may I remind you that I dine with the king every month? Charlotte is not my charity—she's the king's."

Andrew's brows shot up in surprise. He hadn't considered royal support.

"Would you release her," he asked suddenly, "if she wished it?"

The duke studied him carefully. "I'd send her with my blessing—but only if you were willing to support her career publicly. Otherwise, you don't deserve her."

Before Andrew could respond, the duke's attention shifted. "Ah, there she is."

Andrew followed his gaze, his heart skipping despite himself as he watched Chatham stride toward Charlotte's radiant smile.

A low growl escaped Andrew's throat.

"He's gone feral," Preston's voice came from behind him. "Do you suppose he might have contracted rabies?"

"That, gentlemen, is the sound of jealous rage," Hereford chuckled, raising his glass. "Our dear Carlisle has finally met his match."

"You would do well to remember you're at my mercy, eating my food!" Andrew gritted out.

Preston gently removed the champagne glass from Andrew's white-knuckled grip. "Perhaps some air, old friend, before you do something spectacularly foolish?"

AFTER AN EVENING of watching his beloved with another man and his friends taunting him about his unrequited love, Andrew settled into a wingback chair in one of the guest rooms and played the day's events in his mind. He was aware of Lady Lidia's allure—her beauty, impeccable manners, and the connections her family possessed. She seemed to have mastered the art of seduction, and having Wilson as a father-in-law would make the scoundrel less of a threat.

While he hadn't minded the show Lady Lidia had put on, flaunting her bosom and her beautiful neck, he found her overall demeanor insincere. His preference lay with women of substance, those whose intellect captured his attention before anything else. The rest, he considered a bonus, much like Charlotte.

A life with Charlotte might afford him a contented marriage, like those of his friends, who seemed to bask in the glow of their wives' presence. Although the stubborn woman brought little to the table except trouble, her keen intelligence, determination, and generosity were aphrodisiacs to Andrew. He longed for a woman who could understand a self-made man like himself while expertly navigating the intricacies of polite society.

Yearning to talk to her and fill his vision with her loveliness, Andrew walked toward the small library, certain she would have her nose buried deep in documents. Instead, he was distracted by a streak of light emanating from Charlotte's bedchamber.

He knocked, and in the absence of a response, pushed open the door. Two lanterns burned by the bedside, illuminating Charlotte, who sat on the floor with her head resting on the bed, surrounded by piles of books and papers.

"Foolish woman," Andrew muttered under his breath, irritated that she had disobeyed the cardinal rule of any household—never sleep with candles burning. He went over to the slumbering woman and carefully moved the candles out of the way. With her head turned to one side and both hands tucked under her cheek, she snored softly, clad in a worn night rail and an equally threadbare cotton housecoat.

In the warm, orange glow of the lanterns, her beauty overwhelmed him. Her thick, dark lashes fluttered, and her lips parted slightly. A long, gentle exhale escaped her mouth. As Andrew gazed upon her, his indignation evaporated. She possessed an inner flame, perhaps what he found so irresistible. His chest tightened at the sight of her innocent and vulnerable appearance in sleep. The thought of waking up next to that sweet face filled his mind.

Curiosity compelled him to lean over the bed and illuminate the papers, examining the documents she had been drafting. They were primarily cases representing working-class families against their landlords, neighbors, and fraudsters. Undoubtedly, she was diligently fulfilling her duty without compensation.

As he moved to clear the papers, Wilson's name caught his eye, leaping out from one of the documents. Sensing he had stumbled upon something significant, Andrew circled the bed and scrutinized the papers more closely. His curiosity morphed into a scowl as he carefully turned the pages, revealing the names of all the shareholders in his company.

It appeared Charlotte had compiled his company's financial statements and that of Wilson's, for a grievance submitted by his tenants. He smiled at the prospect of Wilson at her mercy but frowned at the impact of the trial on his company. He moved the stacks of paper to the desk.

The rustling of papers caused her thick lashes to flutter, and her eyes suddenly opened. Charlotte gasped and sat up quickly, tightly closing her robe around her neck as she took in her state of undress.

"Andrew, what are you doing here?"

Without pausing in his task of moving papers off the bed, Andrew replied grumpily, "Ensuring your candles don't burn the house down. You ought to know better."

"Oh, my sincerest apologies. I didn't mean to doze off. I am so sorry."

She quickly rose to her feet and examined the piles of papers organized on the desk. "I was going to be cross with you for piling the documents in a nonsensical manner, but you categorized them perfectly."

"I've spent thousands of hours reviewing legal documents and meeting with solicitors. I'm quite familiar with the process." With a teasing glint in his eyes, he added, "Now, I suggest you sleep on the bed rather than using it as a desk. If you're uncertain of their respective purposes, please do speak up now."

Her long lashes swept upward toward him as she said, "Their uses are interchangeable. Don't you agree, Lord Carlisle?"

Andrew was speechless. He was uncertain of his purpose in approaching her, but his feet carried him closer until she needed to tilt her head back to meet his gaze.

He spoke in a low, raspy timbre. "Charlotte, I believe you might have learned a thing or two from the courtesans you associate with."

"You shall never know."

She managed to hold his gaze, but Andrew noticed the tension in her neck and shoulders. She then swallowed and bit her bottom lip. His eyes focused sharply on her mouth, glistening lusciously in the faint glow. Such fullness, like a ripe cherry about to burst. How he wished to taste her sweetness, to feel her surrender beneath his touch.

"What a shame. I could give you much, much more pleasure," he said, his voice hoarse and low.

"Well… I shall learn to live with the loss. I bid you good night, my lord."

With every ounce of willpower he possessed, he stepped away from her and exited the chamber.

He had to admit he had lost the battle of wits against Charlotte Morton.

DISASTER

11 December 1836

ANDREW STARED AT the cause of his fatigue, his gaze transfixed by the sight before him. Charlotte was a vision of loveliness in a silk emerald-green gown, the fabric draping over her to entice. He had hardly slept the previous night, plagued by a raging erection as he thought about her. He had finally given in and had whispered her name as he reached his climax.

She was unadorned around the neck, and he found himself fantasizing about gifting her all the luxuries money could afford. To his chagrin, there was one constant undesirable ornament on her person—the Duke of Chatham. Ever the faithful servant, the duke stood by her side like a devoted husband, if not a territorial lover.

Andrew had managed to distract himself with estate matters during the day while Daisy entertained her friends with a scavenger hunt. But duty called this evening as the orchestra prepared to announce the commencement of the first dance.

"Carlisle, just the man I was looking for." Wilson slapped him on the shoulder, and Andrew grimaced for more reasons than one. The man's breath smelled like sour milk, and he had an inkling as to why Wilson was so eager to see him.

"Wilson," he replied coolly.

"I need to speak with you in private."

Nodding curtly, Andrew led him to a vacant corner, ordering a footman to fetch him a glass of brandy as he did so.

"You and my daughter seem to be getting along quite well.

You would make a very handsome pair," Wilson said without preamble.

"Lady Lidia is undeniably lovely, but I must confess I have no intention of marrying this Season."

"And why not? How does waiting benefit you? You're approaching two and thirty, are you not?"

"I may embark on a long voyage, you see. I don't wish to leave a wife behind, pining for my return."

"A long voyage for investment? Is there something I ought to know about?"

The prospect of profit always managed to catch Wilson's attention, but even more eager was his desire not to miss out on anything other men were pursuing. His weak spine had him panting after whatever other dogs chased, a trait Andrew found rather distasteful.

"Nothing related to your investment, if that's what you're asking."

"If it's a promising venture, I wish to know about it." Wilson's eyes gleamed with greed.

"It's merely an idea I'm exploring currently, to invest personally. I'm afraid I cannot say any more on the subject at present."

Wilson nodded reluctantly. "Yes, well, do let me know when the time is right."

"I shall, of course."

"As I was saying, you and my daughter would make a fine pair, not to mention the advantageous joining of our families," Wilson continued, undeterred by Andrew's lack of enthusiasm.

"I'm honored you're willing to be associated with a *nouveau riche* like myself," Andrew said.

"It seems you cannot be ignored, as even King William thought you worthwhile for an earldom. If you're good enough for the king, you're good enough for me." Wilson puffed out his chest with self-importance.

"I appreciate that. Let us be clear. There is no understanding between you and me, nor between Lady Lidia and myself."

Wilson eyed him suspiciously, his gaze narrowing. "I have a feeling you have no intention toward my daughter."

"She is young, and I worry about her lack of life experience in handling a man like me. But in a year or two, who knows…" Andrew's tone was gentle.

"That is precisely why she would make an ideal wife, one who stays out of your way and doesn't know to make demands. Her best childbearing years are ahead of her."

Andrew internally grimaced at Wilson's notion of an ideal wife. "Even so… Is that what you wished to discuss?"

"There is something else. I saw the grievance statement for your case. You shall hear from the court in the next few days."

"Who is the assigned judge?"

"Abinger… for now."

"He is a liberal."

"That he is. He might even be a suffragette sympathizer," Wilson said with a wince, his distaste for the movement evident in his tone.

"If not a suffragist himself," Andrew added, a hint of amusement in his voice.

"Hoffman might be a better choice." Wilson's words were not a suggestion, but rather a pointed demand, made clear by the look he directed at Andrew.

"Hoffman? I want to win the case." Andrew studied Wilson with a calculating glance.

"You may have the case heard, but you cannot validate a female barrister. We discussed what would happen if you did even if you were to discredit her after the trial."

"I didn't say I would."

"You'd risk all for one cause?" Wilson asked quickly.

In addition to coveting control of Andrew's company, he was hiding something else. The man was tiresome, indeed.

"May I rely on your support when the time comes to expel her?" Wilson asked, a sly grin spreading across his face.

Andrew tensed but forced himself to sound neutral. "How do

you plan on achieving that?"

"I don't have anything concrete yet, but the fact that she lives with doxies is a good place to start."

Andrew frowned at this new knowledge. "She lives with them?"

"That she does. She rents out a room in the Bankside. A woman of low morals cannot possibly defend the public honorably." Wilson's voice was filled with self-righteous indignation.

Andrew narrowed his eyes. "How did you come to know this?"

Wilson shrugged. "I hear things."

"You had her followed," Andrew said, anger surging.

Wilson cleared his throat, confirming his suspicions. In that moment, Lady Lidia joined them with a bright smile, shyly meeting Andrew's eyes. "Papa, the dance is starting."

Andrew bowed over her hand but found himself distracted by the emerald green of Charlotte's dress swirling around the royal blue of the duke's suit in perfect synchronicity.

Chatham was an accomplished dancer and expertly concealed Charlotte's errors, Andrew observed. They laughed together as only close confidants with a special kinship could. Once again, something tugged painfully at his heart.

"Are you not dancing, Carlisle?" Wilson asked, undoubtedly hinting that he ought to ask his daughter for a turn about the room.

Thankfully, Andrew had a perfectly valid excuse.

"I wish I could, but I do not know how."

The lady and her father gasped, as if Andrew had admitted to lacking the knowledge of proper silverware usage.

"Whyever not? You're an earl now, my good man. You'd best start learning if you're to attend balls and maintain your social standing." Wilson's brow furrowed in disapproval.

Andrew scoffed at Wilson's remark, finding the notion of dance lessons utterly ridiculous. "I don't attend balls, except when

I'm hosting. I simply do not have the time for dance lessons, or dancing, for that matter."

Lady Lidia's disappointment was palpable, her crestfallen expression mirroring her father's displeasure. However, Andrew paid them no mind, his attention inexorably drawn back to the woman in green and the duke, their graceful movements captivating him.

As he watched, Andrew's fingers absently twisted a button on his coat, his mind consumed by the sight before him. Charlotte looked up at the duke and laughed, her face alight with joy. In that moment, Andrew's fingers tightened, inadvertently tearing the button from his coat.

The sudden realization of his action jolted him back to the present, and he quickly pocketed the errant button, hoping no one had noticed his momentary lapse in composure. Yet, even as he tried to focus on the conversation at hand, his thoughts remained firmly fixed on the dancing couple, their connection both intriguing and unsettling to him in equal measure.

THE DUKE WAS a graceful dancer, and there was no danger of losing her toes. Charlotte, on the other hand, nearly tripped twice due to misremembered steps. She hadn't danced in at least a decade, and her face flushed with embarrassment.

"Do not concern yourself," His Grace said when she apologized. "I was taught to dance from the tender age of three. My dance lessons only ceased when I began to hide away, causing quite a panic. I can dance more easily than I can sleep."

"You do dance beautifully, Your Grace."

"And you..." He trailed off, regarding her with soft eyes. "You look positively stunning tonight. I don't believe I have ever seen you more beautiful."

"Thank you. You're very kind and perhaps a little blind," she said, managing a playful smile.

He tilted his head back and laughed, a rich, melodious sound. "I may be seven and thirty, but I can see well enough to find you beautiful."

Charlotte tilted her head. "Your Grace? You've never spoken to me this way before."

"True. I've always been careful about crossing the line. No matter how much trust you have in me, I felt it was my duty to protect your reputation as anything, even wearing the wrong frock could land you in hot water. It seems Wilson is in a rush to have you disbarred."

Her visage froze with alarm. "Did you hear something lately?"

The duke did not respond immediately, instead spinning her around before catching her on the other side as the dance continued. "He has an assistant who's been asking about you. The line of questioning makes his intentions quite obvious."

"What can I do?"

Chatham paused as they bowed to conclude the dance. "Come. Let us discuss this further."

Charlotte followed the duke to a secluded corner near the door, her heart racing with anticipation. Chatham rubbed his chin awkwardly, his jewels sparkling impressively under the glow of hundreds of candles. He gazed at her, his eyes searching hers as he spoke.

"We broached the subject yesterday, but I am quite serious. Let us marry," he said firmly.

She nodded, her breath catching in her throat. When she finally tried to speak, her throat felt as dry as sand, the words struggling to form on her tongue. She glanced around, desperate for a passing beverage tray, and the duke, ever attentive, waved a footman over.

"Champagne for the lady; port for me," he said.

They faced each other once more, the duke quietly studying her expression. His countenance was solemn, and his usually sparkly eyes darkened with intensity.

"I... Your Grace, do you mean it? Because if you do, I shall prepare the most advantageous marriage contract in existence," Charlotte managed, her voice trembling slightly.

Chatham laughed, the tension shattering like delicate crystal, and his mirth seemed to grow with each passing moment until his face was flushed a deep shade of purple.

"Are you quite all right?" she asked.

"Aye, aye," he assured her, standing upright and clearing his throat. "I assure you, Charlotte, I am as serious as I can be. You are aware of my situation. I believe we would make an excellent team, you and I. I can't think of anyone who would make a better wife for me."

"Yes, I agree," Charlotte said. "But how on earth would you secure your uncle's approval for such a match? He may have tolerated my pupillage, but he cannot approve of a working duchess, in the courthouse, no less."

"Yes, well... I suppose I would need to confess to the king."

"Impossible. You will not. The risk is too great."

"The king has implied some time ago that he would approve of me taking you as my lover."

"That does not indicate if he would approve of our marriage."

The duke reached for her hand and held it between his palms. "Charlotte—"

"Your Grace, this is hardly the place. Perhaps we can discuss it when we have more privacy."

"Of course. I understand how improper this setting must be. But I've finally made up my mind, and I'm sober enough to remember it. We could announce it now, and there's nothing the king can do about it."

"Except to punish me or us afterwards. He may not be as severe to his nephew, but he may take away my license and exile me to the colonies."

Chatham looked down at her fondly. "I promise I shall follow you should you be exiled. Our strong respect and love for each other shall guarantee our happiness as husband and wife." He leaned forward slightly and said softly, "Come, Charlotte. Wilson would not dare try anything to ruin your career if you become my duchess. You'll be well provided for. We could work together. I would not dream of standing between you and the law."

She smiled warmly. "It does sound like a dream come true, Your Grace."

ANDREW COULDN'T EXPLAIN how he knew, but he knew. In fact, he felt a flurry of panic, anger, and possessiveness before he was even aware of his own actions—before he could articulate his reason. All he knew was that one moment he was draining his champagne glass, and the next, he was striding purposefully toward her. His gaze fixed sharply on their joined hands, her small, delicate hand sandwiched between the duke's bedazzled ones, and all he could think was, *Mine.*

The couple came into sharp focus as he neared, and he saw the ruby ring Chatham removed from his pinkie and Charlotte's surprised face. Without a word, he stepped between them, facing her shocked countenance, and forcing them to release each other's hand. He heard the duke telling him to step aside and felt his hand attempting to push him away.

His mind blank except for seeing the woman he loved. He immediately pulled her to his chest and planted a firm kiss on her mouth. He lingered for a few seconds, both in shock of his own action and savoring the hot quicksand that was her sweet lips. He noted a tantalizing mix of champagne and honey on them as the ballroom fell deafeningly quiet, while his head began to fill with a thunderous cacophony of thoughts.

He forced himself to release her, only to be met with a look of abject horror on her face. Then came a forceful shove and a hard, stinging slap across his cheek.

Gasps broke out and echoed around the ballroom, the sound reverberating off the walls.

The last thing he saw was a fist full of diamonds as the murmurs turned into a surge of voices, rising like a tidal wave.

His last thought, as the world spun around him, was *shite.*

SCHEMING

13 December 1836

IT WAS DARK, and his head spun in a dizzying whirlwind of pain and confusion. A sickening feeling churned in his stomach, and he desperately craved the sweet relief of laudanum. He opened his mouth to speak but found himself unable to utter a word. What a bloody mess he had created.

"Keep your mouth and eyes closed, my lord. Trust me, you don't want to see yourself. You look positively ghastly," his valet said.

"You have caused quite a scandal, my lord." David laughed. "The duke landed his diamond rings right on your nose and below the eyes. Then he swung a left hook to your jaw. He could have blinded you, but I think he knew exactly what he was doing. His Grace has studied the oriental art of fighting. Did you know that? The man looks harmless, but—"

Andrew reached out, pulling on his valet's wrist, then his thin neck. Despite the pain the exertion caused, he couldn't stand hearing the man's name. Every syllable pounded into his head like a sledgehammer.

"Doc… tor," Andrew managed to rasp.

"He's been to see you already. Your nose and cheekbones are broken, so he set them as well as he could. He left you laudanum for the pain. Naught to be done other than waiting, the doc said."

Despite the amount of laudanum he had been given, it wasn't enough. His face hurt like the devil himself had taken up residence there; but he wasn't a stranger to pain, having sustained several broken bones and various injuries at the docks.

"Give me… laudanum. Where's… Miss Morton?" Andrew's words slurred.

"I believe the lady has left with the Duke of Chatham, my lord."

A pitiful whimper escaped Andrew's throat. The sound was foreign to his own ears.

"Get… me… Cooper."

"Yes, sir." David poured a small amount of laudanum into his master's mouth before limping away on his crutch.

Andrew breathed a sigh of relief at the descending silence, but his solitude was short-lived. The door opened, and Cooper's soprano voice pierced his skull like a hot knife. He placed a finger over his lips, and the secretary lowered his voice, approaching gingerly on his toes.

When Cooper leaned in, Andrew whispered through clenched teeth, "Find Miss… Morton's lodging in… Bankside. Get me… the address."

"The lady may have gone to the Duke of Chatham's residence with Lady Gloria," Cooper said.

Andrew frowned, then grimaced as pain shot through his face. "Find out."

"Yes, my lord."

Cooper bowed and left the room, leaving Andrew alone with his thoughts. He closed his eyes, trying to will away the throbbing pain in his skull. Time seemed to stretch on endlessly as he lay there, every minute feeling like an eternity.

Just as he was about to drift off into a restless sleep, a knock at the door jolted him back to awareness. His valet entered, followed by a group of visitors. Andrew growled as he turned his head to see who had arrived, causing a rush of agony to envelop his skull. He groaned, the action sending shockwaves of pain through his jaws.

"You look ghastly," Rogers said, his tone more amused than sympathetic.

"You really are hideous. Try not to scare any children," Wilson added with a laugh.

"Never mind children. He would scare even the bravest of men!" Murphy exclaimed, eliciting a collective burst of laughter from the group.

Andrew snarled, the laudanum helping to dull the pain, but turning his brain to mush in the process.

"Come, come, gentlemen. Let us show some compassion to this man who must loathe himself for making a proper hash of Lady Daisy's birthday," Collins said with a chuckle, his charm ever-present.

"So, was it love that drove you to madness?" Rogers asked with gusto, clearly relishing in Andrew's misfortune.

"Love? Not a chance. It was lust. She does get my bollocks tingling," Wilson said, his voice dripping with crude innuendo.

"Watch… your… mouth," Andrew hissed.

"You've got it all wrong, gentlemen. Don't you see? It was all part of his plan," Collins said jovially. "It's always been his plan to ruin the woman and her career."

"What a relief! The board unanimously opposes your involvement. We were prepared to send you off on a long holiday if you insisted on marrying the chit," Murphy said, his tone a mix of relief and disdain.

"Gentlemen, we haven't confirmed Carlisle's intention. Let him speak," Wilson said with a hint of strain in his voice.

"Drink," Andrew croaked, his throat as dry as sandpaper.

Collins swiftly stuck his head out and summoned a footman. When he returned, Andrew spoke. "I will… marry her."

"What?" Murphy barked, his eyes wide.

"I warned you, gentlemen. He has affections for the woman," Wilson said, relief and smugness staining his tone.

"What is your plan, Carlisle? I do not believe you'd throw away your control over the company for the sake of a woman. Unless…" Collins paused, his expression pensive. "Unless you did it to control Morton and keep her away from Chatham's influence. You're brilliant! This way, Chatham would be forced to sever his ties with her after such a scandal. And as her husband, you'd have complete control over her actions."

"That is genius!" Murphy exclaimed, his eyes alight with admiration.

"Impressive, indeed. This is precisely the reason why I invested in you, Carlisle. Your scheming brain always stays ahead of us, but within the legal realm," Rogers said.

In truth, Andrew had not been thinking at all, but now he saw how publicly ruining Charlotte might force the king and Chatham to withdraw their support for her.

"Well, I think you have given us renewed confidence, Carlisle," Collins said, placing a gentle touch on Andrew's shoulder.

"If this had been your plan all along, why drag my daughter into the talk of matrimony?" Wilson's countenance was rosy with anger.

"Leave that discussion for another day, Wilson. The man can hardly speak," Collins chided.

Except for Wilson, the men left in excellent spirits, chatting animatedly about the brilliance of the Earl of Carlisle. Andrew felt like a piece of dung, his stomach churning with guilt and regret. His intention had been sincere, but in the aftermath of that error in judgment, he realized he had to choose between her happiness and his own, her career or his company, for they could not exist simultaneously.

Before he could progress further in his thoughts, the door slammed open, causing him to flinch at the pounding in his ears.

"What did you tell them?" Daisy's voice was angry, her eyes flashing with fury. "I heard them say your scheme was brilliant. What are they talking about?"

He exhaled, which was likely his last breath before Daisy chewed him up and spat him out.

"I'm marrying... Morton."

He nervously watched his sister's pensive and stoic face, knowing she was too smart to be overjoyed without probing for answers.

She narrowed her eyes, her gaze piercing through him. "Why?"

"I… like her." His words sounded feeble, but they were true.

Her eyes narrowed even further, her suspicion growing with each passing moment. "But why?"

"Smart… kind… brave…" His words came out in short, painful bursts.

"I'm not convinced you were so in love with her that you would publicly ruin her. You hardly even know her. I think you're trying to do your shareholders' bidding and destroy her."

He exhaled deeply, partly frustrated by his slow speech and partly to buy more time. Just before he kissed her, he had been so crazed that all he could think of was she belonged to him, no one else. What he couldn't recall was whether he'd been aware that kissing her might destroy her career.

"No. I shall… apologize… go to her."

Daisy didn't look as pleased as he thought she would. He had even expected her to compliment him for his sense of duty.

"If the duke wishes to still marry her, you ought to let him," she said.

His body went rigid, shooting pain through his head and neck. "No."

"He has more influence and can better protect her should she wish to continue her important work. You must let her."

"No."

"She isn't one of the stocks you buy and trade at a whim. She is a person, and you ought to respect her wishes. Do not force her hand, Andrew. Not in this."

"She is… Charlotte."

"What?"

"Charlotte… my garden…"

Daisy's eyes widened and her mouth opened agape. She plopped into a chair beside the bed. "She's that Charlotte?"

"Yes."

"Oh, my… I am sorry, Andrew. It had not occurred to me they might be the same Charlotte. I thought it was a coincidence."

Andrew watched his sister's mind whirl with possibilities. He could do nothing but stare at her, his mind reeling with the consequences of his actions.

UNFORGIVING

16 December 1836—London

ANDREW WAITED THREE days for the swelling to subside before seeking Madam's counsel. Despite the newspapers' unflattering portrayal of him, he made his way to Madam Tansley's brothel, the place where he had first laid eyes on Charlotte.

In Madam's private parlor, she displayed concern mixed with mild amusement in her voice as she remarked on his appearance. Andrew declined her offer of tea or stronger drink, his head throbbing with pain.

"How is Charlotte faring?" Madam asked, her directness a comfort to Andrew.

"She left with the duke… I haven't seen her since," Andrew replied, wincing at the pain.

"So, tell me. Were your intentions honorable? Or did you act on behalf of those scoundrels you prefer to call shareholders?"

"All I could think about… was her… pledging herself to another."

The older woman's eyes narrowed, her silence enveloping the room. She spoke after a long moment. "What shall you do now?"

"I will offer for her. I shall… dedicate myself to ensuring her happiness."

"And will you allow her to pursue her career?" Madam asked, her words sharp and pointed.

Andrew hesitated, the weight of his responsibilities heavy on his shoulders. "I can't. Not unless I'm prepared to lose... my shareholders and jeopardize... my business. Countless employees... and your charity depend on me."

"Must you destroy a soul to keep your shareholders satisfied?" Madam's disappointment was palpable. "Shame on you, Andrew."

His eyes searched Madam's face for understanding. "My company has been my life, my joy... I have nurtured it for two... decades, pouring my heart and soul into its success."

"You can always start anew," she said. "You will never again face hunger."

Frustration welled up within Andrew as he turned to gaze out at the rain-soaked streets. Madam's words pierced the silence: "You found her after all these years. If you fail to understand the importance of her pursuits, you will lose her once more."

"How I have longed for her..." Andrew admitted, his voice heavy with emotion. "I can't bear the thought... of losing her again."

Madam's final words carried the weight of wisdom: "This is one instance where you cannot have everything you wish."

DISCOURAGED BY MADAM'S words and frustrated by his longing, Andrew climbed into his awaiting carriage. He didn't dare show his face in public when an artist would make a few shillings for a sketch of his hideous face. Instead, he had the driver park in front of London Bank. Adams promptly boarded and, credit to him, didn't flinch upon seeing his friend's mug.

"I'd say good evening, but I suspect it isn't," Adams said with a grimace.

"It sure as hell isn't. I trust... your journey was a productive one?"

"Not entirely."

Andrew frowned, then winced at the pain. "Go on."

"I discovered Miss Morton had paid ten pounds monthly to one of her professors for his silence."

"What is the crook's name?"

"Buckley."

"Buckley… Where do I know that name from?"

"He is now a member of the Parliament. He left Cambridge in Miss Morton's third year. And the chances are, he is utilizing your bank."

"Find him. Make him repay with interest… or I'll take it out of his account at a higher interest rate."

"I shall. There's one more discovery regarding Miss Morton's time at Cambridge."

Andrew waited, his mood darkening at Adams's tone. He sensed something terrible had happened.

"I met a maid for the university who claimed that the lady had a monthly rendezvous with a man."

Andrew's blood turned cold, his stomach dropping as if he'd fallen from a great height.

"Do you know who it was?"

"No. It seems the relationship was a secret. No one else said anything about a love interest. They met at different offices at the university."

Andrew's hands clenched into fists, his knuckles going white. The thought of Charlotte with another man—willingly, repeatedly—sent a surge of jealousy and betrayal through him that nearly made him sick.

"By rendezvous, you mean…"

"I'm afraid so. They occurred late at night. I'm sorry I couldn't discern who it was that the lady met with."

Andrew's fist tightened into a ball. *Did she use her body to silence all the professors?* The thought sickened and enraged him. He dismissed Adams with a grunt and closed his eyes, allowing his mood to fall into the darkness.

Shortly after, Andrew stood before a dilapidated townhouse

in one of London's most impoverished districts. He fervently hoped Charlotte would receive him. Rapping his knuckles forcefully against the door to ensure he was heard over the traffic and rain, Andrew was relieved when the door unlatched and cracked open, revealing her visage.

With a tip of his hat and a bow, he said, "I hope you don't mind me… calling on you unannounced."

As he raised his gaze, Andrew caught the shock that widened her eyes, undoubtedly finding his cuts and bruises ghastly. But in the next breath, Charlotte regarded him with a look that could have curdled fresh milk. Without a word, she turned and walked up the creaky stairs. Andrew rushed after her, dripping rainwater onto the threadbare rug. The house reeked of mold, and the strident voices of two quarrelling women mingled with the faint sounds of copulation. He felt enraged by the squalid conditions in which his beloved resided.

Opening the last door in the hallway, Charlotte held it open until Andrew stepped in.

She crossed her arms and perched against the old wooden desk. He noted the tension coiled in every muscle of her body.

"Why?" she asked.

"I beg your pardon?"

"Why did you ruin me the way you did?"

Andrew sensed her nerves were as frayed as the threadbare rugs beneath their feet.

"I couldn't lose you to Chatham."

Her eyes blazed with fury, which threatened to consume him whole.

"Am I to understand"—her voice trembled with barely contained anger—"that you ruined me for sport because you couldn't bear the thought of losing?"

Andrew felt the weight of her despair, a palpable force that seemed to fill the room, suffocating him with its intensity. He feared he was doomed to live with her wounds forever, a constant companion that would haunt him.

"I came to apologize," he said, his tone measured and controlled. "And to ask for your hand in marriage."

As if to mock him, the sounds of fornication from the neighboring room grew louder. She began to pace, each word that fell from her lips cutting sharper than the one before, a verbal assault that left no room for mercy.

"You wished to break me, the problematic female. Or did your shareholders hold the puppet strings? Do not bother claiming you're in love with me when all you care about is yourself and your precious company."

Andrew could hear the sourness in her voice as she continued, "I find your intention deplorable. You could be the last man on earth, and I wouldn't wish to marry you. You don't love me at all. You're simply too selfish to lose me to another man!"

Andrew flinched at the insult, the motion shooting pain through his head. Desperation clawed at his chest, and words tumbled from his lips before he could stop them.

"You might not wish to wed me," he said, his voice growing harder, "but you have precious few... options left. Pack your things. We shall set... out for York to marry within the week."

When Charlotte's gaze showed defiance, panic seized him. "There's nothing to ponder, and no... point in waiting. We've already... indulged the scandal sheets far too long... If you're married to me... you'll at least have my protection."

The moment the words left his mouth, Andrew recoiled inwardly. This wasn't how he'd planned to propose, wasn't how he'd dreamed of winning her back.

Hostility etched itself into every line of Charlotte's face. "Protection? You mean control. You only wish to claim me, not love me. Will you truly take a woman whose heart belongs to another?"

Her words struck him, but he saw through them—the pain in her eyes, the way her voice trembled with hurt rather than conviction. He stepped closer, his voice dropping to a harsh whisper.

"You don't love him. You're saying that to wound... me, and we both know it." His jaw clenched. "But you're right about one thing... I am selfish. Selfish enough to... want you despite everything, selfish... enough to have ruined you... rather than lose you to him."

She bristled, meeting his gaze without flinching. "Even if you forced me to the altar, you will never truly have me. Chatham would have loved me the way I wished to be loved. I love him from the depths of my soul, and that is one thing you cannot take away from me!"

Andrew staggered back as if she'd struck him, though he knew she was lashing out in anger and pain. The desperation in her voice, the way she clung to Chatham's name like a shield—she was trying to hurt him as he had hurt her.

"Keep telling yourself that," he said quietly, his voice hollow. "But we both know you're lying."

She lifted her chin, her eyes blazing with defiant tears. "You may have my hand, my name, and my body, but you will never have what I gave to Chatham freely. So yes, I will marry you because I must. But do not mistake duty for affection, or submission for love."

He stepped into the hallway, closing the door softly behind him, and stood there for a moment, horrified by his own behavior.

What kind of man had he become? Forcing her into marriage, trapping her with threats and desperation—it sickened him. Outside, he gasped for air, rain mingling with the tears he hadn't realized were falling.

He had lost her completely now, and worse—he had become the blackguard she believed him to be.

CHARLOTTE ENDURED THE long journey to Whitstable in silence, feigning sleep to avoid confronting the reality of her forced betrothal. Upon arrival at Andrew's grand estate, she was struck by the opulence surrounding her. As Mrs. Poulett showed her around the lavender suite, Charlotte's fingers traced the soft velvet drapes and silk counterpane, a glimmer of girlish excitement breaking through her melancholy.

Later, as she sat by the crackling fire in her nightclothes, resentment at her situation warred with grudging appreciation for the security Andrew's wealth provided. However, she couldn't help but compare this to the life she might have had with the duke—a union built on mutual respect, even if it lacked passion. With Andrew, she faced the opposite problem: his commanding presence ignited desire within her, but she feared their relationship would be defined solely by these heated moments rather than the intellectual partnership she craved.

When she heard Andrew's footsteps approach their adjoining door, Charlotte's heart raced. The firm click of the lock brought disappointment mingled with relief. Sinking deeper into the plush armchair, she stared into the dancing flames, wondering if the price of passion would be the sacrifice of her own identity.

THE WEDDING

24 December 1836

THE WEDDING CEREMONY was a simple affair, held in a quaint stone church nestled in the heart of Whitstable. Andrew had insisted on the intimate gathering—only Daisy, Susie, the Duke of Lancaster, and the Marquess of Hereford stood as witnesses to what felt more like a reckoning than a celebration.

He had pleaded with Madam Tansley to attend, but she had adamantly refused, explaining that her presence would sully their reputation irrevocably.

Pale light streamed through the stained glass windows, casting a muted glow over the ancient wooden pews. Andrew stood before the altar in his tailored ivory suit, his throat tight as he watched Charlotte clutch her small bouquet of evergreen sprigs, holly, and herbs. Her hands trembled slightly, and the sight sent a stab of guilt through his chest. She looked resplendent in her pink gown, but he could see the tension in her shoulders, the careful mask she wore to hide her true feelings.

What had he done? The question hammered at him as he gazed upon his bride. He was determined to claim her as his own in every sense of the word, but doubt crept into his mind like poison. Did her thoughts drift to Chatham even now? Could he truly build a life with a woman whose choices he had stripped away?

The ceremony itself was brief, the vicar's words echoing through the hushed church as they exchanged vows that felt more like a business contract than promises of love. When

Charlotte slipped the simple gold band onto his finger, Andrew felt the weight of it like a chain—not binding her to him, but him to the consequences of his actions. Fifteen minutes and multiple signatures later, she became the Countess of Carlisle.

As they turned to face their small audience, Andrew caught Daisy's beaming smile, her eyes glistening with genuine joy while Susie offered Charlotte a reassuring look. Despite Daisy's warning glare, Hereford and Lancaster shook their heads gravely, as if Andrew were about to face the gallows.

Perhaps he was.

His heart ached with the desperate need to make his bride understand that his actions, though brutal, stemmed from a love so consuming it had driven him to madness. But looking at her profile now—proud even in defeat—he realized that love without respect was merely possession. He had won her hand but lost her heart, and the victory felt hollow.

As they took their first steps as husband and wife, Andrew silently vowed to spend his life proving that he could be worthy of her—not the man who had forced her into this union, but the man who might somehow earn her forgiveness, and perhaps, eventually, her love.

CHARLOTTE FELT THE warmth of his hand in hers and hated how her body still betrayed her, yearning for his touch even as her mind rebelled against him. The love she had carried for six years still burned beneath her ribs, but it was tainted now with the bitter knowledge that his love, if it even was love, came with chains. He claimed to want her, yet his actions had shown he would rather break her wings than risk losing her to flight.

As they took their first steps as husband and wife, Charlotte acknowledged the precarious nature of their union sustained by an undeniable connection that refused to die. She could feel the tension radiating from him, sense his desperate need for her forgiveness, but she wasn't ready to grant it. Her enduring feelings battled against the knowledge that loving him might mean losing a part of herself she could never reclaim.

The weight of her new ring felt foreign on her finger—a symbol of union that felt more like surrender. As the cold air bit at her cheeks, Charlotte wondered if she would ever be able to separate the man she had fallen in love with from the one who had stolen her choices. Time would tell whether she would spend her marriage fighting to remain herself.

THE GROUP HEADED to Andrew's estate for the wedding breakfast, with Daisy taking a separate carriage with Susie to give the bride and groom some privacy despite Charlotte's protest. As the carriage rolled through the countryside, Charlotte's gaze fixed on the passing scenery of bare trees and gray skies. Beside her, Andrew studied his bride, his eyes tracing the delicate lines of her profile.

"I apologize for my absence since our arrival in Whitstable," he said, his voice low. "Estate matters demanded my attention before our matrimony."

Silence stretched between them, and his words went unanswered as he had feared. Had he erred in keeping his distance? Time had been scarce, and he, a man more accustomed to roughness than charm, had feared missteps in his attempts to win her favor. Even Daisy, when asked for guidance, had offered little solace, insisting that forgiveness for his transgressions would not come easily.

As the carriage swayed, Andrew's gaze roamed over Charlotte's slight form, drinking in the gentle slope of her shoulders, the fullness of her lips, and the swell of her breasts. Desire, swift and fierce, ignited within him, and he shifted in his seat, his body responding to the mere thought of settling between her thighs. He must have fantasized about this a thousand times since her departure six years ago. However, his wife's countenance was as somber as a mourner's.

As the carriage drew to a halt, Andrew stepped out into the crisp air, his hand extended toward Charlotte. She hesitated for a moment before placing her gloved fingers in his. In one swift motion, he gathered her into his arms, carrying her purposefully toward the front door of the house.

Charlotte's voice rang out in protest, her words tinged with indignation. "Andrew, I demand that you set me down this instant!"

Her plea fell on deaf ears as Andrew ignored her entreaty and crossed the threshold, gently placing her on her feet in the grand hallway. Charlotte, flustered by his bold actions, straightened her skirts and collected her scattered dignity, her cheeks flushed with a becoming rose hue. Andrew, captivated by her loveliness, held back his overwhelming urge to capture her crimson lips in a searing kiss.

"How utterly romantic!" Daisy exclaimed from behind them, her voice filled with girlish delight. For once, Andrew found himself grateful for her timely interruption.

Without preamble, Daisy linked her arm through Charlotte's, drawing her close as she began to lead her on a tour of the house. Susie, her stature dwarfed by her enthusiastic friend, practically jogged to keep pace with Daisy's eager strides.

"When shall the meal be served? I find myself quite famished," Hereford's voice said from behind.

"I must say, this house is not entirely horrible, considering it belongs to an earl," Lancaster remarked, his voice dripping with exaggerated condescension.

Andrew fixed his friend with a withering scowl, prompting Lancaster to flash a disarming grin, his teeth gleaming white in the soft light.

"You must admit, old chap, a mere year-old earldom is—"

"I shall have you stuffed in place of the turkey come Christmas," Andrew said.

"My word, you are in a foul mood for a groom. Shall we adjourn to the drawing room?" Hereford gestured expansively, as if he owned the house in which they stood. The group acquiesced, following him to the elegantly appointed room, where they settled themselves comfortably by the roaring fire.

"Where is Preston?" Andrew asked.

"Alas, he is in court and could not postpone it," Lancaster drawled.

"That's a shame. I was hoping to introduce him to my wife," Andrew said.

"Surely, they must have crossed paths, considering they must attend court regularly," Hereford said.

"Are you certain you want to introduce them? Preston attracts females like flies to rotten meat," Lancaster said.

"Leave him be, Lancaster," Hereford intervened. "It appears Carlisle is unlikely to enjoy any feminine company in the foreseeable future, judging by the chill emanating from his lovely countess."

"Hold your tongue, man!" Andrew snapped.

At that moment, Charlotte returned from her tour of the house, her arrival heralded by a sudden hush that fell over the room. She paused, her gaze drawn to the sight of Andrew's stern visage. With a graceful movement, she settled herself in the plush chair beside Andrew, avoiding her husband's gaze.

"What say you, Lady Carlisle?" Hereford asked with a mischievous grin. "Would you like to meet the most charismatic man in London? We could arrange an introduction to stave off the tedium of married life."

Charlotte, despite her reserve, couldn't suppress a small smile at his audacity. "Why, we must do what we can to prevent such tedium," she remarked, her tone carrying just a hint of playful challenge.

"Ah, so that explains the distinct chill in the air," Hereford drawled, a knowing glint in his eye.

"I beg you, desist," Andrew gritted out. "I fear Lady Carlisle may not be accustomed to your uncouth banter, gentlemen. Perhaps we ought to steer the conversation to more appropriate matters."

"Indeed, shall we discuss your plans to thaw her ladyship's icy demeanor?" Lancaster inquired languidly, his gaze flickering between the newlyweds.

Despite her hands fidgeting nervously, Charlotte favored the group with a faint smile.

"If I may be so bold," Lancaster continued, clearly enjoying Andrew's discomfort, "you would do well to shower your bride with expensive gifts and make grand gestures of apology. Though I suspect a woman of Lady Carlisle's evident intelligence requires more than mere baubles."

"Indeed," Hereford added with theatrical solemnity. "Perhaps you ought not to stifle her considerable talents. After all, you fell in love with a woman of ambition and courage. 'Twould be folly to try changing her now."

Charlotte positively glowed at their words, her eyes shining with appreciation as she regarded Andrew intently. The gentlemen, too, fixed their gazes upon him, their smirks making it clear that they were deriving great amusement from his discomfort.

"Say, I wonder if breakfast is ready," Andrew said, ringing the bell and clearing his throat. He silently prayed that one of his friends would take pity on him and come to his aid, but alas, they seemed content to let him squirm.

Salvation came from an unexpected quarter, however, as Charlotte spoke up, her voice soft but clear. "Lord Carlisle has been instrumental in helping me achieve my goals. Without his support, I fear I would still be toiling away in the brothels, cleaning and scrubbing."

Andrew's heart swelled with gratitude at her words, and he met her gaze to convey his appreciation. Charlotte, however, quickly lowered her lashes, suddenly finding great interest in the intricate pattern of the rug beneath her feet.

At that moment, a servant appeared, announcing that breakfast was served. The group rose, eager for the promise of a hearty meal and further testing their friendship.

THE NEST

S HORTLY AFTER BREAKFAST, the guests embarked on their journey home, and the newlyweds headed to a small cabin Andrew had built a few years prior. The ride was less than an hour, during which time Charlotte dozed, her head eventually resting on his shoulder. Andrew savored the contact, as he had been uncertain if his wife would ever let him touch her.

As the carriage slowed to a stop, Charlotte suddenly sat up, looking around as if lost. Realizing where she was, she touched her hair to assess if anything was amiss. Then an old kerchief came out of her threadbare reticule, and she dabbed her eyes with it. Andrew gently took the kerchief from her and spread it out to examine the Duke of Chatham's coat of arms. Wordlessly, he shoved the kerchief in his pocket, then handed her one of his own. She took his reluctantly and put it in her reticule.

Andrew alighted first, then held out his hand to help her disembark. When she gripped his hand, however, he draped her over his shoulder, against her screaming protest. "Put me down, you brute!"

Andrew laughed jovially, gripping her thigh and bottom firmly, the taut flesh igniting a smoldering fire within him. As the footman unlocked the wooden door to the small cabin, he stepped over the threshold and gently set her down.

"Is this how you intend to treat me? Like a mere sack of potatoes?" Charlotte's eyes flashed with indignation.

The corners of Andrew's lips twitched with a hint of a smile. "I assure you, I'm usually far gentler with a sack of potatoes. They may be hardy, but even they can sustain scrapes. And that would be quite detrimental to business."

Charlotte fixed him with a piercing glare, her eyes sharp as daggers, but as she took in the surroundings of the cabin, her expression softened. Her eyes grew round, sparkling with delight, with a touch of a smile on her lips.

"This place is wonderful. It's perfect."

Andrew exhaled, running his fingers through his hair, a sense of relief and joy washing over him at the sight of his bride's pleasure, a rare occurrence in recent times. "I had it built a few years ago. It's small, as you can see. One bedroom, a kitchen, and a parlor."

Charlotte met his gaze with a smile, a sight he had sorely missed. "And what did you build it for? Hunting, perhaps?"

"No, not at all. I have no fondness for hunting or shooting. I built this cabin as a retreat, a place to be alone and to feel at home."

Charlotte's brows furrowed at his words, a puzzled expression settling on her features. "Home? Does this cabin remind you of your childhood home?"

"Not exactly." Andrew's gaze grew distant as memories flooded his mind. "My parents' home was even smaller than this, more basic in its furnishings. While living in a mansion filled with servants serves its purpose, it often feels like a display, a theatre of sorts, to me. In my eyes, a true home is quaint, a sanctuary where only my family resides. It's a place where I attend to every need, from cooking and cleaning to starting a fire. I suppose I shall never truly be a gentleman, as these roots run deep within me. It's why I find solace in working at the dock. The physical labor and returning to my roots bring me satisfaction."

Andrew abruptly left her standing in the parlor, unable to meet Charlotte's eyes after revealing something of himself. He entered the bedroom, leaving the door open. He unbuttoned his coat and peeled it off, preparing to change before venturing out to chop wood for the fire. The impending darkness and the capricious nature of the weather at this time of year demanded his attention. Charlotte's eyes followed him, he knew, but she quickly diverted her gaze when he glanced in her direction, a flicker of unspoken emotion passing between them.

"One room?" Charlotte asked from the parlor.

"Aye. The pantry should be stocked if you need sustenance or beverage." With those words, he closed the door to their bedchamber, leaving Charlotte alone with her thoughts.

In the solitude of the room, Andrew exhaled deeply, as if the weight of his decision was just settling on his shoulders. He questioned whether he had erred in bringing her to this intimate sanctuary instead of returning to the cottage, where distractions abounded. Here, in the confines of this small cabin, they would be compelled to confront each other and the truth of their emotions, laid bare without the trappings of society to shield them.

Donning an old laborer's shirt, worn and familiar against his skin since the tender age of twenty, Andrew emerged from the bedroom, rolling up his sleeves as he walked. In the kitchen, Charlotte was diligently making a list of the items in the pantry. A surge of warmth blossomed in his stomach as he pondered the happiness that could be theirs if this simple life were all they had. He allowed himself to indulge in a fantasy, imagining Charlotte loved him and a little one was on the way. In this reverie, he was a humble dockworker with a steady income, content with the life they had built together.

Despite the allure of this imagined simplicity, Andrew knew his ambitions could not be so easily quelled. It wasn't the pursuit of wealth that drove him but rather an innate need to conquer, to build and shape the world around him. Madam's words echoed in his mind, reminding him he could start anew, sell his business, and watch it from afar. The mere thought of it, however, caused a wave of unease to wash over him as he envisioned his blood and sweat sinking under the guidance of those who would take the helm in his absence.

As ANDREW EMERGED in his laborer's attire, Charlotte found herself captivated by the sight of him. The realization that he now belonged to her sent her pulse racing, a thrilling undercurrent of possession and desire coursing through her. The worn cotton shirt, likely a remnant from his youth, stretched taut over his bulging muscles, accentuating the slimness of his waist and hips. Charlotte felt a flush of heat rise to her cheeks as her gaze lingered on the firm contours of his behind.

Without a word, Andrew stepped out of the cabin, leaving Charlotte to watch him through the side window. Soon, the rhythmic thudding and cracking of wood being split filled the air, as if a machine were at work. The sound continued in a steady cadence as Charlotte busied herself with baking dessert biscuits, the occasional grunt from Andrew punctuating each strike. He showed no sign of relenting, only stopping once he filled the wooden rack. Charlotte watched from the window as he set down his axe and turned toward the cabin, but several minutes passed without his appearance at the door.

As Charlotte opened the door to investigate the delay between the side window and the front entrance, she was greeted by the sight of Andrew shaking off splinters from his body and hair, reminiscent of a large dog. Laughter bubbled up within her, and she found herself contributing to his efforts, tousling his hair and brushing the debris from his body with her hand. The heat emanating from his skin was startling despite the cold air, and she became acutely aware of the solid muscles lying just beneath the surface.

"Would you like some tea and biscuits before supper?" she asked, her voice soft and inviting.

Andrew paused at the doorway with his gaze intense as it fixed on her.

"Are you all right? Did I say something amiss?" There was a flicker of uncertainty in her tone.

"No, not at all… You baked?"

"Yes."

"I didn't realize you knew how."

"I learned to bake because my housemates enjoyed sweets when they could afford sugar. I hope you don't mind that I used your sugar. I—"

Before she could finish her sentence, Charlotte found herself enveloped in Andrew's arms, his mouth descending upon hers in a passionate kiss. All she could feel was warmth, security, and the stirring of dormant memories as her body recognized his touch.

His lips moved over hers, brushing and nipping, his tongue lightly tapping against her lips in a tantalizing dance of taste and sensation. He was careful not to overwhelm her, tempering his ardor with a gentleness that spoke of his desire to cherish and protect her. In that moment, Charlotte saw him not as the man who had once humiliated and ruined her, but as the man who had saved her, and a husband offering her a haven.

Charlotte stood motionless in his arms, however, as conflicting emotions swirled around her head. Andrew abruptly released her and, without a word, disappeared into the bedchamber, leaving her alone with the bittersweet ache of his touch she'd longed for.

She sought solace in the familiar task of preparing tea while fighting to ignore the conflicting signals of her heart. Meanwhile, Andrew emerged from the bedchamber and set about starting a fire in the parlor. Although the temperature had not yet dipped low enough to necessitate a fire, Charlotte quickly realized that his intentions were to boil water for a bath. Her heart began to race at the thought of their impending wedding night.

Did he mean to consummate their marriage this evening? Of course he did. Why wouldn't he? It was common knowledge that men lived for this moment.

"Make up your mind, you imbecile," she muttered under her breath, frustrated by her desire and fear of physical intimacy.

Just as Charlotte was about to lift the tea tray, Andrew's large hands intervened, gripping the tray and carrying it to the small table. He pulled out a chair and waited for her expectantly, prompting her to sit down and murmur her gratitude awkwardly. When Charlotte moved to pour the tea, Andrew gently stayed her hands.

"Please allow me," he said, his voice warm.

She could do nothing but stare at him in astonishment, her eyes wide.

"You've never seen a man pour tea before?" he asked, the corners of his eyes crinkling as he served her before helping himself.

"Never the master of the house," she said.

"With my sister being only two years old when our parents died, I simply did what was necessary. I also poured for Madam and the ladies at the brothel, as they enjoyed ordering me about and laughing at my expense. I performed many other chores, too, for the few years Daisy and I lived there."

"Madam was the only mother figure Daisy knew, then?"

"Aye," he said, his gaze distant as he delved into his past. "She cared for Daisy during my territorial conflicts with other boys. After three years, I saved enough to move us to a room with a woman who educated Daisy."

Contentment and peace spread over Andrew's visage like nothing she had seen before. He continued, "We left five years later when I could afford to buy us a house and hire tutors for her."

Charlotte swallowed hard before asking, "You were able to purchase a house in just five years?"

"I was. Fortunately, I was taller than most men at only fifteen, which allowed me to secure work at the dock I now own. They were long hours, twenty hours a day, seven days a week, but I didn't mind hard work. I gained the owner's trust and was promoted quickly."

As she sipped on the hot brew, Charlotte found herself lost in thought, imagining the hardships the twelve-year-old Andrew must have endured. In that moment, a newfound understanding and respect blossomed within her, a shared connection born of adversity and resilience.

"Do you miss your family?" he asked, his voice gentle.

Charlotte found herself surprised by the need to ponder before answering his question, her emotions a tangled web of conflicting sentiments.

"I miss the idea of a family." Her words were measured and thoughtful. "I don't particularly regret not having their company. I realize now how miserable I was, living with people who didn't understand me at all and resented me for not using my charms to cultivate better connections for them. My father only thought about Mother. As much as I appreciated his efforts to keep her at home, I wish he had planned for my security and safety."

Andrew's hand moved a bit on the table as if to reach for her, then stopped, catching himself. Charlotte's gaze drifted to his bare forearm, resting flat on the table. She watched, transfixed, as his muscles flexed and thick veins popped along the grooves of his skin, his fist clenching and relaxing in a display of strength.

"I cannot imagine what kind of parents would put their daughter in such a vulnerable position when they had the means to prevent it."

From the tension in his clenched jaw, Charlotte knew he was angry on her behalf.

"Are your parents the reason why you wished to become an officer of the law?" he asked.

She nodded, impressed by his perception. "I did what everyone thought was impossible for the sole purpose of fighting the injustice in this society that treats poverty and illness as crimes."

Andrew leaned back in his chair, rubbing his chin thoughtfully, a shadow of stubble appearing on his square jaw. As he did so, his biceps stretched the fabric impressively, drawing Charlotte's gaze.

Feeling heat rise to her face, Charlotte searched for another topic. She quickly said, "What will you do about Lady Daisy after the trial is over?"

"I suppose I'll find her a good suitor."

"And if she refuses?"

Without meeting her eyes, Andrew fell silent for a moment, lost in thought. "She wouldn't outright refuse," he said at last, his words measured and careful. "She'd be gone before I learned of her true feelings."

"Is that what happened when she went overseas to study?"

"Yes. I didn't know how strongly she felt about it until she disappeared, leaving a note."

Andrew studied her face for an uncomfortably long time, his gaze penetrating and thoughtful, before rubbing the crease between his brows with a finger.

"I thought about you for a long time after you disappeared six years ago," he said, his voice low. "I'd meant every word when I said I wanted to marry you."

Charlotte's fingers tightened around the starched white tablecloth, crumpling the fabric in her grasp as she nodded in acknowledgment. "I believed you then," she said softly, her gaze meeting his. "I left for the same reason I would have rejected your recent proposal if you had given me the chance."

"Your work," he stated, his words heavy with understanding.

"Yes. It was paramount to my happiness then, as it is now."

"Truly?" Andrew's eyes searched hers. "How can you be certain you wouldn't find contentment as a mother and a wife?"

Charlotte regarded him with an indulgent smile, as if addressing a young pupil. "How do you know you wouldn't be happy being a father and a husband while working as a laborer?" Her words were gentle yet pointed.

Andrew's lips pressed into a thin line, but he nodded, acknowledging the truth in her words.

"Did you consider staying and marrying me six years ago?"

"I did. I considered finding you and asking you to make good on your word when life became unbearable. But I persevered."

"When did you stop thinking about me?" Andrew's question hung in the air, surprising her with vulnerability.

Charlotte met his gaze, her heart swelling with a bittersweet ache. "I never have," she confessed. "Women don't forget their first."

With those words, she rose from her seat and began clearing the table, her movements purposeful. She could feel Andrew's eyes boring into her back, his gaze igniting a tremor in her fingers at the mere thought of his attention focused solely on her. Unbidden, her mind conjured up memories of the night they had shared, the carnal pleasures he had introduced her to. Her breath grew shallow, and she placed a hand on her chest, willing her racing heart to calm.

Just as she was about to continue her task, Andrew pushed back his chair with a screech, the sound jarring in the quiet room. He approached her, his presence both comforting and unnerving.

"If you'd like to wash, I'll prepare supper tonight," he said, his voice gentle.

Charlotte's eyes widened in surprise as she looked at him. "You?"

Andrew's smile was warm and genuine. "Why not me?" he asked, his tone teasing.

"Well, you're a man…" Charlotte said, her words trailing off as she realized the absurdity of her own assumption.

"And you're a female barrister. Aren't we perfect for each other?" Andrew regarded her with an unreadable emotion before saying, "I'm not just any man. I'm a man who raised a child and looked after himself for most of his life."

"True." Charlotte allowed a hint of admiration in her tone. "But most men would have paid someone to bring them food or eaten a cooked potato for sustenance."

"I didn't grow this big by eating potatoes, darling wife," he said, pointing to his body. "I offered my strength in exchange for meat."

Charlotte touched her cheek with the back of her hand, attempting to hide the blush that rose at being addressed as his wife. But Andrew's imposing form drew closer, and his warm hand brushed against her face, sending a shiver down her spine.

"I'm sorry if I startled you earlier with that kiss," he said softly. "I was touched that you'd baked and acted impulsively. I know you haven't adjusted to the idea of being with me yet."

Charlotte focused on maintaining a steady rhythm of breath, determined not to let him see how deeply his presence affected her.

"I'd be lying if I said it didn't hurt my pride," he continued, "or my feelings to know you preferred him over me."

She looked up at him, then. "Are you angry with me?"

"I was angry with Chatham for existing and stealing your heart… but I stole you from under his nose, so we're even now," he said, stroking her cheek lightly with his thumb.

"I'm not sure he sees it that way."

"He may not, but I'm not giving you back." His lips curved into a smile, his thumb pausing on her plump lower lip.

"If you think I'm going to forgive you just because you smile and jest, you'll be disappointed," she said as she tried to ignore the fluttering in her stomach.

"I know," he said, lowering his hand. "But you can't stay angry with me forever if you want a chance at happiness. Wouldn't you agree?"

Charlotte narrowed her eyes at him, crossing her arms in a defensive posture. "I shall take as long as I need, if you don't mind."

His face cracked open into a broad grin, his eyes sparkling with mirth. "Yes, Mrs. Creswell."

She flinched at the unfamiliar title. "Mrs. Creswell sounds too personal and Lady Carlisle is too grand. How about Charlotte for now?"

"Very well, Charlotte. Allow me to assist you with your bath." He held out his arm, his gesture gallant, albeit exaggerated.

"With my bath?" Her eyes widened in surprise. "Absolutely not!"

"You misunderstand me. I only meant the bathwater, unless you plan to carry out the labor yourself."

She bit her lower lip as mortification washed over her. "Yes, of course. I'd like that. Thank you."

She was grateful Andrew refrained from teasing her about the misunderstanding. She took his proffered arm, allowing him to guide her into the spacious water closet. As they entered, Charlotte's eyes widened in delight at the sight of the large copper tub, surrounded by rows of colorful bottles adorning the shelves and clean, fluffy towels. A beautiful bouquet of flowers filled a vase beside the tub, adding a touch of elegance to the room.

"This is lovely." She reached for a small pink bottle, unscrewing the cap and inhaling the delightful scent of vanilla and lemon that wafted from within.

"They're for you to wear or drop into the bathwater. I didn't know what you preferred, so I had every scent purchased for you from the apothecary."

Charlotte turned to face him, struck by the sweetness in his expression. He seemed eager to please, his eyes searching hers for approval.

"They are lovely and so very thoughtful of you. Thank you. I'd like to try every single scent before we leave here," she said softly, a shy smile gracing her lips.

"They belong to you. We shall take them home with us, so there's no need to rush."

Charlotte swallowed, her fingers tightening around the small bottle as she studied it intently. "Yes, home," she murmured, her mind racing with the implications of their new life together. "Where will we reside?"

"I apologize for not discussing it earlier," Andrew said, his tone sincere. "I thought we might stay in London, close to our offices."

Charlotte's head snapped up, her eyes searching his face for any sign of deception. Reading the unspoken question on her lips, Andrew quickly added, "I'm not promising anything, but for now, nothing shall change."

"Oh, Andrew," she breathed, her hands clasping together in a gesture of joy and relief. "Thank you!"

Andrew smiled awkwardly before he turned and left her to enjoy a hot, soul-melting bath, the promise of a new beginning lingering in the air.

SWEET SURRENDER

A s CHARLOTTE EMERGED from the bath, her skin as pink as a ripe peach in August, her mind finally quieted and arrived at the possibility she could be happy with Andrew Creswell, the man who had captured her heart all those years ago. If he were willing to support her career, she could ask for nothing more. She would allow herself to fully love him. It was truly a dream come true.

Clad in a soft pink muslin dress, Charlotte pinned her damp hair up in a loose chignon, the tendrils framing her face in a delicate and feminine manner. Following the sounds emanating from the kitchen, she discovered Andrew slicing vegetables, his own hair damp and his appearance fresh, like a man who had indulged in a hot bath.

"Are there two water closets?" she asked.

"There are." His eyes resolutely never left his task.

"Were you lying when you said there was only one bed-chamber?" Charlotte hoped he had.

"I wasn't lying." A sly smile tugged at his mouth. "One bed-chamber. One bed. That was my grand plan for bedding my wife."

A wave of heat swept over Charlotte's face, tinting her cheeks a delightful shade of pink. "Are you determined to turn me into a strawberry?" she asked, feeling annoyed about her incessant blushing.

"Is it working?" He smirked, his hands expertly slicing through the cured ham with practiced precision.

She went closer and leaned against the worktable. "You are very skilled with that knife."

"I am, and yes, strawberry is my goal." Andrew's eyes twinkled with mischief.

In a moment of uncharacteristic boldness, Charlotte playfully touched his arm, only to wonder at the woman she had become, one who flirtatiously touched a man and smiled with the exuberance of a Haymarket ware.

In a matter of minutes, Andrew had produced plates of sliced ham and a vibrant bowl of salad, brimming with spring greens, carrots, and artichokes tossed with vinegar, olive oil, and what she assumed to be salt. He placed the dishes on the table, which was dimly lit by a single candle, casting a romantic glow over the setting. With a gallant flourish, he pulled out a wooden chair, waiting for his bride to be seated first.

Charlotte stared at the food, overwhelmed by the dishes her husband had prepared. They were a visual feast, bursting with vibrance and freshness.

"I've never had fresh greens before," she said.

"Working at the dock, I met numerous foreigners and foreign chefs. For a time, I sailed and worked every job there was to work, including the galley. The French chef there taught me the importance of eating fresh vegetables whenever possible. He believed they prevented all sorts of ailments on the ship."

"That is a very unusual perspective, although not entirely surprising. If citrus fruits can cure scurvy, it stands to reason that other vegetables and fruits must have benefits for various ailments."

Chewing lazily, his jaw muscles bunching and relaxing with each bite, Andrew leaned back in his chair, a contemplative expression on his face. "While that would be the logical way of thinking, the scientific community often rejects such ideas," he said.

"And you don't abide by expert opinions?"

"No, I don't. Most of the time, they're too invested in what they've known, what they've convinced themselves to be the results of empirical research. I'm less biased than they are and capable of drawing my own conclusions."

"I suppose that is consistent with your choice of a wife," Charlotte said, a hint of amusement in her tone. "You don't listen to society and will dictate your own terms."

Her heart melted as his face broke into a wide grin; his handsome features were illuminated by genuine joy. Confound it, he was devastatingly attractive, and his voice flowed like rich, smooth syrup, enveloping her in its warmth.

"Except I try to mold my wife into my life, Mrs. Creswell," he said, a playful glint in his eyes.

Charlotte found herself nearly ignoring the underlying bite in his words, tempted to simply melt under the spell of his baritone timbre.

"And how would you mold me?" To her chagrin, her voice came out soft and coaxing rather than strong and challenging.

"I would seduce you and make you want to surrender to me willingly. Desire so strong you'd obey me despite every rational thought telling you otherwise."

Charlotte felt a surge of disappointment. "Ah, I see. You mistake subjugation for seduction. How wonderfully medieval of you."

"I'm sorry, Charlotte. I want you, but you want a life that I cannot give. And I'm too selfish to let you go. I need you."

"Would you truly turn me into a shell of myself? Wouldn't it be easier for you to choose someone else?"

"No. You're the one I desire. But do not worry. The battle shall resemble a python squeezing a mouse."

His lips were smiling, but his stern gaze alluded to the gravity of his statement. Charlotte stared back at him intently, wondering how he had so quickly become a man to be wary of when they were having a perfectly pleasant conversation only minutes ago.

"What you don't realize is that I'm not an ordinary mouse," she managed to say.

A low chuckle rumbled out of his throat, the sound sending pleasant shivers down her spine. "Thank heavens for that. It's precisely the reason I wanted you from that fateful night." With those words, Andrew stood and held out his hand toward her.

Charlotte's pulse thumped violently in her ears, and a charm of hummingbirds flapped against her ribcage. She stared down at his hand as if he were the grim reaper, a harbinger of both danger and desire.

"Right now, I only wish to feed you," he said.

As Charlotte furrowed her brows, she tilted her head to regard Andrew from a different angle, her eyes taking in the striking contours of his face. The interplay of shadow and orange glow cast by the flickering candlelight chiseled his strong jaw and high cheekbones, lending him an air of mystery and intimidation. Despite the imposing nature of his features, however, a faint smile lingered upon his lips, and his eyes softened with each passing moment, a glimmer of tenderness shining through the darkness.

Unable to temper her curiosity, Charlotte placed her hand in his, allowing him to lead her toward the bedchamber. Though she flinched ever so slightly at the contact, Andrew's keen senses didn't miss the subtle reaction.

"Trust me, Charlotte. Nothing could be further from seduction in what I'm about to do." Despite his words, the tone indicated something else altogether.

Charlotte found herself following his lead, her feet moving of their own accord as if drawn by an invisible force. In truth, what choice did she have? She was bound to him now, and her body was his to thrill and terrify.

As they crossed the threshold of the bedchamber, Charlotte's heart raced, a symphony of anticipation and fear pulsing through her veins.

The room was dominated by a large bed, its plush head and

footboards swathed in ivory, exuding an air of luxury and comfort. The matching vanity and dresser added a touch of elegance to the otherwise uncluttered space. The counterpane and linen, all pristine white, lent the bed a virginal quality.

"Sit on the bed, if you please," Andrew said, his voice gentle yet commanding.

Charlotte glanced at him askance, her steps measured and cautious as she approached the bed. She did as he asked, perching against it. Andrew, meanwhile, retrieved a brush from the vanity, presenting it to her with a flourish. The ivory handle glistened in the candlelight, its smooth surface beckoning to be touched.

Charlotte gingerly took the brush from him and ran her finger over the smooth edge, admiring the intricate etchings of flowers that adorned its back. Turning it over, she discovered an engraving, and the words caused her heart to skip a beat.

"My darling Charlotte... Be mine. Allow me to caress your soul," she read softly. "I have nothing for you," she said, looking up at Andrew.

"You haven't run away, and that's the biggest gift you could bestow upon me."

Andrew took the brush from her and positioned himself behind her on the bed. The mattress dipped beneath her, and Charlotte braced herself with her hands. She sensed his nearness behind her, his body settling like a boulder as he sat back on his heels. He began to brush her hair slowly and thoroughly, sometimes letting the strands flow between his fingers.

The feel of his fingers on her scalp reminded her of the way he had held her hair in that searing kiss so long ago. Her breath hitched as her mind got lost in the memory. When he finally brushed her hair over one shoulder, she felt his warm breath on her neck. She focused on steadying her breath with one hand on her stomach.

Andrew withdrew a long linen fabric from his pocket, holding it up for her to see. "I'm going to blindfold you," he said, his voice low and reassuring. "You can trust me."

With gentle hands, Andrew tied the material around her eyes, plunging her world into darkness.

"Sit back against the headboard. You'll be more comfortable," he said.

She did as she was told and sat still, her senses heightened as she listened to the rustling of his trousers, indicating his movement about the room. The clanking of dishes and utensils from the adjacent space filled her ears until she heard his footsteps return. The mattress dipped slightly as he placed something at the foot of the bed.

"Lean forward a little."

She complied and soon felt a soft pillow being placed behind her back. "Now sit back and relax."

Moments later, she felt a small fabric, no larger than a kerchief, being tied deftly around her neck.

"Now, open your mouth," he commanded.

Having heard far too many stories from the courtesans, Charlotte shook her head vigorously, her heart pounding in her chest.

A faint chuckle and a sigh escaped Andrew's lips before he spoke again. "You know more than you should."

Something cold and metallic nudged her lips apart. Hesitantly, she opened her mouth, and it was instantly filled with a sweet and velvety apple pudding. A gasp of delight escaped her, and she licked her lips, savoring the unexpected treat.

"Open again," Andrew said, his rich timbre slightly breathless.

Charlotte parted her lips once more, and a moan escaped her as a warm and buttery rhubarb tart shocked her taste buds, sending a wave of pleasure coursing through her body. Each subsequent bite brought with it a new and tantalizing sensation, from the creamy richness of the trifle to the sweet and sticky indulgence of the roly-poly jam pudding.

The crisp sweetness of the biscuits gave way to the ethereal lightness of the meringue, and finally, the cool, refreshing burst of iced oranges danced on her tongue. With every morsel, Charlotte found herself moaning, gasping, and exhaling, her senses overwhelmed by the sheer delight of the experience.

"I could listen to you all night," Andrew said darkly, his voice thick with a hunger that likely had little to do with the desserts.

"I can't eat another bite," Charlotte managed to say, her breath coming in short, satisfied gasps. "That was a wonderful surprise. I can't remember the last time I enjoyed something so much."

"Don't you recall our encounter in the library?" he said, his tone seductive.

Feeling the heat rise to her face once more, Charlotte reached up to remove the blindfold.

"Allow me," Andrew said, his fingers brushing against her skin as he easily loosened the knot with a single tug. As the fabric fell away, Charlotte blinked, her eyes adjusting to the sight of her husband, his shirtsleeves still rolled up and the collar open at the neck, a vision of masculine beauty.

"Where did you get all these delicious desserts?" she asked.

"The wife of a nearby innkeeper is known for her desserts. I ordered some before our arrival."

"You remembered that I enjoyed sweets?" Charlotte asked, her heart swelling with surprise and affection.

"Aye," Andrew said, settling himself on the bed beside her, his presence both comforting and electrifying. "You're likely undernourished. I plan to reverse the damage."

A smile bloomed on Charlotte's face, her features softening in his warmth. "I won't complain," she said.

His eyes sparkled with amusement. "It's about time, wife," he said, his voice low and enveloping her like a comforting embrace.

Rising to his feet, Andrew gathered the tray and carried it out of the room. "I boiled water for you if you need it!" he called from the other room, his thoughtfulness causing Charlotte's heart to swell.

Impressed by his attentiveness, Charlotte changed into a simple cotton night rail, a far cry from the silk unmentionables she had once worn. As she cleaned her teeth, her gaze was drawn once more to the hairbrush, the engraved words etching themselves into her essence.

Slipping beneath the counterpane, Charlotte waited anxiously, her knuckles turning white as she gripped the fabric, her mind racing with questions. Would he choose to sleep beside her, or would he remain in the parlor? Surprise dawned on her to realize she wasn't sure which she preferred.

It wasn't long before Andrew strode into the room, his body relaxed and casual, a man at ease in his own skin. With a gentle breath, he extinguished the candle, plunging the room into darkness. Charlotte watched, transfixed, as the shadowy outline of his form moved about the space, his movements fluid and graceful. Her heart raced as he removed his shirt and trousers, the rustling of fabric the only sound in the stillness of the night.

Panic gripped Charlotte as Andrew turned to fold back the counterpane. She quickly rolled over, so her back was to him, her body tense with anticipation and apprehension. The mattress dipped significantly under his weight as he settled beside her, his presence both comforting and strange.

"Good night, Charlotte," he said, his voice a gentle whisper in the darkness.

She replied above the pounding of her heart. "Good night, Andrew."

As the night wore on, Charlotte lay awake, listening to the steady rhythm of Andrew's breathing, her mind a whirlwind of emotions. She found herself sorting through the tumultuous feelings that had taken root in her heart, trying to make sense of the love, distrust, resentment, and longing that now plagued her. When at last Andrew's breaths turned deep and even, Charlotte allowed her own eyes to drift shut.

DAWN AND DUTY

25 December 1836

A S THE FIRST light of dawn crept into the room, Andrew's eyes fluttered open, a silent groan escaping his lips. The night had been a restless one, his sleep interrupted by the constant pull of desire that seemed to emanate from Charlotte's presence.

More than once, he had awoken to find himself pressed against her, his body molding to the curves of her bottom, his throbbing member paying a tribute to the hunger that consumed him. In the darkest hours of the night, he had sought release in his own hand, a temporary relief to the ache that burned within him.

Now, as the sun rose and his wife lay beside him, the devil returned, taunting him with memories of every sensual moan and gasp that had fallen from her lips the previous evening. The way she had licked her lips, leaving them glistening with moisture, was a vision that tortured and enticed him in equal measure.

Turning his head, Andrew's gaze fell on Charlotte, her sleeping form a picture of tranquil beauty. She lay on her stomach, her dark hair fanned out across the pillow, obscuring much of her face but contrasting starkly against the creamy expanse of her bare arm. Beneath the covers, the faint outline of her curves beckoned to him, his imagination running wild with thoughts of how he would take her from behind.

"Bloody hell," he muttered under his breath.

Cautiously, Andrew rose from the bed, his steps measured and quiet as he made his way into the parlor, gently closing the bedroom door behind him. Seeking distraction from the temptation that lay just beyond the threshold, he busied himself with starting fires in both the kitchen and the parlor, his mind drifting to thoughts of showing Charlotte the market. He hoped she could ride, for the last thing he needed was the torture of her sweet arse nestled against his aching cock.

A loud and urgent rap at the front door startled him from his reverie, and Andrew moved swiftly to answer the summons.

"Mr. Brinkley, good morning." He greeted the steward of one of his Whistable estates.

"Good morning, Mr.—um… milord. Pardon me for the intrusion, but I'm afraid we have a situation on our hands."

"What is it?" Andrew asked, gesturing for the man to step inside.

No stranger to emergencies, he led Brinkley to the water closet where he had left his work clothes from the day before. With hurried movements, he cleaned his teeth and changed into the familiar garments as the steward apprised him of the situation.

"I'm afraid there's pox going around at the farm," Brinkley said, his voice grave.

"Has the doctor been summoned?" Andrew's mind raced with plans and possibilities.

"Yes, sir. But Miss Jenny, one of the residents, has an infant, you see. She says she'd like to go to her mum's in Cornwall."

"Her mother a decent woman?" Andrew turned to face the man, his fingers deftly tying the last knot on his neckcloth.

"Yes, milord."

"Very well. Call the coach and have the mother and babe stay somewhere else while waiting. I'll be close behind."

"Right away." Brinkley bowed and hurried out of the cabin, his footsteps echoing in the stillness of the morning.

Andrew approached the bedroom door, opening it quietly.

"I'm awake," Charlotte called out, her voice clear.

He entered the room to find her already dressed in a blue

walking dress, her fingers nimbly arranging her hair. The sight of her sent a thrill through his heart.

"Good morning. I assume the disturbance woke you."

"I heard voices," she said, her gaze meeting his. "It sounded like something was amiss."

"Aye. There's a pox breakout at one of my farms. I need to assess the situation, see if I need to get help for them."

"I will come with you. I've had the pox."

Before Andrew could protest, she strode past him, her steps quick and purposeful.

"Can you ride well?" he asked.

"Yes."

"You can still become ill from it, you realize."

"I'm aware, but I'm not going to sit by idly while I could be of use somewhere else."

Andrew helped her saddle and mount the horse before swinging onto his own steed. As they set off, he turned to her and declared, "You're happiest when helping others! That's your entire reason for being!" A look of profound admiration and pride accompanied his pronouncement.

Charlotte smiled back at him, her eyes sparkling with the joy of a person who had finally been seen, truly and completely.

THEY RODE THROUGH the countryside spotted with occasional green foliage, the unseasonably warm temperature bringing a gentle breeze carrying the scent of the sea. After twenty minutes, they arrived at the sprawling farm, surrounded by grazing sheep and cattle. The farmhouse was not at all what Charlotte had expected. It could have been a mansion in Mayfair or any other affluent neighborhood. It appeared to have dozens of rooms and there were expansive play areas, mazes, gardens, and horse-riding enclosures for children.

Handing their mounts off to a waiting groom, Charlotte followed closely behind Andrew as they entered the building. The sound of crying children and hushed whispers filled the air, a haunting melody that made her feel uneasy.

"My lord, how wonderful to see you." A young woman with chestnut-brown hair approached them, her arms outstretched in a gesture of warm welcome. Charlotte watched, her brows raised in question, as Andrew gripped the woman's hands merrily and placed a gentle kiss on her cheek. Their overfamiliarity sent a pang of jealousy through her heart.

"Cecilia, I wasn't expecting to see you here," Andrew said.

"I happened to be visiting when trouble began." Cecilia smiled brightly, as if there were nothing she couldn't conquer.

"Trouble does like to follow you." Andrew's tone was flirtatious, a stark contrast to the simmering anger that bubbled inside Charlotte. But just as she felt the first tendrils of resentment take hold, Andrew placed a hand on her back, drawing her nearer to his side.

"Charlotte, may I present Miss Cecilia Wood? She works for Madam Tansley."

Forcing a smile to her lips, Charlotte nodded in acknowledgment, her discomfort palpable in the air between them. "Cecilia, this is my wife, Charlotte," Andrew said, his voice filled with pride.

Cecilia's hands flew to her mouth, her eyes wide with surprise and delight. "How wonderful! I heard you became engaged in the most spectacular fashion. I had no idea you'd already be married!"

Before Charlotte could react, Cecilia enveloped Andrew in an enthusiastic embrace, her lips brushing against his cheeks in a display of unbridled joy. Then she turned her attention to Charlotte. The woman's arms wrapped around her rigid form, and the scent of white powder filled her nostrils.

As Cecilia released her, her happiness genuine and unguarded, Charlotte felt a flicker of ease begin to take root. But still, the mysterious purpose of the house nagged at her. Glancing around, she realized the house was filled with young, beautiful women.

"Tell me what's happening here, Cecilia," Andrew said, his voice solemn.

"Come, I'll show you." Cecilia led the way, her steps as confident as the mistress of the house might be. As they walked, maids passed by with warm and welcoming smiles.

"What manner of establishment is this?" Charlotte inquired, as they walked past a modest but well-appointed parlor with its simple wooden furnishings and cheerful yellow curtains.

"Since Lord Carlisle brought you here, I presume I may speak freely. This is a sanctuary for women of unfortunate circumstances, my lady," Cecilia said gently, her weathered hands folded in her lap. "Former ladies of the evening who seek a different path."

Charlotte's eyes widened, her fan snapping shut with an audible click as she turned to regard her husband with newfound curiosity.

"Madam Tansley aids women who have fallen into dire straits," Cecilia continued, gesturing toward the adjoining rooms where the soft murmur of feminine voices could be heard. "The residents are provided shelter here and at several other establishments until they might secure respectable employment, establish modest enterprises, or perhaps make advantageous marriages."

"And pray tell, what part do you play in these charitable endeavors?" Charlotte asked Andrew, one delicate eyebrow arched in inquiry.

"I provide stud services," Andrew replied with perfect gravity, "ensuring a steady supply of orphans for the workhouses."

"Andrew!" Charlotte gasped, her cheeks flushing crimson. "That is neither amusing nor appropriate!"

"Indeed, my lord!" Cecilia scolded, though her lips twitched with suppressed mirth.

"I must respectfully disagree with both of you ladies," he said, his dark eyes dancing with mischief.

Cecilia stopped in front of a door and turned to face them

both. She leaned toward Charlotte and lowered her voice. "Andrew funds the entire operation."

Stunned by this revelation, Charlotte barely noticed Cecilia entering the room and inviting them inside. A young woman was in bed with two young children on her lap. After a brief introduction, Cecilia said, "They were the first ones to become ill. They had just returned from the north, so we're not sure if the villagers were exposed."

"I haven't heard of an epidemic. I shall investigate. How many have fallen ill?" Andrew asked.

From there, Andrew and Charlotte spoke to the villagers, assessing the situation and determining their needs. They confirmed that no villagers were affected, but Andrew dispatched help and supplies lest that changed quickly. They hired a carriage to nearby towns, purchasing toys, mittens, medicine, and locating physicians and nurses to monitor the patients.

Dusk settled when they returned home, during which time Charlotte learned Andrew had been on a rescue mission when he had discovered her with Chatham.

The cabin was immersed in a golden glow from the setting sun when they arrived. Andrew immediately began writing letters to his secretary, physicians, and Madam. Charlotte quietly prepared supper, careful not to disturb his concentration, which was just as well. She needed to digest the fact that her husband, whom she thought lived for wealth only, was, in fact, a philanthropist. And a more honorable cause she could not imagine, because given the secrecy, his involvement would never be publicized or glorified.

While they ate in silence, Charlotte studied him, her heart reaching out to him, and some of the tenderness she had felt toward him all those years ago began to stir. She thought he had become unrecognizable, but perhaps she had judged too quickly. Andrew, engrossed in his work, left his meal untouched. Charlotte stood and placed a spoonful of stew at his lips, nudging him to open. He did her bidding and ate obediently until he looked up in surprise.

"I'm sorry. I didn't realize you were feeding me. I tend to become oblivious when working."

Charlotte smiled. "We have that in common."

He shook his head woefully. "We'll need to hire nurses and nannies to ensure we don't forget to feed our children."

Her heart halted at his words. It was a life she never imagined she could have—a life with husband and children. Could she have it all?

Andrew ate his meal, showering her with praise until she blushed. After they finished eating, they washed the dishes side by side in companionable silence.

They sat on the sofa by the fireplace, Charlotte cradling a cup of tea and Andrew a glass of brandy. It was the closest Charlotte had felt toward Andrew since they'd become reacquainted. Now that the old feelings had begun to seep through her heart, she felt she soon wouldn't be able to stop the flow. Her pulse began to race at the thought of sharing the bed with him again.

Could she press her luck and ask for another night to prepare for the eventual coupling? It wasn't that she did not crave the physical pleasure he could give her, but she feared the connection they were beginning to forge would turn into ashes if she associated their intimate act with the trauma of her past.

Upon feeling his gaze on her, she summoned the courage to meet his eyes. As she glanced at him sideways, he smiled lazily, the flickering light from the candle casting dancing shadows across his pristine white shirt. With a languid movement, he reached up to his neck, loosening the cravat that encircled his throat. Flustered, she hastily averted her gaze, hiding her flushed face behind the delicate teacup.

"Are you nervous?" His voice was low and gentle, with an undercurrent of amusement.

"About what?" she replied, feigning nonchalance.

"I can't say for certain. Perhaps you could enlighten me? You seem rather tense."

"I'm afraid I don't know what you mean."

She wasn't quite ready to discuss such a sensitive topic with him. How could she explain the shame that consumed her over Cambridge—over giving what should have been his to a stranger out of sheer desperation? Though Andrew surely believed the duke had claimed that prize, the truth was somehow worse: She had traded her innocence not for love or even desire, but for silence and survival.

Despite the magical nature of their previous encounters, a cold fear gripped her heart. What if, when the moment came, her body betrayed her? What if the memory of that Cambridge night—the revulsion, the powerlessness—intruded upon what should be beautiful between them? She had enjoyed Andrew's kisses, his touch, but would intimacy awaken the trauma she had buried so carefully?

The thought of flinching from her own husband, of him witnessing her break apart from ghosts he knew nothing about, filled her with a dread that had nothing to do with inexperience and everything to do with the scars invisible wounds could leave upon one's soul.

"Shall I venture a guess, since you seem either unsure or too abashed to say?" Without awaiting her response, he leaned back against the sofa, his eyes narrowing as he regarded her intently. "Perhaps you find yourself astonished by your good fortune in securing a husband as dashing as myself, and yet you feel nervous about expressing your gratitude."

Unable to suppress the smile that tugged at her lips, she shook her head in denial.

"Could it be that you're concealing a rather large mole upon your person, and the thought of revealing it to me fills you with embarrassment?"

Once more, she shook her head, amusement dancing in her eyes. With an air of exaggerated pensiveness, he rested his chin on his hand, the muscles of his biceps flexing and straining against the fabric of his shirt. Noticing her appreciative gaze, Andrew smugly unfastened the top four buttons of his shirt, exposing a tantalizing glimpse of his chest. She found herself unable to look away, transfixed by the sight of his tanned skin.

"Or perhaps," he murmured, his voice a low, seductive rumble that sent shivers down her spine, "you fear that I may have turned feral since our last encounter, and that I might devour you whole when we retire to our bedchamber." There could be no mistaking the intimate promise behind his words, the unspoken desire that hung heavy in the air between them.

His confidence, the practiced way he spoke of such intimate matters, made her acutely aware of her own inexperience.

"Surely, you must have known the touch of skilled women," she blurted, the words escaping her lips before she could think better of them.

He fell silent, his expression unreadable as he regarded her with an intensity that made her heart race.

"What leads you to believe such a thing? Is it because of my work with Madame Tansley?"

Charlotte felt a pang of remorse, sensing that she had somehow offended him with her remark.

"You do have connections to them, and I cannot imagine that any woman would deny you," she said softly, her gaze downcast.

He arched a brow and reached for a strand of her hair. "Why, Mrs. Creswell, that sounded remarkably like a compliment, and an acknowledgment of your excellent taste in husbands."

Charlotte rose abruptly from her seat, a sudden wave of fear and anxiety gripping her heart. She felt the need to escape, to find solace in solitude and gather her thoughts.

"If it would not be too great an imposition, I should like to take a bath," she said, her voice trembling slightly.

Andrew, ever the gentleman, inclined his head politely, choosing not to remark on her hasty request. "Of course. I shall see to the preparations at once."

As he busied himself with the task of boiling water and filling the tub, Charlotte slipped away to change into her bathing gown.

The thin, worn cotton felt like a flimsy shield against the turmoil that raged within her, but she clung to it nonetheless, her fingers tightly gripping the front as if it were a suit of armor.

She knew the coupling with her husband would be pleasant. However, her body repelled the thought of joining with a man, making her stomach queasy as her heart tried to escape her body.

When at last Andrew announced that her bath was ready, Charlotte could not bring herself to meet his gaze, fearing that her inner turmoil would be all too apparent in her eyes. She kept her head bowed as she made her way to the bathing chamber.

Upon entering the room, Charlotte was greeted by the soft, inviting glow of a dozen candles, their flickering light casting a warm ambiance that instantly soothed her frayed nerves. She let her housecoat fall to the floor, and with a sigh of contentment, lowered herself into the steaming water, allowing her eyes to drift shut as she savored the sensation of the liquid heat enveloping her body. The gentle lapping of the water against the sides of the tub, combined with the delicate scent of lemon that perfumed the air, worked to ease the tension from her muscles and quiet the chaos of her thoughts.

Lost in the tranquility of the moment, Charlotte failed to hear the soft click of the door as Andrew entered the bathing chamber. It was only when the floorboards creaked beneath his weight that her eyes flew open, her heart leaping into her throat at the sight of him standing before her, his gaze dark with unspoken desire.

ANDREW OPENED THE door to the bathing chamber with a glass of champagne. As he stepped into the room, a wave of hot, damp air enveloped him, the steam clinging to his skin and clothing. Cautiously, he peered around the corner, only to be met with a sight that drew a low groan from his lips.

Charlotte's eyes flew open and stopped her ministrations

before she moved to sit up hastily.

"Forgive me," he murmured, his voice low and rough. "I thought you might enjoy chilled champagne in a hot bath."

Charlotte felt her cheeks flush with heat, a potent blend of embarrassment and gratitude. She made to cover herself, to shield her nakedness from his piercing gaze, but Andrew stayed her hand with a gentle touch.

"Please," he whispered, his fingers brushing against the delicate skin of her wrist. "Do not hide yourself from me. You are a vision of loveliness."

Slowly, hesitantly, she allowed her arms to fall away, exposing herself to his appreciative gaze. Andrew's eyes roamed over her form, drinking in the sight of her like a man parched, his breath coming in shallow pants as he fought to maintain his composure.

"Charlotte," he breathed. "I am undone by you, my love. You have bewitched me, and I fear I shall never be the same."

He watched Charlotte's gaze drift downward, eyes widening at the evidence of his arousal, his trousers stretching taut over his erection. Her teeth sank into her plump lower lip as she toyed with a strand of her hair. Slowly, almost hesitantly, her hand disappeared beneath the water's surface once more, and Andrew knew she had resumed her previous ministrations.

She leaned back, immersing herself fully in the scented water, her dark hair fanning out around her like the wings of a crow, shimmering in the candlelight. Her eyes sparkled with desire as she watched him, transfixed by the sight of his own hand sliding lower to cup the aching hardness that strained against his falls.

With a groan of surrender, he sank to his knees beside the tub, his hand coming to rest upon her shoulder while his other hand rubbed his aching cock. Charlotte let out a soft gasp as his fingers began to move, tracing the delicate lines of her collarbones before dipping lower, skimming the tops of her breasts where they peeked above the waterline.

She arched into his caress, silently begging for more, and

Andrew was all too happy to oblige. His hand slid lower, beneath the water's surface, his fingers grazing the silken skin of her thigh before delving into the slick heat of her most intimate place.

Charlotte's head fell back against the edge of the tub, a low moan escaping her parted lips as his fingers found her swollen bud, stroking and teasing until she was writhing beneath his touch, desperate for release. With a final, expert caress of his thumb, he sent her flying over the edge, her inner muscles convulsing around his fingers with the force of her climax as wave after wave of ecstasy crashed over her.

The sight of her, lost in the throes of passion, combined with the exquisite sensation of her body's response to his touch, proved too much for Andrew to bear. With a low groan, he found his own release, the pleasure surging through him with an intensity that left him weak and trembling.

As the haze of passion cleared, their breathing gradually slowed and the world came back into focus. Andrew pulled her closer, pressing his lips to her temple as something profound and unnamed settled between them—a connection that transcended mere physical desire.

THE GAME

26 December 1836

O N A CRISP winter evening near the cottage, the village of Whistable was alive with the glow of lanterns and the joyful strains of a fiddle. The community had gathered in the newly built assembly room to celebrate the nuptials of Lord and Lady Carlisle.

The assembly room, a testament to Andrew's generosity, was resplendent with garlands of hollies and fragrant herbs, their delicate scent mingling with the aroma of freshly baked bread and roasted meats that wafted from the heavily laden tables. At the far end of the room, a group of musicians played a lively tune, their feet tapping in time to the beat as couples whirled and spun across the dance floor, their faces alight with merriment.

As Charlotte and Andrew made their grand entrance, a re-sounding cheer erupted from the assembled crowd, their faces beaming with gratitude and admiration. The villagers, young and old alike, surged forward to offer their heartfelt thanks and felicitations, their hands clasped in sincere appreciation for all that Andrew had done for their community.

"Lord Carlisle, words cannot express the depth of our grati-tude for your boundless kindness," the vicar said, his voice trembling with emotion. "Your generous supply of medicine and extra hands may very well save countless lives. And now, with the new classrooms and teachers you've so graciously provided, our children will have opportunities that other villages can scarcely dream of."

Andrew, his hand resting lightly on the small of Charlotte's back, inclined his head graciously. "It is my honor and privilege to serve this wonderful community," he replied.

As the evening wore on, Charlotte found herself observing her husband with a sense of wonder and admiration. She realized how gravely she had misjudged his character while she watched him graciously accept the villagers' thanks and laugh with carefree abandon alongside the village children.

Nevertheless, a niggling doubt lingered in the back of her mind even as her heart swelled with a newfound affection for her husband, wondering if his words could truly be trusted when it came to her career.

As his strong, capable hands guided her through the crowd with a gentle touch, she felt a rush of warmth suffuse her being, and memories of their time apart came flooding back—the long, lonely nights at Cambridge, the ache of missing him that had never quite faded, even as she threw herself into her studies with a singular focus.

She recalled the moment at Cambridge when she had given herself to another man, a desperate attempt to hold on to her dream, her life's purpose. The memory brought with it a pang of shame and regret, disgust churning her stomach at the thought of the man she had lain with.

"Oh, please, Lord Carlisle! Won't you dance with us?" The eager voices of the young women pleading with Andrew roused Charlotte from her painful reverie. The ladies inched closer to him, their advances inadvertently forcing him away from his bride.

"I'm afraid I must decline," he stammered, his face flushing a delicate shade of pink.

Charlotte observed him with keen interest, curious as to what could cause her formidable husband to blush like a schoolboy. Just as she began to feel a prickle of annoyance toward the brazen women who shamelessly pressed closer to Andrew, offering him an unobstructed view of their ample bosoms, he cast a beseeching glance in her direction. To her amusement, he seemed to be silently imploring her for assistance.

With a graceful step, Charlotte approached and took Andrew's hand in hers, offering the ladies a polite smile. "If you'll excuse us, his lordship has promised me the honor of the first three dances."

Paying no heed to their collective murmurs of disappointment, the newlyweds made their way toward the group of villagers dancing merrily by the musicians.

"I'm curious. What happened to make you so terrified of a few young girls?" she asked.

Andrew rubbed the back of his neck, a sheepish gesture. "I wasn't frightened."

"Judging by the scarlet hue of your face, it was either fear or shyness," she teased.

Averting his gaze, he said, "I've never been particularly adept at conversing with women, especially when they gather in groups."

A chuckle bubbled up from her throat and spilled past her lips, eliciting a look of mild annoyance from her husband.

"Forgive me," she said, her eyes sparkling with mirth. "I simply didn't expect Andrew Creswell, the giant of a man and businessman, to be afraid of women. You didn't seem particularly shy when we first met."

"I was, in truth, but you appeared disinterested in me, which came as a relief. Then, when you spoke, your words caught me so off guard that I quite forgot myself."

Charlotte beamed, delighted by this discovery. "And what is your usual course of action when a woman attempts to seduce you?"

He shrugged. "I find myself staring at whatever is deemed appropriate—the dance floor, the musicians, the empty space…"

"So, have all your past encounters been initiated by the woman in question?"

She waited patiently as he traced invisible patterns on the

floor with the toe of his boot.

"That many?" she asked when the silence stretched on.

"Three," he blurted, his cheeks coloring once more.

Her mouth fell open. "Three? Only three?"

He nodded slowly, his eyes still fixed on the floor.

"Well, that's not many at all," Charlotte mused, smiling softly as she gazed up at her husband in a new and endearing light.

"Three, if you count the twelve strokes," he mumbled, his words almost lost in the din of the room.

"I beg your pardon?" Charlotte's eyes widened, certain she must have misheard.

He shifted his weight from one foot to the other, his hands burrowing deeper into his pockets. "I was asleep, you see, and I awoke to find a woman... she was doing things to me. She managed a dozen strokes before I was alert enough to leap from the bed."

Charlotte gasped, her hand flying to her mouth as she struggled to decide whether to laugh at the absurdity of the situation or be utterly scandalized by the woman's audacity.

"And the others?" she asked, her curiosity getting the better of her jealousy.

"An older woman, when I was nineteen."

"How much older?"

"Eight years, or thereabouts. She never did confide her exact age."

"And what became of that liaison?"

He exhaled heavily, running a hand through his hair as if the memory weighed on him. "I proposed, and she declined."

Charlotte's hand climbed to her throat, the air suddenly seeming to vanish from her lungs. "Is it your habit, then, to propose to every woman who catches your fancy?"

He looked up then, his gaze locking with hers, intense and unwavering. "Yes, for when I love, I do so deeply. I have no interest in dallying with women for whom I hold no deep affection. Emily and I were together for four years. When I was finally earning a comfortable income, I asked for her hand, only to discover that her heart had been claimed by another—a young aristocrat of twenty."

Charlotte felt a sting of resentment as his gaze turned pensive once more, his foot resuming its invisible tracings on the floor. She wondered if his foot might be tracing her name—Emily.

"And the third?" Her voice took on a sharp edge.

He raised his eyes to hers, the corner of his mouth lifting in a smile that made her heart flutter. Stepping closer, he rested his hand gently on her waist, the heat of his touch seeping through the layers of her gown. Charlotte tilted her head back, her eyes searching his.

"The third, my sweet, is you," he whispered, his breath warm against her cheek.

"Me?" She sucked in a breath.

He chuckled, the sound low and rich. "Surely you haven't forgotten the intimacy we shared?"

"No, of course not, but… are you saying you've been with no other woman since our encounter?"

"Aye, that's precisely what I'm saying."

"Not even for a single night?"

Leaning toward her, he whispered in her ear, "Not even for a moment if you don't count the woman with my prick in her mouth."

"Oh, my…" Charlotte's voice quavered as his words blazed hotly inside her.

"Lord Carlisle, won't you join us for a dance now?" the same young women called out, their voices rising above the lively music.

"I'm afraid I must decline, ladies. Dancing is not among my talents."

"You don't dance?" Charlotte echoed, her eyebrows arching in surprise.

"No, I never learned how. I never found the time."

"Well, that can be easily remedied," she declared, taking his hand and leading him toward an empty space on the dance floor.

At first, Andrew appeared hesitant, his movements stiff and uncertain as he tried to follow the intricate steps of the country dance. His brow furrowed in concentration as he struggled to keep pace with the music.

But Charlotte simply laughed, her eyes sparkling with warmth and encouragement as she squeezed his hand reassuringly.

"Don't fret," she whispered, leaning in close so that her words were meant for his ears alone. Andrew's arm came around her waist possessively, holding her close for a moment longer before releasing her.

With infinite patience, Charlotte began to steer Andrew through the steps, her body moving with grace and fluidity. She twirled and spun, her skirts billowing about her ankles as she moved in perfect time to the music, her hand never leaving Andrew's as she guided him gently.

Soon, the two of them were laughing and spinning together as they twirled and dipped and swayed. The rest of the world fell away until there was nothing but the magic of the moment.

As the carriage carried them homeward, Andrew sat with his eyes closed, his body coiled with a palpable tension that seemed to fill the confined space. Charlotte half-expected to see lightning crackling above his head at any moment.

For the next twenty minutes, until they arrived at their destination, Charlotte found herself wringing her hands, silently willing the butterflies in her stomach to settle. How could her husband transform from sweet to terrifying in the span of a single breath, evoking laughter from her one minute and trembling with fear the next?

Glancing out the window, Charlotte felt the weight of the

night pressing down on her. Uncertainty gripped her heart as she pondered whether Andrew intended to consummate their marriage this evening or if she might be granted a reprieve for one more night. The mere thought of joining with a man sent tremors through her body and beads of perspiration dotting her brow.

And yet, the memory of Andrew's tender ministrations in the bath chamber, the exquisite sensation of his hand upon her heated flesh, had her rubbing her thighs together. Perhaps she would fare better if they could avoid the bed... if she could see his face during the act.

As the carriage rolled to a stop, Andrew seemed to come to life once more, swiftly moving to assist Charlotte as she alighted. Without so much as a glance in her direction, he busied himself with the task of lighting candles and stoking the fires in the hearths. Once he had prepared her bathwater, he hastily took his leave, leaving Charlotte alone with her thoughts in the bedchamber.

Unable to find solace in the bath, her anxiety mounting as the darkness closed in around her, Charlotte washed with hurried efficiency, donning a shift and housecoat. Then an idea occurred to her to possibly make the coupling more comfortable for her. The last thing she wanted was for her to respond with revulsion when he entered her. That would surely expose her and ruin their intimacy. With that thought, Charlotte donned the garter and stockings beneath her shift and ventured out to face whatever the night might bring.

"Shall I pour you a cup of tea, Charlotte?" Andrew's voice cut through the heavy silence.

"Yes, please. Thank you." Her words were soft, almost lost in the crackling of the fire.

Toweling her damp hair, Charlotte made her way into the parlor, where she found Andrew standing before the hearth, a steaming cup clasped in his hand as he stared into the dancing flames. He, too, had already bathed and changed, wearing a simple shirt and trousers beneath his own housecoat.

Charlotte lingered by the fire, trying to gauge her husband's mood as she searched his face for any hint of his thoughts. Andrew met her gaze, his eyes seeming to pierce straight through her. His attention drifted deliberately downward to her stockings, one brow lifting while his expression remained dark and unfathomable.

Then with excruciating slowness, his gaze traced a burning path from the swell of her breasts to the curve of her hips.

He came to her slowly and pulled her body flush against him, one hand pulling up her shift to press his knee between her thighs. Despite the hunger evident in his shallow breaths and ardent caresses, Andrew's kiss was impossibly tender. He brushed his lips softly against hers, nipping and exploring with a gentleness that left her motionless.

Charlotte allowed him to explore her mouth, relishing the softness of his lips, the warmth of his breath, and the way his hands roamed her body. When his large hands cupped her bottom and pulled against his shaft, she gasped in surprise. She wrapped her arms around his neck and stroked his short hair. She marveled at its softness.

"Give me your tongue. Let me taste you," he whispered against her mouth, his husky voice sending shivers down her spine.

As she offered her tongue hesitantly, Andrew's mouth claimed hers in a deep, possessive kiss, his tongue delving inside to explore every crevice that left her weak and trembling. He spread his palm over her back, caressing the curve of her buttocks before squeezing, a low moan escaping his throat. His fingers trailed up her spine, then gripped her head to press her lips more firmly against his own.

ANDREW LOST ALL sense of who he was and what he wanted, consumed by a burning thirst that only she could quench. Cupping her round bottom, he ground his aching member against her.

Gently, Charlotte's hands pressed against his chest, breaking the kiss. They stared at each other, panting, her lips swollen and bright red from his fervent assault.

"Could we not delay intimacy?" she whispered, her voice trembling slightly.

He stilled, studying her thoughtfully. "Why?"

"We are scarcely acquainted… physically. You have kept yourself chaste… whereas I…" Her words trailed off, and even in the dim light, Andrew could see the shame in her eyes.

Andrew loosened his arms, eventually releasing her and stepping back. Her countenance changed from shame to wounded, her eyes readily accepting his disappointment. As much as he longed for the oblivion of claiming her, even sleep would be preferable over a discussion, he sensed this conversation was of great importance to the woman he had drawn into his orbit.

"I am no aristocrat, save for my title, and I do not subscribe to their notions of feminine purity," he said. "A true woman is not some untouched paragon, but rather one who has lived, endured, and triumphed over adversity. You, my sweet, embody that indomitable spirit—a woman who has overcome, yet refused to let it break her."

As he spoke, Andrew slowly divested himself of his house-coat, Charlotte's eyes following his every movement. The garment slipped from his broad shoulders, revealing the open shirt and trousers beneath. Her gaze was drawn to the expanse of his chest, tapering to a trim waist, before skipping involuntarily to the unmistakable protrusion along his thigh. This time, there was no laughter in her eyes.

"You are my wife, Charlotte, whether it pleases you or not," Andrew said, his voice tinged with weariness. "Delaying the inevitable will only breed discomfort between us. Besides, I find myself aching for your touch. It has been so long since I last lay with a woman... I can only hope I remember how it is done."

He studied Charlotte's countenance, noting the way her expression seemed to waver between a chuckle and a cry. A sense of unease settled over him, an instinct that whispered all was not as it seemed with her.

"I... I would like to propose a means of easing this process of... bedding, if I may," Charlotte said.

Andrew stepped closer, lifting her chin with the tip of his finger until her gaze met his. "Are you afraid of me?" he asked softly, his eyes searching hers.

She shook her head rapidly, words seeming to fail her.

"Do I repulse you?"

"No, of course not," she whispered. "I am merely nervous."

Nodding, Andrew released her, accepting her explanation. "What did you have in mind to make you more comfortable?"

"A game," she said.

Andrew lifted his brows. Rolling up his sleeves, the fabric sliding over his muscular forearms, he fixed her with an appraising look. "And what sort of game did you have in mind, my clever wife?"

Her smile widened; her countenance became more relaxed. "I shall pose to you a series of legal questions, and for each incorrect answer, you must remove one article of your clothing. But should you answer correctly, it is I who shall shed a garment."

A deep, rumbling laugh escaped Andrew's lips as he crossed his arms over his broad chest. "Hardly an equitable arrangement, Lady Carlisle. You are, after all, a professional in such matters."

"Ah, but a professional of limited experience. And you, my lord, are a seasoned man of business. We could, if you prefer, restrict the questions to matters of contract and corporate law."

Andrew's gaze drifted longingly to the housecoat he had so recently discarded, now draped haphazardly over the divan. "I find myself regretting my earlier decision to make myself more comfortable."

Charlotte shrugged. "What's the worst that could befall you, should you find yourself standing before me in nothing but your skin?"

"That you might flee, and I, in my state of undress, would be powerless to give chase," he said.

"Cowardice has never been a trait I've associated with you, my lord. Do you accept the challenge?"

With a nod of his head, Andrew acquiesced. "I do, my lady wife. You may begin."

Charlotte crossed her arms, pacing the room with an air of pensive contemplation. After several long, torturous moments, designed to stoke the fires of his anticipation and unease, she turned to him, her eyes full of mischief.

"Please tell me, my lord, what is the legal term for an individual who meets their demise without leaving behind a valid will?"

"An intestate," Andrew replied without hesitation.

Charlotte stared at him, her lips parted in surprise.

"I must point out, my sweet," he said, a teasing note in his voice, "that your question bears little relevance to the realm of business. I can't help but suspect you of attempting to swindle me."

A flicker of panic danced across her face, but she quickly masked her unease with a tight smile. "My apologies, my lord. Let us begin anew."

"No," Andrew said firmly, his gaze intense. "I'm waiting."

Taking a deep, steadying breath, Charlotte tugged at the strings on her housecoat, her fingers trembling slightly as she removed the garment. It was hardly an act that should have caused such apprehension, given what had transpired in the bath closet, but the power he held over her, the way he could make her tremble with a single look, thrilled her in ways she dared not admit.

Collecting herself, Charlotte stood tall in her night rail, the soft fabric clinging to her curves as she posed another question. "In the realm of contract law, what term is used to describe a clause that stipulates the sum of damages to be paid by a party who fails to fulfill their contractual obligations?"

A slow, wicked smile spread across Andrew's handsome face. "A penalty clause," he answered, his voice low and rich with amusement. "If I didn't know better, my wife, I might suspect that you harbored a secret desire to divest yourself of your clothing."

A soft, breathy laugh escaped her lips, more from anxiety than mirth. Without uttering a response, she sat down and reached for her garter, careful not to lift her shift in the process.

"No," Andrew said, his voice low and rasping. The sound sent shivers down her spine. Charlotte's gaze snapped up to meet his, and she watched his eyes darken, his jaw tightening with barely restrained desire. "Leave your stockings on."

Swallowing hard, Charlotte stood and untied the ribbon on one shoulder, holding her night rail in place. She pulled on it with deliberate slowness, her movements carefully measured to reveal as little as possible. She had underestimated him, she realized, and would need to pose more challenging questions if she hoped to maintain any semblance of modesty.

With one ribbon untied, Charlotte lifted her chin, trying to collect as much dignity as she could muster. A quirk of his brow and the upward curve of one corner of his lip was his only response as he stepped closer until he could reach out and touch her. With one long finger, he reached for the ribbon lying loosely against her flesh. Avoiding direct contact, he brushed the ribbon aside, sucking in a sharp breath as the action revealed one perfect, round breast. The rosy, pink peak tightened under his heated gaze.

Charlotte studied the play of emotions across his face, fascinated by the way desire warred with restraint, before allowing her gaze to drift lower, to the thick shaft that strained against the confines of his trousers.

Steadying her own breath, Charlotte pressed on, her voice trembling slightly as she spoke. "In the context of a contract for the sale of goods, what legal principle allows a seller to recover the full contract price from a buyer who wrongfully refuses to accept and pay for the goods?"

"The action for goods bargained and sold," Andrew replied, his gaze fixed upon her with an intensity that made her knees weak.

With shaking hands, Charlotte tugged on the ribbon at her other shoulder, carefully untying only the first knot, silently praying that the remaining knot would hold. To her relief, it did, but Andrew, it seemed, would not allow it.

With an impatient tug, he pulled at the ribbon, and the night rail pooled at her feet, leaving her bare save for her garters and stockings. An audible groan escaped his throat, his breathing growing shallow as she watched his eyes drink in the sight of her: the swell of her breasts, the delicate peaks of her nipples, and the allure of the apex between her thighs.

Instinctively, Charlotte moved to cover herself, but with a speed that left her breathless, Andrew had her pinned against the wall, her arms shackled above her head by his powerful grip. His eyes, half-hooded with desire, roved over her breasts again and again until she felt she might faint from the sheer intensity of his gaze. But her pride demanded to be restored, and so, with a breathless whisper, she continued.

"W-what is the legal concept that allows a party to a contract to be excused"—she swallowed hard, her voice trembling—"from performance due to an unforeseen event that renders performance impossible or impractical?"

"Sweet Jesus… I can't think, and I don't care…" Andrew rasped, his voice rough.

When Charlotte remained silent, a smile playing about her lips like that of a cat with its prey, he rolled his eyes and released her arms. With deft movements, he removed his own shirt, leaving Charlotte to stare in open admiration. He was an impressive specimen, every sinewy muscle proof of his strength and power. Her gaze settled on a long scar she had noticed before, now realizing it extended the length of his back.

Noticing her curiosity, Andrew spoke, his words tumbling out in a rush. "A chain broke off a thousand-pound crate, whipping me in the process. I would've been crushed under the weight if a fellow docker, David, hadn't pushed me out of the way."

Charlotte's hand flew to her lips, her own state of undress momentarily forgotten. "I am so sorry. How... how fared David?"

"His leg was crushed and had to be amputated. Otherwise, he continues to be a thorn in my side as my valet," Andrew replied with a wry smile.

Tossing his shirt onto the divan, he fixed her with a heated stare. "Are we quite finished with this game?"

Sensing that his patience was wearing thin, Charlotte hastily posed one final question. "Under the Statute of Frauds, which types of contracts must be made in writing to be legally enforceable?"

Andrew closed his eyes, searching for the answer. "Contracts for the sale of land, contracts that cannot be performed within one year, and... Bloody hell, woman!" he growled.

Before Charlotte could fully comprehend what was happening, Andrew pulled her into his arms. "Enough," he rasped, his voice raw with need, before capturing her lips in a searing kiss that set her body ablaze.

His lips were hot and soft, a delicious contrast to the hard, unyielding planes of his body. He enveloped her completely, his larger frame dwarfing her own as he held her close, his embrace all-consuming. His tongue sought hers with a frenzied desperation, a man starved for the taste of her, and she yielded to him willingly, eagerly.

His long, elegant fingers tangled in her hair, tilting her head back as he deepened the kiss, plundering her mouth with a skill that left her weak. She clung to him, her own hands roaming the broad expanse of his back, reveling in the play of muscles beneath his heated skin.

As he kissed her with the passion of a man who had at last found his salvation, his hands began to wander, mapping the curves and valleys of her naked form. He cupped the plump globes of her buttocks, kneading the soft flesh, before skimming upward to tease the hardened peaks of her breasts. Charlotte gasped into his mouth, arching into his touch, silently begging for more.

Lost in the heat of his ardor, Charlotte wound her arms around his neck, her fingers burying into the thick, silken strands of his hair. She pressed herself closer, molding her body to his, desperate to eliminate even the tiniest space between them. She kissed him back with equal fervor, nipping at his bottom lip, then soothing the sting with her tongue, until he growled low in his throat, the sound vibrating through her core.

In his arms, Charlotte felt a sense of belonging, a rightness that defied explanation. She wanted to lose herself in him, to take shelter in the strength of his embrace and the steadfastness of his heart. With him, she could forget the pain of her past, could start anew, unburdened by the ghosts that had haunted her.

She burrowed into him, seeking his warmth, his protection, his love. He was her salvation, her only hope for a future filled with happiness and joy. In his kiss, in his touch, she found a glimmer of that long-sought peace, a balm for her weary soul.

She surrendered to him, to the desire that coursed through her veins, to the love that had taken root in her heart.

ANDREW'S HANDS GLIDED down the smooth expanse of Charlotte's back, coming to rest on the luscious curves of her bottom. Her flesh, soft and yielding, fit perfectly in his large, work-roughened palms. With a low growl of desire, he lifted her, his mouth never leaving hers as he carried her to the nearby divan.

Charlotte instinctively wrapped her legs around his waist, the heat of her core pressing deliciously against the hard ridge of his arousal, eliciting a groan of approval from deep within his chest.

As he settled onto the divan with Charlotte straddling his lap on her knees, Andrew trailed a path of heated kisses along the column of her throat, his lips and tongue worshipping the delicate skin he found there. His hands deftly unfastened his falls, releasing the thick shaft that jutted out with hunger.

Driven by an overwhelming need to taste her, to bring her to the heights of ecstasy, Andrew lowered his head to her breasts, drawing one rosy nipple into the wet heat of his mouth. He suckled and teased, his tongue swirling around the hardened peak, while his fingers plucked and rolled its twin. Charlotte arched into his touch, her fingers tangling in his hair as she held him to her, silently begging for more.

When at last, she lowered herself onto his lap, the touch of her slick quim against his burning cock nearly brought him undone. Charlotte ground her hips against his. The friction of her wet heat against his engorged erection drove him to the brink of madness. With a groan of surrender, Andrew tore his mouth from her breast, his breathing ragged and uneven.

"Charlotte," he rasped, his voice rough with need. "I need to taste you, to feel you come undone beneath my tongue."

She stilled atop him, her eyes wide and uncertain. At his nudging, she stood hesitantly, her feet bracketing his thighs. Impatiently, he gripped her hips firmly and brought her closer until her glistening folds were a mere breath away from his eager mouth.

"Your cunny is exquisite," he breathed. "And it's mine."

The first swipe of his tongue had them both moaning in unison, the taste of her desire a heady elixir on his lips. While his pulsing erection jerked at every opportunity for attention, Andrew licked and caressed her folds, gently scraped her swollen bud with his teeth, then soothed it with his tongue. Panting and moaning more and more without inhibition, Charlotte finally whispered his name.

"Andrew. Oh my, Andrew…"

He knew then that she was close. Bracing himself for the overwhelming pleasure that was to come, he nudged her hips away from him. Before she could protest, he said huskily, "Get on your knees, Charlotte. Now."

She did his bidding, and even before her knees touched the soft cushion, he lowered her quim over his rigid cock. She screamed as her orgasm broke over his cockhead and screamed again when the climax crested and crashed upon being filled completely. The silky muscles of her heat fluttered around his hard cock in waves, as his unyielding grip lifted her over his member, then thrust into her again.

"Christ…" he rasped.

His own orgasm rose higher and higher, then he fell over the peak, plunging into the weightless abyss. He floated until another surge of pleasure thrust forcefully through him, again and again, as his body lurched forward, holding his wife close in his arms. She was the redemption he had needed all along.

With the pleasures of their joining humming in their heads and hearts, they remained in each other's embrace. He stroked her hair tenderly while she drew circles around his scar, their racing hearts gradually slowing to a more even rhythm. Andrew gradually became aware of a dampness on his shoulder, the saltiness of Charlotte's tears mingling with the sheen of sweat on his skin. Alarm coursed through him, and he tilted her chin up, forcing her to meet his gaze.

"What troubles you, my love?" His voice was a mix of concern and fear. Had he hurt her in some way? Did she regret their joining, longing instead for the duke she had left behind?

But Charlotte merely shook her head, burying her face in the crook of his neck as she clung to him, her tears flowing anew. Understanding that she was not yet ready to voice the demons that haunted her, Andrew simply held her tighter, his hands stroking her back in soothing circles, pouring all his heart into the embrace, grateful that he had this second chance with the woman he had burned for over the past six years.

ANDREW AND CHARLOTTE embarked on a blissful life together in their London townhouse. With Charlotte's law office now relocated to Andrew's London Bank building, they fell into a delightful routine of breakfasting together each morning before arriving at the office arm in arm. As they parted ways to attend to their respective duties, Andrew would give her a sidelong glance filled with longing, a promise of the passion that awaited them.

Throughout the day, as they immersed themselves in their work, Andrew would find himself drawn to her office, unable to resist the pull of her presence. He would coax her to leave, to return home with him, his eyes smoldering with desire.

In the evenings, when they attended gatherings or soirées, Andrew's jealousy would often get the better of him. The sight of other men's gazes raking over his beautiful wife would stoke a fire within him, a primal need to claim her as his own. In those moments, he would pull her into a secluded linen closet or an empty room, his hands roaming her body with a desperate urgency.

"I thought I'd die without being inside you this very moment," he'd growl against her ear, his voice needy. "The way all those men were looking at you, I must remind you to whom your pleasure belongs." And remind her he did, his thick, rigid member plunging into her depths with a fervor that left her trembling.

CHARLOTTE FOUND HERSELF falling head over heels for this man, so desperate and transparent in his need for her. She performed her legal duties with diligence, then floated around their townhouse, attending to her countess duties and meeting with lawyers to oversee Andrew's charitable endeavors. She pored over finances and sought ways to improve operations, her heart swelling with pride at the good they were doing together.

At night, Andrew would storm into the parlor, the study, wherever she happened to be, and sweep her into his arms, devouring her with a hunger that never seemed to be sated.

"I missed you all day," he'd confess, his eyes dark with longing.

Charlotte would laugh, her head tilted back in joy, and he would trail kisses along the taut lines of her neck, then lower to her breasts.

Sometimes, his lovemaking was tender, filled with gentle warnings and nudging caresses. Other times, he would surprise her as she lay on her stomach, lost in a book. He'd sneak up on her silently, slip his hands beneath her night rail, spread her legs, and take her with such fervor that it left her gasping and clinging to him.

When she yelped in surprise, he'd whisper hotly against her skin, "Next time, I better find you touching yourself, thinking of me, or I shall take you until you can't remember your name."

They would discuss law, politics, and philosophy, engaging in passionate debates that often ended with Andrew throwing in the towel in the name of peace and pleasure.

"Ride my tongue, and I shall declare you the winner," he'd say darkly.

Every time they came together, the sexual tension between them was electric. They could do nothing but cling to each other, screaming one another's names in ecstasy until they collapsed into the blissful oblivion of sleep.

"Will you tell me why you won't let me mount you on your back?" he asked gently one day.

She shook her head, her eyes growing distant.

"Tell me why, then," he pressed softly, concern threading

through his voice.

She remained silent, unable to voice the memories that haunted her.

Andrew studied her face, recognizing the shadows that crossed her features. Understanding that some wounds needed time to heal, he simply pulled her closer, content to love her in the ways that brought her only pleasure.

Theirs was a love that consumed them, body and soul, a love that burned brighter with each passing day. Within the sanctuary of their embrace, they found a peace and contentment that knew no bounds.

POISON

12 January 1837

THE BUSTLING ATMOSPHERE of the gentleman's club provided a welcome respite from the chaos of London's streets. The soft murmur of conversations and the clink of glasses created a soothing ambiance, allowing members to relax and unwind after a long day.

Tucked away in a quiet corner of the club, Andrew sat engrossed in a contract, his brow furrowed in concentration. He relished these rare moments of solitude, away from the demands of his business empire.

However, his peace was short-lived. The sound of approaching footsteps drew his attention, and he looked up just in time to see the smug face of Wilson appear before him. Andrew's jaw clenched, a flicker of annoyance passing over his features at the unwelcome intrusion.

"Ah, Carlisle, I believe congratulations are in order," Wilson declared, his voice cutting through the quiet hum of the club.

"Thank you," Andrew replied tersely, his eyes never leaving the document in his hands. He had no desire to engage in small talk with the man, whose presence always seemed to grate on his nerves.

Wilson, undeterred by the cool reception, glanced about for a servant and barked, "Brandy!" before settling himself in the chair opposite Andrew. He leaned back, crossing his legs and regarding Andrew with a self-satisfied smile.

"Do you know why I recommended you for the position of

an honorary bencher, Carlisle?" he asked, his expression one of self-satisfaction.

"To have me at your beck and call, I presume." Andrew's gaze moved across the document.

Wilson chuckled, a grating sound that set Andrew's teeth on edge. "You are as obedient as an ill-tempered feline. No, that would be a foolish endeavor. In truth, I was doing you a favor. As an honorary bencher, you could vote on court policies that may impact your business practices. And now, you have the means to keep a watchful eye on Chatham and your lovely wife."

At the mention of Charlotte, Andrew's gaze lifted to meet Wilson's, his countenance hardening. "Speak one disparaging word about my wife, Wilson, and I shall ensure my face is the last thing you'll see before drawing your final breath," he hissed.

Wilson, seemingly unfazed by the threat, took a languid sip of his brandy before setting the glass upon the table. "I meant no offense to Lady Carlisle, of course. But you know how men can be, Carlisle, and Chatham is no exception to that rule."

A shadow passed over Andrew's features, his brow furrowing with suspicion.

"He seems to seek out your wife's company when she is in court. They are often seen together, engaged in conversation. Nothing improper, mind you, but a glance here, a touch there... I merely thought it prudent to inform you, as I would hate for my new bride to be gallivanting about with a former lo... colleague, causing tongues to wag. It would not bode well for our company if rumors of your being cuckolded were to spread."

Andrew's eyes narrowed, his grip tightening on the document he was holding. "Our company?"

Wilson shifted uncomfortably, realizing his slip of the tongue. "What I meant to say is that I have a vested interest in the success of your enterprise, Carlisle."

Tossing the papers onto the table, Andrew leaned back in his seat, his gaze never wavering from Wilson's face. Though his initial impulse was to storm out and confront Chatham directly, he knew such an action would be the height of folly. He had not built his empire by acting on childish whims.

Some foolish men might call the scoundrel out, demanding satisfaction, but Andrew had never understood how putting a bullet in the man would bring about any desirable change. Besides, there would be ample time for that later, after he had gotten to the bottom of Wilson's true motives.

"What is it that you want, Wilson? Surely, you're not informing me of my wife's impending infidelity out of the goodness of your heart."

Wilson laughed, a forced, awkward sound. "Your reputation is at stake, Carlisle. As the president of the company, any rumors regarding your lack of control, be it over your business or your household, may sow seeds of doubt in the minds of our investors."

Andrew regarded the man with an unwavering gaze, then chuckled softly. Wilson started in his seat. Was this a veiled threat, or was Wilson revealing his hand? Either way, the message was clear. He wanted her out of the Inner Temple and away from Chatham's influence.

"You have taken up enough of my time, Wilson. I shall be sure to convey your regards to His Majesty when I see him tomorrow," Andrew said.

At the mention of Andrew's royal connections, Wilson blanched, his earlier bravado faltering. With a curt nod, he turned to leave but paused briefly to deliver a parting shot.

"The agenda for the next bencher's meeting shall include a vote on Lady Carlisle's disbarment," he said, then beat a hasty retreat.

As Andrew sat, his mind roared with conflicting emotions. The conversation with Wilson had left him unsettled, a nagging sense of unease lingering in the pit of his stomach. Though he knew better than to take the man's words at face value, jealousy flooded his mind at the thought of Charlotte spending time with Chatham, even if it was in a purely professional capacity.

He trusted his wife implicitly, knew that she would never betray him, but the knowledge did little to quell the irrational fear that gnawed at his insides. Chatham was a handsome, charming man, a far cry from the rough-hewn docker Andrew was. What if, in the course of their work together, Charlotte found herself drawn to the duke's refined manners and cultured ways? What if she came to regret returning his affection, longing for a life of elegance and sophistication that Andrew couldn't provide?

Even as these dark thoughts swirled through his mind, Andrew knew he could not stand in the way of Charlotte's dreams. She had worked so hard, sacrificed so much, to become a barrister, to make a name for herself in a world that sought to deny her existence. How could he, who loved her, be the one to crush her reason for being?

But the thought of losing her, of watching her slip away from him and into the arms of another man, was a prospect too terrible to contemplate. And yet, he knew any attempt to control her, to limit her interactions with Chatham or any other man, would only serve to drive a wedge between them.

Torn between his desire to protect what was his and his need to support his wife's aspirations, not to mention what his investors might demand if he didn't support their agenda, Andrew felt as though he were being pulled in all directions.

TRIAL

22 January 1837—London

T HE OLD BAILEY'S imposing stone facade cast long shadows in the winter morning light as Charlotte prepared to represent the Earl of Carlisle's family in what many considered an unwinnable case. Lord Byron had publicly accused Lady Daisy Creswell of compromising herself during their betrothal, leaving her reputation and her brother's business interests hanging in the balance.

"If it pleases the court, I am here to represent the Earl of Carlisle, Andrew—"

"I am well aware of who he is, Miss Morton. The question is, are you a qualified barrister?" Judge Hoffman's voice dripped with condescension.

Charlotte straightened her spine, meeting the judge's gaze. "Indeed, Your Honor. I graduated at the top of my class at Cambridge—"

"This court has no patience for boasting and self-aggrandizement, Miss Morton," the judge snapped. "A true lady would know better as would a qualified barrister."

A hush fell over the courtroom as Charlotte's voice rang out. "If I were not qualified to stand before you today, Your Honor, then I'm afraid the court has made a grave error in allowing me to enter, to don this robe and wig, and to take my place at this bench."

From his seat, Andrew quirked a brow at the judge, whose face now matched the hue of his bulbous, red nose. Andrew had never been fond of the man and was even less inclined to be now.

"Are you suggesting, Miss Morton, that my court is inept?" the judge shrieked.

"Certainly not, Your Honor," Charlotte replied, her tone even and measured. "I merely wished to emphasize that a court as esteemed as yours would never make such a grievous mistake. I have passed the bar under the tutelage of the Duke of Chatham, and I am here today to represent Lord Carlisle in this matter."

The judge leaned forward, his eyes narrowing. "There is a fundamental injustice at play here, wouldn't you agree, Miss Morton?"

Charlotte met his gaze unflinchingly. "I'm afraid I don't follow, Your Honor."

"The fact that you are a woman may prove advantageous," the judge said with a hint of a sneer. "As the sole female in this courtroom, I imagine some men might be swayed by sympathy, seeing you as the fairer sex, easy on the eye."

Andrew gritted his teeth, imagining the most painful ways to tear the man apart. But he soon relaxed as he watched Charlotte's fingers curl beneath the wooden table, her nails digging into the surface. Her claws were out, he mused. He felt proud she would grow stronger before animosity and fight her own battle, although he would gladly assist.

"I have the utmost faith, Your Honor," Charlotte began, her voice ringing with conviction, "that you will ensure the objectivity of all present. I also trust in your impartiality, as well as that of our learned colleague representing Lord Byron today. After all, I am but a humble representative of the court. The matter at hand, the accounts of the journalists, and your ultimate judgment will bear consequence only for Lord Carlisle and his family."

Judge Hoffman fixed Charlotte with a piercing stare, his voice echoing through the courtroom. "Were there written applications submitted for the presence of these journalists?"

"Yes, Your Honor," Charlotte replied.

"Provide me with their names." The judge's command hung

heavy in the air, a palpable weight pressing down on the proceedings.

As the interrogation wore on, Hoffman's interruptions became increasingly frequent, his questions serving as a barrier, preventing Charlotte from presenting her case in full. Andrew, observing the spectacle with growing frustration, cleared his throat pointedly, sending a warning to the judge to tread carefully.

The court listened, rapt, as the tale of injustice suffered by Daisy Creswell unfolded—Lord Byron's broken promise, his false claims that she had deliberately compromised her virtue to escape their engagement, and the harassment endured by an unchaperoned lady whose only crime was pursuing an education. However, when the time came for judgment, Lord Byron's reprimand was little more than a slap on the wrist, a mere crown to be paid in recompense.

From Andrew's perspective, Charlotte had emerged victorious on paper, and that was all the law would allow them. He recognized the inadequacy of the judgment even as he accepted its strategic value—they had established Byron as a liar in the public record.

THREE HOURS LATER, the Creswell family sat at a teashop, Andrew feeling proud of his wife's legal prowess despite the hollow nature of their victory. Across from him, Charlotte and Daisy sat rigidly, their faces set in stony expressions. Charlotte's fingers clenched and unclenched in her lap.

"You won. Be happy," Andrew said, though his tone suggested he understood the bitter taste of such limited justice.

Daisy's eyes flashed with indignation, her voice trembling with barely contained fury. "The compensation is humiliating. It might have been better if Byron wasn't fined at all."

Andrew rubbed his temples, the familiar weight of protecting his family while navigating society's constraints pressing down on him. "Byron was sufficiently embarrassed in a court of law, and the record shows him as a liar. I have my own methods of ensuring he pays his due for what he attempted to do to you."

Daisy's voice trembled with barely contained rage. "And the way the judge insulted Charlotte... I nearly leapt to my feet in outrage."

"He may have behaved if you had advised him to call you Lady Carlisle, Charlotte," Andrew said, though privately he seethed at the disrespect shown to his wife.

"Why should she not receive the respect she deserves merely for being a barrister? She was called to the bar by the Inns of Court and had every right to be there! And wasn't his insult indirectly directed at you, Andrew? Why aren't you angry?" Daisy exclaimed.

"I'm angry at the system that creates such injustices," Andrew said carefully, "but public displays of temper would only harm Charlotte's standing. Byron will answer for his lies through other means."

The weight of what they had accomplished—and what they could not—settled over the table. Charlotte had proven a woman could argue law as competently as any man, even if the system still refused to grant them equal justice.

Andrew's thoughts turned to securing his sister's future happiness, knowing that Byron's defeat, however limited, had at least cleared the path for better prospects. The afternoon's legal victory, modest though it was, had demonstrated that the Creswell family would not suffer attacks on their honor without consequence.

"I've been considering Lord Bridgewater as a potential suitor," Andrew said, watching Daisy's reaction carefully. "With Byron's accusations now publicly discredited, we can move forward with confidence."

Daisy's shoulders slumped, her earlier defiance giving way to weariness. "Who do you have in mind now?" she asked, her voice resigned and barely audible over the clatter of the carriage wheels.

"Lord Bridgewater. Have you made his acquaintance?"

A faint smile brightened Daisy's features. "Yes, I had the pleasure of dancing with him once."

Andrew leaned forward, his elbows resting on his knees. "And what was your impression of him?"

"He made for easy company."

Nodding, Andrew sat back, a look of satisfaction crossing his visage. "That aligns with my own assessment. He seems a decent man, not prone to fits of temper. To my knowledge, he has no vices. He is well-connected, and his wealth should ensure your comfort."

Shaking her head, Daisy sighed. "I need more time to find the right man. I don't expect a love match, but at the very least, someone with whom I can cultivate a friendship."

"That will come once you're married," he said, turning away from his sister's misery.

ANDREW STEPPED INTO the gentlemen's club, his eyes scanning the room until they landed on Lord Bridgewater. The viscount's self-assured countenance contradicted his slight frame as he sat stoically, a cigar in one hand and a document in the other. With a nod to a passing waiter, Andrew ordered a drink and settled into the plush leather chair across from his acquaintance.

"Good afternoon, Bridgewater," Andrew greeted pleasantly.

Bridgewater glanced up from his papers, a flicker of curiosity in his eyes. "Good day to you, Carlisle. To what do I owe the pleasure of your company? I don't recall having a meeting scheduled."

Andrew took a sip of his drink, leaning back in his chair and crossing his legs with an air of nonchalance. "No, we don't have a meeting, but I wished to discuss a matter of some importance with you." He paused, studying the viscount's reaction before continuing. "I'd like to propose the formation of an alliance between our families."

A frown creased Bridgewater's brow. "Am I to understand you're suggesting a matrimonial alliance?"

"Indeed. I assume a man of your age and station must be considering settling down. You're only a year my junior, after all."

Bridgewater shrugged, his expression noncommittal. "I'm in no particular rush since my previous betrothal ended in humiliation."

"So, you're not currently courting anyone?" Andrew pressed, his voice carefully neutral.

"No, I am not."

"Excellent. I believe you've been formally introduced to my sister, Daisy." He brought his glass to his lips, his eyes never leaving Bridgewater's face as he gauged the man's reaction.

"Yes, before the lady's betrothal to Lord Byron," Bridgewater remarked.

Andrew bristled at the mention of Byron, the callous reference to his sister's past a clear indication of Bridgewater's negotiating tactics. He sharpened his gaze, watching as the viscount set aside his document and focused on his cigar.

"I read that the judgment was in your favor," Bridgewater said, exhaling a plume of smoke.

"That's correct. Byron was found to have falsely accused my sister to avoid fulfilling his promised investment."

Bridgewater nodded, a calculating look in his eyes. "Regardless of the judgment, I trust you understand my reservations."

"I have no doubt as to Daisy's innocence," Andrew said firmly.

"Of course, of course," Bridgewater murmured, waving a hand dismissively. "I assume you're eager to see Lady Daisy betrothed once more, to put this unpleasantness behind her."

Andrew leaned forward, his elbows resting on his knees. "On the contrary, Bridgewater. My eagerness stems from the fact that I'd like to take my new bride on an extended honeymoon." The lie rolled smoothly off his tongue, a necessary evil in the game of negotiation. "I'd like to take her for at least three months, and naturally, I want to ensure my sister's protection in my absence."

Bridgewater considered this, tapping his cigar against the ashtray. "And how does Lady Daisy feel about this arrangement?"

"She is amenable," Andrew assured him. "In fact, she has quite a positive impression of you."

A smile ghosted across Bridgewater's lips. "I'm grateful for her kindness." He paused, taking a long drag on his cigar before fixing Andrew with a piercing stare. "Tell me, Carlisle, are you in search of new shareholders?"

Andrew caught the underlying meaning in Bridgewater's words. "Capital is not a necessity, but I am seeking to add a name to approximately a thousand shares."

He suppressed a smile, pleased that Bridgewater had broached the subject of shares first. It was a clear indication of the viscount's eagerness to negotiate the terms of the marriage contract. And why wouldn't he? Daisy was quite the prize— beautiful, healthy, charming, and wealthy.

Bridgewater leaned back in his chair, studying Andrew with a calculating gaze. "Of all the women in the world, it's intriguing that you chose such a complex lady."

A wry smile tugged at Andrew's lips. "The heart wants what it wants, unfortunately."

"I must say, I find your sister to be quite amicable. If I'm not mistaken, she has studied medicine, has she not?"

And there it was. The negotiation was now in full swing, the winds of bargaining billowing the sails of their conversation.

Andrew nodded, his eyes glinting with pride. "She has, in-deed. Daisy is accomplished in many areas. Your children will undoubtedly be clever."

"I believe she harbors a desire to practice medicine," Bridge-water mused, his tone carefully neutral.

"You're well-informed. She does, but she also understands and respects her place within the household. What are your thoughts on career-minded women, Bridgewater?"

"Not favorable, I'm afraid."

Andrew nodded, feeling a flicker of disappointment. He had hoped to find Daisy a husband who would, at the very least, tolerate his sister's lifelong dream, even if he couldn't openly support her.

"Daisy possesses more energy and good cheer than anyone I know," he said, his voice warm with affection. "Life with her will never be dull."

Bridgewater smiled, but there was a hint of reservation in his eyes. "I am pleased to hear it. However, as much as I admire both you and your sister, I hope you'll understand that I must conduct my own investigation before agreeing to the betrothal. It's not a matter of trust, but rather for the sake of appearances."

"Of course," Andrew agreed, his expression somber. "In fact, I would prefer that you do so, to ensure there will be no lingering doubts about her innocence in the minds of the *ton* when you wed."

"Might I have two weeks to reach a decision?"

"Certainly."

Andrew drained the last of his drink and rose from his chair. "It was a pleasure, Bridgewater."

The two men shook hands, each gauging the strength and resolve of the other's grip.

THE LETTER

4 February 1837

ANDREW STOOD MOTIONLESS in the doorway, his heart breaking at the sight of her anguish, knowing all too well the cause of her pain. Her fingers tore at a letter written in an expert hand, her distress evident in every movement.

When she finally turned to face him, the tracks of her tears glistened on her visage, but her eyes blazed. "These are tears of frustration, not weakness or defeat!" she exclaimed.

Andrew stepped closer, his arms outstretched in a silent offer of comfort. Charlotte fell into his embrace, her body melding to his as he stroked her hair and pressed tender kisses to her forehead.

"I know, love. I know," he murmured.

As her breathing gradually steadied, Charlotte gently extricated herself from his arms, her gaze searching his face for answers. "They've disbarred me because you kissed me in public. How was that my fault?"

Andrew wiped away the tears staining her cheeks. "It wasn't, and I'm sorry," he said softly.

"Did you know?"

"I learned of it a few days ago."

"Why didn't you tell me?"

"I didn't think informing you ahead of time would help in any way."

Charlotte sank onto the chaise by the window, her gaze fixed on the world outside, a world that seemed to be crumbling around her. Andrew had known that losing her law license would devastate her, but the depth of her anger and suffering was even more acute than he had ever imagined.

"Is there anything you can do? You know what I was willing to give up for a career in law. I beg of you to help me. I don't ask for anything. Only this." Her voice was small, pleading.

"I shall do what I can, love."

Charlotte gestured to the letter, now lying in tatters on the floor. "I can't believe one letter is all it took to change my life. No appeal, no opportunity to prove my innocence. Surely, they know the truth of what happened. But they're shackling the victim."

Andrew's mind raced, searching for a way to ease her pain, though he knew his own actions had contributed to this catastrophe. The weight of his guilt threatened to crush him—he had been so consumed with protecting his empire that he had failed to protect the woman he loved most. "Why don't you put your energy toward finding a replacement for yourself?"

Charlotte studied his face, noting the raw anguish in his eyes, the way his shoulders sagged with remorse. For a moment, she glimpsed the depth of his regret, but the wound was too fresh for forgiveness.

She nodded, dabbing at her eyes with a lace-trimmed handkerchief bearing Andrew's initials.

In the days that followed, Charlotte threw herself into her work with quiet determination, finding solace in the only legal work still available to her. Though she could no longer practice as a barrister, she could still use her knowledge to help those who needed it most. Andrew watched from a distance, his guilt evident in every glance, but he respected her need for space even as it tore at his heart. The house felt heavy with unspoken words and the weight of a future that seemed increasingly uncertain.

THE TERRIBLE TRUTH

27 February 1837

THREE WEEKS LATER, Charlotte sat at her desk, the flickering candlelight casting shadows across the scattered papers before her. Her once pristine barrister's robes hung limply on a nearby hook, a painful reminder of the career she had lost. The grief of being disbarred still weighed heavily on her, a constant ache that seemed to permeate her heart and occasionally gave it a painful squeeze.

Despite her grief, Charlotte found purpose in crafting documents for women and girls rescued from brothels and workhouses. These papers would provide them with new opportunities for jobs, marriages, and even emigration.

As she worked, Charlotte reflected on Andrew's involvement in these rescue missions, feeling a newfound respect for her husband's compassion. Sealing the final document, she felt fulfilled. She gathered the papers in ordinary-looking envelopes and pushed a cart toward the post office, her steps light with purpose.

Suddenly, a figure emerged from the shadows of a dark alleyway, causing Charlotte to yelp in surprise, her heart leaping into her throat. "What is the meaning of this, sir? You nearly frightened me to death!"

The man bowed his head in apology, his voice low and contrite. "I beg your pardon, Lady Carlisle. I have been waiting for an opportunity to speak with you in private."

Charlotte's brow furrowed in confusion, her eyes narrowing

as she studied the stranger's face. Upon recognition, Charlotte felt a flicker of unease, her body tensing as she wondered what possible reason this man could have for seeking her out. "You are Lord Byron, are you not? But why should you wish to speak with me?"

She cast a furtive glance over his person, searching for any sign of a concealed weapon, but found none. The presence of the cart between them and the bustling street nearby provided a measure of comfort, but still, she couldn't help but wonder how Andrew would react if he were to stumble upon them together.

Schooling her features into a mask of calm, Charlotte addressed the man before her. "What can I do for you, Lord Byron?"

Lord Byron's expression turned serious, his voice carrying a bitter edge. "I came to warn you, Lady Carlisle, though I confess my motives are not entirely pure. Your husband humiliated me publicly—made me appear a fool and a liar before all of London society. My reputation shall never recover from that courtroom spectacle." His hands clenched at his sides. "But even in my anger, I cannot stand by and watch him destroy an innocent woman with the same calculated cruelty he showed me."

Charlotte remained silent, her heart beginning to race as she sensed the gravity of what he was about to reveal.

"Your husband planned your disbarment from the start. He promised his shareholders he'd ruin you after the case. He even voted against reinstating your license. I heard this directly from Wilson and other Sovereign Seas shareholders. They boasted of it at their club, speaking of you as if you were merely a business obstacle to be removed." His voice grew quieter, more intense. "I may despise your husband, Lady Carlisle, but I recognize that you are a victim of his machinations. You deserve to know the truth of his betrayal."

With a curt nod, Lord Byron melted back into the shadows, leaving Charlotte alone with her thoughts, her mind reeling from the shocking accusation.

As the weight of Byron's words sank in, each syllable a dagger plunging deeper into her heart, Charlotte felt her world tilt on its axis. Her eyes widened in disbelief, her mouth falling open in a silent gasp of shock and betrayal. The air around her seemed to grow thick and heavy, as if conspiring to suffocate her with the awful truth of her husband's deceit.

"No," she whispered, her voice faint above the roaring of blood in her ears. "No… he wouldn't…"

But even as the words left her lips, Charlotte knew in her heart that it was all-too plausible. The pieces of the puzzle began to fall into place with sickening clarity—how Andrew had ruined her so publicly, his investors' interests, his guilty expression when she'd been disbarred.

A wave of nausea washed over her, her vision blurring with unshed tears as the bitter sting of betrayal mingled with the searing pain of shattered trust. How could the man she loved, the one to whom she had given her heart and soul, be capable of such cruelty, such calculated manipulation? The thought was too terrible to bear, and yet, the evidence was mounting, painting a picture of a marriage built on lies and deception.

With trembling hands, Charlotte gripped the cart for support, her knuckles turning white as she fought to maintain her composure. She knew she couldn't break down here, not in the middle of the street where anyone might see.

Squaring her shoulders, Charlotte pushed the cart forward, her steps no longer light and carefree, but heavy with the burden of knowledge and the weight of the difficult path that lay ahead.

CHARLOTTE'S FIRST STOP was the Duke of Chatham's office at the Inner Temple. As she entered, she found him in his court dress, complete with a powdered wig, holding a piece of paper. He stared at her like a startled hare.

"Charlotte! What on earth brings you here?" He leapt from his chair and strode toward her, his eyes wide with surprise and concern.

Quickly, she closed the door behind her. He enveloped her in a tight embrace, his hands stroking her back as he rocked her gently from side to side.

"I am overjoyed to see you, my dear. I've missed you terribly. How has Carlisle been treating you?" He held her at arm's length, his hands resting on her shoulders as he studied her face intently. "What troubles you? What has happened?"

Charlotte shook her head, her voice trembling slightly as she replied, "I am well enough. I've come to seek your assistance." She examined his countenance more closely, her brow furrowing. "You appear unwell yourself. Are you feeling ill?"

The duke sighed deeply, shaking his head as he gestured for her to take a seat. He poured them each a glass of brandy, which Charlotte accepted with a grateful nod, sipping the amber liquid cautiously to calm her frayed nerves.

"Suffice it to say, I have not slept well since your nuptials," he confessed, settling into the chair beside her.

"Have you been lonely, then?"

"Immensely so. I feel as though an arrow has pierced my heart. Though we correspond, it is a poor substitute."

Charlotte took a deep breath, steeling herself for the words that would follow. "Then perhaps fortune smiles upon you, for I may soon be leaving my husband."

Chatham's eyes widened in shock. "Why ever would you do such a thing? I was under the impression that you and Carlisle were quite content together."

Unable to meet his gaze, Charlotte lowered her head, blinking back the tears that threatened to fall. "I may have loved a different man, an illusion of the one I thought I knew. It seems I loved the version of himself that he presented to me. It has come to light that he may have been plotting my disbarment and ruination from the very beginning. Now, I find myself questioning everything I once held true."

The duke leaned forward, his voice gentle and coaxing as he offered her a crisp linen kerchief. "Tell me, what has led you to suspect such treachery on Carlisle's part?"

Charlotte accepted the kerchief gratefully, dabbing at her reddened eyes as she spoke. "It was Lord Byron who came to me, claiming that Lord Wilson and other shareholders had confessed the plot."

"He wouldn't be the most impartial source. However, I've heard Wilson repeat the same confession to anyone who would listen. It seems he is determined to make your life miserable."

She nodded and raised her gaze to meet Chatham's, her face half-hidden behind his kerchief. "Do you believe these allegations are true?"

The duke's expression turned regretful. "If it were Wilson alone, I may doubt his words, but other shareholders have verified the claim."

A thin shriek of despair escaped her throat as she covered her mouth with the soft fabric and began to wail. Chatham reached out, embracing her tightly, his visage absorbing some of her pain. After a long while, when her cries became sniffles, he grasped Charlotte's hand tightly in his own. "I shall do anything you wish, Charlotte. How can I assist you now?"

Charlotte took a deep breath, squaring her shoulders as she met his gaze. "I suppose I must speak with him, confront him." Her voice trembled slightly from the fear of the pain that threatened to overwhelm her.

Chatham's grip on her hand tightened, his thumb stroking the delicate skin of her wrist. "Will you be all right to face him alone?"

She smiled faintly, an attempt to put His Grace's mind at ease. "Yes, I believe so," she said, her voice steadier than before.

Chatham's eyes softened, a flicker of tenderness amidst the concern that etched his features. "You are always welcome to stay with me, Charlotte, if you can bear the scandal that may follow."

Dimples appeared in her cheeks, a brief flash of humor in the face of her despair. "Thank you, but I may ask Madam Tansley if I may stay with her for a while. It may be the perfect location for us to rendezvous if you wished."

The duke's countenance brightened, making him look much younger in an instant. Rising to her feet, Charlotte disentangled her hand from Chatham's, her fingers lingering for a moment in his warm, comforting grasp. "I cannot thank you enough for your kindness and your unwavering support."

Chatham stood as well, bowing his head in a gesture of respect and affection. "Think nothing of it. I am, and always shall be, your most devoted friend."

With a final, grateful smile, Charlotte turned and made her way toward the door, her skirts swishing softly against the polished wood floor. As she stepped out into the corridor, she could feel the weight of Chatham's gaze upon her back.

As she walked through the halls of the Inner Temple, Charlotte's heart was a battleground of emotions. Despair and hope mingled in a dizzying dance. The thought of confronting Andrew, of facing the man who had so callously betrayed her trust, filled her with a sickening dread, but beneath that fear, there was a spark of the indomitable spirit that had carried her through so many challenges before.

And so, with a deep breath and a lifted chin, Charlotte stepped out into the bustling streets of London.

THE BREAKING POINT

ANDREW'S VOICE THUNDERED through the halls, his anger palpable in every syllable, when Charlotte crossed the threshold of their home. "Where have you been?" he roared, his eyes flashing.

Acutely aware of the servants' presence, Charlotte chose not to respond, instead striding past him with purposeful steps toward their bedchamber. Andrew followed closely behind, his silence a heavy weight upon the air between them. Once they were secluded within the privacy of their room, he closed the door with a resolute click, his gaze fixed on her face.

Charlotte turned to face him, her heart pounding in her chest as she took in his expression. In an instant, the anger that had contorted his features melted away, replaced by a look of deep concern. "What happened?"

The tenderness in his voice made her heart ache.

"Lord Byron intercepted me on the street," she replied, her tone even and controlled, betraying the tumult of emotions that raged within her.

Andrew's eyes narrowed, his jaw clenching as he registered the implications of her words. "Did he hurt you?" he asked, his voice sharp as a dagger's edge.

"Not in the way you might think," Charlotte said, her gaze never wavering from his. "He told me you had planned all along to destroy my career to appease your shareholders. Is it true?"

As the words left her lips, Andrew's face drained of color, his skin turning an ashen hue that reminded her of the sands of an hourglass, slipping away before her very eyes. In that moment, she knew, with a certainty that pierced her to the core, that he was guilty of the accusation laid at his feet.

A bitter laugh escaped her, the sound harsh and grating to her own ears. "What a fool I have been, to believe your love for me had conquered your aversion to my chosen path. You had planned to destroy me from the very beginning." Her voice broke on the last word, the weight of her realization threatening to crush her where she stood.

Unable to remain still, Charlotte began to pace the room, her skirts swishing around her ankles as she moved, her agitation evident in every line of her body.

"Why did you marry me?" she asked, her voice rising with each word. "You could have ruined me and been done with it, left me with some shred of dignity intact. Was it to control me? To keep me under your thumb? Or was it some twisted way of conquering the one woman who had dared to defy the system that men like you have built? Or perhaps it was nothing more than base lust, a desire to possess my body?"

She halted abruptly, her gaze raking over his form, taking in the rigid set of his shoulders, the stony expression on his face. He stood before her like a statue, unmoving and unfeeling, a far cry from the passionate, devoted husband she had thought him to be.

When at last he spoke, his voice was even, almost clinical in its detachment. "I hired you because I needed a barrister, and you were the only one willing to take on my case. I told my investors that I would ruin your career once the trial was over, a means to placate them for the time being. I meant it to a degree, but I was also conflicted. But I did not marry you out of spite, or some perverse need to conquer you. My affections, my love for you, were genuine. I fell in love with you because I've never known a woman as kind, as courageous, as utterly remarkable as you. I've loved you from the first day we met at Madam's."

Charlotte's heart clenched at his words, a part of her longing to believe him, to trust in the sincerity that shone in his eyes. But the bitter sting of betrayal was still too raw, the wound too fresh to be so easily soothed.

"Did you vote to have me disbarred?" she asked, her voice choking with emotion, dreading the answer as she knew, with a sickening certainty, what it would be.

"Yes." The single word fell from his lips like a condemnation, a final, damning blow to the fragile trust that had once bound them together.

Charlotte stared at him in stunned silence, her mind reeling as she tried to reconcile the man she had loved with the stranger who stood before her now.

"I cannot live with your betrayal," she said at last, her voice trembling with the force of her emotions. "I cannot bear to look at you, to be reminded every day of the fool I have been, the trusting, naive girl who believed in the illusion of your love."

With shaking hands, she began to pack her valise, her movements swift and purposeful as she gathered her belongings, the remnants of a life she could no longer claim as her own.

"Charlotte, please," Andrew said, his voice urgent. "I know I've hurt you, that you may never find it in your heart to forgive me. But we're married, bound together in the eyes of God and the law. We must work to heal the rift between us, to find a way to live together."

Charlotte shook her head, her eyes bright with unshed tears. "I have no desire to heal anything related to you, Andrew. Your very presence is a reminder of my own foolishness, my own blindness to the truth that was staring me in the face all along."

"You may not believe me"—his voice broke on the words— "but I love you, Charlotte. The thought of losing you, of living without you by my side, is too painful to bear. I cannot breathe without you. Please, I beg of you, do not leave me."

Charlotte's eyes flashed with anger and pain, her voice rising with each word as she confronted her husband. "You love your empire and your pride more than you could ever love me. You have no idea what I sacrificed to earn my degree, to secure my place at the Inns of Court!" Her hands clenched into fists at her sides, her body quivering with the strength of her despair. "I gave up so much, and you, who claim to love me, contributed to the very destruction of all I held dear!"

Andrew's face crumpled, his shoulders sagging under the weight of his guilt and shame. "I am sorry, Charlotte. I know I've been selfish, that my actions were wrong. It was my own fear and insecurity that influenced my vote." He took a step toward her, his eyes pleading for understanding. "I was terrified you would see me for the brute I truly am, that you would leave me for the duke. When Wilson told me you and Chatham were spending time together at the Inn, I couldn't bear the thought of losing you."

Charlotte's eyes widened in disbelief, her mouth falling open in shock. "Wilson? That snake told you the duke and I were close, and you believed him?" She shook her head, a bitter laugh escaping her lips.

"Not entirely," Andrew admitted, his gaze dropping to the floor. "But you'd been lovers once, and I was afraid."

"I was never the duke's lover, you stupid man!" Charlotte cried, her voice cracking with emotion.

Andrew raised his head, his brow furrowing in confusion. "What do you mean?"

"You saw us together, yes, but we weren't there alone."

"Someone else was in the room? Was she hiding?" Andrew frowned, his mind struggling to make sense of her words.

"Not a woman. A man, concealed behind the curtains."

Andrew's face further reflected his confusion. "Are you saying you and two men?"

Her complexion turning crimson, she exclaimed, "No! *They* feared being discovered." Charlotte took a deep breath, steeling herself to explain. "After the duke helped me at Cambridge, I returned the favor by pretending to be his lover, in case someone stumbled upon them, as you did that night."

Andrew staggered backward as if struck, his face draining of all color. Charlotte watched in stunned silence as the realization seemed to crash over him. She could see the exact moment when the full magnitude of what he had done hit him—the destruction of their marriage, her career, everything they had built together, all based on lies and his own fears.

"I've ruined us," he whispered, his voice hollow with horror. "I've destroyed our marriage, your career, everything... over nothing. Over lies." His hands shook as he pressed them to his temples. "Christ, Charlotte, what have I done? What have I done?"

He sank into a chair, his head falling into his hands as the magnitude of his failure seemed to overwhelm him. For several long moments, only his ragged breathing filled the silence.

When he finally looked up, his eyes were red-rimmed with unshed tears. "If not the duke, then who?"

Charlotte shook her head. The weight of her secret, the shame and pain she had carried for so long, threatened to crush her. She braced herself to speak the awful truth she'd been avoiding, denying. Her hands trembled as she clutched the kerchief tighter, her knuckles turning white with the force of her grip. She opened her mouth to speak, but the words caught in her throat, choking her with their intensity.

Charlotte inhaled deeply, summoning every ounce of courage she possessed. "Wilson," she said from behind the kerchief, her voice uneven.

The name hung in the air between them like a poison. Charlotte watched Andrew's face turn completely white, his eyes widening in shock as if she had struck him. His mouth opened, then closed, no sound emerging. For several heartbeats, the only sound in the room was her own ragged breathing.

Finally, she forced herself to continue. "He was the dean of the school. He threatened to expose me if I didn't... lie with him."

The words physically pained her, her face contorting as if the memories were shards of glass slicing her anew. "I had already completed nearly three years of study, sacrificed so much... I couldn't bear the thought of it all being for nothing."

Andrew stared at her in horrified silence, and Charlotte could see something breaking behind his eyes. His hands slowly curled into fists at his sides, his whole body radiating a fury that seemed desperate for an enemy to pummel, to punish, for daring to lay a hand on the woman he loved.

"Charlotte..." he choked out, the syllables jagged in his throat. "My God, I... I am so sorry. That I didn't protect you, that I unknowingly aligned myself with the monster who..."

Tears spilled down his cheeks as he reached for her with a shaking hand. Charlotte flinched instinctively, and she watched anguish twist his features. Slowly, giving her time to pull away, he brushed his fingers over her trembling ones.

"What can I do?" he implored, his voice cracking with agony. "How can I possibly atone for my part in your suffering? Tell me, and it shall be done, no matter the cost to myself."

Unable to face his reaction any longer, Charlotte covered her face fully, weeping bitterly as the excruciating memories washed over her. Her body shook with the force of her sobs, years of agony and shame pouring out of her in a torrent of tears. She had braced herself for Andrew's anger, his disgust, his rejection, but in that moment, all she could feel was the overwhelming relief of finally unburdening herself of the terrible truth.

Through her tears, she felt Andrew's arms encircle her, drawing her against his chest. "I'm sorry. I am so deeply sorry," he whispered, his voice thick with anguish.

At first, Charlotte's body remained rigid in his embrace, every muscle tense with the weight of betrayal and pain. But as her sobs continued to wrack her frame, she found herself gradually melting into his warmth, her resistance crumbling under the force of her own grief. She pressed her face against his chest, letting his familiar scent and the steady rhythm of his heartbeat anchor her as years of suppressed torment poured out of her.

His hands stroked her hair with infinite tenderness, and she heard him murmuring words of love and apology against the top of her head. For a moment—just a moment—she allowed herself to believe that his comfort could heal the wounds that had festered for so long.

But reality crashed back too quickly. This was the same man who had voted to destroy her career, who had chosen his investors over her dreams. The same man who had aligned himself with her tormentor.

Charlotte pulled away from his embrace, her heart already beginning to harden against the vulnerability she had just shown. She could not—would not—let his remorse undo the necessity of what came next.

Without meeting his eyes, she turned toward the door, each step carrying her further from the life they had built together. Behind her, she could feel Andrew's devastation, but she did not look back. The soft click of the door closing behind her was the final, irreversible ending of everything they had once been.

THE RECKONING

13 March 1837

S TANDING BEFORE HIS major shareholders in his study, Andrew's shoulders slumped, and his eyes were hollow with misery. He had foregone the comfort of a chair, too agitated to sit still.

In the days since his wife's departure, his rage had boiled over time and again, leading him to shatter every breakable item within reach and topple anything that wasn't bolted down. David, his ever-faithful valet, had carefully wrapped his bruised and bloodied knuckles after he had dented a wooden post with his bare fists, only for Andrew to turn his wrath upon another, lest he damage the supporting beam beyond repair.

Now, fresh blood seeped through the bandages, evidence of his unrelenting torment. He welcomed the physical pain, finding solace in the way it distracted him from the gaping wound in his chest where his heart had once been. In truth, he believed he deserved far worse, but he refrained from punishing himself to the point of incapacitation. He needed to maintain his faculties, to keep his mind sharp and focused on the task at hand—exacting his revenge upon the filth of a man, Wilson. That man would pay for hurting Charlotte, Andrew vowed to himself, his jaw clenching with barely contained fury.

Sensing the dark cloud that hung over their host, the four men summoned to his study sat in uneasy silence, their eyes fixed upon Andrew's disheveled form. He was clad in the rumpled laborer's clothes he had slept in for the past three days. Leaning against the window behind his desk, Andrew stared out into the lifeless garden, even the evergreens seeming to have deemed him unworthy of their vibrant hues.

As his heart clenched painfully once more at the thought of his beloved Charlotte, Andrew cleared his throat, the sound harsh and grating in the oppressive stillness of the room.

"Gentlemen," he began, his voice devoid of emotion, "I will spare you a lengthy explanation. I have called you here to inform you that I am transferring the ownership of the Sovereign Seas Trading Corporation to a charity, effective immediately."

A chorus of shocked exclamations filled the air, the men leaping to their feet in a flurry of agitated movement.

"What? Why?"

"You've gone mad, Carlisle!"

"Explain yourself at once!"

Andrew remained impassive, his gaze still fixed on the barren landscape beyond the window. "You have no need to know my reasons," he said coolly. "As the majority shareholder, I'm not obligated to inform you of my plans. Consider this a courtesy, nothing more."

"You cannot simply donate one of the most profitable companies in all of England, Carlisle! Who will operate the business? Surely, not the charity?" Rogers shouted, his face flushed with anger as he jabbed a finger in Andrew's direction.

"I'll do what I want with what I built with my own two hands if I please, and when I please." Andrew's eyes flashed dangerously as he turned to face the irate man. "Sit down, Rogers, before I forget myself and do something we'll both regret."

Chastened by the barely leashed violence in Andrew's tone, Rogers sank back into his chair, his mouth set in a grim line.

Andrew's gaze swept over the assembled men, his expression hard and unyielding. "I will return your investments for the expansion with interest and buy back your shares at a fair price, then proceed to give away every brick and mortar of this company to the charitable organization. I will walk away from it all, and you'll receive your payment once everything is finalized, provided you keep this matter strictly between yourselves. No one, and I mean no one, must know of this, especially Wilson."

"Why not Wilson?" Murphy asked, his brow furrowed.

"Because," Andrew said, his voice low and menacing, "he is the cause of this decision, and I plan to destroy him."

"Surely you jest, Carlisle," Rogers scoffed. "You would burn everything to the ground, all to avenge yourself upon one man?"

"What could Wilson possibly have done to warrant such drastic action?" Collins inquired, his tone somber.

Andrew's eyes narrowed, his jaw clenching with barely contained rage. "That is between me and Wilson. Suffice it to say, gentlemen, he committed an unforgivable act against my family. He will not receive a single penny from this company from now on. His fortune will evaporate overnight."

"He will be ruined," Murphy said, understanding dawning in his voice. "He could sell his secondary and tertiary homes, but he has nothing else."

"I'll allow him to keep those for the sake of his family. But I strongly advise you to withdraw all dealings with the man, be they business or personal, unless you're prepared for my wrath. And do not think to deceive me in this matter, for I did not rise to my current position by playing the fool. Now," he gestured to the stack of documents on his desk, "sign the papers and take your leave. I have nothing further to say on the matter."

As the men filed out of the room, their faces expressing shock, anger, and unease, Andrew remained motionless for several long minutes, staring at the closed door. The magnitude of what he had just done—dismantling the empire he had spent decades building—should have devastated him. Instead, he felt only a hollow emptiness where his ambition had once burned.

An hour later, Andrew made his way to the parlor, where his dear friend, the Marquess of Hereford, awaited him. Without a word, he poured himself a generous measure of brandy and sank into the chair beside his companion, his eyes fixed unseeing on the flickering flames of the hearth.

"You look positively dreadful, old chap," Hereford remarked, his tone gentle despite the bluntness of his words. "And I must say, you could do with a good scrubbing. The scent of wretchedness clings to you like a second skin."

Andrew remained silent, his gaze never wavering from the dancing flames.

"Do you know where she is?" Hereford asked.

Andrew nodded, his throat working as he swallowed back the lump that had taken up permanent residence there. "With Madam," he said hoarsely.

Hereford nodded, unsurprised by Charlotte's chosen refuge. They sat in companionable silence for a time, the only sound the crackling of the fire and the distant ticking of the grandfather clock in the hall.

"Will you go to her?" Hereford asked at length, his eyes searching Andrew's haggard face.

At this, Andrew's composure crumbled, his eyes filling with torment. "I can't," he whispered. "I have no right to lay my eyes on her, not after what I've done." With a shuddering sigh, he dropped his head into his hands, his fingers twisting in his hair as he pulled until the pain brought tears to his eyes.

Hereford placed a comforting hand on his friend's shoulder, his grip firm and steadying. "You love her, do you not?"

Andrew nodded, unable to speak past the tightness in his throat.

"Then that, my friend, is more than she believes she has at this moment. Love her in the best way you know how, in the way that she deserves. From what you've told me, I believe you've already begun to do just that."

Andrew nodded once more, a flicker of light sparking to life in his haunted eyes. "They signed the papers without further protest. Wilson will rue the day he dared to cause her even a moment's pain."

Hereford regarded his friend with sympathy. "Are you certain you wouldn't rather continue operating the company?"

Andrew shook his head. "That company was everything I had, everything I knew. It turns out it taught me nothing and gave me nothing. I lost the only woman I truly loved because I thought my business meant something. But there's no meaning to any of it without her."

His friend quirked his brows, then nodded approvingly. "I am honored to take over the operation on your behalf. Does the madam know?"

Andrew shook his head. "I shall visit Madam Tansley this afternoon."

Hereford stood and offered his hand. "You have work to do. Whatever you need, you only need to ask."

Andrew clasped his friend's hand and inclined his head in acknowledgement before rushing out of the parlor shouting, "David!"

ANDREW STEPPED INTO the brothel, feeling rather foolish in the formal attire his valet, David, had insisted upon. When Andrew mentioned his desire to appear presentable should he encounter Lady Carlisle, David had set aside his usual concern for his master's melancholy and thrown himself into the task with determined efficiency, selecting a suit of vibrant royal-blue to emphasize Andrew's broad shoulders.

His heart pumped arduously within his ribcage, seemingly too large to be contained. With a deep, steadying breath, he glanced around the room, his eyes searching for any sign of Charlotte.

"Why, Andrew!" A veteran of the brothel, Miss Amy, greeted him with a warm smile, her eyes twinkling with genuine affection. "Have you come to see Madam, my lord?"

"Indeed, I have," Andrew replied, inclining his head.

"You'll find her in her office, if you wish to proceed directly," Amy said, gesturing down the corridor.

As Andrew turned to take his leave, Amy called out after him, "Your wife is a true gem, my lord. Such an intelligent and kind-hearted woman!"

At the mention of Charlotte, Andrew's heart gave a mighty thump, his step faltering for the briefest of moments. Without responding, he continued down the hallway, his knuckles rapping gently on the door to Madam's office.

Madam, as always, was the picture of refinement and grace, her appearance so polished that one might think she was expecting a visit from the royal family. With a warm smile, she welcomed Andrew into her embrace, her arms opening wide to receive him. He bent to place a chaste kiss on her cheeks, his own arms encircling her petite frame with the utmost care, lest he crush her.

As Madam settled herself into her favorite armchair, a ghastly combination of red, orange, and green that never failed to offend Andrew's sensibilities, she fixed him with a pointed look.

"So, you've made quite the mess of things, haven't you?" she remarked, her tone more observational than accusatory.

Andrew sank onto the settee opposite her, his head bowed low, unable to meet her penetrating gaze.

"Have you come to see her?" Absent was any sympathy in her voice.

"No."

Madam sighed, her fingers lacing together in her lap. "She's doing remarkably well, all things considered. I'm not certain I would have fared half so admirably at her age."

At this, Andrew shrank further into himself, his shoulders hunching as if to protect him from the weight of his own guilt and regret.

"If you didn't come to see her, then why are you here? Surely you didn't think I would welcome you with open arms, not after what you've done?"

Andrew glanced up at her then, a sheepish expression on his face. "You did, though," he muttered.

Madam waved a dismissive hand, her eyes twinkling with affection. "That was me greeting the boy I've come to love as my own. This, however, is me speaking to my son, wondering how on earth I managed to raise such a scoundrel."

At her words, Andrew dropped his head into his hands, his fingers raking through his hair in a gesture of frustration and despair.

"You do look very handsome today, I must say," Madam continued, her tone softening once more. "You ought to dress like this more often, though I'm not so naïve as to believe you did it for my benefit." She paused, studying his face intently. "Are you quite certain you didn't come here hoping to see her?"

Andrew sat up straight, his shoulders squaring as he met Madam's gaze. "Would she agree to see me if I asked?"

Madam shook her head. "No, my dear."

With a grunt of frustration, Andrew rose from his seat and began to pace the room, his agitation evident in every line of his body. Suddenly, he turned to face the wall, one hand braced against the smooth surface as if to steady himself.

"How is she, truly?" he blurted. "Is she eating? Sleeping? Does she... does she speak of me at all?"

Madam remained silent for a moment, her expression thoughtful as she considered her response. When at last she spoke, her voice was gentle. "She doesn't sleep much, I'm afraid. And when she does, it's often fitful, plagued by dreams that leave her weeping. She's thrown herself into her work, spending long hours in this office to distract herself from the pain." She paused, her eyes meeting Andrew's with a knowing look. "She hasn't mentioned you by name, but she doesn't need to. It's clear in the sorrow that haunts her eyes just how deeply she misses you."

Andrew's hands clenched at his sides, the image of Charlotte weeping alone in the darkness nearly bringing him to his knees. He felt the sting of tears behind his own eyes, and he swallowed hard against the tightness that gripped his throat. "Do you truly believe that? That she misses me, even after all I've done?"

"Yes, my darling boy. I know she does." Madam's hand came to rest on his shoulder.

Desperate to maintain some semblance of composure, to cling to the tattered remnants of his pride, Andrew sought to steer the conversation to safer ground. He stepped away from Madam's touch as he spoke. "I've made a decision. I intend to sign over the ownership of the Sovereign Seas to your charity."

A stunned silence followed his words, and when Andrew turned to gauge Madam's reaction, he found her standing motionless, her eyes wide.

"Ma?" he said softly, the childhood endearment slipping from his lips.

A deep furrow appeared between Madam's brows, and she reached into her pocket to retrieve a delicate lace kerchief, dabbing at her eyes with a trembling hand. "Oh, Andrew. The proudest day of my life was when you learned to read. Do you remember? You were such a bright boy, with a heart so full of honor and a desire to do what was right. I feared that your wealth and success might have led you astray, but I see now that I was wrong. Today, my dear, is the second proudest day of my life. I am truly blessed to call you my son."

Overwhelmed, Andrew crossed the room in a few long strides, gathering Madam into his arms and holding her close. He buried his face in her hair, inhaling the familiar scent that had always meant comfort and safety to him, even in his darkest moments.

"Ma," he whispered, his voice choked with tears. "Do you think she could ever find it in her heart to forgive me?"

Madam rubbed soothing circles on his back, her voice soft and reassuring. "I cannot say for certain, my darling. But you must try. You must fight for her."

Andrew released her then, his head bowed once more, but this time, there was a glimmer of hope in his eyes. "I miss her so much. But I fear seeing her now would only cause her more pain."

Madam nodded, her expression one of understanding. "I agree, my dear. The hurt is still too raw, the memories too fresh. Give her time. I will tell her how wretched you looked, though I must say, your suit is quite dashing."

A faint smile graced Andrew's features, the first since Charlotte's departure. "Hereford has agreed to oversee the company and manage the finances for the charity," he said.

"Ah, Lord Hereford. I've always liked that man."

"Indeed. I have no doubt he will excel in his duties."

Madam studied Andrew's face, her eyes searching his. "And what of you, my dear? What will you do once the ownership is transferred?"

Andrew sighed, rubbing his face. "In truth, I don't know. So much depends on whether Charlotte will allow me back into her life when all is said and done. Perhaps I will travel, see the world while I nurse my wounds, and try to find my way back to the man I once was."

Madam reached out, taking his hand in hers and giving it a gentle squeeze. "You are a good man, Andrew Creswell, and I have every faith that you will find your way back to happiness, back to the woman who holds your heart."

With a final, grateful embrace, Andrew took his leave, his steps heavy but his heart lightened by the knowledge that Charlotte was not lost to him completely.

DAISY'S WEDDING

T HE CHURCH BUZZED with excitement as the wedding party gathered, awaiting the bride's entrance. Lord Bridgewater stood stoically at the altar, resplendent in his white suit and purple cravat.

Andrew, surprised by the grand scale of the celebration, felt grateful for his sister's acceptance of her groom. His mind, however, was preoccupied with thoughts of Charlotte. The past month had been agonizing, each moment an eternity of suffering. Nights were the worst, haunted by memories of her smile, her laughter, and the crushing reality of her absence.

As Andrew paced restlessly, the church doors swung open. He turned, his breath catching as his eyes met Charlotte's. For a moment, time stood still, the world fading away, leaving only them and their shared memory. When at last the spell was broken, Andrew found himself struggling to find his voice, his tongue heavy and clumsy in his mouth. "Good morning," he managed, bowing stiffly as she curtsied before him.

"My lord," she replied, her voice soft and tentative. "I apologize if my presence comes as a surprise. Daisy was kind enough to extend an invitation, and I found myself quite unable to refuse."

"Of course, you are most welcome," he said, his eyes observing the dark circles under her eyes and her form, which appeared even more delicate than before.

"I ought to find my seat," she said, her eyes evading his.

Andrew nodded toward a nearby footman instead of escorting Charlotte himself, a silent signal that he was aware of her discomfort around him. He watched as she made her way to her seat, greeting the footman with a smile that sent a spike of jealousy through his heart. Her proximity set every nerve alight with longing so intense he thought he might go blind.

He fought to keep his gaze from straying to where she sat, knowing that the sight of her would only serve to deepen the ache in his chest. Yet, he could not help but be aware of her, his senses attuned to her every movement, every shift of attention.

Forcing himself to focus on the ceremony ahead, Andrew turned as the sound of approaching footsteps drew him from his tortured reverie. He saw his sister descending the stairs, her bridal attendants trailing carefully behind her. Daisy's face was lined with nervous excitement, her smile tremulous as she met her brother's gaze. Andrew forced himself to return the smile, though he feared it came across as more of a grimace, a poor facsimile of the joy he knew he ought to feel on this momentous occasion.

As Daisy reached the bottom of the stairs, Andrew extended his hand, clasping hers tightly in his own. "How are you faring, my dear?"

"I am well, Andrew. Truly." Daisy searched his face, her brow furrowing slightly. "But what of you? You look quite shaken."

Andrew swallowed hard, fighting to maintain his composure in the face of his sister's gentle inquiry. "I am fine. Please, do not trouble yourself on my account."

A look of understanding passed over Daisy's features, her eyes softening with sympathy. "I take it you have seen Charlotte, then?"

"I have. A bit of warning might have been appreciated."

Daisy's face fell, her eyes filling with tears. "Oh, Andrew, I am so sorry. I wanted her here, to share in my happiness. I was uncertain if she would come."

Andrew sighed. "It's all right, Daisy. I am a grown man, and she is your sister-in-law. This is your day, and you should not have to worry about my feelings."

Daisy attempted a watery smile, but the tears continued to gather in her eyes, threatening to spill over at any moment. Andrew pulled her into a gentle embrace, mindful of her delicate gown and carefully arranged hair.

"Hush now. This is a day for joy and celebration, not for tears shed on my behalf. You look radiant, and I wish you and Lord Bridgewater find every happiness together."

Daisy clung to him for a moment longer before she pulled away. With a final, reassuring squeeze of her hand, Andrew escorted his sister to the entrance of the church, ready to guide her down the aisle and into the waiting arms of her groom. And though his own heart was heavy with the weight of his loss, he could not help but feel a flicker of hope at the sight of Daisy's luminous smile.

As the music swelled and the congregation rose to their feet, Andrew took his place beside his sister, his head held high, and his shoulders squared.

CHARLOTTE HAD ANTICIPATED seeing Andrew at the wedding, but nothing could have prepared her for the surge of emotions that coursed through her upon laying eyes on him. The mere sight of him sent a jolt of electricity through her veins, leaving her simultaneously overstimulated and bereft of coherent thought.

As the bridal march began, Charlotte took in the elegant decorations and the sizeable gathering of guests. Then, Andrew appeared, escorting Daisy down the aisle. Charlotte noticed the sharper angles of his jawline and the dark circles under his eyes. Though he didn't meet her gaze directly, she knew he was acutely aware of her presence.

Daisy was radiant in her white-and-lavender gown, with a lengthy train and a crown of flowers. Susie followed behind in a matching lavender dress, both women a vision of beauty as they made their way down the aisle.

Suddenly, in a single, heart-stopping moment, Daisy stumbled, her foot catching on the hem of her gown. The congregation watched in horrified silence as the delicate fabric tore along the front seam, exposing her from groin to knee in a gaping wound of ruined silk. A collective gasp filled the air as Andrew leapt forward, positioning himself in front of his sister to shield her from prying eyes. With deft movements, he removed his own coat, tying it around her waist to preserve her modesty.

For a long, tense moment, no one else moved, not even Susie. They seemed frozen in place by the shock of the incident. It was Charlotte who sprang into action, hurrying to the bride's side and gathering up the long train. Together, the three of them made their way to the waiting carriage, the tin cans tied to the rear clattering loudly as they drove away from the church.

Inside the carriage, Daisy sat with Andrew's coat draped across her lap, her body shaking with the force of her sobs as she clung to Charlotte for comfort. Andrew, seated opposite them, stared out the window in stony silence, his face an inscrutable mask of gloom. Not a word passed between them during the long journey to Whistable, the only sound the muffled cries of the distraught bride and the rhythmic clip-clop of the horses' hooves against the cobblestones.

Eventually, exhausted by her tears, Daisy drifted off to sleep, her head coming to rest on Charlotte's shoulder. Careful not to disturb her sleep, Charlotte reached out to adjust the coat that had begun to slip from her lap. As she did so, her gaze fell on the torn seam of the gown, and a sudden, chilling realization struck her like a bolt of lightning.

The stitches along the inner layer of the seam had been cut with deliberate precision, weakening the fabric and causing it to give way at the slightest provocation. It was no wonder Daisy had stepped on her hem, for the altered gown had left her particularly vulnerable to such an accident. It was most likely that was precisely what Daisy had hoped for. Charlotte's instinct told her there was no foul play to consider.

A shiver of unease ran down Charlotte's spine as the pieces of the puzzle began to fall into place. She recalled the mysterious circumstances surrounding the loss of Daisy's virtue. Could it be that the young woman had intentionally orchestrated these events, deliberately causing herself harm and humiliation? The thought was almost too frightful to contemplate, but Charlotte could not shake the growing sense of dread that settled in the pit of her stomach.

As the carriage rolled to a stop before the entrance of the cottage, Andrew leapt from the vehicle, waving away the footman who rushed to assist them. With a gentleness that belied his stern expression, he helped first his sister and then Charlotte to alight, his hand lingering for the briefest of moments in Charlotte's own before he released her and bounded up the stairs, taking them two at a time in his haste to see to his sister's comfort.

Barking orders at the assembled servants, Andrew quickly had a contingent of maids surrounding the distraught bride, ushering her up the grand staircase and toward the privacy of her chambers.

As she watched Daisy disappear, her slight frame supported by the attendants, Charlotte couldn't help but wonder what secret pain had driven the young woman to such a desperate act.

Charlotte lingered at the entrance of the drawing room, her mind awhirl with the unanswered questions that plagued her thoughts. Andrew was engaged in hushed conversations with various members of the staff, his voice low and urgent as he issued a series of orders and directives. Finally, after what seemed an eternity, he turned his attention to her, his expression hardening as he fought to control the simmering anger that bubbled just beneath the surface.

"Would you care for some tea, Miss Morton?" he asked, his tone clipped and formal, his address implying the end of their marriage.

"Yes, I would. Thank you, Lord Carlisle." Charlotte bobbed a small curtsy in acknowledgment of his offer.

Without another word, Andrew turned on his heel and strode toward the small drawing room, his long legs carrying him swiftly across the polished parquet floor. Charlotte hurried to follow, her steps quickening to keep pace with his determined gait, feeling for all the world like a wayward pupil being summoned to the headmaster's office.

Andrew made a beeline for the bar in the drawing room, his movements brusque and purposeful as he poured himself a generous measure of amber liquid. Charlotte silently watched him drain the glass in a single, swift gulp, the muscles of his throat working as he swallowed. He refilled the glass immediately, offering it to her with a raised brow, but she declined with a small shake of her head, her stomach churning with unease.

Shrugging, Andrew tossed back the second drink, the empty glass clinking sharply against the polished wood of the bar as he set it down. He made no move to invite her to sit, his body radiating a tense, coiled energy that set her nerves on edge.

Seeking to put some distance between them, Charlotte settled herself in the farthest chair from where he stood, her hands folded primly in her lap as she studied his profile. She could practically feel the waves of anger and frustration rolling off him, and she found herself holding her breath, waiting for the inevitable explosion.

Andrew, for his part, seemed indifferent toward the silence, his jaw clenched tightly as he stared into the fireplace, his hands gripping the mantelpiece with such force that his knuckles turned white.

But the eruption never came. Instead, after several long, tense moments, Andrew seemed to collect himself, his shoulders straightening as he drew in a deep, steadying breath. But there was no mistaking the undercurrent of rage that threaded through his body.

As Andrew drained the third glass of brandy, a mirthless chuckle escaped his lips, the sound harsh and grating in the oppressive silence of the drawing room. In a twisted way, he found himself welcoming the anger that coursed through his veins, preferring its familiar bite to the relentless onslaught of pain that had plagued him for the past month.

His mind churned with a maelstrom of fury and frustration, each thought stoking the flames of his ire. The groom had stood by like a useless figurehead while his bride suffered such humiliation. His own incompetence, his inability to prevent Daisy from falling, from being subjected to such indignity.

And then there was Charlotte… The mere thought of the suffering he had caused her was enough to reduce him to a sobbing wreck of a man.

The arrival of the tea tray brought a momentary respite, and Charlotte favored the maid with a weak smile, her hands trembling slightly as she accepted a cup of the steaming brew. She had positioned herself as far away from him as the room would allow, a fact that did not escape his notice. With a heavy sigh, he lowered himself into a chair, another glass of brandy clutched tightly in his hand.

"I am grateful for your aid," he said, his voice low and gruff. "You were the only one who had the presence of mind to come to Daisy's assistance."

Charlotte inclined her head. "I am deeply sorry that today has been such a trying ordeal for you and Daisy."

"Yes, well…" Andrew trailed off, his gaze fixed on the amber liquid in his glass as he swirled it absently.

They lapsed into silence once more, each lost in their own thoughts as they sipped their respective drinks. Charlotte's hands were pale and trembling, her face devoid of any vibrant hue. He longed to reach out to her, to offer some measure of comfort, but he held himself back, knowing he had lost the right to such intimacies.

"Are you well?" he asked tenderly.

Clearing her throat, she met his gaze with some effort, but her voice was steady. "Yes, quite well. And you?"

A wry smile appeared at his mouth, a humorless thing that did not reach his eyes. He said nothing. What could he say when an apology was wholly inadequate, and his pain nothing like what she had endured? Especially when he had exercised his power while she had been helpless against him, against Wilson. He buried his face behind his hands, her silent screams and misery beneath Wilson choking him.

"I should like to see how Daisy is faring, if I may," she said. "Could you perhaps have someone escort me to her chambers?"

Andrew nodded, rising to his feet. "I shall take you myself."

"All right. Thank you."

"You will tell me, won't you?" he asked, his eyes searching her face intently. "If you discover something that might affect her well-being?"

"Yes, of course," Charlotte said, her expression full of sympathy.

They made their way up the grand staircase and down the long corridor in silence, the air between them heavy with unspoken words and unresolved emotions. Each step felt like a surrender, a tacit acknowledgment of the chasm that now yawned between them.

⟫⟫⟫⟫⟪⟪⟪⟪

ANDREW CAME TO an abrupt halt, his eyes locking with Charlotte's in a gaze that made her feel exposed, as if he could see every secret longing, every hidden desire that she had buried deep within her heart.

"Are you comfortable at Madam's establishment?" he asked

with some hesitation.

"Yes." She kept her tone carefully neutral.

Andrew's brow furrowed, a flicker of concern passing over his handsome features. "Would you not be more comfortable at our townhouse? You would have greater privacy, more assistance and luxuries at your disposal."

Charlotte smiled faintly. "Thank you for your kind offer, but I am quite content at Madam's. It is convenient, being able to meet with the rescue women on site. And it is less lonely with the company of others."

Andrew fell silent, his gaze searching her face as if trying to understand how she could so easily replace him with a group of virtual strangers. Charlotte met his eyes briefly, her heart aching with the void left in her life.

She pined for him, longed for his touch, his presence, with an intensity that bordered on physical pain. But he had stolen the light from her spirit despite her efforts to persevere, and for that, she could not forgive him.

With a curt nod, he turned on his heel and retraced his steps down the corridor, his long strides carrying him swiftly away from her. Charlotte watched him go, her vision blurring with unshed tears, her heart shattering into a thousand jagged pieces for the loss of hope.

She allowed the tears to fall freely, her shoulders shaking with the force of her silent sobs as she mourned the loss of all that had once been, and all that could never be again. The weight of her heartbreak crushed her chest and stole the air from her lungs. She leaned against the door, her knees threatening to buckle under the strain of her emotions.

She remained frozen in the hallway for several minutes, struggling to compose herself before facing Daisy. Taking a shuddering breath, she forced her feet to carry her the remaining distance to her sister-in-law's door, steeling herself to push aside her own heartbreak in favor of the crisis at hand.

With a perfunctory knock, Charlotte announced herself and

slipped inside Daisy's room, the click of the latch behind her a welcome relief from the suffocating presence of the man she loved.

Daisy sat propped up in her bed, watching her sister-in-law, with her eyes red and swollen from crying. Her face was pale, her usually vibrant features drawn and haunted. Charlotte made her way to the bedside, her steps heavy and unsteady. She climbed in beside Daisy, the mattress dipping under her weight as she wrapped her arms around the young woman in a comforting embrace. Daisy rested her head on Charlotte's shoulder, her body shaking with the aftermath of her tears, her breath coming in shuddering gasps.

"Have you been crying too, Charlotte?" Daisy asked.

"Yes, but I'm all right."

"Is it because of Andrew? He told me what transpired between you two."

"Yes, but don't concern yourself about us. I'm more concerned about you. That was quite an interesting turn of events, wasn't it?" Charlotte remarked, keeping her tone carefully neutral as she studied Daisy's tear-streaked face.

Daisy let out a watery chuckle, the sound bordering on hysteria. "Interesting? That's rather a mild word for the complete and utter ruination of my life. Catastrophic, doomed, disastrous... take your pick. They all apply."

Charlotte reached out to clasp Daisy's hands, her heart aching for the palpable pain that emanated from the young woman. "But it wasn't truly a disaster, was it? Because you planned it that way."

Daisy's head snapped up, her red-rimmed eyes wide and panicked. "I don't know what you mean."

"I think you do." Charlotte kept her voice soft, coaxing. "I noticed the cuts you made in the fabric of your gown. Deliberate, strategic cuts. You couldn't have missed them when you were dressing. In fact, you would have had to be careful to ensure the seam didn't come apart."

Daisy seemed to crumple in on herself, a broken marionette whose strings had been cut. A keening sound tore from her throat as fresh tears spilled over, the dam of her composure shattering under the weight of Charlotte's gentle persuasion.

"I couldn't do it," she gasped, the words ragged and thin. "I couldn't condemn myself to a life shackled to a man I could never love, never be truly myself with." Her hands twisted in her skirts, the ruined silk bunching and tearing. "I thought if I could just ruin myself, make myself undesirable, I could escape."

With a groan, Daisy buried her face in her hands, her fingers tangling in her hair. "I am so deeply ashamed," she whispered, her voice muffled by her palms.

"Ashamed of what, exactly?"

"Of deceiving you and Andrew." Daisy's shoulders slumped in defeat.

Charlotte reached out, placing a comforting hand on the younger woman's arm, her touch gentle and reassuring. "I trust you felt you had no other option than to take such drastic measures."

Daisy nodded, her eyes filling with fresh tears, her breath hitching in her throat. "When I realized Andrew would not give up his search for suitors for me, I felt frantic to escape the assault." Her words tumbled out in a rush, as if a dam had broken within her.

"Assault?" Charlotte's eyes widened as she began to piece together the fragments of Daisy's confession.

"Yes… the marriage… with a man," Daisy said, her hands twisting in the fabric of her skirt. "I couldn't bear the thought of being trapped in a loveless union, living a lie for the rest of my days."

The realization hit Charlotte like a gust of hot wind, the pieces of the puzzle falling into place with startling clarity. Daisy hugged her knees to her chest, burying her face in the folds of her skirt, her body wracked with sobs. Overcome with heartache for the young woman, Charlotte wrapped her arms around her shrunken figure, holding her close, rocking her gently as she wept.

"Oh, Daisy," she murmured, her voice thick with compassion, her own tears falling silently onto the top of Daisy's head. "How you must have suffered, bearing this burden alone." The thought of Daisy's pain, of the secret she had carried for so long, was almost too much to ponder.

Daisy shook her head, her voice muffled against her knees. "I wasn't alone. I had Susie." The words were barely audible, but Charlotte heard them as clearly as if they had been shouted from the rooftops.

"Is she the one you love, then?" Charlotte asked, her hand lightly rubbing soothing circles on Daisy's back.

Daisy nodded, her sobs intensifying, her entire body shaking with the force of her emotions. "Yes," she managed to choke out between gasps for air. "I love her with all my heart."

"You did nothing wrong, Daisy. You acted out of love, and there is no shame in that." Charlotte held Daisy tighter, pouring all her love and acceptance into the embrace.

Slowly, Daisy lifted her head, her eyes hesitant and uncertain, searching Charlotte's face for any sign of judgment or disapproval. "You're not angry with me?" she asked, her voice small and fearful.

"No, of course not. What choice did you have? I only wish you had spoken to your brother instead of creating these crises."

"He wouldn't have understood."

"He loves you very much. It's unfair to assume he would react poorly without giving him a chance." Charlotte's words were gentle but firm. She hoped Andrew would prove her right.

Daisy sat up straighter, blowing her nose and fixing Charlotte with a searching gaze. "After what he's done to you, you still defend him?"

A wistful smile tugged at Charlotte's mouth, her eyes filled with sadness and affection, a bittersweet mix of emotions that seemed to encompass the entirety of her relationship with

Andrew. "He may have betrayed me, but that doesn't change the depth of his love for you. All he wants is for you to be happy." The words were a painful truth, a reminder of the man she had once believed him to be.

"But he is so antiquated in his thinking," Daisy protested, grimacing in frustration. "I doubt he would have ceased his search for potential suitors on my behalf."

Charlotte shook her head, her expression thoughtful. "I really believe he might not be as antiquated as he appears. Perhaps it is merely a facade to appease his shareholders. After all, he allowed you to study in Jamaica without a chaperone, did he not?"

"Yes."

"You see? Talk to him, Daisy. I'll be right by your side if he reacts poorly or spouts any nonsense." Charlotte gave the younger woman's hand a reassuring squeeze.

Daisy reached out, clasping Charlotte's hand tightly in both of her own. "Thank you, Charlotte. Your support means more to me than I can possibly express."

"There's no rush. We shall stay here until you gather enough courage to face your brother. And when you do, I will be with you every step of the way."

⇥⟫⟩⟨⟪⇤

ANDREW RECLINED IN his chair, his head lolling back as he closed his eyes, savoring the smooth, potent taste of the brandy on his tongue. For weeks, he had been haunted by visions of Charlotte whenever he dared to rest his weary eyes—her sparkling gaze, her dimpled smile, and her clever, tempting mouth.

With her sleeping beneath his roof this night, he knew he would need to drain the entire bottle of brandy before he could hope to find even a moment's respite. His greatest fear was that, in his inebriated state, he might unintentionally find his way to her bed, frightening her with his unwelcome presence.

A sharp rap at the door startled him from his musings, and he looked up, his eyes wide and alert. He had assumed that the women had long since retired for the evening, given the late hour. With a gruff shout, he bade them to enter, and to his surprise, both his wife and sister appeared in the doorway, clad in their housecoats.

Despite his best efforts, Andrew's gaze lingered on Charlotte's form, the casual attire evoking bittersweet memories of happier times. With a force of will, he tore his eyes away, focusing instead on the weariness that etched deep lines into Daisy's face.

The two women settled themselves on the sofa across from him, their hands clasped tightly together. Andrew noticed the way Charlotte gave Daisy's hand a reassuring squeeze. Daisy cleared her throat, her voice husky from the tears she had shed.

"Andrew," she began, her tone hesitant and unsure. "I sabotaged my own wedding... because I... I do not feel drawn to men in the way that society expects."

For a long moment, Andrew simply stared at his sister, his brow furrowed in confusion as he struggled to comprehend her words. As the realization of her meaning sank in, he inhaled sharply, his eyes widened in shock. Abruptly, he rose to his feet, strode to the bar, and poured himself a generous measure of brandy with trembling hands.

When at last he returned his attention to the women, he opened his mouth as if to speak, but the words seemed to stick in his throat, refusing to be given voice. He tilted his head, his expression one of bewilderment. "What are you saying, Daisy?"

Charlotte, her hand resting gently on Daisy's shoulder, spoke slowly and carefully, as if to ensure that her words penetrated the fog of Andrew's shock. "Daisy cut the stitches on her wedding gown with the sole purpose of exposing herself to the *ton*, thereby publicly humiliating herself and ensuring no man would wish to marry her."

Andrew's gaze darted between the two women, his eyes wide

and unblinking. Daisy had curled in on herself, hugging her knees to her chest in a posture of vulnerability and fear, a position he had not seen her adopt since she was a little girl. Charlotte met his gaze steadily, her expression one of gentle plea and warning as she allowed him time to process the revelation.

Rising to his feet once more, Andrew began to pace the room, his steps heavy and agitated as he tried to encourage circulation to his addled brain. Suddenly, he stopped, whirling to face the women, appearing profoundly disturbed.

"And the incident with Lord Byron? The rupture of your…" He trailed off, unable to give voice to the delicate matter.

Charlotte's arm tightened on Daisy's trembling form, her voice even as she replied, "She caused the injury herself to avoid the marriage."

A look of horror passed over Andrew's visage, his mouth falling open in a silent gasp as he ran a palm over his face. He muttered under his breath about the dangers of such an act. After a moment, he composed himself, his eyes seeking out his sister's huddled form.

"Daisy," he said gently, his voice filled with a tenderness that belied his shock. "Have you always been drawn to women?"

From her self-imposed cocoon, Daisy nodded, a single, jerky movement that spoke volumes of her fear and uncertainty. Andrew sank back into his chair, his mind wheeling as he tried to reconcile this new information.

For a long moment, silence reigned in the room, broken only by the crackling of the fire in the grate and the soft, hitching breaths of the three occupants. At last, Andrew leaned forward, his elbows resting on his knees as he clasped his hands together, his gaze fixed on the floor.

"I can't believe how blind I've been… I thought I knew what was best for you… To think that I've put you through such immense pain because of my views and actions…"

Andrew tousled his hair and rested his head in his palm, his eyes closed. After a while, he sat up and met his sister's gaze.

"Daisy," he said, his voice low and rough with emotion. "I cannot pretend to understand the depths of your struggles, the pain you must have endured in keeping this secret for so long. But I want you to know that no matter what, you are my sister, and I love you with all my heart. Nothing could ever change that."

At his words, a soft, broken sob escaped Daisy's lips, and she uncurled herself from her protective ball, throwing herself into her brother's arms. Andrew held her close, his own eyes glistening with unshed tears as he stroked her hair, murmuring words of comfort and reassurance.

Gently resting his hand on Daisy's shoulder while she blew her nose, Andrew fixed his sister with a probing gaze. "Do you have a special woman in your life now?"

Daisy nodded, her cheeks flushing as she avoided her brother's eyes and whispered, "Susie."

Andrew took a deep breath, shaking his head with a rueful smile.

"Are you very angry, Andrew?" Daisy asked.

"No, darling. We are all aware of the tragically foolish mistakes I've made in recent months. I'm hardly in a position to cast stones," he huffed, catching a glimmer of amusement in Charlotte's eyes that warmed his heart and eased the tension in his chest.

"I must admit, I don't believe I would have had the courage to do what you did," he continued, his tone light and teasing. "Your plan was certainly effective. I daresay there isn't a man in all of England who would dare to propose marriage to you now, not after two such public scandals. But did you really have to wait until I had spent a fortune on the wedding?"

The women chuckled, the sound warming his heart. Somehow, the gravity of the situation seemed to lessen in the face of their shared mirth.

Growing serious once more, Andrew asked, "What do you wish to do now?"

Charlotte glanced at Daisy, who nodded in silent approval. "We believe that Daisy ought to consider a marriage to the Duke of Chatham."

"Chatham…" Andrew nodded slowly, understanding.

"He is drawn exclusively to men," Daisy said, confirming what he'd suspected since Charlotte's confession.

"And you agree to this?" Andrew asked his sister, who nodded shyly. Turning to Charlotte, he inquired, "Do you think he'd be amenable to the idea?"

"Yes. I believe he would deem it a perfect solution to his dilemma. He has someone important to him."

Andrew sat in pensive silence, marveling at the strength and resilience of the two women, the loves of his life. He also realized how arrogant he'd been about what he thought he knew, how he had caused so much anguish to the women he loved, and how close he'd come to losing them. Perhaps he had already lost Charlotte forever.

Gazing at both women, he rose to his feet. "We better get some sleep. We have a long day of travel tomorrow." Enthusiastically, Daisy hopped out of her chair, hugging her brother once more. "Thank you," she whispered.

Kissing the top of her head, Andrew said softly, "I am so sorry I've been blind. I know the duke to be a good man, and pray you find happiness with him." Releasing her and offering his arm to his sister, he said, "Let us continue this discussion during our travel tomorrow. We have much to consider."

Andrew tamped down his compulsion to hold Charlotte back, and instead, watched her follow Daisy out of the room. Though his heart ached with the knowledge that Charlotte may never again be his, he took solace in the fact that she was here, by his side, to face whatever trials lay ahead. It was a small comfort, but one he clung to with all his might.

BORROWED TIME

AFTER SHE ENSURED Daisy was tucked snuggly in her bed, Charlotte returned to her room at approximately one o'clock in the morning and stood by the open window, the gentle breeze providing a welcome respite from the tumultuous emotions that had consumed her. As she gazed at the sliver of a moon, a shifting shadow in the garden caught her attention. There, illuminated by the soft moonlight, sat a tall figure dressed in trousers and a housecoat, his head cradled in his hands. The sight of his anguished form mirrored the pain in her own heart.

Despite the hurt and resentment she had felt since his betrayal, Charlotte couldn't help but admire the kindness and generosity he had shown his sister. It was a demonstration of his inherent goodness, even if he had betrayed her trust. But now, it was time to close this chapter of their lives and their union.

Donning her pelisse and slippers, Charlotte made her way to the garden, the gravel path crunching softly beneath her feet. As she approached his still form, he hastily wiped his face with the sleeve of his housecoat and looked up, his eyes glistening with tears and filled with sorrow. He rose to his feet, his hands digging deep into the pockets of his housecoat, and dropped his head.

"Are you all right, Andrew?" she asked softly.

He shook his head slowly, his shoulders sagging with the weight of his emotions. "I've been a fool, Charlotte. A damned, arrogant fool. I thought I knew what was best for you and Daisy, that I had all the answers. But the realization of the pain I've caused you both… it's tearing me apart inside. I'm ashamed and wish I knew how to make amends."

He approached her, anguish etched in his features as he clasped her hand between his own. The warmth of his touch sent a shiver down her spine, memories of their shared past flooding her mind. He brought her hand to his lips, kissing her knuckles with reverence. His eyes bore into hers as he spoke, his voice raw with regret.

"I am so deeply sorry, Charlotte. What I thought was love was nothing more than a selfish desire to control and possess you. But I'm ready to love you the way you deserve, with all the respect and adoration you merit. I know I don't deserve your forgiveness, not yet. The wounds I've inflicted will take time to heal. But I'm begging you, please don't give up on us. Give me one more chance to prove my love for you."

"Andrew, I—"

"Even if you want nothing to do with me, I want to give you everything I can. We'll go on our honeymoon. We'll visit the finest modiste in Paris, and you'll have your pick of gowns, shoes, and bonnets. And the townhouse, it's yours. I'll have the deed in your name within a week. If you don't like it, you can have any of my properties, all of them if you want. I have—"

"Andrew!" Charlotte interjected, her fingers brushing against his wrist to silence him. As he met her gaze, she inhaled deeply, steeling herself for the words that would shatter his world. "I am leaving."

The air rushed from his lungs as if he'd been struck. His eyes widened in disbelief, his mouth falling open in a silent cry of anguish. He staggered back a step, his hand slipping from hers. As though he couldn't maintain the weight, he leaned against the stone table.

"Please," he whispered, his voice broken and pleading. "Please don't go. I can't… I can't lose you, Charlotte. You are everything to me."

"I'm sorry, Andrew, but I must follow my heart's true calling. I am bound for Ohio, in the United States of America, where a school that accepts female students awaits me. There, I can live with dignity and purpose."

"Does this mean we shall become strangers once again? Won't you give me a chance to salvage our marriage, regain your trust before you go?"

"Unfortunately, the summer holiday begins in just a month. I must leave in a fortnight to catch a ship bound for America, to plead with the dean to admit me. Otherwise, they shall become unreachable over the summer."

A heavy silence hung between them, the weight of her words settling upon his shoulders like a lead shroud.

"I wished to inform you in person while I had the chance," Charlotte said softly, her eyes downcast. "I shall not see you again after we speak to the duke." Glancing up at his form briefly, she muttered, "Good night."

She turned to head back inside, her heart heavy with the burden of their parting. She had taken but a few steps when she felt his strong arms envelop her from behind, drawing her back against the solid warmth of his chest.

"Charlotte," he whispered, his voice cracking with raw emotion. "I cannot bear to let you go. The thought of living without you by my side is too much to endure. My love for you consumes me, body and soul. I know my actions were unforgivable, but I beseech you—do not condemn me to a life of misery. Please, I implore you, stay a while longer. Grant me a month to prove my devotion and to regain your trust."

Charlotte closed her eyes, her resolve wavering as she felt the heat of his embrace, the strength of his hold both comforting and unsettling. As if sensing her inner turmoil, he tightened his arms around her. Summoning her courage, she spoke the words she knew must be said.

"I suffer as you do. I loved you deeply and wished nothing more than to be a good and faithful wife. But it is clear now that we are ill-suited. You must find a wife willing to devote herself wholly to your needs and those of your household. With your connections and influence, I have no doubt you shall secure an annulment on the grounds of your wife's abandonment."

"Damn it, Charlotte," he growled, his sudden vehemence startling her as he spun her to face him. Cradling her face in his hands, he searched her eyes desperately, silently pleading for mercy. "It is you I love, and you alone. Since the day we met, no other woman has captured my thoughts or stirred my heart. There can be no other."

He raised his arm and pointed to the lights. "This, all this, was for you. I pored over these lights to distract my incessant longing, to stay connected to you since our very first meeting. Come. I'll show you."

Charlotte turned her gaze to the sky as she followed his gesture, but from their position in the garden, she could only see scattered points of light. When Andrew took her hand, his fingers trembling with urgency, she didn't resist.

"From here, you cannot see…" he said, his voice thick with emotion. "Please, Charlotte. Let me show you what I've carried in my heart all these years."

He led her inside, his long strides purposeful yet careful not to outpace her completely. They moved through the dimly lit corridor, Andrew's hand a warm anchor as he guided her up the grand staircase. One flight, then another, then a third, their footsteps echoing softly in the sleeping house. Charlotte's heart hammered against her ribs, not from the exertion, but from the desperate hope in Andrew's eyes and the promise of revelation that awaited.

Finally, he stopped before the large windows overlooking the garden, his breathing slightly labored. With gentle hands, he positioned her beside him and gestured toward the view below.

"Now," he whispered. "Now you can see."

Slowly, she registered what she was seeing and gasped. Charlotte's heart raced, pounding against her ribcage as a whirlwind of emotions surged through her. She stood transfixed, her eyes wide with wonder and disbelief as she took in the sight before her. The twinkling lights, arranged with such care and precision, spelled out her name—*Charlotte*—a declaration of love that took her breath away. Tears welled up in her eyes, blurring the stunning display, because he had pined for her and because of the dream that would never be realized.

But perhaps she could dare to dream for one night. One more night before she released him forever from her heart.

In a fleeting moment of reckless abandon, she stood on her toes and kissed him, brushing her lips over his, side to side. He stood frozen for a moment in a stunned silence, then captured her mouth with his, pouring every ounce of his longing into the heated kiss. Charlotte found her body responding to his ardent attentions, a breathless moan escaping her lips.

Andrew claimed her mouth, swallowing her gasp of surprise as he slanted his lips over hers. His tongue delved deep, stroking and tangling with her own until she was dizzy with need, sparks of pleasure shooting down her spine. Charlotte surrendered to the onslaught of sensation, her hands fisting in his shirt, tugging frantically to feel the heat of his skin against her palms.

Removing his housecoat, his mouth never leaving hers, he draped it over Charlotte's shoulders. She opened his shirt and ran her hands over the hard muscles of his torso. Andrew cupped her bottom in his hands and pressed her against him before walking backward into a dark room.

Charlotte followed, running a hand firmly over his erection, eliciting a grunt and ragged breaths. The air in the room was cool against her heated skin, carrying the faint scent of leather and ink that marked it as his private domain. When his back met a table, Andrew's hand squeezed her breast over the night rail, his thumb brushing over the taut nipple. She desperately sought the buttons on his falls.

Charlotte opened the third button and gripped the source of her incessant craving. A sigh of relief left her lips as she took liberties she had been yearning for since their separation. His member was hot and rigid, the veins pulsing under her fingers. Gripping it firmly, she began to stroke.

"Sweetheart…" he panted against her mouth and steadied her hand. "I need to taste you."

With that, he lifted her onto the table, nudging her to lie back with her knees bent. Andrew pushed the hem of her shift to her waist. Feeling shy against his intense scrutiny, she closed her knees together, but he gently pushed them apart, his breathing and eyelids becoming heavier.

His gaze met hers, fire blazing within them, then he knelt on the rug.

Sliding his arms beneath her thighs, he gripped her hips firmly, and his mouth dove into her wet heat. He latched on to her sensitive bud, licking her and feeling her swell under his tongue. She could feel her arousal drip down her thighs when he rewarded her with groans from deep in his chest.

As she stiffened and whispered his name with her thighs squeezing tight, Andrew entered her heat with his tongue, licking and caressing. The orgasm peaked sharply under his skilled attention, causing Charlotte to gasp at the intensity. She muffled her scream with her fist and rode his mouth until wave after wave of her peak carried her into euphoria. When her climax settled, Andrew rose to his feet with his hard shaft in his hand.

"Not like this," she whispered.

Resting his member against her entrance, Andrew gently asked the painful question. "Is this how Wilson took you?"

Her eyes widened, then tears flowed. He didn't ask anymore. Instead, he peered into her eyes with tenderness.

"My love, I'm not he, and he'll never touch you again. This is me, your husband. Let me love you this way." Despite his throbbing manhood, he waited patiently.

"Yes," she said weakly.

"Keep your eyes on me, Charlotte. This is me loving you."

Andrew eased into her heat, inch by tortuous inch, his gaze

locked on her face. A guttural sound, part groan, part sigh, rumbled low in his throat as her silken walls enveloped him, drawing him deeper.

Charlotte drank in the sight of his unraveling control, a heady cocktail of power and affection bubbling through her veins. With Wilson, the desperation and hunger had felt like dominance. With Andrew… this felt like his surrender.

Andrew entered her gently, releasing a silent scream when he buried his cock inside her completely, his eyes becoming half hooded as his head tilted back.

He leaned forward, one hand lifting her hips up to deepen the penetration. He thrust in and out of her, kissing her mouth, her neck, and looking into her eyes, reminding her who was filling her, claiming her, loving her.

Then, as he began to lose control, he hugged her in a cocoon-like embrace, plunging into her. With a sharp inhale, all his muscles tightened, his powerful form giving in helplessly to the paralyzing sensation. He screamed into her nape, lurching forward and trembling from the sheer force of the climax. He thrust his hips in powerful motion, driving his cock into her over and over until he drained the last drop of his pleasure into her quim. With a groan, Andrew rested his head on her shoulder while his arms held her tight.

They lingered in their embrace, each lost in contemplation of the consequences of their passionate union. Rising upon his elbows, Andrew tenderly cleaned away the evidence of their ardor with his housecoat.

Gazing deeply into her eyes, he inquired softly, "Are you all right, my love?"

"Yes," she whispered.

"Was I wrong to insist on this position?" He studied her intently, his brow furrowed with concern.

"I am glad you did," she replied with a weak smile.

He drew her tightly into his embrace once more before rising slowly. He helped her to sit up, his touch lingering on her delicate frame.

"When…" he began, his voice heavy with sorrow. "When do you intend to take your leave?"

"A fortnight hence, as soon as my duties here are fulfilled," she replied, her gaze downcast. "I shall continue my charitable work in America, guiding and assisting those women who seek a new life in that land."

Andrew perched on the table beside her, his shoulders sagging with the weight of her impending departure. "When are your courses due to arrive?" he asked.

"It should be upon me presently," she said shyly.

He nodded, his disappointment evident at the realization that she had little time to reconsider her voyage.

"You will tell me if you find yourself with child?" he asked, his eyes searching hers.

"Yes, of course."

He nodded. "You ought to retire and get some rest. We have a long and trying day ahead of us, visiting Chatham tomorrow."

Charlotte studied his features one last time, noting the vulnerability and weariness etched on his countenance. She pressed a soft, lingering kiss on his cheek and reluctantly turned to make her way back to her chamber, her heart heavy with the knowledge that their paths would soon diverge, perhaps forever.

PUNISHMENT

30 April 1837

"I BESEECH YOU, my lord," the courtesan implored, her voice dripping with honey as she leaned in close, her ample bosom brushing against Andrew's arm. "Would you be so kind as to indulge me with another glass of brandy? A lady must keep up her strength, after all." Her eyes fluttered seductively, and her ruby lips pouted in a calculated display of feminine wiles.

Andrew cast a sidelong glance at Wilson whose fingers were grazing his companion's arm while engaging in a whispered conversation. "I have no doubt that Madam Tansley dines on the finest delicacies London has to offer," Andrew replied smoothly. "Surely, she has no need for my assistance in lining her pockets."

Wilson, his face flushed with drink and merriment, let out a hearty chuckle that echoed through the dimly lit room. "Come now, Carlisle! Don't be such a miser," he chided, wagging a finger in Andrew's direction. "A man of your considerable means has more than enough to spare for these lovely creatures. The more they imbibe, the merrier our evening shall be!" He punctuated his words with a suggestive wink, his eyes gleaming with lust.

With a tight-lipped smile that didn't quite reach his eyes, Andrew affected an air of reluctance. "Every penny I possess is hard-earned, Wilson," he said, his voice low and measured. "Unlike you, who tries to cut corners at every opportunity."

"Do you know why I am the way I am, Carlisle?" Wilson asked, swirling the amber liquid in his glass.

Andrew remained silent, sensing that the question was rhetorical.

"I was like you once," Wilson continued, his gaze distant, as if seeing into some long-buried past. "Young, idealistic, determined to change the world through sheer force of will." A bitter laugh escaped him. "But the world has a way of grinding down those rough edges, of teaching hard lessons to those foolish enough to challenge the hierarchy."

He drained his glass in one swift motion, wincing as the alcohol burned a fiery path down his throat. "I learned those lessons, learned them well. And now I pass them on to bright young sparks like you, so that you don't make the same mistakes I did. The only way to thrive is to create your own game, let them play until there's only one left, then steal it from the winner."

"And what if I don't care to be that underhanded?" Andrew bit out, pushing down the disgust beneath his skin.

Wilson shrugged. "Then you'd best prepare yourself for a world of pain and disappointment, my boy. A world that will chew you up and spit you out without a second thought."

Andrew drained his glass to get rid of the foul taste in his mouth. "You speak the truth, Wilson. Perhaps it is time to reap the rewards of my labors. I shall procure another three rounds." He signaled to a passing servant, who hastened to fulfill his request.

The courtesans erupted in a chorus of applause and delighted squeals at the prospect of more alcohol. Wilson joined in their enthusiastic cheers, his voice booming above the din. It had occurred to Andrew that Wilson's persistent attempts to disqualify Charlotte may have been to muzzle her before she could reveal what kind of repugnant beast he was. Andrew, his smile now smug and self-satisfied, fought to suppress the loathing that churned in his gut. Oh, how he longed to pummel the scoundrel until his knuckles were raw and bleeding, to feel the satisfying crunch of bone beneath his fists. But he held fast, reminding himself that he had a far worse fate in store for the despicable man.

Much to Andrew's delight, Wilson tossed back the fourth glass of brandy in a single swallow, too foxed to notice the bitter taste of the laudanum Madam had discreetly prepared earlier in the evening. As the drug began to take effect, Wilson's movements grew increasingly clumsy and uncoordinated. A moment later, his head hit the table with a resounding thud, his body going limp as he succumbed to the sedative.

Rising slowly to his feet, Andrew fixed the unconscious man with a look of utter contempt, his lip curling in disgust. "I shall await Judge Hoffman's arrival," he announced, his voice cutting through the haze of smoke and perfume. "See to it that this wretch doesn't leave your sight." With deliberate movements, he withdrew a carefully folded document from his pocket, lifted Wilson's head, and deftly slid the incriminating papers beneath before allowing it to drop back onto the table with a satisfying thump.

With a curt nod to the two courtesans, who promptly positioned themselves on either side of Wilson, Andrew took his leave. He made his way to the parlor, his steps purposeful and measured, where he sprawled himself upon the plush divan, feigning intoxication alongside another courtesan he had entrusted with the crucial task of attending to Hoffman upon his arrival.

Andrew was quite certain that once the esteemed judge laid eyes upon the damning document in Wilson's possession, he would have little appetite for the night's revelries, his sense of duty and moral outrage overriding any base desires. Andrew settled in comfortably, prepared to wait as long as necessary. The pompous fool was notorious for his tardiness.

As he reclined on the divan, his thoughts drifted unbidden to Charlotte, her face swimming before his mind's eye, tormenting him with memories of their shared past and the uncertain future that stretched out before them. For a moment, he considered imbibing the laudanum-fortified brandy himself, if only to dull the ache in his chest and quiet the clamoring of his own traitorous heart.

As the evening progressed, the once stately parlor of the brothel grew increasingly lively and raucous with each passing moment. The air was thick and heavy, redolent with the scent of expensive perfume, spilled alcohol, and the unmistakable musk of desire that seemed to permeate every corner of the room. Andrew, still sprawled out on the divan in a carefully affected posture of drunken repose, kept a watchful eye on the entrance, his senses attuned to any sign of Judge Hoffman's impending entrance.

The sudden sound of a carriage pulling up outside caught Andrew's attention, and the courtesan beside him rose gracefully to her feet, adjusting her bodice to better showcase her ample bosom, the creamy swell of her flesh almost spilling over the confines of her tightly laced corset. As Judge Hoffman stepped through the door, his portly frame filling the doorway, the courtesan bent over toward Andrew conspiratorially and said loudly, "I don't believe Lord Wilson is capable of such dishonor. He is the Master of Bench at the Inner Temple, is he not?"

"He is," Andrew slurred, pitching his voice just loud enough to ensure that the judge, who had halted a few feet away and was currently eavesdropping on their conversation with a look of avid interest, would hear every word. "But greed will make a fool out of any man, no matter how high and mighty he may believe himself to be. I saw it with my own eyes, the proof…"

He let his voice trail off, as if suddenly realizing he had said too much. With an exaggerated gesture, he placed a finger over his lips. "But don't tell a soul about this," he said, his words slightly slurred. "I wouldn't wish for anyone to blame the honorable judges…"

"What is this all about, Carlisle?" Hoffman boomed, his voice cutting through the din of the room. "What exactly might the judges be blamed for?" He strode forward, his face flushed with a combination of righteous indignation and barely contained curiosity.

Andrew turned around, affecting a look of surprise and unsteadiness as he caught sight of the judge looming over him. He stood up hastily, swaying slightly and grabbing onto the furniture to keep his balance, the very picture of a man deep in his cups. He bowed clumsily, the gesture made all the more comical by the courtesan trying to hold him steady.

"My apologies, my lord." His words were a barely coherent jumble. "I didn't mean to trouble you with such unpleasant matters. Please, pay no heed to the ramblings of a drunken fool such as myself. I implore you, enjoy your evening and think no more of it." He waved a hand dismissively, as if to banish the topic from the room.

The green-eyed beauty walked over to Hoffman and hung onto his arm tightly, her smile never wavering as she tried to steer him toward the more private chambers. But the judge shook off her touch impatiently, his attention fully focused on Andrew.

"I must insist that you tell me everything you know, Carlisle," he said, his voice low and urgent. "If it is related to the Inner Temple, then it is a matter of utmost importance and cannot be ignored."

Andrew hesitated, rubbing his chin pensively as if deep in thought. He let the silence stretch out for a long moment, building the tension until it was almost unbearable. "Very well, my lord," he said at last, his voice tinged with grim resignation.

Andrew gestured for the judge to follow him. He led the way down the dimly lit hallway. They entered the room where Wilson lay unconscious, the two courtesans keeping watch over his prone form.

Andrew pointed at the papers peeking out from beneath Wilson's head, acting appropriately reluctant to make accusations. Judge Hoffman approached the table and lifted Wilson's head and retrieved the incriminating document, his eyes scanning the neat columns of figures and notations with growing horror and rage. Wilson, still deep in slumber, did not move a muscle.

"Embezzlement? From the Inner Temple, no less?" he roared. "This is a grave offense, a betrayal of the highest order. The fool has sealed his own fate with his greed and arrogance. I shall see to it that he pays dearly for every penny he has stolen, that he spends the rest of his miserable life rotting in the darkest, dankest cell the Tower has to offer." He looked up at Andrew with an expression of self-importance. "You have done a great service today, Carlisle, in bringing this matter to light, albeit reluctantly. I shall handle things from here. Wait for me, if you please. I may have further questions for you once I have alerted my colleagues."

With that, Hoffman turned on his heel and strode purposefully out of the room, the tails of his coat flapping behind him. Andrew leaned against the wall, a sense of deep satisfaction settling over him as he watched Wilson's motionless form. He took out a cigar and lit it with a steady hand, savoring the rich, earthy flavor as he puffed out a stream of fragrant smoke.

It was a pity, he mused, that he wouldn't have the pleasure of squeezing the life out of Wilson with his own bare hands, of watching the light fade from the bastard's eyes as he gasped out his last, rattling breath. But there was a certain poetic justice in knowing that the man would be tormented and die a slow death in a filthy cell.

HEALING

6 May 1837

As DAWN BROKE, the dock bustled with activity. Sailors hustled about, loading supplies and cargo onto the waiting ship. The creaking of ropes and groaning of wooden planks mingled with shouts and laughter, creating a symphony of human endeavor.

Amidst this chaos stood Charlotte, her trunk at her feet and her heart heavy with a mixture of fear and anticipation. Taking a deep breath of salty air, Charlotte made her way to the gangplank. The creaking wood beneath her feet seemed to echo the uncertainty in her heart as she boarded the ship that would carry her away from everything she'd ever known.

After showing her ticket, she paused to gaze at the country she was leaving behind. Doubt crept in, but she steeled herself, remembering the knowledge and freedom awaiting her across the ocean.

"May I help you, Miss?" A sailor tipped his hat.

"Oh, yes." Charlotte handed him her ticket. "Could you direct me to my berth, please?"

Glancing at the ticket, the sailor paused briefly, then said, "Yes, of course. Oakley at your service, Miss Morton. Follow me, please." He took the trunk from her and led the way.

As they ascended through the ship, Charlotte grew increasingly confused. She had purchased the cheapest ticket available, yet they climbed higher and higher. Finally, they reached an ornate door that seemed far too grand for her modest fare.

As Oakley turned the lock, Charlotte's eyes widened in disbelief. The suite before her was a marvel of luxury and opulence. Rich wood paneling covered the walls, plush carpets cushioned her steps, and exquisite furniture filled the space. A large four-poster bed dominated the room, promising a level of comfort Charlotte had known only with Andrew.

"There must be some mistake," Charlotte said, bewildered. "I couldn't possibly afford this."

Oakley smiled knowingly. "No mistake, Miss. This is your room for the voyage."

As he left, Charlotte sank onto the bed, her fingers tracing the smooth wood. She was convinced Andrew had arranged this unexpected luxury. Here, in this opulent suite, she imagined drifting off to sleep, lulled by the roar of waves and howling winds—a stark contrast to the constant activity that had made sleep a rare commodity at Madam Tansley's brothel.

A sharp rap at the door startled Charlotte to her feet. "Come in," she called out.

The door swung open, revealing Andrew's imposing figure. Charlotte's breath caught in her throat, and for a moment, she was certain her heart had ceased to beat. It had felt like an eternity since their last encounter, and the sight of him, thinner and paler than she remembered, only confirmed her suspicion that he, too, had been suffering in their time apart.

"Andrew," she managed, swallowing the lump that had formed in her throat. "What a surprise."

"Hello, Charlotte," he replied, closing the distance between them until he stood a mere arm's length away. "This is a momentous day for you. Congratulations." His smile was genuine, almost boyish, a stark contrast to the ruthless businessman she had known. In that instant, he was simply a man, humbled.

"Thank you for arranging this accommodation," she said, gesturing to the room. "You really didn't have to."

"I know, but I couldn't bear the thought of you falling prey to rats in the steerage."

Charlotte wrinkled her nose at the unpleasant image.

"How are you, Charlotte?" Andrew's voice was solemn, yet tender.

"I am both excited and terrified. I haven't received word from the school, so I'm not certain of my admission. Regardless, I intend to find work there and forge my own path."

"You know that's unnecessary. I would gladly provide for you, no matter what happens between us, for the rest of your days."

She inclined her head in gratitude. "Thank you, but you may remarry, and I cannot rely on your generosity indefinitely."

Something flickered in Andrew's eyes, an intensity she couldn't quite decipher. Their conversation was interrupted by the ship's horn, announcing its imminent departure.

"Oh, you must hurry. The ship is leaving," she urged.

Andrew's eyes, dark and intense, locked onto hers. "I'm not going anywhere, Charlotte. I intend to journey with you."

The meaning of his words hung in the air between them. Charlotte felt as though the ground had shifted beneath her feet. "What? Why?"

Andrew took a step closer, his presence filling the room. "I'm here because I hope to earn your forgiveness, if you'll allow me the chance to prove myself worthy of your trust once more."

Charlotte shook her head, struggling to comprehend the magnitude of his decision. "Andrew, that is not something that will happen within the duration of this voyage. You can't simply abandon your life, your business…"

"You are my life… my family, Charlotte," he said, his voice low and fervent. "I love you, and I'm willing to spend whatever time it takes to become the man you deserve, if you'll let me."

The intensity of his gaze made her breath catch. She watched as he reached into his coat, producing a neatly folded newspaper. "There's something you should see," he said, handing it to her.

As Charlotte unfolded the paper, her eyes widened in disbelief. The bold headline proclaimed Lord Wilson's arrest, detailing his embezzlement from the Inner Temple. She looked up at Andrew, her mind reeling.

"You did this?" she asked, her voice trembling.

Andrew nodded. "I have you to thank for that."

"Me? How so?"

"The night I entered your room because you had fallen asleep with candles burning, I noticed the date on which one of his properties was purchased. It aroused my suspicions, as I knew he lacked the funds. That led me to investigate further."

Tears welled in Charlotte's eyes as the full impact of Andrew's actions washed over her. This man, who had once betrayed her trust, had not only brought her tormentor to justice but was now willing to uproot his entire life to follow her across an ocean.

"Your company," she began, her voice thick with emotion. "Your life in London—"

"None of it matters without you," Andrew said softly, closing the distance between them. "I've realized that my empire, my wealth, my status—they're hollow achievements if I don't have you by my side."

Charlotte felt the walls she had built around her heart begin to crumble. The man before her was not the same person who had hurt her so deeply. This Andrew was humbled and unafraid to lay bare his vulnerabilities.

"I don't expect your forgiveness to come easily or quickly," he continued, his voice rough with emotion. "But I'm prepared to spend every day loving you the way you ought to be loved and become the partner you need."

As Charlotte gazed into his eyes, she saw the depth of his commitment to right his wrongs. The realization that Andrew was willing to leave behind everything he had built, to start anew in a foreign land, all for the chance to rebuild what they had lost—it shook her to her core.

For the first time since their estrangement, she allowed herself to imagine a future where love and trust could flourish once more.

As the night deepened, Charlotte found herself adrift in a sea of sleeplessness, her thoughts an endless stream of conflicting emotions. The knowledge that Andrew was aboard, a mere whisper away, his presence both a balm and a torment, consumed her. His determination to journey alongside her for the fortnight ahead stirred a dangerous elation within her heart, one she knew she ought to temper given the wounds of his past betrayal.

His absence from the dining room, where she had observed fellow passengers embarking on their own odysseys of family reunion or fresh beginnings, puzzled her. For a man so intent on earning her forgiveness, his scarcity seemed a curious strategy indeed.

At last, unable to bear the restless confinement of her cabin any longer, Charlotte arose. With careful movements, she donned her pelisse and bonnet, steeling herself against the night air. As she ventured onto the deck, she found the world shrouded in an inky darkness, the moon having abandoned its post in the sky. Only the faint, flickering beacon of the wheelhouse offered any respite from the overwhelming blackness.

Gripping the railing with tentative fingers, Charlotte made her way to the lower deck, each step a small victory against the ship's gentle sway. As she reached her destination, the icy caress of the wind against her cheeks brought with it a sense of exhilaration, a reminder of the vast unknown that lay ahead, both in her journey across the ocean and in the uncharted waters of her heart.

"Charlotte?"

She yelped in surprise. "Andrew?"

A shadow emerged from the darkness near the wheelhouse, and as he drew closer, his face became visible, a few feet away from her own. Charlotte's heart soared with joy, only to plummet when a second shadow materialized beside him, the silhouette of a woman.

The shock must have registered on her face for he hastily introduced the shadow. "This is Lily, from Madam's program. In fact, there are half a dozen ladies traveling from the program."

"Hello," Charlotte greeted the woman, her voice uncertain. "I remember your name, Miss Bailey. I arranged for all of you to travel on another ship two days earlier. What happened?"

Charlotte used the woman's last name deliberately to show Andrew the propriety of addressing a stranger. He wasn't in Madam's parlor. He was in the presence of his wife, for goodness' sake.

"There wasn't enough room on the other ship, so I offered to bring them on this one," Andrew said.

"I see… You had more than one reason to be here, then," Charlotte said, disappointed and angry.

He stepped closer to her and lowered his voice when he spoke. "I had only one objective. The other was a coincidence. I didn't plan for the other ship to be overbooked, after all."

That still didn't explain why her husband was alone with a woman in the middle of the night.

"We were just discussing our plans," Andrew said, as if to read her mind. Charlotte remained silent, waiting for further explanation.

"If I may," Lily began, "I'm in danger, Miss Morton. Mr. Creswell and I were discussing a safe place for me to stay once we arrive in the United States. He has kindly offered for me to stay with him."

The unexpected statement forced Charlotte to ignore the fact that the woman didn't know she was his wife. Her eyes darted to Andrew. "Did he?" she said with enough chill to freeze his bollocks.

"Yes. He said he'll have guards to look out for my husband who'll surely discover I have left for America. I have no doubt he'll come looking for me."

And why would he need to be there if she had guards with

her? The question burned in Charlotte's mind.

"Lily, I mean Miss Bailey, won't be the only woman there," Andrew added hastily. "Cynthia and Molly will be there also."

Charlotte fixed him with a glare, though she doubted he could see it in the darkness. She hoped, however, that her withering disapproval would somehow radiate through the night air. "So… you'll have three women living with you…"

Andrew rubbed his chin, looking sheepish. "It looks that way. The other two ladies are more temporary until their lodgings are ready. Miss Bailey might be more long-term until her husband is apprehended."

Charlotte's initial surge of jealousy gave way to a sobering realization as the woman's words sank in. *A dangerous husband who would cross an ocean to hunt her down.* This wasn't about romantic rivalry—this was about a woman fleeing for her life.

Charlotte nodded, understanding the gravity of the situation. The danger to this woman was real, and having someone like Andrew as her protector was crucial. There was no room for petty jealousy.

Yet even as she told herself this, Charlotte couldn't ignore the sharp stab of possessiveness that pierced her chest at the thought of Andrew sharing his home with three women. The intensity of her reaction was unexpected. She had convinced herself she was prepared to build a life without him. But based on her strong aversion to the idea of Andrew's proximity to another woman, Charlotte realized she needed to reassess her willingness to lose him.

"You'll be as safe as you can be with Mr. Creswell," she assured Lily, who smiled gratefully in return. "You must have more to discuss," she addressed Andrew and the woman. With a polite incline of her head, Charlotte turned and headed back to her suite.

Once in the privacy of her room, Charlotte sat up against the headboard, her mind even more unsettled than before. She tried to untangle the web of her emotions, weighing the fear of losing

Andrew against the fear of a broken heart.

A soft knock at the door had her leaping out of bed, her heart racing.

"Yes?" she called out softly.

"It's Andrew."

On trembling legs, she opened the door and motioned for him to enter. Andrew stood in the middle of the room, his overcoat draped over one arm.

"I didn't want any misunderstandings lingering between us before you went to bed," he began. "I'm sorry about that. I seem to become a bumbling fool in your presence."

Charlotte, realizing she was only in her night rail, hurriedly climbed onto the bed and slipped under the counterpane. Sitting up against the headboard and pulling the blanket up to her neck, she met his gaze, now riveted on her form.

Andrew quickly turned away from her. "I'm sorry, I should've asked if you'd be all right with me offering my home to strangers."

Charlotte's eyes widened. "How do you have a home already? What has become of your company?"

"I no longer own it. The charity does, and Hereford will guide it along."

"Andrew, that company meant more to you than anything."

"I thought it did. I realized too late that it didn't. But I'm here to do the right thing by you, Charlotte. I only want to be near you, to help with your studies and career in whatever way I can. I want to cook for you, study with you, chase away other men... I'm afraid that will never change." He smiled woefully.

"I don't know what to say..."

"You deserve far more than I can offer, but I'm willing to give it all and become the best husband in between murdering a man or two who ogle at you."

Charlotte emitted a soft laugh, her eyes glistening with unshed tears as she delicately dabbed at them with her handkerchief.

"If the notion of my residing with three comely ladies displeases you," Andrew offered, his voice tinged with a hint of playfulness, "I could, perchance, take up residence in your abode instead."

Arching a delicate brow, Charlotte retorted, "Or perhaps the ladies might find sanctuary under my roof?"

"And expose you to danger? I think not," Andrew said. "Speaking of which, I have taken the liberty of procuring two estates in your name, situated in close proximity to your place of study. Your home shall stand adjacent to mine, though separated by sufficient acreage to afford you privacy."

Her hands flew to her mouth. "You have purchased properties for me? I am most grateful. I don't know what to say."

"This is not an attempt to purchase your forgiveness. My sole desire is to ensure your safety and comfort, regardless of the path our relationship may take."

"I am deeply moved by your generosity," Charlotte murmured, her voice breaking. "Yet, I must insist that I am quite capable of tending to my own needs. There is no call for you to assume the role of my steward."

"But I must. I am compelled to maintain some connection to you, to atone for my transgressions. Charlotte, I have been utterly bereft in your absence. I implore you, allow me this small comfort, as much for my sake as for yours."

Overwhelmed, Charlotte could only nod her assent.

"I shall take my leave and allow you to rest," Andrew said, moving toward the door. As his hand grasped the handle, he paused, turning to face her once more. "I love you, my lady wife," he whispered, his voice laden with tender affection.

As Andrew's footsteps faded into the distance, Charlotte remained motionless, her heart pounding a fierce tattoo against her ribcage. For the first time in her life, she would not face the world alone, but with a devoted companion to share her burdens.

EPILOGUE

23 February 1838—Oberlin, Ohio

A s CHARLOTTE SURVEYED the faces of her young classmates gathered in the parlor, a mix of determination and apprehension hung in the air. These women, aspiring lawyers, judges, and politicians were about to embark on their first protest against the barring of female students from law schools.

Safety concerns had initially dampened their enthusiasm, but interest surged when Andrew generously offered to hire guards to protect them from harassment. They had poured their hearts into the preparations, working tirelessly through evenings and weekends. Andrew had even joked that they might face deportation before they could finish unpacking their trunks.

Charlotte took a deep breath, her voice steady as she addressed the group. "Very well, ladies. We shall meet in front of the State Capitol building tomorrow morning at eight o'clock. Don't forget the pamphlets, signs, food and drink, and a list of your emergency contacts. Bring pen and paper in case we need to write an urgent correspondence. Be prepared for a long day and an even longer fight. Are there any questions?"

The room fell silent, a palpable sense of anticipation and solidarity settling over the gathering. After they exchanged a few more words, the women rose to their feet, ready to depart. But all the heads turned when Andrew entered the parlor, his presence commanding attention. He dipped his head in greeting, a charming smile on his lips that seemed to make the lovesick females swoon. Charlotte couldn't fault them for their admiration. Andrew was, indeed, an impressive man.

He made his way through the room, his eyes seeking out Charlotte. Upon reaching her, he placed a gentle kiss on her cheek, a gesture that sent a flutter through her stomach. "How was the meeting?" he asked, his voice low and intimate.

"Fine, I think," Charlotte replied, a hint of uncertainty in her tone. "We are as ready as we will ever be. Is everything prepared on your end?"

"I believe so. I will have two dozen men with me."

Charlotte's eyes widened in surprise. "You'll be there as well?"

"Of course. Why do you sound so surprised?"

"I didn't think you could join us. You are usually so busy with your new venture."

Andrew's gaze softened, a tenderness in his expression that made Charlotte's breath catch.

"I'm never too busy for you, sweetheart." His brow furrowed slightly as a thought occurred to him. "Did you serve the refreshments I made?"

Charlotte's hands flew to her mouth. "Oh no… I completely forgot."

"Charlotte… you'll starve to death before you even begin the protest."

"I'm sorry. You went through all that trouble of making them. I should have eaten while they were hot."

Andrew waved off her apology, his smile reassuring. "No matter. They can be heated. I'll pack them in case some of your guests wish to take them home."

Andrew busied himself with packing the mini meat pies he had prepared into small paper bags. These meetings served a vital political purpose, but Andrew's thoughtful gesture of providing food for the students who couldn't afford proper meals touched her deeply. As she watched him, her heart swelled with love and appreciation for the man he was.

Charlotte resided alone, which proved to be a blessing, as

every room in her house had been transformed into either a study or a war office, where she meticulously planned events and stockpiled signs. Andrew, on the other hand, had shared his home with three women, but now only Lily remained under his roof.

Together, Charlotte and Andrew had been teaching the young woman secretarial skills, hoping to help her find work in the field. As it turned out, Lily possessed a natural talent for the job, and Andrew wasted no time in hiring her to work at his newly purchased textile factory.

After the last of the guests had departed, Charlotte busied herself with tidying up, fluffing cushions and gathering her notes. Lost in thought, she barely registered Andrew's presence as he gently took her hands in his.

"Charlotte," he said softly, his voice laden with solemnity.

The grave tone of his voice snapped her to attention. "What is it?" she asked, her brows furrowing with concern.

"We apprehended Lily's husband."

"You did?" Charlotte's eyes widened, and she threw her arms around Andrew, hugging him with unbridled glee. She bounced on her feet, her heart swelling with relief. Andrew's arms encircled her waist, pulling her close, nuzzling his nose in her hair. "I'm so glad. The poor thing must be so relieved. When did this happen?"

Releasing her hold on his neck, Charlotte stepped back, her hands already reaching for the tea trays as she waited for his answer.

"This morning."

She looked up at him. "That is wonderful, Andrew. You've accomplished what the sheriff couldn't. I'm so proud of you."

"I was desperate. I spared no expense to capture that blackguard."

"Yes. Lily's safety has been weighing heavily upon you."

"That's not what I meant," he said. "I was eager to spend more time with you. Even spend the night here if you'd allow me."

At his remark, Charlotte froze, her posture stiffening. A single, breathless sound escaped her lips. "Oh..."

His brows drew together, his distress evident. "Your countenance betrays a lack of enthusiasm. Have you forgotten I'm your husband?"

"No, I... I simply found myself unprepared to broach the subject of our marriage," Charlotte replied, her voice barely above a whisper.

Andrew closed the distance between them with purposeful strides, relieving her of the tea trays. After placing them aside, he gently rested his hands on her waist. "Are you content with our present arrangement?" His eyes searched hers with an intensity that made her breath catch.

"Indeed, I could not ask for more." A timid smile graced her features as her heart thundered.

He bowed his head, nodding solemnly before withdrawing his touch and thrusting his hands into his pockets. "Do you not yearn for something beyond our current... state?"

"To what do you refer?" A mixture of confusion and curiosity swirled in her heart.

"I..." Andrew turned abruptly, a low growl escaping his throat. He paced the room, hand rubbing his jaw as he exhaled deeply. "It has required every ounce of my self-restraint to maintain a respectful distance, to honor your need for time. Though I know my past transgressions were grievous, I had dared to hope you might find it in your heart to grant me a second chance. I fear..." He paused, swallowing hard as his hand moved to massage the nape of his neck. "I fear I may have forever lost my claim to you as my wife. If you believe you can never truly forgive me... never love me as more than a mere companion, I implore you to speak plainly, that I might steel myself for the inevitable."

He crossed his arms, as if bracing himself against an impending blow to his heart.

"The inevitable?" she echoed, perplexed by his train of thought.

How could he possibly imagine her affections had not been

rekindled after all he had done to make amends? He had proven himself a steadfast champion of her causes and aspirations, leveraging his connections to smooth her path. He had catered to her every whim without condition, betraying no hint of his carnal desires save for the scorching gaze that often compelled her to avert her eyes.

For months, Charlotte had grappled with a most unseemly jealousy regarding the women who shared Andrew's abode, partaking of meals with him and perchance passing his chambers nightly in their night attire, as his need for feminine company surely smoldered. On more than one occasion, she had been sorely tempted to yield to her own desires, to quell the restless yearning that grew ever stronger. Yet she had abstained, reminding herself of his past betrayal and resolving that the opportune moment must arrive on her own terms. He must prove the strength of his devotion, rather than her succumbing to her own insecurities.

Andrew had proven himself as steadfast in his loyalty to her as a barrister to his wig. She had been most relieved to discover from the women who shared his home that he had not strayed. Yet he had not voiced yearning of anything more until this moment.

Exhaling deeply, Andrew tried once more. "Do you not pine for… our tender moments? Our… intimate encounters?"

She shrugged, her eyes staring at her toes while her cheeks flushed crimson with embarrassment.

He paced the room, his agitation evident in his movements, then whirled about abruptly. "Has another captured your affections?"

"I beg your pardon?"

Returning to her side, he fixed her with an intense gaze, his voice quavering. "You are a woman of beauty and intelligence. Surely your professors are predominantly gentlemen, are they not? And these American men… They are of a different ilk. They are exceedingly forward in their pursuit of the fairer sex. Have you perhaps encountered someone whose company you prefer to mine?"

"Certainly not."

"You speak the truth?"

"Indeed. How could you imagine I would fall so far from grace? I have never forgotten my station as a married woman."

Andrew shielded his eyes with his hand, his breath coming in heavy inhalations. Charlotte wondered if he might submit to tears.

When at last he revealed his countenance, it bore an expression of profound vulnerability and trepidation. His words left him in haste. "What, then, is to become of us? Have you remained faithful merely out of a sense of duty? Or does your heart harbor affection for me? Might you ever come to love me truly? Do you desire a union in the fullest sense, with love, devotion, and the pleasures of both mind and body?"

"I…" She held his gaze for a moment, torn between revealing the truth and protecting her heart. "Yes, I want it all," she whispered, her voice breaking on the words. Tears she hadn't expected spilled down her cheeks as the confession unlocked something deep within her chest that she'd kept carefully guarded. She felt exposed, vulnerable, as if she'd just handed him her heart on a silver platter.

His hand flew to his mouth, his eyes closing with relief. When he opened them, his eyes were bright with moisture. "I-I am humbled and most grateful for your generosity, truly. I shall endeavor with all my being to ensure you never rue this decision."

She nodded, feeling a warmth suffuse her being at the prospect of resuming their marital relations. With a deep breath, she sought a final assurance. "I need to know… have there been others?"

"Upon my honor, I have not."

Nodding once more, she wrapped her arms about her torso, suddenly feeling awkward. Andrew approached with measured steps. When but a hairsbreadth separated them, his broad chest filling her vision, he asked softly, "Might I kiss you?"

Averting her gaze, she nodded, her throat suddenly parched.

His hand reached out, caressing her chin, then tilting it upward with the gentlest pressure. His dark eyes pierced hers.

"I am filled with immeasurable pride in you, Charlotte. Your strength, your passion, your unwavering commitment... these are the qualities that have captured my heart. It pains me that I realized this only after inflicting grievous harm, and for that, I am profoundly sorry."

Andrew's arm encircled her waist, drawing her closer. "I wish you to know that I have no desire to alter your essence. My sole aim is to support you, to stand beside you as you reshape the world. I hope you believe me."

Feeling a familiar sting in her nose, her vision blurred with welling tears.

"I do," she said, her voice thick with emotion. "Your steadfast support these past eight months has been my anchor during the most trying of times. I now place my complete trust in you."

"My sweet, my heart," he breathed, his voice reverent. "You are far too good to be my wife."

When words failed her, Andrew dipped his head, capturing her lips in a tender, reverent kiss. Charlotte felt herself melting as he took his time, his mouth moving against hers with a gentleness that made her heart race. The familiar taste of him, the warmth of his breath mingling with her own, sent waves of longing through her that she'd suppressed for far too long. Her hands found purchase on his arms, her fingers reveling in the unyielding strength beneath his skin as she returned his kiss with equal fervor, pouring every ounce of her desire into the embrace.

Andrew's arm snaked around her bottom, lifting her against him. Charlotte wrapped her legs around his hips, the evidence of his longing pressing against her. She gasped at the sheer power of his strength, his yearning. Her body trembled with anticipation.

"Christ," he rasped, his voice rough with barely restrained

need. "I don't want to hurt you, but I fear I may become too rough from my sheer need of you. I need you, more than I've ever needed anything in my life."

Charlotte gazed up at him, grateful for the friendship she had cultivated with the three women and for their tutelage in the art of pleasure.

"Andrew, could you wait for me in my bedchamber?"

He swallowed and gawked as if he'd been told seven virgins awaited him. Without a word, Andrew spun on his heels and climbed the steps three at a time.

"In my bed!" she called after him with a chuckle.

"Dear God, I fear I shall expire from anticipation before you even arrive!" he replied, his voice echoing through the corridor.

Laughing, Charlotte quickly removed her drawers and washed, her heart pounding in her ears.

She hastily went upstairs and with trembling hands, opened the bedroom door. Andrew sat up in bed, his back against the headboard, his long legs stretched out in front of him. He had removed his coat and cravat, his feet bare and shirt collars open, revealing a glimpse of his sculpted chest. The room glowed with the warm, orange light of the candles, illuminating his jawline and the enticing dip between his collarbones.

She stood across from him at the end of the room, her gaze dropping to the floor as her body buzzed with nerves. Without a word, she began to unbutton her bodice, her fingers trembling, slowing the process. She stole a quick glance at Andrew, his eyes transfixed on her as she opened the bodice fully.

Remembering what the courtesans had told her about the most powerful aphrodisiac being a tease, she stretched the thin linen shift taut over her breasts as she removed the bodice with deliberate slowness. To her satisfaction, Andrew's jaw dropped, his eyes darkening with hunger, and she couldn't help but notice the way his cock strained against his trousers, already hard with want.

The air between them crackled with electricity, anticipation coiling tighter with each passing heartbeat. Charlotte's pulse quickened, her skin flushed and tingling under the scorching intensity of Andrew's gaze.

Without breaking eye contact, she turned slowly, presenting her back to him. Her fingers worked at the ties of her skirts with maddening leisure before she bent forward to slip them off, the movement deliberate and provocative. His sharp intake of breath sent a thrill through her. Before straightening, she gathered the shift tight against her curves, the fabric molding to every line of her body.

"Christ… your curves could tempt the angels to sin," he groaned, his voice thick with need.

She turned to face him again, one hand trailing up to cup her breast through the gossamer fabric, her thumb circling the peaked nipple. "Come to me," he commanded, his voice rough with desire. "I need to feel you."

"No." The single word fell between them like a gauntlet. "You cannot touch me until I give permission."

"Charlotte, please…" His plea was raw, desperate. "Do not torment me so."

"I am in control now, Andrew." Her voice was silk and steel. "It will serve you well to surrender to it."

"Wicked creature…"

She smiled at his frustration, then slowly raised one leg, placing her foot on the bed's edge. His eyes followed the movement hungrily as she untied her garter with painstaking care, then rolled the stocking down inch by agonizing inch, letting her knee fall open to afford him a tantalizing glimpse.

"God…" His breathing had turned ragged, his knuckles white where they gripped the bedsheets.

Turning away once more, she gathered the shift in front, baring herself completely to his view. The sound he made—half groan, half prayer—sent liquid heat pooling low in her belly.

"I cannot… I shall spend myself if you continue this sweet torture," he rasped.

She faced him again, close enough now that she could see the pulse hammering in his throat. "Then you had better learn restraint, my lord."

"Do you wish an untimely death upon me?"

"Don't you think I deserve this after what you've put me through?" She let the words hang between them as she slowly lowered the strap of her shift, baring one breast to his hungry gaze.

"Yes…" he breathed, his voice rough with want as his eyes fixed on the rosy peak that crowned her pale flesh.

"Then follow my rules, or you shall not touch me at all." Her voice was velvet wrapped around steel. "Do you understand?"

His gaze riveted on her nipple, his hand moved instinctively toward his straining cock.

"No." The command cracked like a whip.

A tortured groan tore from his throat. "You'll pay for this torment, wife. When you're finished playing your games, I shall claim every inch of you."

The threat sent heat spiraling through her core. Charlotte approached with feline grace, letting the shift pool at her feet like spilled moonlight.

"Are you losing control, my lord?" Her fingers found the buttons of his shirt, working them free with deliberate slowness until his sculpted chest was bared to her touch. The chiseled planes of muscle drew a soft moan from her lips as her impatience finally broke through. Her hands flew to his falls, freeing him with urgent efficiency.

His manhood sprang free, thick and proud, the sight of him making her mouth water with anticipation. Without breaking the spell of his desperate gaze, she straddled his thighs, one hand finding her aching center while the other cupped her breast.

"Christ…" The word was barely human, torn from somewhere deep in his chest.

She began to move against her own touch, her body responding to months of denied longing. When his hand jerked toward her, she caught his wrist. "Not yet," she whispered, but as her pleasure built to a crescendo, she leaned forward, offering her breast to his waiting mouth.

He seized the gift hungrily, his tongue circling and teeth grazing until she cried out, her body arching as waves of sensation crashed over her. Every muscle in his frame was taut with restraint, his breath coming in harsh pants.

"Please," he begged against her skin. "I'm dying for you, Charlotte."

Instead of answering, she turned in his lap, her back to his chest, and wrapped her fingers around his rigid length. The contact made him buck beneath her, a strangled curse escaping his lips as she began to stroke him with maddening precision.

"Sweet Jesus," he gasped.

Rising on her knees, she positioned herself above him, then took him into her mouth in one fluid motion. His shout of pleasure echoed through the room as his control finally shattered, his hands tangling in her hair as she drove them both toward the edge of reason.

He cried out her name as his release claimed him, his body shuddering with the force of his climax as she took everything he gave. When the last tremor subsided, Andrew's hands found her waist, drawing her up his body until she straddled his hips, her slick heat pressed against his softening length.

"Magnificent," he breathed, his voice rough with satisfaction and renewed hunger. "Come here."

With a fierce growl of possession, Andrew captured her lips, his mouth claiming hers with desperate intensity. This kiss was different—deeper, more consuming—a declaration that went beyond mere desire. His hands tangled in her hair as they melted into each other, their bodies fitting together as if they'd been crafted for this very moment.

When he finally tore his mouth from hers, they were both breathless, her lips swollen and glistening from his ardent attention. The passion-glazed look in his eyes made something primal stir within her once more.

"I need to taste you," he said, his voice a dark promise. He urged her to her feet, guiding her hands to the headboard. "Hold tight, love. Don't let go."

The first touch of his mouth against her sensitive center made her cry out, her fingers gripping the carved wood as sensation crashed over her. He was relentless in his worship, his tongue mapping every sensitive fold with devastating precision. Each stroke sent lightning through her—sometimes gentle as a whisper, sometimes demanding as his hunger grew.

His hands gripped her hips, holding her steady as she began to move against him, chasing the pleasure that built with each caress of his tongue. When he sealed his lips around her most sensitive spot and sucked gently, she nearly lost her grip on the headboard.

"Andrew," she gasped, her head falling back as the tension coiled tighter within her.

He answered with a low moan that vibrated against her flesh, the sound pushing her closer to the edge. When his tongue delved deep inside her, she rode the sensation with abandon, her body moving in an ancient rhythm until ecstasy finally claimed her, leaving her trembling and breathless in his arms.

In one fluid motion, he swept her beneath him, her body yielding to his strength as he positioned her on her back. She felt boneless, pliant, completely at his mercy as he settled between her thighs.

"Andrew, I—"

"I have you," he whispered against her lips, his voice thick with need and tenderness. "I am your husband, and I love you. Let me claim you properly this time."

The blunt head of his arousal pressed against her entrance, hot and demanding. His eyes, dark with desire, held hers captive. "Tell me who I am," he commanded softly.

"My husband," she breathed.

The words were barely past her lips when he surged forward, filling her completely in one devastating stroke. Her back arched as a cry tore from her throat, her body stretching to accommodate his size while pleasure and possession warred within her.

"And who is taking you now?" His voice was strained as he

began to move, each thrust deliberate and claiming.

"My husband," she gasped, her nails digging into his shoulders.

"That's right." His rhythm intensified, powerful and relentless. "You belong to me, just as I belong to you. Say my name, Charlotte. Let me hear it."

"Andrew…" The name fell from her lips like a prayer.

"Again." His control was fraying, each movement more urgent than the last.

"Andrew!"

"Once more," he demanded, his gaze never leaving her face as he drove them both toward the precipice.

"Andrew! Oh, Andrew!"

Her release crashed over her like a tidal wave, her body convulsing around him as ecstasy claimed every nerve. The sight and feel of her surrender seemingly shattered his restraint. With a hoarse shout, he followed her over the edge, his body shuddering as he poured himself into her welcoming heat.

Afterwards, they lay entwined in the golden aftermath, Andrew's arms encircling her as he drew the covers over their cooling bodies. The silence was profound, broken only by their gradually slowing breaths and the distant sound of their hearts beating in tandem.

"Andrew," she whispered into the darkness.

"Mmm?"

"Should we not consider… preventing conception?"

His lips found her temple, pressing a tender kiss there. "If we are blessed with a child, I would count it the greatest gift imaginable. To be your husband is honor enough, but to father your children…" His voice caught with emotion. "There could be no greater privilege."

Tears she hadn't expected spilled down her cheeks at his words, the depth of his love washing over her like a benediction. He pulled her closer still, as if he could shelter her from every hurt the world might offer.

"Are these tears of joy or sorrow?" he asked softly.

"Joy," she whispered, her voice thick with emotion.

With a deep exhalation, he bestowed a kiss on her shoulder.

"I fear I may be barred from attending lectures should I find myself in a delicate condition," she said.

"Then we shall prevail upon the professors to instruct you privately."

"And if I am denied entry to the school of law?"

"Then I shall establish one for women."

Charlotte turned to face him, her countenance alight with suspended disbelief. "Do you speak in earnest? Is such a thing possible?"

"Indeed. I have already broached the subject with several influential members of the Ohio Board of Education and prominent educators in Oberlin." Andrew's tone betrayed no hint of the momentous nature of his words.

With a cry of delight, Charlotte flung her arms about his neck. Andrew's rich laughter filled the air as he enfolded her in his embrace.

"Rest now, Mrs. Creswell," he murmured. "You must conserve your strength if you are to reshape the world."

Lulled by the steady rhythm of his breathing against her ear, Charlotte drifted into a peaceful slumber, secure in the knowledge that her beloved's devotion to their love would never waver.

The End

Thank you for reading. Please consider leaving a review on Amazon and/or Goodreads.

For updates, promos, and ARC opportunities, please sign up for my newsletter at www.mihwawrites.com

For any updates on my new Dragonblade releases, please follow me at www.dragonbladepublishing.com/team/mihwa-lee

About the Author

Mihwa Lee is NOT a New York Times, USA Today, or Amazon Best Selling Author. But what she is not, she makes up for with her sense of humour, unusual life experiences, and imagination. The combination of these qualities can yield entertaining stories and parties. As a result, she is a sought-after guest at all parties and karaoke except those that have banned her.

Mihwa became a writer after retiring as a medical expert witness in brain injury (like Law & Order but boring) because she hates disposable income and thought it would be fun to piss off her teenagers. She has bookmarked her favourite steamy scenes in her books for her children in case they need her advice once she's gone. Her children are mortified but tolerate her legacy because of the potential for a passive income.

Mihwa is passionate about equalising the world population through education. She has set up a scholarship in Costa Rica (where she used to live) to send underprivileged Latin American youths to university and/or fund their entrepreneurial ventures.

Mihwa believes in living life to the fullest. Therefore, she writes steamy historical romance like a woman possessed.

linktr.ee/mihwawrites
FB reader group: Mihwa's Den of TMI
TikTok: @mihwa.lee
IG: mihwawrites
YouTube: @DesireDialogue